# Nightingale's Code

• • • • • • • • • • • •

## A poetic study of Bob Dylan

• • • • • • • • • • • •

## John Gibbens

WITH PHOTOGRAPHS BY

## Keith Baugh

TOUCHED
PRESS

First published in 2001
by Touched Press
4 Varley House
County Street
London SE1 6AL

British Library Cataloguing-in-Publication Data
A catalogue record for this book is
available from the British Library

ISBN 0-9539153-1-X

Designed and set in Caslon 9.5/12 by Touched Type
Printed and bound in England by
Bookcraft, Midsomer Norton, Somerset

*Dedicated
to the memory of
P.J. Fahy
poet and musician*

but he would have us remember most of all
to be enthusiastic over the night,
    not only for the sense of wonder
  it alone has to offer, but also

because it needs our love. With large sad eyes
its delectable creatures look up and beg
    us dumbly to ask them to follow:
  they are exiles who long for the future

that lies in our power, they too would rejoice
if allowed to serve enlightenment like him,
    even to bear our cry of "Judas",
  as he did and all must bear who serve it.

       (W.H. Auden, 'In Memory Of Sigmund Freud')

# Contents

Foreword: A Walking Antique                                              ix

## Part I: I Ain't Different Than Anyone                                  1

1. To Fenario   The roots of folk                                         6
2. Burning Coal   Folk and Romanticism                                  10
3. Pierrot! Pierrot!   Folk and the unconscious                         13
4. Written Somewhere Down In The United States
                                  Folk, art & commerce                  21
5. So All Souls Can See It   Folk as creed                              25
6. Am I Hearin' Ya Right?   The synthetic tradition                     29
7. Bob Dylan's Blues   Some musical sources                             33
8. Jokerman Dance   Myth and persona                                    41
9. Into The Narrow Lanes   The road                                     55
10. The Longest Road I Know   Highway 61                                66
11. My Name It Is Nothing   The sea                                     94

Interchapter: Watching the River Flow                                   107

## Part II: A Little Upside Down                                        115

1. Something Is Happening Here
                  1964: politics, pop, drugs & blues                   118
2. Reels Of Rhyme
   *Another Side of Bob Dylan, Bringing It All Back Home*               125
3. Who Are You Anyway?   Dialogue                                       137
4. I Plan It All And I Take My Place   The shape of an LP               147
5. The Arrow On The Doorway
                  *The Times They Are A-Changin'*                       154
6. Talking To The Folks   MY BACK PAGES, CHIMES OF FREEDOM              171
7. The Springtime Turned   TO RAMONA and some arcana                    180

Interchapter: Upon the Steps of Time                                    193

## Part III: In the Final End                                          199

1.  Savage Rose & Fixable  DESOLATION ROW                             214

2.  The Dark Is Just Beginning  1965 singles; *Blonde on Blonde*      235

3.  The First Lesson in Chinese  *Blonde on Blonde* concluded         244

4.  Scald Like Molten Lead  *The Basement Tapes*                      253

5.  Standing Where It Ought Not  *John Wesley Harding*                257

6.  A Key to Your Door  *John Wesley Harding* concluded               277

7.  By Golly, What More Can I Say?
                        *Nashville Skyline, Self Portrait*            281

8.  Builder of Rainbows  *New Morning*                                286

9.  The Gone World  *Planet Waves*                                    291

10. Iron Gates Of Life
                        *Before the Flood* and other live recordings 296

11. I Do It For You  *Blood on the Tracks*                            303

12. To Grasp And Let Go In A Heavenly Way  *Desire*                   306

13. Here Comes The Story  *Desire*, Side 1                            311

14. King Of The Streets  JOEY                                         317

15. Serpent Eyes  JOEY and ROMANCE IN DURANGO                         324

16. The Righteous With The Wicked  BLACK DIAMOND BAY                  328

17. Another Hard Luck Story  SARA                                     337


Afterword:  A Diamond Voice                                          343


Postscript:  For What  *Love and Theft*                              356


Index                                                                362

# Foreword

• • • • • • • • • • • • • • • • • • •

# A Walking Antique

• • • • • • • • • • • • • • • • • • •

I started this book about twenty years ago, after meeting Keith Baugh at a party. It was going to be a quick job, supplying the text that would accompany a selection of his photographs of Bob Dylan on stage. Writing about a musician who'd already given me so much pleasure, encouragement and inspiration soon proved to present a few obstacles, however.

I'd known some of his records – *Bringing It All Back Home*, *Highway 61 Revisited*, *John Wesley Harding* – since I was a child, while *Blood on the Tracks* and *Desire* were companions of my adolescence; but I hadn't heard all of his officially released music, nor did I know that much about the culture in which it was rooted. I never intended to write encyclopaedically, but this knowledge seemed indispensable if I was going to sound off at all.

This was before the advent of the CD and the wealth of reissues which it has made possible. American roots music was not easy to come by, especially for those without deep pockets. For example, there were no Woody Guthrie LPs in print in the UK when I began my study. Nor was there a fraction of the historical information on popular music that is available now. With conscientious attendance at the second-hand record dealers and bookshops, I began to piece together a picture as best I could.

A second obstacle to my project was that I didn't know what to say about the songs I already knew. A third was that I didn't know how to write down my thoughts once I had them.

In the course of my first exploration, which ran aground on shoals of confusion, I did learn the rough topography of the territory I had to describe. This first draft was called *Be In My Dream* ("You can be in my dream if I can be in yours" – TALKIN' WORLD WAR III BLUES). When I returned to the wreck with a view to salvage, I discovered that it contained some observations that still seemed sound and had not been made elsewhere. These I condensed into a second draft, *Walking Antique*, which took its title from the peculiar emphasis its subject gave to those words when I heard him sing SHE BELONGS TO ME at Hammersmith eight years ago. From that sketchy and not altogether articulate skeleton I took the bare bones of this book, which I began in 2000.

What follows is not a continuous commentary on Dylan's career. The bulk of the music I have written about is from the 1960s and early 1970s (which is also, at the moment, the era that Dylan's own shows concentrate on). This is not because I think the later work has declined, but because it's easier to outline a body of art by tracing the course of its growth, and the resources of the later work are implicit in the earlier. The more recent songs are also less subject to my sort of commentary, I think: their poetics are more and more inseparable from the driftwood texture and sculpture of Dylan's voice, though the verbal and visual fireworks go on:

> There's a woman on my lap and she's drinking champagne.
> She's got white skin, got assassin's eyes,
> I'm starin' up into the sapphire-tinted skies.
> I'm well-dressed, waitin' on the last train.

I hope anyway that my comments on the examples I have chosen will shed light elsewhere, and that "if you want any more you can sing it yourself".

# A note on sources

During this long gestation I have had recourse to many articles and books, and quite a few that are no longer on my shelves after several house-removals. I read three lives, for example: Antony Scaduto's *Bob Dylan: An Intimate Biography*, Robert Shelton's *No Direction Home* and Bob Spitz's *Dylan: A Biography*. I read the first two volumes of Paul Williams's *Bob Dylan: Performing Artist*, an early edition of Paul Cable's *Unreleased Recordings*, Larry Sloman's *Rolling with the Thunder*, and so on. In lieu of a full bibliography, I have listed below the books which were to hand while I wrote, and a few more which contributed either background or inspiration or both:

*Bessie: Empress of the Blues*, Chris Albertson, Abacus 1975.

*Wanted Man: In Search of Bob Dylan*, edited by John Bauldie,
    Penguin 1992.

*Rythm Oil: A Journey Through the Music of the American South*,
    Stanley Booth, Jonathan Cape 1991.

*Black Gospel: An Illustrated History of the Gospel Sound*,
    Viv Broughton, Blandford Press 1985.

*The Illustrated Encyclopaedia of Jazz*, Brian Case and Stan Britt,
    Salamander 1978.

*Are You Ready for the Country?: Elvis, Dylan, Parsons and the
    Roots of Country Rock*, Peter Doggett, Viking 2000.

*Hank Williams: The Biography*, Colin Escott with George
    Merritt and William MacEwen, Little, Brown 1995.

*Tommy Johnson*, David Evans, Studio Vista 1971.

*More Rock Family Trees*, Pete Frame, Omnibus Press 1998.

*Woman With Guitar: Memphis Minnie's Blues*, Paul and Beth
    Garon, Da Capo Press 1992.

*The Sound of the City*, Charlie Gillett, Souvenir Press 1983.

*Song & Dance Man: The Art of Bob Dylan*, Michael Gray,
    Hamlyn 1981.

*All Across the Telegraph: A Bob Dylan Handbook*, edited by
    Michael Gray and John Bauldie, Futura 1987.
*Feel Like Going Home: Portraits in Blues and Rock'n'Roll*,
    Peter Guralnick, Penguin 1992.
*Lost Highway: Journeys and Arrivals of American Musicians*,
    Peter Guralnick, Penguin 1992.
*Last Train to Memphis: The Rise of Elvis Presley*,
    Peter Guralnick, Abacus 1995.
*Careless Love: The Unmaking of Elvis Presley*, Peter Guralnick,
    Little, Brown 1999.
*Bound for Glory*, Woody Guthrie, Dolphin Books [a stained
    and battered US paperback, *circa* 1959].
*The Nearly Complete Collection of Woody Guthrie Folk Songs*,
    Ludlow Music Inc./Tro Essex Music Ltd 1973.
*Pastures of Plenty* [unpublished writings of Woody Guthrie],
    edited by Dave Marsh and Harold Leventhal,
    HarperCollins 1990.
*Dylan: Behind Closed Doors: The Recording Sessions (1960–1994)*,
    Clinton Heylin, Penguin 1996.
*American Music: A Panorama*, Daniel Kingman, Schirmer Books
    1990.
*Revolution in the Head: The Beatles' Records and the Sixties*,
    Ian MacDonald, Pimlico 1995.
*Country Music USA*, Bill C. Malone, University of Texas Press
    1985.
*Mystery Train: Images of America in Rock'n'Roll Music*,
    Greil Marcus, E.P. Dutton 1982.
*Invisible Republic: Bob Dylan's Basement Tapes*, Greil Marcus,
    Picador 1997.
*Almost Grown: The Rise of Rock*, James Miller, Heinemann, 1999.
*Shots from the Hip*, Charles Shaar Murray, Penguin 1991.
*The Story of the Blues*, Paul Oliver, Penguin 1972.
*Rolling Thunder Logbook*, Sam Shepard, Penguin 1978.
*Down the Highway: The Life of Bob Dylan*, Howard Sounes,
    Transworld 2001.

*The Dylan Companion*, edited by Elizabeth Thomson and
    David Gutman, Macmillan 1990.
*Bob Dylan In His Own Words*, edited by Chris Williams,
    Omnibus Press 1993.
*Bob Dylan: Watching the River Flow: Observations on his art-in-
    progress, 1966–1995*, Paul Williams, Omnibus Press 1996.

My handy reference for Dylan's words was *Lyrics 1962–1985* (HarperCollins 1994), though I have transcribed my quotes from the records, and punctuated them according to how I hear them. That text is far from reliable – for example, it appears to depict Rubin 'Hurricane' Carter as an artist's model rather than a middleweight boxer: "Rubin could take a man out with just one pouch…"

Nearly all of the recorded music I refer to in the book I have on long-unavailable vinyl, which it would be pointless to list. I don't think there's anything quoted that can't be found on a current CD.

# Acknowledgments

O ver the years I've shared an enthusiasm – which might be mistaken for obsession – with a number of friends, or inflicted it on them. My thanks to these in particular who helped to educate this book: Peter Amlot, Esmé Butterfield, John Butterfield, Richard Daventry, Tim Drummond, John Froude, David Gibbens, Richard Gibbens, Jeremy from Wales (for the Earl's Court '78 cassette), Steve Mann, Paul Milican, Gerry O'Donovan, Judith Ososki, David Remfry, Jackie Remfry, Gareth Roscoe, Julie Silk, George Stuhler, Max Williams, Rhys Williams.

Keith Baugh's superb portfolio of photographs will be forthcoming in book form before too long, I hope. My thanks to him for allowing me the use of the illustrations here.

My thanks also to a few of the songwriters and musicians from whom I learned more about the nerve and the lifeblood of music-making than I ever did from records: John Arthur, Peter Astor, Heidi Berry, Peter Cadle, Julia Doyle, Dan Driscoll, Bertie Fritsch, David Goulding, Nigel Goulding, Nigel Melia, Dave Russell, Chris Schuler, Steve and Rachel (the Saving Graces), Kath Tait, Piece Thompson, Jon Owen Williams.

And to Armorel, who is the one without whom.

*Elephant & Castle, June 2001*

• • • • • • • • • • • •

# Part I

• • • • • • • • • • • •

# I Ain't Different
# Than Anyone

• • • • • • • • • • • • • • • • • •

*"I've been around this whole country," he says, "and I've never yet found –* Fenario." *And then he sings:*

> As we marched down,
> > as we marched down,
> > > as we marched down to Fenario…

*So where is Fenario, and who is this boy who tells us that it doesn't exist, and then that he's been there?*

H e'd come out of nowhere, as it were, claiming to be from nowhere, or from everywhere. Some saw it as a con from early on, but most found the show worth the suspension of disbelief. And looking back, it is hard to believe that it was ever believed, with what we now know of how green and provincial the young Robert Zimmerman actually was. But then we can easily miss how precisely Bob-Dylan-shaped was the space in people's expectations, the people who were drawn to the folk revival, and how precisely he shaped himself for it.

More than any of the comparable entertainers, more than Elvis or the Beatles or the Rolling Stones, say, Dylan came out of his corner ready, punching from the first chime of the bell. He seems to have understood from the off that in the arena of the media, among the injection-moulded facts, the rhetoric and the hemi-demi-semi-information, he was not under any obligation to tell the truth. His lies, however – the dead parents, the circus he ran away with, the teenage years of hoboing, the spells under the wings of bluesmen and folksingers – did not really amount to an alternative, fictitious biography so much as an *evasion* of biography. The important thing was not that he should be from somewhere other than where he came from, but that he should be from nowhere in particular; not that he should be someone other than who he was, but that he should be a kind of Everyman.

There is, of course, a clichéd (not necessarily trivial) American glamour-figure behind this non-identity: that Western hero who appears at his cheesiest as the Lone Ranger; more mythically, as the Man with No Name in Sergio Leone's films with Clint Eastwood – *A Fistful of Dollars*, *For a Few Dollars More*, *The Good, the Bad and the Ugly*. That character is at his most numinous in Eastwood's own *High Plains Drifter*, where he becomes a spirit and is reassumed into the 'heaven' of archetypal figures.

As a legend, the cowboy plain and simple has always had this quality: unattached, self-sufficient, set alone in the vastness with every direction open, yet readily drawn to the west. If barely any of her immigrants found their America to be like this, the early establishment of the cowboy as legend (virtually simultaneous with the fact), his apotheosis as an ideal American, shows the strength of their desire to believe it could be so. He continued to represent, if not an actual, quotidian independence, at least that spirit of self-reliance which the nation appeared to require and the freedom it appeared to offer them to reinvent themselves.

Outside the American context, there is also a tendency for the hero to appear, in one of his phases, as the unknown, or in disguise: Achilles in the *Iliad*, concealed among the women;

"wily" Odysseus, the wanderer, telling the Cyclops his name is No-man, and later coming into his own home as a beggar. Spies and private eyes, perhaps that elementary hero Sherlock Holmes, may be our modern equivalents.

We are touching here on the heroic or divine archetype who is known as the Trickster, who has had a vigorous life in the United States. As a divine image, this figure represents, ultimately, the unsearchable nature of God – the Spirit which Jesus, in John's Gospel, likens to the wind, which "bloweth where it listeth, and thou hearest the sound thereof, but canst not tell whence it cometh, and whither it goeth". As a human image, it could be said to represent our own heroic nature, which is so often in hiding.

Insofar as such a naturally fleeting character can be said to persist, we shall return to the persistence of the wanderer and the Trickster as emblems of 'I' within Dylan's songs, long after his own tricks had been exposed and his first persona allowed to fade. First we must ask why he chose to adopt a persona at all. Yes, it lent glamour, but it also had something of necessity about it; a necessity which sprang from being a folksinger. Or we could say, using a distinction which the ailing Woody Guthrie drew between his young imitator and other performers of the revival, that the persona was entailed by Dylan's desire to be – his feat of being – "a folksinger" rather than "a singer of folk songs". In that milieu, this was the master's seal of approval, the stamp of authenticity. It was also a case of like recognising like, because Guthrie too had *created* himself as a folksinger.

In order to understand his distinction, we have to ask, what is folk?

## · 1 ·

# To Fenario

It's a hard subject in which to make a beginning since folk by definition has no beginnings, only a continuous succession of revivals. But let's start with the word. Folk as an area of study, as in folklore, folk song, folk customs and so on, was named by the German scholars of the last part of the eighteenth century who initiated the natural history of oral culture. As a mark of their efforts, the German dictionary still has far more compound nouns under this head than the English. As well as *Volkslied*, folk song, there are, for example, *Volksweise*, folk tune, *Volksmärche*, folk tale, *Volksstück*, folk play, *Volksdichter*, folk poet.

While in German, however, the word *Volk* is just the ordinary word for "people", and in some contexts for the nation (as for example, *Volksversammlung*, national assembly), taken over into English it has another connotation. The *Shorter Oxford English Dictionary* gives "folk-lore", coined in 1846, alongside such older compounds as "folkland", "folkmoot" and "folkright". A folkmoot is an "assembly of a town, city, or shire". Folkright is another term for "common law" – which is in turn defined as "the unwritten law of England". And folkland perhaps brings out the word's English connotations most clearly: it is the opposite of bookland in Old English law, an antithesis interpreted by some scholars as distinguishing between land held according to ancient custom – by folkright – and land held by written charter. In other words, while the German terms, arising out of that general enterprise of forming a national culture which began in the late eighteenth century, speak of things which belong to the Germans as a people, as a whole, the

English term 'folk' already carries connotations of the ancient, the unwritten and also of the local. Divided from the everyday synonym 'people' by the great Norman/Saxon fault-line that runs through the language, 'folk' are implicitly of the land and of the past.

Before the name stuck, though, and even before the German studies got under way, what came to be called folk art had begun to work its eventually decisive influence on British culture. George Saintsbury in his *Short History of English Literature* (1898) traces an interest in the old ballads right back to the beginning of the eighteenth century, but settles on 1765 as the watershed date, when the anthology compiled by Bishop Thomas Percy, *Reliques of Ancient Poetry*, was published. Its popularity both signalled and accelerated that sea-change in English literature that came to be called the Romantic Revival. Also in the 1760s came the excitement and controversy of the 'Ossian' poems published by William Macpherson. Though presented as translations of an oral epic tradition from the Gaelic, they were substantially the compositions of their supposed translator.

A second literary stream, distinct from but eventually converging with the taste for 'folk' poetry, was that of 'country' verse, which gradually opened the garden gates of the pastoral convention to less tidy rustic things. Again the well-spring can be traced back to the early years of the century, with the appearance of James Thomson's *Seasons* in the 1720s, going on through Goldsmith's 'Deserted Village' to Cowper and Crabbe, and of course Burns, in whom the two streams of ballad form and rural setting may be said to merge.

Critical consensus finds a third forerunner of Romantic revolution in the work of William Collins and Thomas Gray in the mid-century. In the Interchapter preceding 'The Triumph of Romance', the tenth book of his *History*, Saintsbury writes: "the same mixture of conventional externals and Romantic spirit [as in Thomson] meets us in the scanty but intense poetical work of Collins [and] in the almost as scanty and less intense, but curiously 'questing', poetical work of Gray". And here finally we arrive at the question to which this perilously abbreviated digression into literary history has been leading. Why is it that these three things, not apparently related – the contemplation of natural scenes and rural life, the return to archaic forms, particularly the ballad, and the qualities of intensity and "questing" – are seen as part of the one thing, the emergence of Romanticism? Is it an illusion of hindsight, because all three were subsequently amalgamated in the poetry of Wordsworth and Coleridge, or do they have their own underlying unity?

For Saintsbury, what these foreshadowings have in common is that they are all reactions against Convention (he capitalises it himself) – a series of cracks running up the facade of the Classical temple which one further tremor – the influence of the French Revolution – was to bring crashing down. But he doesn't consider them as having a single seismic source. Their common ground, in other words, is simply the ground of exclusion, and it was this ground, whatever happened to remain outside the temple precincts, which the authors of the *Lyrical Ballads* seized upon. But this would suggest a "Romantic spirit" that was completely inorganic, an expedient coalition bound only by a common enemy, rather than a power in its own right. How then account for *The Ancient Mariner*, for example, in which ballad form combines with "questing" intensity; in which Coleridge, journeying into psychic depths beyond his own power even to interpret, also happens to produce the one authored poem which truly lives in the atmosphere of the ballads?

It seems to me that the pre-Romantic stirrings we have looked at, which all took their important places in the first era of English Romanticism, are aspects of a single movement and have a common orientation, towards rather than against something. They are different appearances of a single vector which can be said to point, depending on the frame of reference, backward or downward or inward.

Backward, first, into the past. New movements often see themselves as the revivals of something older and more authentic – the leap forward setting its foot on a timeless rock. The Renaissance is a conspicuous case in point – the rebirth of the culture of the Classical world. Modernism too took some of its impetus from its contact with the 'primitive'. So Romanticism, appealing to qualities of feeling – the "spontaneous overflow of powerful emotion", in Wordsworth's formula – the freedom of fancy and incantatory power which were excluded by the Classical model, found its voice through "ancient" poetry. We can subsume under that heading the medieval forgeries of the precocious Thomas Chatterton, the Ossian poems and Gray's versions from Norse and Welsh literature as well as the more authentic ballads and early pieces collected in Percy's *Reliques*. Special mention should be made here of Gray's famous poem 'The Bard', in which the last of the Welsh bards to survive the extermination of Edward I of England, as he curses the king, prophesies a resurrection of the bardic spirit under a Welsh dynasty (i.e. the Tudors). Gray, in other words, appropriates Shakespeare, the very touchstone of English literature, for the 'excluded' tradition.

## · 2 ·

# Burning Coal

What seems characteristic of the Romantic retrospect, in English poetry at least, drawn to borderlands of history like the 'Celtic fringes' of the British Isles and the realm of Arthurian legend, is its nostalgia, its sense of the irretrievability of the past, 'lost in the mists of time'. Despite the voice of Gray's bard (who is, after all, prophesying before he flings himself to his death over a precipice), Romanticism misses that supreme self-confidence which enables Vasari, in his *Lives of the Artists*, not only to chronicle the gradual revival of the Classical canon of art, but also to claim that, in Michelangelo and Raphael particularly, the Renaissance had come to surpass the Ancients. In the same way that the most 'romantic' stories, in the modern sense, are often those of unattainable loves, Romanticism yearns for its past. The unresolvable longing of the knight-at-arms for the fairy queen in Keats's beautiful ballad 'La Belle Dame Sans Merci' is also that of the poem itself for knights-at-arms and Faëry. Perhaps the mood reflects the increasingly scientific practice of history, and a new sense of the irrevocability and inevitability of historical change and of 'progress'.

The desire toward an object which is ineradicable and irretrievable, the Orphic backward glance at the crack between the worlds, for a Eurydice who is seen in twilight, on the threshold, sinking back among the shades – these find frequent voice in Dylan's later songs. Of course there is recollection of a lost beloved as early as GIRL OF THE NORTH COUNTRY in 1963, and *Blonde on Blonde* is wholly suspended between the poles of Eros and absence, which reach their fullest charge in the haunted VISIONS OF JOHANNA. But the tenderest songs of the 1980s and '90s almost all seem to turn to a woman in the past – from IN THE SUMMERTIME, I'LL REMEMBER YOU and BROWNSVILLE GIRL, through MOST OF THE TIME and SHOOTING STAR and BORN IN TIME, to DELIA, on the folk album *World Gone Wrong*, with its forlorn refrain, "All the friends I ever had are gone." Latterly, it's not just a woman, it's a whole world that's gone missing.

In 1988, at about the nadir of this troubled passage in Dylan's career, a strong moment on what is perhaps the weakest of his studio LPs, *Down in the Groove*, is the concluding country song, RANK STRANGERS TO ME:

> I wandered again
>     to my home in the mountains
> Where in youth's early dawn
>     I was happy and free.
> I looked for my friends
>     but I never could find 'em.
> I found they were all
>     rank strangers to me.

In fact the little trio of covers at the end of *Down in the Groove* – NINETY MILES AN HOUR (DOWN A DEAD END STREET), SHENANDOAH and this one – seemed to point a way back to Dylan's missing world and missing muse; a way which had been beckoning ever since 1985, with the convincingly stark acoustic finale, DARK EYES, to the largely unconvincing *Empire Burlesque*. But it was not until 1992, with a collection of solo performances of blues and ballads, *Good As I Been to You*, that Dylan finally returned to his roots – a return eventually vindicated by the resurgence of his songwriting on the utterly lovelorn *Time Out of Mind* in 1997. Nevertheless, in the fiercely polemical sleevenotes to the second and more powerful of his latterday folk albums, *World Gone Wrong*

(1993), Dylan expresses an unshakeable sense of the songs as emanating, albeit undiminished, from a dimension utterly divorced from our own time. Like the album's final track, LONE PILGRIM, in which a dead man sings from the grave, these are Ghost Songs, heard in a place, as Ezra Pound wrote in a late fragment of *The Cantos*,

> where the dead walked
>> and the living were made of cardboard

## · 3 ·

# Pierrot! Pierrot!

The concomitant of the Romantic look backward through historical time is the look backward through personal time, to childhood, as the locus of imaginative freedom and direct feeling, but equally irrecoverable. Here the backward look intertwines with the inward one, into the unconscious, though that would not be named until Freud came to show how these two perspectives might be one. This could also be called the 'downward' look, the search for roots and subterranean springs, both of culture and of the individual mind. And all three are entwined in the idea of 'folk'.

As we saw earlier, the German word for folk song, *Volkslied*, might as well be translated 'people's song' or even 'national song', and only as the term is taken over into English does it come to imply a division of the populace into two parties, the folk and the non-folk. This pointless-seeming distinction lies behind the old crack (Hank Williams's or Big Bill Broonzy's? – I've seen both attributions) that all songs are folk songs – "leastways, I never heard of no horse singing one". However, by the time the modern English usage was coined in the mid-nineteenth century, there really was, perhaps for the first time in history, a non-folk, an urbanised industrial society for whose members the country was becoming *another country*. In this perspective, the 'folk', despite their contemporary existence, belonged to the past, as the historical ground on which the modern world had arisen. They could also be seen as the 'childhood' of which the modern world was the adulthood, and their oral and traditional culture as the 'unconscious' of which the literate urban world was the consciousness.

It's intriguing to see how often, and in what various contexts, these roles are rolled into one. In the conclusion to his preface to *The Oxford Book of Ballads*, for example, Sir Arthur Quiller Couch admits that the ballads do not stand up well alongside lyric poetry from the literary tradition when juxtaposed in anthologies, "so that I have sometimes been forced to reconsider my affection, and ask 'Are these ballads really beautiful as they have always appeared to me?' In truth (as I take it) the contrast is unfair to them, much as any contrast between children and grown folk would be unfair. They appealed to something young in the national mind, and the young still ramp through Percy's Reliques – as I hope they will through this book – 'trailing clouds of glory'…" (His quote is from Wordsworth's 'Ode: Intimations of Immortality from Recollections of Early Childhood').

The irony is that at the time of his preface, in 1910, the work of collecting the folk songs of the British Isles from the oral tradition was in full swing, in the hands of Ralph Vaughan Williams and Cecil Sharp and others: the childhood, the past to which the ballads were supposed to belong was still the present. In fact the same is true of Bishop Percy's original collection of ballads: although some of his pieces dated back to the fourteenth century, many were no older than the reign of Charles I. Nobody in the 1760s would have thought to call works contemporary with these, like Milton's, say, "ancient poetry".

From Quiller Couch's idea of the ballads as expressions of a cultural childhood, we pass to the representation of the folk tradition as a kind of cultural Id. Words like instinctive, un-self-conscious, unconscious crop up frequently in folk commentary, for example in Maud Karpeles's *Introduction to English Folk Song* (OUP, 1974): "It is impersonal, because it is the expression of the community and not merely of the individual. It is sincere because it has been evolved unconsciously…" Or this, from the Statement of Purpose on the back of a Woody Guthrie album released some time in the mid-60s as part of an Archive of Folk Music series by Everest Records of Hollywood, California:

> With the current renaissance of folk music there has come a proliferation of so-called "folk" recordings. By its very definition, folk music cannot be "manufactured". Most of these efforts are rather slick and facile popularizations of either traditional tunes or "composed" folk tunes. Though pleasant, these are not folk music.
>
> Authentic performances of indigenous and unselfconscious music of the people by the "minstrels" of the people seldom have enjoyed the benefit of big-city recording studios and techniques. However, some of these were recorded, albeit under rather difficult conditions and on not so high-fi 78 r.p.m. discs during the thirties and forties. Most of them have been out of print for years and exist only as well worn 78's in the collections of a few buffs.
>
> It is the avowed purpose of the Archive of Folk Music to seek out original recordings and to selectively and carefully make them available to the public as relatively high quality L.P.'s at reasonable prices.
>
> The illustrious names represented in this line have long been known and revered by dedicated folk buffs. Now for the first time these historic recordings may be enjoyed by the modern generation, most of whom were not even born when these historic slices of folklore and heritage were performed. …
>
> The Archive of Folk Music is proud to bring these recordings to you. If your reactions are favorable, we can continue the "good fight" and bring you more great performances – Good listening!

I quote it at length to convey something of the atmosphere in which folk music moved in Bob Dylan's early years – the atmosphere in which he precipitated a thunderstorm.

The album itself is a well-made selection from the

recordings (now "Electronically Stereotized") made with Cisco Houston and Sonny Terry for Folkways in New York in the early '40s. I have another, obviously slightly later Everest Records release, which is a sampler of the definitive bluegrass sides that Lester Flatt and Earl Scruggs cut for Mercury between 1948 and 1950. The label has moved to 2020 Ave. of the Stars, Los Angeles, and the series has now become the Archive of Folk & Jazz Music, with the Statement of Purpose tweaked accordingly, but these are still "authentic performances of indigenous and unselfconscious music" and, though less than twenty years old, "historic slices of folklore and heritage". These are quality records and their purpose seems sincere, or as sincere as Hollywood gets, but the notes illustrate perfectly how 'folk' can generate time-space anomalies sufficient to provide for a whole series of *Star Trek: Voyager*.

Woody Guthrie has some of these absurdities skewered to a nicety in an episode towards the end of his highly coloured autobiography, *Bound for Glory*. He's auditioning in the Rainbow Room on the top floor of the Rockefeller Center, New York, and the managers of the cabaret are trying to work out how to stage him:

> "I have it! Listen! I have it!" The lady rose up from her table with a look on her face like she was in a trance of some kind, and she walked over across the carpet to where I was standing, saying, "I have it! Pierrot! We shall dress him in a Pierrot costume! One of those darling clown suits! It will bring out the life and the pep and the giddy humour of his period! Isn't that a simply swell idea?" She folded her hands under her chin again and swayed over against my shoulder as I side-stepped to miss her. "Imagine! What the proper costuming will bring out in these people! Their carefree life! Open skies! The quaint simplicity. Pierrot! Pierrot!" She was dragging me across the floor by the arm, and we left the room

with everybody talking at once. Some taking tryouts said, "Gosh! Gon'ta catch on!"

Outside, on a high glass porch of some kind, where wild tangled green things growed all along the floor by the windows, she shoved me down in a leather chair by a plastic table and sighed and puffed like she'd done an honest day's work. "Now, let me see, oh yes, now my impression of the slight sample of your work is a bit, so to say, incomplete, that is, as far as the cultural traditions represented and the exchange and interrelationships and overlappings of these same cultural patterns are concerned, especially here in America, where we have, well, such a mixing bowl of culture, such a stew-pot of shades and colors. But, nevertheless, I think the clown costume will represent a large portion of the humorous spirit of all of them – and – "

I let my ears bend away from her talking and I let my eyes drift out the window and down sixty-five stories where the town of old New York was standing up living and breathing and cussing and laughing down yonder acrost that long island.

The key phrase, in the present context, is "his period": "the life and the pep and the giddy humour of his period!" But the whole passage is illuminating. While it's not impossible, or even implausible, that someone suggested a Pierrot costume to Woody, that sudden shift from luvvie-speak to cod sociology makes it clear that this lady is an emblem, an amalgam of attitudes to folk, to "these people". And perhaps she represents an ambivalence, not only about the ways he was presented and represented, but also about ways he had presented himself, as a source of "giddy humour" or as a walking piece of social history; his role as what Bob Dylan called "a *glorified* folksinger".

In fact, the choice of Pierrot really is an inspiration – probably of Guthrie's – because the clown has been one of the chief conduits of folk into a more sophisticated arena. Where Shakespeare is closest to folk, for example, is often in the songs in the mouths of his Fools. Indeed, the word 'clown' itself originally meant a peasant. The clown is an irruption of the Other, and a containment of it; the Other being the uncivilised 'remnant' of society and also of the individual mind. The white-face make-up, concealing the performer's identity, offers us a grotesque reflection of ourselves. The clown's relation to the unconscious, and particularly uncon-scious fears and aggression, shows through in the moments where he goes beyond the ritual boundaries which contain his salutary anarchy; where he becomes an image of something deeply sinister and menacing, or of bitterness and desolation. (Perhaps the poignancy of the heartbroken clown lies more in the contrast between aggression and tenderness than in the contrast between laughter and sadness…)

Two historical moments should be mentioned in this connection. One is the moment in the first dawn of Modernist art when Picasso, dispersing the melancholy of his Blue Period, prefaced the full-frontal incursion of the 'primi-tive' in *Les Demoiselles d'Avignon* with the clown and circus imagery of his Rose Period. The second is the earliest dis-semination of black music in America, or at least an inkling of its spirit, through the agency of "nigger minstrels" – usual-ly, but not exclusively, white performers wearing black-face, in a peculiar negative of the usual clown's face. There is still something of the harlequin in Hank Williams, whose songs introduced hillbilly sensibility into the crooning pop main-stream of the early 1950s. His rhinestone flash, descended from the musical cowboys of Hollywood (who got it from the circus riders of the old Wild West shows), was inherited by Elvis, who brought it to a ridiculous sublimity, or sublime ridiculousness.

In *Bound for Glory*, however, Woody Guthrie proposes for himself a different form of entry into the metropolitan world, other than as a clown. At the end of the episode quoted above, as his mind wanders away from the chatter of the theatrical lady and his eyes wander out across New York, he has this vision:

> Limp papers whipped and beat upwards, rose into the air and fell head over heels, curving over backwards and sideways, over and over, loose sheets of newspaper with pictures of people and stories of people printed somewhere on them, turning loops in the air. And it was blow, little paper, blow! Twist and turn and stay up as long as you can, and when you come down, come down on a pent-house porch, come down easy so's not to hurt your self. Come down and lay there in the rain and the wind and the soot and smoke and the grit that gets in your eyes in the big city – and lay there in the sun and get faded and rotten. But keep on trying to tell your message, and keep on trying to be a picture of a man, because without that story and without that message printed on you there, you wouldn't be much. Remember, it's just maybe, some day, sometime, somebody will pick you up and look at your picture and read your message, and carry you in his pocket, and lay you on his shelf, and burn you in his stove. But he'll have your message in his head and he'll talk it and it'll get around. I'm blowing, and just as wild and whirling as you are, and lots of times I've been picked up, throwed down, and picked up; but my eyes have been my camera taking pictures of the world and my songs has been messages that I tried to scatter across the back sides and along the steps of the escapes and on the window sills and through the dark halls.

This passage seems a likely source for the refrain of Dylan's BLOWIN' IN THE WIND – *Bound for Glory*, after all, was practically holy writ for him in his late teens. For the moment, though, notice Guthrie's version of the 'folk process', an intriguing reversal of convention as expressed, for example, by the Archive of Folk Music. There the oral tradition is captured by the modern media, almost inadvertently it appears, at a technical and commercial level too rudimentary to have interfered with the "unselfconscious" art. In Woody's metaphor, the process passes from the industrial media (the scrap of newspaper), through a process of natural selection, as it were (the random forces of wind, rain, sun), into oral tradition. The perversity of this as folklore science, following straight on from the parody of folk-phoniness in the Pierrot episode, is probably quite deliberate. It also proved to be prophetic.*

"The answer, my friend, is blowin' in the wind": perhaps behind the enigma of Dylan's chorus there lies the thought that these questions he asks have been answered already – in messages that Woody Guthrie "tried to scatter", that had been "picked up, throwed down, and picked up". If so, the song that evokes that vision also came to fulfil it. BLOWIN' IN THE WIND became, if anything in the modern world can be, a 'folk song', on a national and international scale – but only because it was propagated mechanically, in printed form and, more importantly, as a record. This is not quite the same thing as the old line that 'pop music is modern folk music': the crucial difference with this song of Dylan's is that it was widely *sung*, not just widely heard. But it spread with a rapidity and to a distance that was simply not possible through oral transmission.

Well before he convulsed the scene by going electric, Dylan had found an ambiguity in folk orthodoxy, a place of ambivalence and tension, and hence of energy – a place that could be called Fenario. It wasn't hard for him to find: following in Woody Guthrie's footsteps led him there, because it was where Woody came from.

---

* The unsigned sleevenote to one of the most influential LPs of the 1960s, *Robert Johnson: King of the Delta Blues Singers*, issued in 1961, takes up the same metaphor: "Robert Johnson appeared and disappeared, much in the same fashion as a sheet of newspaper twisting and twirling down a dark and windy midnight street."

# · 4 ·

# Written Somewhere Down In The United States

L et's go back for a moment to Maud Karpeles's *Introduction to English Folk Song*. It provides us with a plain definition of folk song, as adopted in 1954 by the International Folk Music Council, of which the author was a founder member. Karpeles was a collaborator with the great folk scholar Cecil Sharp on his trips to the Appalachian Mountains, where they collected hundreds of songs and thousands of tune variants descended from the near-moribund English tradition (published in *Folk Songs from the Southern Appalachians*, 1917). It seems fair to take the late summary of her life's study presented in the *Introduction* (1974) as representative of folklore orthodoxy in the first half of the last century. I shall paraphrase the IFMC's definition briefly.

The essential point is oral composition and transmission – songs written down or transmitted primarily in print or on records are not folk. Then there are three subsidiary but also cardinal points which we might call extension, adaptation and selection. First, extension: to belong properly to the tradition, a song must have proved its fitness in a Darwinian way by 'reproducing' in space and time – being passed from one singer to another and handed down from one generation to the next. Then, adaptation: as it spreads, a song should also mutate, subsequent singers bringing their own improvements to the original. Finally, selection: the oral tradition which causes the versions to proliferate should also preserve its favourites, perhaps also recombining them as it does so.

Karpeles notes that "among the early German Romantic writers" folk song seems sometimes to be viewed "as a kind of mysterious, spontaneous product of the folk soul". For all its scientific clarity, though, is the IFMC's creed any less mystical? It's an ideal prescriptive formula: if you wanted to produce a folk song, "an expression of the community and not merely of the individual", to quote Karpeles again, this would certainly be the way to do it. Whether it describes what the tradition actually contains, or whether it would be useful to curtail the tradition to only what fits the formula, is another matter.

Leaving aside the dynamic chaos of America, even in the more stable English context much, and perhaps most, 'folk' must break one or other of these rules. The aim is to democratise the art, to make sure as many people as possible take a hand and to remove it as far as possible from the "merely" individual. But however communal the process we envisage, unless we think of a piece going from door to door, begging a line here and a melodic phrase there, which the scholars agree is absurd, then we must assume that somewhere, in some form, the songs had individual composers. Of course, they had ready-made material to hand, and their composition might shade imperceptibly into adaptation: a new song could be made by fitting new words to an existing tune, or vice versa; familiar cadences could be combined in a new melody, old tales retold, stock situations reworked. But if originality was not a criterion either for these songmakers or their audiences, and if the rewards of fame and money were not on offer as they might be for the art or the commercial composer, still there is no reason to suppose that their creative thinking was fundamentally different from that of other musicians. It might be no trifling reward simply to be known as a maker of good songs, or to know yourself as one. How, then, can the individual, conscious artist be written out of the folk equation, even if they would never refer to themselves as artists – any more than they would refer to themselves as folk?

Again, if we acknowledge the beauty and subtlety and force of folk songs, why should we suppose that those who contributed them were capable only of good bits, lines or verses or phrases, and not whole works? And if a song was good and complete, why should it be altered? The oral tradition is fertile in variation, undoubtedly, but it also seems to be capable of startlingly exact transmission. The brothers Grimm, for example, recorded how one old lady from whom they were taking down fairy-tales would stop to correct herself when she hadn't told a part of her story in *exactly* the right form of words. In fact, there is much evidence – startling to literate and untrained people like us – of the prodigies of precise memory achieved by oral traditions. Karpeles herself gives an instance, an eleven-verse Robin Hood ballad collected by Cecil Sharp which proved to be identical, virtually word for word, with a version printed, but not widely circulated, two centuries earlier. So it is not impossible that some folk songs, being entirely the works of individuals, have also come down to us in the form in which they were first created.

So much for tradition and the individual talent: so far we have just been hypothesising on the basis of a purely oral community, which rural England has not been for many hundreds of years. Literacy may not have been common among the peasantry but it was hardly unknown, and those who were not literate themselves could still be influenced by literary culture. Those same "clowns" who bring a folk element into Shakespeare, for example, also take Shakespeare away with them, being among the groundlings at the Globe. Similarly, lutes were hung on the walls of barbershops in Elizabethan towns, so that the gentlemen might show their accomplishment in song. Even if this was a milieu of the genteel, in which the courtly madrigal prevailed, we may assume that these shops or booths had doorways which opened onto the streets: that the achievements of the sophisticated and the simple musician, in other words, could never have been that far from influencing each other.

We also know that the printed word – and its world of urban commerce and industry – had an important place in folk culture. In fact, there was a class of professional folksingers in England: the broadsheet pedlars who sang ballads and sold the sheet music, particularly at fairs. In Ben Jonson's *Bartholomew Fair* (1614), the witless Bartholomew Cokes discovers that he doesn't have the coin to buy the sheet of the ballad – an admonition to cutpurses – which he's just heard sung, because his purse has been stolen as he listened by the cutpurse Edgworth, an accomplice of the ballad-singer, Nightingale. Jonson's editor, William Gifford (1756-1826) provides this footnote to the scene: "In Jonson's time scarcely any ballad was printed without a wooden cut, illustrative of its subject. ... The houses of the common people, especially those of the distant counties, seem to have had little other ornamental tapestry than was supplied by these fugitive pieces, which came out every term in incredible numbers, and were rapidly dispersed over the kingdom by shoals of itinerant syrens."

In the introduction to a fine anthology, *The Common Muse: Popular British ballad poetry from the 15th to the 20th century* (Chatto & Windus, 1957; Penguin, 1965), the editors, V. de Sola Pinto and A. E. Rodway, cite the scholar Chappell as having traced more than two hundred and fifty ballad publishers in London in the seventeenth century. And despite Gifford's past tense, the ballad trade was still thriving in his time and continued to do so till the mid-nineteenth century, when it began to be superseded as popular song by the music hall and as sensationalism by the "penny dreadful" newspapers. In the early nineteenth century there were lucrative ballad publishing businesses not only in London but in every major city in England, providing teams of singing pedlars with their wares, the distributors also acting as collectors, bringing back songs that they picked up on their rounds – or perhaps that they composed themselves. Grisly murder ballads were the "great goes" as a ballad seller, a "running patterer", told Henry Mayhew, author of *London Labour and the London Poor*, in the mid-nineteenth century. Mayhew cites a single murder ballad selling two and a half million copies in 1849.

The main concern of de Sola Pinto and Rodway's introduction is to show how the contemporary street ballad, more even than the "ancient" ballad, was a source of vigour for English poetry, known at first hand and adopted by writers from the Elizabethans through to the Romantics. In passing, they suggest how the reverse was also true, to some extent at least, that literary poetry entered into the popular forms – often by way of parody, but not exclusively. They mention, for example, that Wordsworth's ballad-influenced poem 'We Are Seven' was itself circulated as a penny broadsheet in the early nineteenth century. And certainly they make it clear that *written* ballads were so popular and so widespread that we cannot conceive of a popular song tradition in England which remained untouched by them.

· 5 ·

# So All Souls Can See It

The tenets I have been contending with are no longer articles of faith for folklorists. In *American Music: A Panorama*, Daniel Kingman writes:

So intertwined for centuries have been the printed and oral traditions that the notion of a "pure" oral tradition, existing uninterruptedly for generations, aloof from the contaminating populism or professionalism of printed media, is a myth with no more relation to actuality than the romantic but discredited notion of the spontaneous "communal creation" of ballads. The facts are, first, that a ballad, however it may have changed over time, was originally the product of a single individual (who can even be identified in some cases); and, second, that the older it is, the more likely it is to have been in and out of print over the course of its history.

Kingman does also say, however: "Among folklorists, oral transmission still retains its preeminence as the ideal medium of folk song."

What matters for our purposes is that when both Woody Guthrie and Bob Dylan were coming up, these tenets still underpinned the folk movement. In America, though, folk acquired further layers of ideology, particularly through its association with communism. After the Russian Revolution, the Soviet example endorsed folk art as a vehicle for propaganda, while the bitter struggle for unionisation and vicious anti-union repression in the US, notably in the coal-mines of Kentucky, inspired a new kind of ballad, drawing on traditional materials but with topical and partisan lyrics – the protest song, in a word.

The British proletariat had, of course, produced songs of social criticism for as long as it had existed (a selection of them makes up the second section of *The Common Muse*); but these tend more to the type of the complaint and the petition than to the rallying cry. In 'The Coal-Owner and the Pitman's Wife', for example, from the 1840s, the poor woman tricks the rich man into believing she has returned from hell, which is evicting its poor occupants to make way for the vast influx of the wealthy damned, and persuades him he should treat his workers better if he wants to stay out of the devil's clutches. The blend of poignancy and mischief, and the dash of the sulphurously supernatural, give this a true ballad flavour – but it hardly makes for sound Marxist politics. In America, though, the new confluence of a politically conscious class struggle with folk music proved a potent combination for the urban intelligentsia.

From the beginning I believe there was a moral undertone to the 'classical' view of folk song. The definition we looked at earlier does not really serve to explain a tradition or how it came to be, but it aims to circumscribe an art which is pure because it is free of certain motives, notably personal gain or glory. (I am not arguing that there is no such area of music-making – it may be the very lifeblood of music – but I don't believe in its isolation as a pure form. After all, blood circulates, and collects impurities.) In the US, cultural purity combined with the ethical superiority of the proletariat, as the vanguard of the revolution (although the folk of the folklorists and Marx's proletariat were hardly identical), to lend folk music a freight of righteousness of religious proportions. So, with Woody Guthrie, socialism takes on the aura of the Christian millennium –

> Jesus of Nazareth told my people one and all,
> You got to join my union army when you hear my union call,
> It's my good old union feeling in my soul…

– while with Bob Dylan the promulgation of revolution becomes eschatological prophecy of an unmistakably biblical kind. This is the faith that fuelled the passionate controversy about Dylan's 'going electric', which crystallised in that inspired yell at the Free Trade Hall, Manchester, in May 1966: "JUDAS!"

With uncanny accuracy, Dylan hit two sore points simultaneously. He managed to 'sell out', ascending to a whole new level of personal wealth and popularity, even as he adopted an aesthetic of 'pure' personal expression, of unrepentant obscurity and, it was felt, elitism, with a clique-language of bohemian references impenetrable to 'ordinary people'. In other words, he gave himself to *both* of the areas which folk was circumscribed against – selfish art music and greedy commercial music – *at the same time*. It almost looks deliberate…

## · 6 ·

# Am I Hearin' Ya Right?

We have surveyed the charged field that young Bob Dylan entered, and the zones of slippage running through it. There is still one more peculiarity of folk in the American context to be dealt with. In America, folk song has been primarily a matter of recordings, not just texts or tune transcriptions. Of course, folk collectors like Cecil Sharp used recording technology as soon as it was available to them, realising that the manner of what they were preserving was as distinctive as the matter. In America, though, the commercial recording industry struck a motherlode in the early 1920s when it discovered that rural people, both black and white, would pay good money to hear their own songs on records – that there was a market which actually preferred its music 'raw'. The great advantage of this was that the records cost hardly anything to make – no arrangers, composers, orchestras, and even, once the field recording unit came in, no studios. Set up in a hotel in a provincial centre somewhere, put the word out through the local press, pay a few dollars per side to the musicians... Some of the most enduring music of the twentieth century was made in this way.

The name to mention here is Ralph Peer, one of the pivotal figures in the history of music recording, and hence of modern music altogether. In August 1920, working for the Okeh label of the General Phonograph Corporation, he assisted in the making of the first black blues record – 'Crazy Blues' by Mamie Smith and Her Jazz Hounds – which launched the whole business of 'Race' and subsequently 'Rhythm & Blues' recordings that drove the sound of

America in the last century. If jazz was America's musical laboratory, this was its dynamo.

Peer had the nous to realise that the best way to serve the vast black market revealed by 'Crazy Blues' was to go out and record musicians in the most natural way possible, near to home, playing just what they played to please the home-folks. With his pioneering field recording unit, he was then struck by cultural lightning again, in Atlanta in June 1923 – though he didn't realise it. His recordings of Fiddlin' John Carson, already a star on local radio, were only pressed up on the insistence of the record-shop manager, Polk Brockman, who'd brought Carson to his attention. Once Brockman had sold the first five hundred copies (unlabelled) in the first month, Peer saw the error of his ways, gave the record an Okeh catalogue number and reissued it nationally, effectively inaugurating the 'Hillbilly' record business as well. As if this wasn't enough, in the first week of August 1927, in a town called Bristol, Peer caught two more thunderbolts in quick succession, whose reverberations would shape country music up to the present day: the Carter Family and Jimmie Rodgers.

In 1999, Steve Earle paid a little tribute to Bristol, the border town, on his bluegrass album *The Mountain*, in the song 'Carrie Brown':

> I walked around in Bristol town, a bitter broken man,
> A heart that pined for Carrie Brown and a pistol in my hand.
> We met again on State Street, poor Billy Wise and me.
> I shot him in Virginia and he died in Tennessee.

The song might have been written for the sake of that last line.

Hank Williams paid a kind of tribute to Bristol too, on that last, long midnight ride on which he died. Either in his final hours or shortly after them, he – or his corpse – was driven through the birthplace of country music. The details of the journey conflict from one witness to another, but some claim to have seen him walking and talking in Bristol that night. If so, then it was the last place he did so; and if not, then not a bad place for his ghost to show.

We shall be returning to the Carters and to Jimmie Rodgers. As for Ralph Peer, his memory will never be far away, since he first broke this ground that Bob Dylan and thousands of others have cultivated.

A t first glance, recordings might be seen as just a technical extension of the oral tradition, but in fact they radically altered it. They allowed a new speed and range of dissemination; they allowed regional styles to escape and cross-fertilise; but above all they froze time. They kept the styles of powerful individual performers intact, and in effect removed them from the tradition. There is no mileage in being the reincarnation of Jimmie Rodgers, say, if Jimmie Rodgers himself is still available. And the paradoxical effect of this freezing of time was to speed it up: the achievements preserved in recordings put the next generation of musicians under an obligation of change, of development.

Despite their commercial contamination, records were gladly accepted into the folk music canon in America. (They were supplemented, it should be pointed out, by the devoted labours of researchers – especially John and Alan Lomax, father and son – collecting the music of communities too small, poor or marginal to have had any commercial potential, like the Sea Islands of the southeastern seaboard, where black music retained its strongest African echoes, or the chain-gangs of southern penitentiaries, whose work-songs remembered the voices of the field-slaves of the plantations.) The canonical collection for the student folksingers of the 1950s and '60s was the *Anthology of American Folk Music*, three boxed sets of two LPs each, compiled by Harry Smith and released by Folkways of New York in 1952. Smith deliberately limited his selection to records which had achieved a degree of commercial success, not (or not only) to subvert conventional views, but on the grounds that it provided an actual measure of popularity, of representativeness. Following this democratic principle, he mapped out an "invisible republic", to borrow Greil Marcus's term. Arranging his material thematically, ignoring lines of influence, of chronology or geography, Smith's anthology effectively creates a synthetic pan-American folk music. And it is this essentially modern, universalising movement in which Bob Dylan took his place. Behind his early Everyman persona, behind the image of a drifter who's "been around this whole country", of a folksinger who acquires his songs and style from everywhere, but from nowhere in particular, there obviously lies such a tradition: the delocalised and atemporal kind of tradition which was created by recordings and which crystallised in Smith's *Anthology*. Yet this is only half the equation. As a folk artist, Dylan was shaped by another consequence of recording, namely, a new premium placed on originality.

While the scholars are occupied with transcribing words and tunes, their sources are treated as clear founts, as it were – impersonal outlets from which the age-old waters flow, unsullied by individual quirks. But when the scholars begin to be collectors of sound, and can capture and ponder how a region, a history, an ancestry, a life can shape the grain of a voice, the way prevailing wind sculpts a tree on a mountainside, then the twists and angles and rugosities of that voice come to be valued, and divergence and idiosyncrasy become almost the badge of authenticity. In America, the country blues especially (or the folk blues as it was often called) put the individuality of the performer in the foreground.

## · 7 ·

# Bob Dylan's Blues

ylan's first record is steeped in the blues, as is his latest. It's the strongest single thread running through all his music, and among his major collections of songs I can think of only one, *Desire*, which does not use the form at least once. Such a bias to the blues may reflect the milieu and the period in which his talent first blossomed, but it's hardly an idiosyncrasy.

The blues is the matrix of American popular music, mythologically at least. If Jazz & Blues are often listed together as though they were siblings, the blues is thought of as the elder, and even (on little historical ground) as the parent, the soil out of which jazz grew. In the mid twentieth century, the ability to play sincere and meaningful blues was an acid test of the improvising soloist. As for the form that came to dominate the popular music market, Willie Dixon, the bassist, producer and songwriter – who entitled his autobiography *I Am the Blues* – put it simply in the title of a song: 'The Blues Had a Baby (And They Called It Rock'n'Roll)'.

When Dylan 'went electric' in 1965, it wasn't really rock'n'roll in its original sense that he returned to, but a descendant of the electrified Rhythm & Blues that he would have heard pouring out of 'Gatemouth' Page's radio show from Little Rock, Arkansas when he was a teenager. Like other changes of direction – like the later country phase, revealing the influence of one of his earliest models, Hank Williams, but also catching the current backing of the countercultural wind – the shift to electric blues was a personal revival but a timely one as well.

Slouching behind the front line of British pop groups that

capitalised on the Beatles' storming of America in 1964 – the likes of the Dave Clark Five and Herman's Hermits – had come the R&B groups like the Animals and the Rolling Stones, and behind them came the serious gunslingers of blues-rock (though the tribal demarcations of 'beat' enthusiasts and rhythm and blues purists, so important back home, got blurred in the general melee of the 'British invasion'). Dylan's electric music has recently been credited (in a *Q* magazine special) with marking the point where 'rock' was born. But the transition from 'pop', with its rapidly moving harmonies, to the more monolithic patterns of 'rock' (to take up a distinction used by the Beatles scholar, Ian MacDonald) can be seen in the emergence – explosion, more like – of the new breed of bands like John Mayall's Bluesbreakers and the Paul Butterfield Blues Band, playing the blues with the flying beats of rock'n'roll and with hot young soloists who could fill extended numbers with fierce virtuosity.

It was the nucleus of Butterfield's band – which had the slight advantage over its British counterparts of hailing from Chicago and learning at the feet of the great originators like Muddy Waters and Howlin' Wolf – that Dylan took on stage with him for that first electrified performance at the Newport Folk Festival in 1965. He had surely heard the LP of socking electric blues that the Muddy Waters Band had recorded at the festival's forerunner, the Newport Jazz Festival, way back in 1956, without anyone trying to take an axe to the power cables. But a style appreciated by the jazz audience was still not tolerable as folk a decade later, even though by then the electric blues had a history going back a good 20 years.

The country blues, on the other hand, was a folk dream: an apparently self-sufficient oral tradition created by a people – the black rural poor – whom racism, poverty, poor education and geographical remoteness had largely excluded from the mainstream culture of modern America. Here was an artform contiguous with the life of the folklorist, yet so alien as to be almost a secret language; with ancient roots (possibly: the question of African retentions in the blues is still open), yet only truly alive when it is created in the moment. It radically altered the idea of folk in America, shifting the weight of definition from the process to the people: those who made the blues were folk, therefore the blues was folk. But the most striking thing about the blues singers – the solo country blues singers especially – is the unique sonic universe each one inhabits.

Big Joe Williams, Blind Willie McTell, Blind Lemon Jefferson, Lightnin' Hopkins: from the first notes, their songs are stamped with their individuality. Each has a timbre to his voice, a way of tuning, a style of playing, a rhythmic movement and an interplay between the singing and the guitar which are his own, and which soon become unmistakable. Within a single stream of the tradition, like the great family of the Mississippi blues, almost every member – those who attain to their majority, as it were – is *sui generis*: compare Skip James with John Lee Hooker, Mississippi John Hurt with Furry Lewis, or the second Sonny Boy Williamson with Howlin' Wolf. Even where we can trace a direct line of artistic descent, for example from Charley Patton through Son House to Robert Johnson, and then on to Muddy Waters, the different and powerful impact of each personality is much more immediately striking than their stylistic common ground. Out of the same few basic elements, each of these blues musicians appears to have built a world of his own. Indeed it is this spirit of originality, of singularity, which seems to be their essential link, the real substance of their tradition. (That's why the traduction of the blues into a musical Esperanto – the twelve-bar plod, less Howlin' Wolf than howling waffle – seems so contrary.)

There's an obvious social reason for the assertion of the self in the blues: it was created by black people in a place and time where, by and large, a person with darker skin was practically not a person at all. There might also be a marketplace meaning to the blues' self-reliant aesthetic: the advantage of establishing a distinct individual 'brand'. What concerns us for the moment is the influence of this individualism on the philosophy of the folk revival, and what Bob Dylan learned from it.

His mentor, Woody Guthrie, is a good example of how the paradigm of folk in the United States differed from – and almost inverted – that of the Old World. Leadbelly, Woody's contemporary on the East Coast folk circuit, is another. In the firmament of the folk revival, these two were the leading lights, the respective repositories of black and white traditions, and their names have been yoked together ever since. Hence the joint tribute album, *A Vision Shared*, put out by Folkways Records in 1988, on which Dylan sings 'Pretty Boy Floyd' and shows, with beguiling simplicity, that he really did absorb Woody Guthrie as thoroughly as any living musician. (And on which Little Richard – who was Bob's last idol before his "last idol", Woody – whips out a cracking 'Rock Island Line', backed by Fishbone. And on which the most beautiful pairing, and one of the least likely in American music, is of Brian Wilson and Leadbelly on 'Goodnight Irene'.)

Certainly Leadbelly had a repertoire that embraced all kinds of songs, from blues and chain-gang hollers to children's rhymes and cowboy ballads. But – whether it's his voice, his twelve-string guitar style, or his monumental rhythmic power – there is not another bluesman on record who sounds remotely like him. With a face worthy of a Mount Rushmore, Leadbelly was a prize in the museum of living folklore, a one-man cross-section of 'the voice of the Negro'; but like each of those bluesmen mentioned above, he didn't represent a tradition so much as remake it in his own image.

The same is true of Woody Guthrie, but the case is altered. The sources from which he derived his style were basic and few – essentially, it was composed of equal parts Jimmie Rodgers and the Carter Family, which would be rather a narrow foundation were not each of the sources in itself so broad.

The Carters could be called the motherlode of the music of the Appalachian Mountains, of 'hillbilly' and everything it subsequently became. But the metaphor of ore is misleading, because their music is far from unrefined. The prime mover of the group, Alvin Pleasant 'Doc' Carter, who formed the original trio with his wife Sara and his brother's wife Maybelle, was not an "unconscious" folk artist, but a folklorist himself, though one who happened to live *in situ*. Raised in a strictly religious household, he loved the forbidden fiddle music of his Clinch Mountain home. An insider-outsider, his 'folk' is both deep-rooted and deliberate. The original Carters' records are crystalline, an essence, almost an abstract of a tradition; and these records themselves became a tradition – one of the things people had to hold on to as the Great Depression decimated populations in the southern states. Yet for all the spirit of place which informs them, and the familial closeness of the ensemble, some unthawed isolation remains. A high, keening lonesomeness shivers in the harmonies and runs like silver wire through the heart of the songs.

Moving counter to the Carters' homeward gravity, the voice of Jimmie Rodgers leans out and onward, towards the horizon. So often the wanderer in his songs, whether hobo or cowboy or high-roller, he sounds like a man who would never want for company; and this companionable quality and the confidence in which he travels is perhaps what most endeared him to a community threatened and fractured by migrations. He has been dubbed the Father of Country Music, but his thought is on a continental scale and no parish can hold him. From the Cumberland Gap to the Delta, from New Orleans to Tin Pan Alley, and from Memphis to the western plains, he roamed with inspiring assurance, like Elvis Presley's, across the whole terrain of popular music. There is a state, according to William Blake, beyond the contraries of innocence and experience, which he calls "organised innocence". That is the sound of Jimmie Rodgers.

Woody Guthrie had from him (though surely influenced, too, by Chaplin's rebounding tramp) the indomitable little-man persona and his backbone of blues; and from the Carters, a fund of songs and Maybelle's guitar style – the musical materials that were readiest to hand in his time and place – which he organised into a new world. He was folk in the sense that he had a solid foundation of busking – playing to try and please the crowd in public places, and speaking from the same level as them, rather than raised up on a stage. But *Bound for Glory* makes it clear that he took up music as a form of *self-expression*: "I just felt like I was going out of my wits if I didn't find some way of saying what I was thinking."

He thought, he says, of being a lawyer, then a preacher, then a doctor; he read voraciously in all subjects; and then he took up painting: "The world didn't mean any more than a smear to me if I couldn't find ways of putting it down on something." So when he started to play, he was already an artist: "I made up new words to old tunes and sung them everywhere I'd go. ... [B]efore long I was invited in and boot-ed out of every public place of entertainment in that country."

His explanation for the particular attraction of music is entirely economical (by the time he wrote *Bound for Glory* he was well-versed in Marxism, of course): "A picture – you buy it once and it bothers you for forty years; but with a song, you sing it out, and it soaks in people's ears and they all jump up and down and sing it with you, and then when you quit singing, it's gone, and you get a job singing it again." It is iron-ic, given how much of Guthrie's own art seems to have been acquired from the phonograph, that this is an economy large-ly obliterated by the commodification of music through recordings. (Bob Dylan, however, is one 'commodity' musician who still lives by his old mentor's philosophy, though not really for materialist reasons.) The flip-side of this fixing of the folk song as an object was that, from the mid-Twenties on, as people took the old tunes home with them on shellac, there was an opening for an artist like Guthrie to develop a 'unique selling point' by giving the mass-produced versions a local and topical reference – reappropriating the commodity, as it were.

> Then I got a little braver and made up songs telling what I thought was wrong and how to make it right, songs that said what everybody in that country was thinking.
>
> And this has held me ever since.

Woody Guthrie created the template from which Bob Dylan worked: he established the idea that an original individual artist could be 'folk', and new compositions could be folk songs. From the start, though – or at least from very early on – Dylan seems to have seen that this was a contradiction. Perhaps the change came when he got to know Woody personally. After their first encounter, he proclaimed (in a postcard to friends): "I know Woody… I know him and met him… He's the greatest holiest godliest one in the world." Clearly, he believed in this man as an incarnation of the goodwill of the People. A couple of years later, in one of his '11 Outlined Epitaphs', he wrote that Woody "taught me / face t' face / that men are men / shatterin' even himself / as an idol / and that men have reasons / for what they do". His understanding of folk ideology as myth is clear on his first album, though. It lies behind the crack about Fenario, pitting his own (mythical) experience against the hallowed truth-to-life of the tradition. In another introductory rap, he has another dig, juxtaposing the ideal of oral transmission with the academic milieu in which folk was fostered: "I learned this song from Ric von Schmidt. Ric's a blues guitar player and I met him in the green pastures of – Harvard University." And then there's the ironic comment in TALKIN' NEW YORK:

> I got up on the stage to sing and play,
> Man there said, 'Come back some other day.
> You sound like a hillbilly.
> We want folksingers here.'

The unerring aim for the point of weakness that would be demonstrated in his "truth attacks" on friends and acquaintances in the mid-Sixties was already in evidence from the beginning.

## · 8 ·

# Jokerman Dance

Now we have seen how 'Bob Dylan', the persona of his earliest appearance before the general public, the 'hero' of his first two records – *Bob Dylan* and *The Freewheelin' Bob Dylan* – was shaped by the requirements of the folk revival. I referred, near the beginning of the present part, to wider and deeper resonances of this figure and how it persisted, as the initial pretences were gradually put away – and still does to this day. It is this we should turn to now.

A persona originally meant the mask assumed by an actor in the Greek theatre, and so far we have been treating 'Bob Dylan' in this sense, as a kind of disguise. But this persona, as was said before, was not an assumed identity so much as an erasure of identity: the mundane self negated to make way for the Imagination, in the words of Blake, "the Real Man which liveth for ever". Despite the falsified biography, 'Bob Dylan' depicted something profound and true about the soul of the artist. And now, at sixty, having averaged over a hundred performances a year all over the world for the last twelve years, he has actually become the incessant wanderer that he claimed to have been at twenty.

At first, 'Bob Dylan', drawn from a mythical realm, was a figure larger than his creator, and encompassed him. The early songs are written and sung from within the role, forming a composite portrait like the separate speeches and scenes that build up a part in a play. The character contains the music, as it were. Later, the relation is reversed: as the world of the songs grows broader, deeper and rounder, this original persona is absorbed into it. The wanderer, the character like Huck Finn – tough but not hardened, with an untutored vision piercing the snares of the world that wants to "sivilize" him – or like Charlie Chaplin, mischievous yet innocent, sly yet naive – this character persists as an actor within the songs, and particularly often as the actor called "I". But we no longer have to identify him with the composer of the songs.

We know that the Little Tramp was a conscious resource of Dylan's. "My biggest idol on stage," he said in 1962, "even off stage, running all through my head all the time, was Charlie Chaplin." As for *The Adventures of Huckleberry Finn*, while it's quite likely that Dylan read it in his youth, its influence was probably transmitted more strongly through *Bound for Glory*. Guthrie's vernacular prose is founded on Twain's, and towards the end of his opening chapter, where Woody and the "colored rider", John, are riding through the hard rain and rolling thunder on the roof of a box-car, there's a clear echo of the storm in *Huckleberry Finn*, with Huck and Jim, the runaway slave, floating on a raft down the Mississippi. Funnily enough, when Huck finally decides to "light out for the Territory ahead of the rest", so that they won't "sivilize" him, one of the places he could be going is Woody Guthrie's birth-state, Oklahoma, part of the former Indian Territory.

Two more books, both central to American literature, should be mentioned here, in relation to the wanderer: Melville's *Moby Dick* and Whitman's original *Leaves of Grass*. Dylan's early persona is very much like Whitman's, the man of the people who is also an Everyman: "Walt Whitman, an American, one of the roughs, a kosmos." There are the same references to the open road, and the same lack of a fixed habitation or any circumscribing details of family or occupation.

The narrator of *Moby Dick*, Ishmael – whose biblical namesake, the first son of Abraham, "dwelt in the wilderness" – is likewise strangely blank. Where he is most vividly an actor is in the odd, Chaplinesque scene, early on, in which he shares a bed with the giant, tattooed harpooner, Queequeg.

Once the voyage of the *Pequod* is under way, though, he becomes largely transparent, simply the story's witness (and its sole survivor). By the end of the book, we really know nothing more about him – who he is, where he's from – than the name he gives us in the first sentence: "Call me Ishmael." And that suggests that it's not his real name.

In Dylan's most slapstick, Chaplinesque song, BOB DYLAN'S 115TH DREAM, he plays an Ishmael of sorts:

> I was riding on the Mayflower
> When I thought I spied some land.
> I yelled for Captain Arab,
> I'll have you understand,
> Who came running on the deck,
> Said, 'Boys, forget the whale…'

(The pun on Captain Ahab's name is neat, since the Arabs were said traditionally to be Ishmaelites, the descendants of Ishmael.) Moby Dick becomes America itself, and its madness unfolds before a bewildered Dylan's eyes as the madness of the hunt does before Ishmael's (though the song's "I" is more of an actor). In the end, as Dylan, like Ishmael, escapes alone, the implication is that America, like the white whale, is a devouring monster, unstoppable, and best left to its own devices. It's still one of his funniest songs.

In terms of the universal archetypes proposed by students of symbolism such as Carl Jung and Joseph Campbell, the figure we are dealing with here, as mentioned at the beginning of this chapter, is known as the Trickster.

I don't know much of either African or Native American traditions, but as I understand it, the United States has inherited through them, in however suppressed a form, two mythologies in which Trickster figures play a large part.

Coyote is the name of the Trickster in Indian tales, and in African ones it is Ananse, the spider – Ananse who is also, in some myths, the creator of the world, spinning it out of nothing as the spider does its web.

Another African Trickster is the hare, as for example in the story of the hare and the moon. The moon sends a bird to tell human beings that, just as the moon's light passes away and returns again, so they will die and come back to life. But the hare, meeting the messenger on the way and learning the message, runs on ahead and tells the people that, just as the moon's light is blotted out entirely, so our lives will wane and vanish into darkness – and this is how death came into the world. (A Christian story, it seems to me: the original messenger, who comes afterwards to give the news of eternal life, is the one who is not believed.)

In the Classical mythology with which I'm more familiar, the Trickster deity is the Greek Hermes or Roman Mercury (which, for the astrologically minded, is the ruling planet of Dylan's birth-sign, Gemini). The cult of Hermes had its origin in the sacred stones, or herms, which were erected at crossroads. Hence he is the god of travellers, merchants, heralds, messengers – and also of thieves. His first divine act was a theft – rustling some of his older brother, Apollo's beloved cattle and making the first stringed instrument by stringing a tortoiseshell with their guts. He would be – or once was, I suppose – the deity of musicians, but when he is arraigned for his crime in the court of their father, Zeus, he gives his invention to Apollo, or 'sells' it, in exchange for clemency. (Does this passage of the lyre from one to the other perhaps memorialise the transition from a wandering minstrelsy to the establishment of musicians in courts and cities?) Zeus pardons Hermes and offers him the post of heavenly messenger, on the condition that he must not lie. He accepts on the condition that he is not obliged always to tell the whole truth.

More solemnly, Hermes was the conductor of the souls of the dead to the underworld, and in this role he is the equivalent of the Egyptian god Anubis – who, bringing us back round to the Coyote of the Indians, was depicted with the head of a jackal.

We seem a long way from the little figure we started out with, but the links can be traced through the guises of the clown and the Fool, who in his Shakespearean garb is definitely an aspect of the Trickster. The Trickster may be the weakling who wins by a ruse – like that reincarnation of the African hare, Brer Rabbit outwitting Brer Fox. He or she can also be the youngster or the simpleton of the fairy-tale, who succeeds where the endeavours of elders and betters have failed. Chaplin's Little Tramp, quicker-thinking and at the same time more foolish than his adversaries, conveys this duality beautifully.

The connection of larger mythical forms, of gods and heroes with our guitar-strumming hobo is made explicit by Dylan himself in JOKERMAN, from 1983. When it first came out, the song seemed to mark a sudden resurgence, a re-eruption even, of the symbolist strain in Dylan's writing. EVERY GRAIN OF SAND, at the end of the preceding album, *Shot of Love*, was rich in images, but of a fairly conventional kind, and steadily unfolding, nothing like the leaping allusiveness of JOKERMAN. Before that, for the two albums of his born-again phase, *Slow Train Coming* and *Saved*, Dylan's language had largely been sober and shorn of any but the most conventional symbolism.

It turned out that JOKERMAN did have some forerunners, recorded at the *Shot of Love* sessions and only released later – the dense and ambivalent ANGELINA, GROOM STILL WAITING AT THE ALTAR and CARIBBEAN WIND. However, it seemed at the time that to find a precedent you had to look back to 1978 and the album recorded just before Dylan's conversion, *Street-Legal*. There is the same array of mythic imagery and archetypal characters; and more particularly, there is the same reliance on the symbols of the Tarot.

*Desire*, from 1976, gives a first hint of the Tarot's influence, displaying on its sleeve the Empress card from the popular Waite-Rider pack, first published in 1910, which was designed by a young Jamaican artist, Pamela Coleman Smith, under the instruction of the occult scholar Alfred Waite. In 1978, having spent much of the intervening year making the giant symbolist collage of his film *Renaldo & Clara*, Dylan quotes a number of Tarot cards directly in *Street-Legal* – the Magician, the King and Queen of Swords, the Empress again, Death, the Tower – and much of the imagery has a similar medieval feel to that of the Waite-Rider cards – angels and warlords, merchants and thieves, veil and fountain, palace and painted wagon.

More broadly, both album and film are remarkable for their omnivorous appetite for symbols – an eclecticism that also underlies the Waite-Rider pack, as revealed in the *Key to the Tarot* which Waite published to accompany it. Here he indicates the plethora of gnostic reference which he poured into the cards – borrowings from the Cabala, Freemasonry, Rosicrucianism, the Old Testament, alchemy, Classical and Egyptian mythology, and so on and so forth. He suggests obliquely – for much of his commentary takes the form of hints at esoteric knowledge which he is not at liberty to reveal to the uninitiated – that the twenty-two cards of the major arcana are not coincidentally the same in number as the letters of the Hebrew alphabet, and that they constitute a universal symbolic set which in its various combinations can 'spell' all the conditions of this life.

The songs of *Street-Legal* divide quite cleanly in two, into a set of fairly straightforward man/woman songs, and a set of four apocalyptic, symbolist pieces – CHANGING OF THE

GUARD, NO TIME TO THINK, SEÑOR (TALES OF YANKEE POWER) and WHERE ARE YOU TONIGHT? (JOURNEY THROUGH DARK HEAT). This last group have more than just imagery from the cards; the Tarot seems to have soaked into their artistic method. While earlier adventures in Dylanland are replete with enigmatic visions, they have their rationale in their sense of presence: the listener may not be able to tease out their meaning but there is no doubt that they are *there*. On *Street-Legal*, lines like the following have a painted, flat, diagrammatic quality, while the persistent pulling apart of melodic and syntactic flow only adds to their unnatural air:

> He was torn between Jupiter and Apollo.
> A messenger arrived with a black nightingale.
> I seen her on the stairs and I could not help but follow,
> Follow her down past the fountain where they lifted her veil.

These are more than enigmatic – they seem deliberately cryptic images, as though Dylan has reversed the usual Tarot practice. Where the discrete symbols of the cards are laid down in a pattern and the relations between them read off in connection with the life of the enquirer, here the conditions of life appear to have been translated *into* these emblems dealt out in rapid succession.

The spiritual aspiration in this 'archetyping' is clear enough, but the spiritual constitution of *Street-Legal* is afflicted, profoundly world-weary, full of *accidie*, the torpor and resulting sense of futility which are the enemy of the soul. To reverse the process of fortune-telling implies a terrible kind of predetermination: the permutations of the images are numerous but finite, and experience is finally reduced to a perpetual shuffling and redealing of the same few elements.

The surprising thing with JOKERMAN is how, with a similar vein of imagery, a similar vision of "a shadowy world", as the song puts it, the spirit can be so different. There is a really balletic suppleness and definition to Dylan's vocal performance, which describes an almost untraceable curve that touches on wonder and defiance and fury and joy.

If there is an emotion that predominates on *Infidels*, which JOKERMAN introduces, it is dread, both in its common sense and in the broader, revelatory sense used by Rastafarians, indicating the terrible and challenging state of the world that is clarified by the approach of its End Times, and also that fear of God which is the beginning of wisdom. JOKERMAN is the obverse of the *Street-Legal* songs: instead of an endless and deathly reiteration, it sees an inspiring and terrifying co-existence of states: all the Jokerman has ever been is simultaneously present in him now. In this, the Jokerman is much like the Fool of Waite's Tarot:

> You're a man of the mountains, you can walk on
> > the clouds…

says one verse, and in another we find him

> Half-asleep 'neath the stars with a small dog licking
> > your face.

Or, in an earlier take of the song, and more Chaplinesquely:

> So drunk, standing in the middle of the street,
> Directing traffic, with a small dog at your feet.

In the early Marseilles Tarot, the Fool is a hapless, ragged beggar pursued by a dog; but in Waite's pack his tatters have become the frills and finery of a young prince, who is journeying on a mountain path and about to step blissfully over the edge of a precipice, with a lap-dog fawning at his heels. In the *Key to the Tarot*, Waite describes the Fool as representing the soul on its passage through the world. Its relation to the twenty-one numbered cards of the 'major arcana' – running from the Magician, number I, to the World, number XXI – is like that of the Joker to a conventional pack of cards. As the Joker can be given the value of any card, so the Fool, numbered zero, takes on each of the twenty-one phases – the apparent world – and yet remains essentially unchanged: an Oriental conception of the soul.

After subduing his art to the service of the Gospel, JOKERMAN is a bold reassertion of imaginative freedom, of Dylan's essential nature as a maker and mover of symbols: "manipulator of crowds, you're a dream-twister". But this nature is seen in a wholly new light, and on a scale that brings it both urgency and its burden of dread.


With its far resonance and troubling ambivalence, JOKERMAN touches on another American depiction of the Trickster, of the dark side of the figure, and perhaps the most concentrated in all American literature, in Melville's extraordinary novel *The Confidence-Man: His Masquerade*. A succession of frauds is perpetrated among the passengers of a Mississippi river-boat, by a deceiver whose changes of guise are so radical as to seem supernatural (if indeed they are all one person, which is never resolved). This character could only be called benign or divine, though, in the sense that he so thoroughly reveals to his fellow passengers their own follies – after he has so cunningly and ruthlessly exploited them.

His mythic stature becomes fuller as the novel progresses, till at the very end, as "the cosmopolitan", Frank Goodman, we find him identified with the god Hermes, conductor of the souls of the dead. He extinguishes the last lamp in the cabin, whose glass is richly decorated with images of a horned altar and of a robed man:

The next moment the waning lamp expired, and with it the waning flames of the horned altar, and the waning halo round the robed man's brow; while in the darkness which ensued, the cosmopolitan kindly led the old man away. Something further may follow of this Masquerade.

This "cosmopolitan" – a man of the world, but literally a citizen of the cosmos – this Frank who is far from frank – this Goodman who is not – on board the steamer *Fidèle*, or Faithful – might remind us of that trickster Frank who is the hero of the short story which Dylan provided as a sleevenote to the album *John Wesley Harding*:

> "Faith is the key!" said the first king. "No, froth is the key!" said the second. "You're both wrong," said the third, "the key is Frank!"

In which case, it may not be true that "When that steamboat whistle blows, I'm gonna give you all I've got to give". And equally, the rich young man who was one of the most famous people in the western world at the time may not be "a lonesome hobo without family or friends". It may be a masquerade.

Before we leave the Trickster, there is one further reference to suggest how strong is his presence in Dylan's art. It comes from John Lennon, who said of his song 'I'm a Loser': "Yeah, that's me in my Dylan period, cos it's got the word 'clown' in it. I had always objected to the word 'clown' but Dylan had used it so I thought it was alright and it rhymed with whatever I was doing."

What is intriguing here is that the song was recorded by the Beatles on 14th August 1964 (just two weeks before they met Dylan, on their first American tour), at which time only his first three albums were out, and in those the word "clown" appears only once: "I heard the sound of a clown who cried in the alley" in A HARD RAIN'S A-GONNA FALL. Of course, later albums would have more clowns, though not many, and *Bringing It All Back Home* and *Highway 61 Revisited* in particular are full of other circus and carnival imagery, so that *now is does* seem a characteristic word. Whatever the confusions of hindsight in Lennon's explanation, though, it is an appropriate intuition that the clown is somehow essentially Dylanesque.

Now we have been out to the farther reaches of the hobo persona, there is also one small and particular prototype to consider. In the opening chapter of *Bound for Glory*, we find Woody riding a box-car crowded with hobos, where a fight breaks out. Someone tries to push him out of the door but his friend, "a long tall Negro boy" whom he's just met, grabs him by the arm. Then the assailant tries to push them both out together, but a sudden jerk of the brakes sends him flying instead – "over the slope of the steep cinder grading, rolling, knocking and plowing cinders twenty feet he chugged into the water of the lake."

Woody and the "colored rider" – we learn later that he is called John – also pitch out but land on their feet and manage to swing back onto the train. They climb up on the box-car roof, where they are joined by two boys, "a tall skinny one about fifteen, and a little scrawny runt that couldn't be over ten or eleven." When a huge thunderstorm rolls over them, they all donate their shirts to keeping the rain off Woody's "meal ticket", his guitar.

> Then I pulled the guitar over to where I was laying down. I tied the leather strap around a plank in the boardwalk, ducked my head down behind the guitar and tapped the runty kid on the shoulder.
>
> "Hey, squirt!"

"Whaddaya want?"

"Not much of a windbreak, but it at least knocks a little of th' blister out of that rain! Roll yer head over here an' keep it ducked down behind this music box!"

"Yeeehh." He flipped over like a little frog and smiled all over his face and said, "Music's good fer somethin', ain't it?" …

"T'ink I could eva' play one uv dem?" The little kid was shaking and trembling all over, and I could hear his lips and nose blow the rain away, and his teeth chatter like a jack-hammer. He scooted his body closer to me, and I laid an arm down so he could rest his head. …

Who's this kid? Where's he from, and where's he headed for? Will he be me when he grows up? Was I like him when I was just his size? Let me remember. Let me go back. Let me get up and walk back down the road I come.

And this is the beginning of his reminiscence. It would not have escaped Bobby Zimmerman's notice in the first flush of his Guthrie romance, as a drop-out student in the Twin Cities, Minneapolis-St Paul, playing Woody's songs in the folk clubs and reading the autobiography over and over again, that this "train bound for glory" which the book begins with had pulled out of St Paul and was rolling through Minnesota.

I wonder, did Woody remember his fictive adopted son, the "scrawny runt" in whom he sees himself, when the skinny youth from Minnesota came and played his songs to him?

In the notes that accompany the *Biograph* compilation of 1985, Cameron Crowe gives an account of Dylan's setting out from the Twin Cities: " … he was playing at a St Paul local coffee house and pizza parlour called The Purple Onion. The Purple Onion was located next to the main highway heading out of town. [The owner] took a liking to Dylan and occasionally allowed him to sleep in the back room."

There's still a Purple Onion pizza café in the Twin Cities, but now it's on University Avenue, Minneapolis, in the heart of the campus district, Dinkytown. The one that Dylan knew was further east, at 721 Snelling Avenue North in St Paul. It's the Ginkgo Coffeehouse now, and still an acoustic music venue (unlike another of his haunts, the Ten O'Clock Scholar, which is the site of a Burger King). Snelling Avenue is not "the main highway heading out of town" but about half a mile south of where the Purple Onion used to be, it crosses University Avenue which was then, before the building of Interstate 95, the main east-west route through the Twin Cities.

"Recalled Dylan: 'I just got up one morning and left. I'd spent so much time thinking about it I couldn't think about it anymore. Snow or no snow, it was time for me to go. … I stood on the highway during a blizzard snowstorm believing in the mercy of the world and headed East, didn't have nothing but my guitar and suitcase. That was my whole world. The first ride I got, you know, was from some old guy in a jalopy, sort of a Bela Lugosi type, who carried me into Wisconsin. Of all the rides I've ever gotten it's the only one that stands out in my mind.'"

Heading for Wisconsin, they're likely to have taken University Avenue all the way across town, through the centre of St Paul, and then turned south-east onto the highway that runs down the western bank of the Mississippi. This 'birth trip', then, that took Bobby Zimmerman from Minneapolis in December 1960 and brought Bob Dylan to New York on 24th January 1961, began literally on the trail of Woody Guthrie, by retracing the journey that frames *Bound for Glory*.

Woody's itinerary is pretty clear: "… this morning? St Paul. Yes. The morning before? Bismarck, North Dakota. And the morning before that? Miles City, Montana. Week ago, I was a piano player in Seattle."

He could have come by a number of routes, but there were two lines, the Northern Pacific and the Chicago Milwaukee St Paul & Pacific, that went all the way, linking Seattle with Chicago. As they negotiate the rugged state of Washington from Seattle to Spokane, both lines come across the Columbia River – celebrated in some of Guthrie's finest songs, like 'Grand Coulee Dam' – before heading out over the narrow northern neck of Idaho into Montana. They run beside each other for a while, through the Bitteroot Mountains to Butte, Montana; but once across the young Missouri River, the CMSP&P diverges to the northeast, through the Crazy Mountains, while the Northern Pacific goes southeast, over the Bozeman Pass, which was once the key route through the Rockies for the settlers' wagon trains. The two railroads are reunited on the banks of the Yellowstone River and run parallel into Miles City. From there, the Northern Pacific would have taken Woody to Bismarck, North Dakota, then on in an almost unwavering straight line, 180 miles due east to Fargo. From Fargo to Minneapolis he had a choice of three roads, Northern Pacific, CMSP&P, and Great Northern. However, on the leg of the journey that he's travelling when the book begins, from St Paul towards Chicago through the "lake country" of "Minnesoty", he's almost certainly on the Chicago Milwaukee Saint Paul & Pacific, hugging the western bank of the Mississippi River.

On the TerraServer website, which offers detailed aerial photos of 97 per cent of the United States, you can follow this track running along the riverside, and for quite a lot of the way the road that Dylan was on runs close by, and sometimes absolutely cheek-by-jowl. The detail is so fine (the pictures, copyright "Sovinform-Sputnik", are old Russian military intelligence that has been sold off) you can even make out a stretch of the railway where you could indeed fall off a train, roll down the embankment and land in a lake. It's along between Red Wing and Wabasha, beside Lake Pepin, which is really a widening of the Mississippi. There the road is so close that if that character had been propelled out of the boxcar on the other side and tumbled to the bottom of the cinder grading, he'd have come to rest on the blacktop of Highway 61.

· 9 ·

# Into The Narrow Lanes

No symbol is more central to Dylan than the road. The first lines of the first of his own songs on record speak of it:

> I'm out here a thousand miles from my home,
> Walkin' a road other men have gone down.
> I'm seein' your world of people and things,
> Your paupers and peasants and princes and kings.

And the first question that the world at large heard him ask, in BLOWIN' IN THE WIND, was:

> How many roads must a man walk down
> Before you call him a man?

Given all that has been said about the wanderer, frequent references to the road are perhaps not surprising; but there is a distinction to be drawn, and Dylan draws it in his very first use of the image. When we use the journey as a metaphor for life, substituting space for time, we may be thinking of life's transience, that we are always having to face new things and leave old ones behind, and that we must always be prepared to encounter the unknown. Morally, the metaphor encourages us in progressive effort and in the setting of successive goals. It lends a purposive weight to our ineluctable forward movement in time, and reminds us that our transit, in birth and death, has a starting point and a destination. In this sense, there is an ordained 'road of life' which we must all travel, and Dylan's images of travelling can often be taken in just this general way. But the road is also something else. It was there before we took it and is there after we leave it; our single journey does not make the road. It is a communal creation, something that "other men have gone down".

When Dylan sings, in the opening line of SONG TO WOODY, "I'm out here a thousand miles from my home", in his hobo role we hear that "out here" as 'somewhere, anywhere, far off, in the wilds'; but if you put a ruler to the map you'll see that it's 1,000 miles (and a bit) from Minneapolis, where he last resided, and 1,000 miles (pretty much bang on) from Duluth, his birthplace, to Morristown, New Jersey, where Guthrie lay dying. This song is sung *to* Woody and "here" is at his bedside – so this "walking" and this "road" are clearly metaphorical. On one level, we could say it is the road of a musical life, already trodden by Woody, and "Cisco and Sonny and Leadbelly too / And all the good people who travelled with you". More specifically, it is a road built of songs – the repertoire of Woody's compositions that Dylan had so assiduously learned.

So the "world of people and things" seen from this road is an imaginative world, inside the songs – as he makes clear with the Old World terms, "Your paupers and peasants and princes and kings". Strictly speaking, America does not have peasants, princes or kings, but she does have paupers, and she does have her rich. The slight analogical shift from pauper to peasant slips past easily enough, and we are prepared for the natural poverty/wealth contrast to follow. Since the linking of peasant and prince is established by usage, we are then led on to accept "princes and kings" as valid terms. Yes, the wealthy in America are effectively an aristocracy. Yet the whole starting point of the United States was that they should not have aristocrats or kings. So through the archaic words we receive a very live political critique. In these few words, the young disciple has conveyed his sense of Guthrie's songs as abiding, having an authority like that born of ancient tradition, and also as still cutting and pertinent.

The road for Dylan is the example set by his models, the musicians whom he set out to emulate. It is also that road of songs which he himself has laid down, the permanent tracks that he has left in the passing times. His initial and persistent intuition of this artistic continuity gives his work one of its distinguishing qualities. Part of the reason for the long-surviving fascination with Dylan is the sense, for the persevering listener, of a story unfolding, in which each new album, particularly, takes its place as a new chapter. The very concept of Progressive Rock was shaped by Dylan, along with the Beatles, of course; and his precedent especially has led to many an unfortunate and ridiculous 'new thing'. But for all the radical changes of musical style, of message and image that he has undergone, the thread linking them remains strong and easy to grasp, at least in retrospect. Though the road may twist and take surprising turns, it doesn't just jump about at random.

Whether deliberately or by instinct, Dylan has sometimes fostered this sense of continuity by establishing a close literal connection between the ending of one album and the beginning of the next. A very clear example is between the last lines of *Bringing It All Back Home* and the first of *Highway 61 Revisited* (though this is an unusual case in that the span of time that was bridged was barely more than half a year any-way). *Back Home* ends:

> The vagabond who's rapping at your door
> Is standing in the clothes that you once wore.
> Strike another match, go, start anew,
> And it's all over now, baby blue.

And *Highway 61* starts:

> Once upon a time you dressed so fine,
> Threw the bums a dime in your prime,
> Didn't you?

The images of tramps and clothing are carried over direct from one to the next.

To add another, more oblique example: *World Gone Wrong*, the second of his folk albums of the 1990s, ended with LONE PILGRIM, a song sung from beyond the grave:

> I came to the place where the lone pilgrim lay
> And pensively stood by his tomb,
> When in a low whisper I heard something say,
> 'How sweetly I sleep here alone.'

His next release was the *Unplugged* live album, on which he treated his own material in a spirit of what might be called detachment, if that did not carry a connotation of indifference; in a fashion, anyway, informed by his recent re-immersion in traditional music, handling his songs with a sense of rediscovery, an unburdened freshness and freedom and also respect, as though he had just drawn them too out of the tradition. The opening song is an abbreviated version of TOMBSTONE BLUES, off *Highway 61*, which, although its title is a play on all the other place-name blues – 'St Louis Blues',

'Kansas City Blues' and so on – is actually also a song about death and survival, with its references (in the original) to reincarnation, ghosts, graves, crucifixion (if we take that to be the allusion of "torturing a thief"); to dying "happily ever after" and the monuments of the illustrious dead (if that is the meaning of the flagpole that stands "where Ma Rainey and Beethoven once unwrapped a bedroll").

By threads like these, and by broader developments of theme and musical mode from one record to the next, Dylan has built and signed his road of songs. Now, to shed more light on the meaning of the road within that road, his use of the word itself, we can look at how it occurs in the work of other songwriters.

One who springs to mind is Jackson Browne, the strength of whose lyrics lies in their natural, conversational tone. His use of metaphor is generally straightforward and close to common usage, and the road for him is almost always an image of the individual's journey, that life-path which diverges from all others and which each must take alone – its most usual sense; though it may also stand for the course of a relationship – "for a while our path did seem to climb"; and there is also a community to be found along the way of one's "changes" (a favourite word of Browne's, along with "dreams"):

> The road is filled with homeless souls,
> Every woman, child and man,
> Who have no idea where they will go
> But they'll help you if they can.
> ('Rock Me on the Water', 1972)

Dylan's road is not really about development in this way. The recurring compulsion to "bid farewell and be down the road" obviously relates to the pursuit of his art, as a force stronger than all mundane attachments, but there isn't a 'personal growth' dimension to his journeying; it's not leading

him to something 'more' or 'other'. The road offers just itself
– which is to say, freedom, the opportunity to go on further,
to experience; it has no rainbow at its end. On the contrary,
it promises hardship: "It takes rocks and gravel, baby, to build
a solid road."

In another verse from his first album, Jackson Browne
indicates Dylan – who else can he mean? – as a source of his
road imagery, and also generously acknowledges his founding
inspiration as a songwriter. If a further clue were needed, the
opening "Ah—" is a close approximation to one of Dylan's
most characteristic vocal signatures:

> Ah, the great song-traveller passed through here
> And he opened my eyes to the view,
> And I was among those who called him a prophet
> And I asked him what was true,
> Until the distance had shown
> How the road remains alone.
> Now I'm looking in my life for a truth that is my own.
>    ('Looking Into You', 1972)

Another singer whose way began quite clearly from Dylan's
footsteps is Bruce Springsteen, in whose songs the imagery of
the road has been a central strand. Or, more precisely, the
imagery of the car. His double album *The River* has so many
automobiles it might better have been titled *The Driver*.

In Dylan's world, on the other hand, the car hardly exists;
and it's interesting, in the two sightings that come to mind,
that when it does appear, it is seen from the point of view of
the pedestrian. One is in TANGLED UP IN BLUE:

> We drove that car as far as we could, abandoned it out west,
> Split up on a dark sad night both agreeing it was best,
> And you turned around to look at me as I was walking
>                    away...

And the other is in BROWNSVILLE GIRL:

> I can still see the day you came to me on the Painted Desert
> In your broken-down Ford with your platform heels.
> I couldn't figure out why you chose that particular place
> to meet.
> Oh but you were right, it was perfect, as I slipped in behind
> the wheel.

The speeding, uncoiling movement of the first and the long syncopated lines of the second both carry echoes of the "bop prosody" of Kerouac and the Beat poets, suggesting that it was *On the Road*, very much an automotive odyssey, that gave the car such mythic status as it has with Dylan. The motoring school of Fifties rock'n'roll doesn't really seem to have made much impression on him. His is primarily a walker's road, a wanderer's road, whereas Springsteen's is the road as fact of American life, or at least it became so.

He originally inherited it, from Dylan and from rock imagery generally, as the place of freedom and possibility, the portal of another world: "The night's busting open, these two lanes could take us anywhere." This 'Thunder Road' of his, on *Born to Run*, can certainly be traced back, like Dylan's, to the Beats and ultimately to Whitman's Open Road; and Springsteen has something of the physical exhilaration of Whitman, singing the body electric:

> And you're in love with all the wonder it brings
> And every muscle in your body sings
> As the highway ignites.
> You work nine to five and somehow you survive till the night.
> ('The Night)

In 'Born to Run' itself, Springsteen endows the road and the car with their wildest dreams:

> In the day we sweat it out on the streets of a runaway
> American dream.
> At night we ride through mansions of glory in suicide
> machines.

The road *is* the American dream for Springsteen – the promise of freedom. But even in this early 'romantic' period the songs circle the question of what will survive in the collision of dream and reality. And from here on, his road becomes less and less an escape, a road *away*, and more and more a road *towards*, a connection, even for the loners of *Darkness on the Edge of Town*:

> There's a dark cloud rising from the desert floor.
> I packed my bags and I'm heading straight into the storm.
> Gonna be a twister to blow everything down
> That ain't got the faith to stand its ground.

Its destination may be transcendental, but he demands that it have one; just to get *out* is not enough:

> Tonight my baby and me we're gonna ride to the sea
> And wash these sins off our hands.
> ('Racing in the Streets')

Dylan's, almost invariably, is a road *away* – it parts people – while Springsteen's, most explicitly here where it is used as an emblem, is a road *between*:

> It's a long dark highway and a thin white line
> Connecting, baby, your heart to mine.
> ('The Ties That Bind', *The River*)

Though it goes away from here, the hope is always that the road leads *home*, to a place of truer belonging.

Springsteen is a writer of social relations in a way that Dylan never really has been. Notice, even in the two quotes from *Born to Run*, the references to the working day – sweating it out, nine till five. And 'The Promised Land', which contains the apocalyptic verse above, about the storm, still begins with brass tacks:

> On a rattlesnake speedway in the Utah desert
> I pick up my money and head back into town.
> Driving across the Waynesboro county line
> I've got the radio on but, man, I'm just killing time.
> Working all day in my daddy's garage,
> Driving all night chasing some mirage.

We're confronted with two fundamental aspects of most people's day to day living – i.e. work and family – which barely appear in Dylan's oeuvre. The relations which concern him are almost exclusively romantic, and as for him having a job, well, there's this:

> I had a job in the great north woods
> Working as a cook for a spell
> But I never did like it all that much
> And one day the axe just fell.
>     (TANGLED UP IN BLUE)

And there's this:

> The only decent thing I did
> When I worked as a postal clerk
> Was to haul your picture down off the wall
> Near the cage where I used to work.
>     (UP TO ME)

And that's about it. Not only is he not going to work on

Maggie's farm no more, for the most part he's not going to work anywhere else either.

Gradually, as Springsteen followed the line of his thought, the highway went from being the great promise to being the great temptation, as in 'Cautious Man' on *Tunnel of Love*. Bill Horton, with the words Love and Fear tattooed on his knuckles, is almost drawn by it into "betrayal" of his wife and child:

> He got dressed in the moonlight and down to the highway
> he strode
> But when he got there he didn't see nothing but road.

Intriguingly, on this record which is so much concerned with the trials of commitment, Springsteen's characters are most often found on foot: Bill Horton "walked looking over his shoulder", and we have 'Walk Like a Man' and 'One Step Up' (and two steps back) and even, in a near-repeat of an earlier image:

> The road is dark
> And it's a thin, thin line
> But I want you to know I'll walk it for you any time.
>     ('Tougher Than the Rest')

On the drastically underrated *Lucky Town* – a rough-and-ready making, from the usually meticulous craftsman, which contains some of his finest writing and singing – his new fatherhood inspires even more heartfelt images of staying put:

> When it comes to luck, we make our own.
> Tonight I got dirt on my hands but I'm building me a home.
>     ('Lucky Town')

> I'm gonna build me a wall so high nothing can tear it down
> Right here on my own piece of dirty ground.

In that last-quoted song, 'Souls of the Departed', his old sense of economic brass tacks is honed to a razor-sharpness:

> I ply my trade in the land of king dollar
> Where you get paid and your silence passes as honour
> And all the hatred and dirty little lies
> Been written off the books and into decent men's eyes.

By the time of *The Ghost of Tom Joad*, his latest and starkest record, the road has passed from being a promise to being a lie:

> The highway is alive tonight,
> Nobody's kidding nobody about where it goes.
>   ('The Ghost of Tom Joad')

And in the skeletal Bonnie-and-Clyde romance of 'Highway 29', a fatal lie.

On his road of songs, Springsteen has gone on in a straight line, following the implications of his work with a single-mindedness unique among songwriters of his generation, as far as I know. Dylan's road doesn't have this kind of directness. It seems a lane of many windings by comparison, or perhaps a spiral where at each turning we come back to the same point but at a higher level, like the road that winds about the "huge hill" of Truth, according to John Donne, which cannot be reached by direct approach, so that who would climb it "about must, and about must go".

## · 10 ·

# The Longest Road I Know

When he brought his work to its first fulfilment, as he felt at the time, Dylan named the results after a road, *Highway 61 Revisited*. Why "revisited"? Because there was already a 'Highway 61', a blues by Mississippi Fred McDowell which Dylan could have heard him sing at the Newport Folk Festival in 1964:

> That 61 highway, it's the longest road I know.
> It runs from up Wisconsin way, down to the Gulf of Mexico.

Actually, it runs further than that – or ran, since the US Highway network has been superseded by the Interstates, and the original "blue highways" have largely disappeared under other numbering systems. We'll be following it as it still was in 1965, when the album was released.

> My left hand hooks you round the waist,
> My right hand points to landscapes of continents, and
> a plain public road.
>
> (*Leaves of Grass*, 1855)

The road begins as Canadian Highway 61 and runs along the northwestern shore of Lake Superior from Thunder Bay, Ontario, towards the US border, which is marked by the crossing of the Pigeon River into the Grand Portage Indian Reservation. Now in Minnesota, it follows the lakeshore at the foot of the Misquah Hills, roughly parallel with the Mesabi Iron Range about 70 miles to the west, in the middle of which lies Hibbing, the mining town where Dylan grew up.

Hibbing is often depicted in writing about Dylan – one of the few places where it has cause to be mentioned – as a kind of Nowheresville. But the 1958 Rand McNally *Popular World Atlas* that I refer to (which grants each state a double-page spread, and which shows the entire railway network and not a single road), marks Hibbing – though it is listed in the gazetteer with a population of only 16,276 – on a map which covers the whole of North America from Colombia to the North Pole. As a source of iron, it was a place of continental importance.

About 140 miles southwest of its border crossing, the first sizeable settlement that Highway 61 reaches – there are precious few of any description along that stretch of Superior's shore – is Duluth, where Dylan was born, the iron-ore port at the westernmost point of the gigantic Great Lakes navigation. From among the earlier inhabitants of this country, the

Ojibwa tribe of Indians, America's first international 'star' arose – the hero of Longfellow's poem *Hiawatha*.

Now, following the St Croix River upstream, a little west of south, 61 heads for the Twin Cities, Minneapolis-St Paul, on the banks of the Mississippi. Here Dylan was briefly at college, swiftly found his place in the beatnik/folkie scene that accompanied the University, and was turned on to much of the spectrum of poetry and music whose influences would eventually be integrated in *Highway 61 Revisited*. The most fateful of those discoveries, of course, was the songs and writings of Woody Guthrie.

When he left Minneapolis, as I have surmised, Dylan probably went some distance on 61, following the Mississippi perhaps even as far as La Crosse, Wisconsin, 120-odd miles downstream. I wonder whether he spotted, as he rode in that "jalopy" with the "Bela Lugosi type", a turning on the right, just past the town of Whitman, for a little place a couple of miles to the west called Rollingstone.

At some point he turned east towards Chicago, while Highway 61 keeps on south through Wisconsin, first on the east side of the Mississippi, then crossing back to the west bank at Dubuque and heading straight down through Iowa, cutting out a great eastward curve of the river, but rejoining it at Davenport, which lies just across the water from Rock Island, Illinois.

That town was the hub of an extraordinary network, the Chicago Rock Island & Pacific railroad, which stretched down to Galveston on the Texan coast and out to Colorado and New Mexico in the west, to bring livestock to the abattoirs of Chicago – as in the song that keeps its fame, Leadbelly's 'Rock Island Line'. Lonnie Donnegan made the tune a big British hit, and even broke into the American Top 10 with it, in 1956. But so what? The record would be a barely pertinent footnote to this American journey were it not both a forerunner and a direct cause of 1964's 'British invasion' of beat groups, which in turn inspired the new, electric Dylan of *Highway 61 Revisited*. Donnegan's 'Rock Island Line' boosted a keen and long-standing, though small-scale, enthusiasm for American roots music, which would eventually send the likes of the Rolling Stones and the Animals across the Atlantic; and it launched, pretty much single-handedly, the skiffle boom which prompted British youth by the thousands to pick up guitars – among them, the Beatles-to-be.

From here on, 61 belongs to the river, seldom straying far from its side for the 800 miles between Rock Island and the sea. Further downstream, it passes through Hannibal, Missouri, the birthplace of Mark Twain and fictitious home, under the name of St Petersburg, to his hero Huckleberry Finn – the author whom H.L. Mencken called "true father of our national heritage" and the boy whose adventures Ernest Hemingway called "the best book we've had. All American writing comes from that."

Then comes St Louis, Missouri, at the junction of the Mississippi with the Missouri River. Over the water in Illinois is East St Louis, where Chuck Berry was born and raised. He created definitive rock'n'roll styles on two instruments simultaneously – the electric guitar and the English language – and when it came time for Dylan's rebirth as a rock star in 1965, he announced it with SUBTERRANEAN HOMESICK BLUES, a wild exaggeration of Berry's proto-rap song 'Too Much Monkey Business'.

In St Louis itself, T.S. Eliot was born and spent his childhood. Until Dylan's day, the creator of the duck-walk and the creator of J. Alfred Prufrock had remained strangers to each other; but if there is anywhere that 'Johnny B. Goode' meets *The Waste Land*, it is on *Highway 61 Revisited*.

In 1869, about twenty years before Eliot was born, an engineer came to St Louis to work on a new scheme for purifying the Missouri's muddy current to provide drinking water for the burgeoning city. He was Thomas Jefferson Whitman, known as Jeff, younger brother of the poet Walt. The two brothers had passed through St Louis together in 1848, steaming up the Mississippi on their way back to New York after a three-month sojourn in New Orleans, where Walt had been editing a newspaper, *The Crescent*.

In trying to explain the transformation of the not-especially-distinguished journalist of the 1840s into the visionary poet who published the anonymous first edition of *Leaves of Grass* in 1855, some critics have traced it to this so-called "New Orleans experience" of 1848. While the personification of the American Everyman – "I am large . . . . I contain multitudes" – stems from Walt's life in teeming New York, his vision of the land concentred on himself, and of himself on a scale with the land, surely arose from this transcontinental trek:

> My ties and ballasts leave me . . . . I travel . . . . I sail . . . .
> my elbows rest in the sea-gaps,
> I skirt the sierras . . . . my palms cover continents,
> I am afoot with my vision.

This vision recurs, with more geographic substance, in the magical rhetoric of Whitman's Preface to the 1855 *Leaves of Grass*:

> [The spirit of the American poet] responds to his country's spirit . . . . he incarnates its geography and natural life and rivers and lakes. Mississippi with annual freshets and changing chutes, Missouri and Columbia and Ohio and Saint Lawrence with the falls and beautiful masculine Hudson, do not embouchure where they spend themselves more than they embouchure into him. … When the long Atlantic coast stretches longer and the Pacific coast stretches longer he easily stretches with them north or south. He spans between them also from east to west and reflects what is between them.

This certainly suggests the perspective of the Mississippi, the central axis of the United States, dividing east and west, joining the north and south. Underlying that description of a poet's relation to the land, I read a perception, which his journey would have offered, not only of the sheer scale of the country extending around him, but also of its flowing towards him, its gravitational focus on the river. Highway 61, running alongside, is a modern, man-made accompaniment to that natural axis of the Mississippi.

From St Louis – where the child Eliot drank water provided by Walt Whitman's younger brother – 61 keeps heading south, still on the west bank of the river. In southern Missouri it crosses its numerical neighbour, Highway 62, a road of even grander proportions which runs 2,200 miles from Niagara in the north-east to El Paso in the south-west. For a stretch of about 20 miles, south of Sikeston, Missouri, they are in fact one road; then Highway 62 heads out to the west, to Arkansas, Oklahoma, Texas and the Rio Grande; but we'll have cause to rejoin it later in the book. Now Highway 61, after cutting across the corner of Arkansas, finally crosses to the eastern bank of the Mississippi again, and into Memphis, Tennessee.

*Horace Logan, MC:* They've been looking for something new in the folk music field for a long time, and I think you've got it.
*Elvis Presley:* We hope so.
    [The *Louisiana Hayride* radio show, *c.*1956.]

Dylan was aware of Elvis from the beginning, he has said, from 'Blue Moon of Kentucky' – the flipside of 'That's Alright,

Mama', released in July '54 – which he presumably heard on the radio shows where he'd already discovered Hank Williams.

The first effect of Elvis's music was surely a sudden sense of openness. It was wild and free and fearless, yet it was simple enough to be within reach. Unlike the other sounds of 'roots' radio, you didn't have to be anyone to make that music – neither a good ol' boy with a smile that was misery upside-down, nor one of the cats with a mojo hand: you could be anyone. Elvis seemed to have stepped away from all cultural conditioning, yet his music also seemed drawn from the deepest, clearest wellsprings.

In the creation myths of rock'n'roll, sex is supposed to underlie the music's innovative power: certainly it became the great bugbear of the reaction *against* rock'n'roll. But compared to some of the 'adult' music of the day, rock'n'roll is not particularly erotic: listen to Julie London's 'Go Slow' from 1957 to hear how naughty a piece of mainstream jazz-pop could be. The physical exuberance of rock'n'roll was largely just that. Elvis's movements, though he did learn to play with their forbidden dimension, were not primarily 'suggestive' but *expressive*. The uninhibitedness of the early rock'n'rollers – Little Richard, Jerry Lee Lewis, Chuck Berry, Gene Vincent, Eddie Cochran – was not really a matter of lewdness, but just that they were more themselves than their pop predecessors. That was the shock they imparted: that they had exploded into view in the entertainment firmament without having been groomed for it. (Now that our view is once again so crowded with corporate properties, we can actually imagine what this must have been like.) And the implication, again, was that if they could do it, *anyone could*.

Beyond the initial excitement, Elvis's lasting contribution was the scale of possibility that he revealed, as he grew up from "the folk music field" to bestride the whole range of popular music. Even from the records of his first pre-Army period, '54-57, it's clear that the Memphis Flash, the Hillbilly

Cat (i.e., in the slang of the day, the white black man), the King of Western Bop, and finally just the King of Rock'n'Roll was thinking of the bigger picture. What is rock'n'roll, after all? Just a dance beat – a backbeat obvious and insistent enough not to be lost by white kids unused to rhythmic sophistication. Or is it perhaps the final betrothal of the black and the white vernacular musics of America, so long alongside each other, of which that 4/4 was simply the ring – and another step towards the eventual disappearance of the fatal false concept of 'races' in our species?

Musicologically, rock'n'roll is a catch-all name for the grab-bag of styles which came out on top when the tendency of young paler-skinned people to buy records and listen to radio programmes intended for young darker-skinned people – a phenomenon which had been bubbling under for a number of years, and in some form or other ever since the Jazz Age of the Twenties – came to be a national excitement, and emergency, in the mid-Fifties.

*Elvis: The '56 Sessions*, Volumes 1 and 2, the pink and the purple LPs that came out in 1978, just after he died, and which were one of the first attempts to present his music systematically as art rather than product, show him at his most consistently rock'n'roll, before movie soundtracks distracted him. (Though even here there are the Hollywood hoedowns of 'We're Gonna Move' and 'Poor Boy' from his first film, *Love Me Tender*.) Recording in New York, Nashville and Hollywood, keeping the sound crisp and swift, he ranges across all the grooves, revealing the menagerie of beats that made up the Big Beat, and writing the rocking handbook for the next decade at least. But he also embraces the slow, from the achingly wistful 'How's the World Treating You?' to the full-blooded romanticism of 'Love Me' and 'Anyway You Want Me'.

That last title could be his motto: hence his cheerful willingness to play the silver-screen hayseed for those *Love Me*

*Tender* songs – the very hick stereotype that 'his own music' defied in every note. The quotation marks are necessary because Elvis really did embrace it all, no matter how ersatz, kitsch or schmaltzy. The worker's pride in his ability to do the job, whatever; the boy who wanted to please; and perhaps the born democrat in him tried to make every song as good as it could be. It's this sense of breadth, of boundlessness, that Dylan inherited from him – as, of course, did the Beatles. Without that influence, I'm not sure we'd have had any occasion here to trace the cultural connections of Highway 61 or invoke the continental "democratic vistas" of Whitman in connection with a pop music LP.

It's salutary to remember, when wondering how Elvis could have 'lost it', that even by 1956 he'd almost run out of things to win. *The '56 Sessions* begins in January when 'Heartbreak Hotel' was recorded, the single that would prove rock'n'roll, and Elvis, a force to kick down time-honoured fences, climbing the country, rhythm and blues and pop charts simultaneously. By August, he was recording 'Love Me Tender', sung to an acoustic guitar, completely unadorned, which would do the same thing, but without being country or R&B or pop. It showed that Elvis-music was larger than genre. In its (daring) quietness and intimacy, it was really his triumphal moment. It was also where the rot set in: as the theme-tune of his first movie, a cross-media tie-in, it was an early example of the kind of beast that has ended up eating the heart out of pop music.

By the time of his last Fifties session, 10 June 1958, when he recorded five hit singles ('I Got Stung', 'A Fool Such As I', 'I Need Your Love Tonight', 'Ain't That Loving You Baby', 'Big Hunk o' Love') in a single night, Elvis had polished his rock'n'roll to a seamless, ripe, fat, fast funk – and had established an amalgam whose suggestions and implications people would still be working out for years to come. He'd taken 'roots' music and made it the flower and the fruit of pop music.

We could trace his continuance in the two diversely brilliant albums with which he greeted the new decade – the blues of *Elvis Is Back!* and the gospel of *His Hand in Mine*, both released in 1960 – though it turned out, dispiritingly, that what he did as a musician didn't make much difference by then, one way or the other, and the thin soundtrack to the year's movie, *G.I. Blues*, far outsold his own creations.

But to get back on 61, we should look back instead, and see how it was not only Elvis the man, but the broad musical vision he carried that had its origins along our road.

"Here's a song, friends, that's real hot around the nation and in some parts of Africa."

Even after Peter Guralnick's exhaustive and probably definitive two-part biography (*Last Train to Memphis*, 1994, and *Careless Love*, 1999), the personality of Elvis Presley remains oddly elusive. His traits of grandiosity and modesty, of confidence, drive, assertion and of insecurity, lassitude and tractability are still perhaps best understood in the light of his protean vocal style. His voice is not especially distinguished in its power, agility or 'grain', but in its 'transparency'; his control of colour and timbre and his adaptation of sound to song remain unsurpassed among popular singers.

I've spoken of Elvis's musical vision, but he never spoke of such a thing himself; indeed any kind of sayings from him about music are few and far between – and often, again, elusive. A couple of times in the recordings of his early radio performances, he makes that little aside quoted above, about "some parts of Africa", which is surely a gratified reference to his records' appearance in the Rhythm & Blues chart, a cryptic proclamation of the convergence that was happening. Still, a cynical reading of his output might just see in its seemingly indiscriminate breadth the influence of the forceful personality of his manager, 'Colonel' Tom Parker, seeking to ensure that his boy's career wasn't tied to a fad and that his appeal was as wide as possible. Guralnick's biography belies this, however, making it clear that the Colonel, while he did try to sway the choice of songs for financial reasons, was adamant that all musical responsibility was finally with Elvis; and that the latter was effectively producer and arranger as well as star of his recordings.

Back at the beginning, though, back in Memphis, the matter of his vision is less easy to determine. His mentor, Sam Phillips of Sun Records, was clearly a man of zeal, of a quiet and efficacious rather than a polemical kind. Sun itself arose from his belief in the beauty of black music; and I can't help wondering if his seemingly poetic sensibility didn't fix upon the premises for his recording business – which his one close associate Marion Keisker says he was absolutely set on – partly because of the name of the street: 706 Union Avenue. Anyway, his venture became one of the most effective agents of racial integration of its time.

When the eighteen-year-old Elvis dropped in at 706 Union one Saturday in August 1953, as Marion Keisker recalled him, he was all "negative capability", a yin counterpart to Sun's yang:

> "What kind of singer are you?"
> He said, "I sing all kinds."
> I said, "Who do you sound like?"
> "I don't sound like nobody."

The story of those months of casual trial and error that Elvis and Scotty Moore and Bill Black and Sam Phillips went through before they made their first record doesn't speak to me of the singer's malleability, a simple willingness to receive his producer's impress, but rather of a radical indeterminacy, in which Phillips had to find that new thing he promised to be. But that in turn bespeaks Presley's determination not to be anything that had already been.

Even apart from Elvis, the part that Sun Records played in the story of popular music is too big to cover properly here, and anyway it's already been told too well elsewhere, notably by Peter Guralnick (in *Feel Like Going Home)*, Greil Marcus (in *Mystery Train)*, and Colin Escott and Martin Hawkins (in *Good Rockin' Tonight: Sun Records and the Birth of Rock'n'Roll*). In connection with our subject, we might just note that the roster of brilliant individual stylists – like Johnny Cash, Charlie Rich, Jerry Lee Lewis, Carl Perkins – whose careers were launched by Sam Phillips after Elvis, also includes Dylan's sometime collaborator in the Travelling Wilburys, Roy Orbison. Before Elvis, though, there was an important style and a great artist that came up through Sun which we can't leave Memphis without mentioning.

The type of blues that combines the 'urban' ingredients of pounding beat and piercing electric guitar with country blues themes and a rural-rooted looseness (and togetherness) is usually called Chicago blues, but it was mainly formed in Memphis, at 706 Union, in the first years of the Fifties. None of the blues performers Sam Phillips recorded then could be accused of being polished. Their shots at the smooth-rolling New Orleans R&B style, or at the kind of tight jump-blues perfected by T-Bone Walker and Louis Jordan, are all dogged by that rough-and-tumble spontaneity that came to be summed up in the adjective 'rock'n'roll'. Most typical of the Sun blues sound, however, is a hard, over-driven guitar – often Willie Johnson's – and the steady thump of the rhythm section.

The paragon of this harsh, electrified music is the great artist mentioned above, Howlin' Wolf, who cut brilliant tracks in Sam Phillips' studio between 1950 and '52. Their steely, driving sound became the template for 'rock' – the heavy, blues-based, improvisatory style that predominated in the later Sixties. On *Highway 61 Revisited*, this piece of 61's history lives on in the switchblade picking of Mike Bloomfield – though the attack of Wolf's guitarists has been tempered by the more fluent, still biting style of B.B. King, perhaps the most influential blues guitar player of all, and another whose first recordings were made by Sam Phillips.

For all their importance, the contributions of Sun Records are still only a portion of the musical legacy of Memphis. From the mid-point of the century, when Sam Phillips founded his venture, we can look ahead to a Southern soul sound largely formed in the city's Stax studio – that new confluence in which the passion and hope of the Sixties found such full expression; and also to the best of Elvis Presley's recordings, made in January and February 1969 at the American Studio – the smooth amalgam of country, gospel, soul, rock and blues which first appeared on the LP *From Elvis in Memphis*. And looking the other way, we can trace a musical history stretching back to the beginning of the century, and further.

> Handy's cast in bronze
> And he's standing in a little park
> With his trumpet in his hand
> Like he's listening back to the good old bands
> And the click of high-heel shoes.
> (Joni Mitchell, 'Furry Sings the Blues')

W.C. Handy, the Memphian bandleader who took the title Father of the Blues, was not, of course, the form's progenitor – Rich Uncle of the Blues has been suggested as a more accurate honorific – but he did play a key role in propagating the music. His compositions (of which 'St

Louis Blues' has proved the most enduring) were often com-
pilations of folk pieces that he'd heard, and they provided an
important conduit through which the blues began its passage
from the obscure confines of rural poverty to the mainstream
of global entertainment. For when Handy published his
'Memphis Blues' in 1912, the first song to appear as a 'blues'
before the general public, it marked a vital stage in that development whereby the voice of poor southern blacks – among
the least-heard people in America – came to be heard and to
find an echo around the world.

Memphis itself was crucial in this history. The Capital of
the Cotton Country, a major river-port and railhead, it was a
magnet for musicians from miles around, and its Beale Street
was one of the main centres of black entertainment in the
southern United States. Here the nascent forms of the blues
– which appear only to have coalesced about the turn of the
century, though from elements of a long tradition – were
moulded into an ensemble music, particularly by the jug
bands, like Gus Cannon's Jug Stompers and Will Shade's
Memphis Jug Band, which were a speciality of the city. The
freedom of the solo blues, which adapted for instrumental
accompaniment the even freer vocal style heard in the 'field
holler' and religious 'shout' – was regulated for band purposes and gradually settled into the twelve-bar, three-chord,
AAB verse form which has become universally familiar.

The blues of Memphis, on the recorded evidence of the
1920s and '30s, tend to be livelier and lighter-hearted than
those of the Mississippi Delta, into which we shall shortly be
heading – those dark and doom-ridden sounds that have long
been cherished as the blues' quintessence. The city's music, fed
by the Delta as surely as its economy was fed by the Delta's cot-
tonfields, was more geared to entertainment and set a precedent for the gradual mingling of the blues into the mainstream.
Another key factor in that process was the founding of the
Theatre Owners' Booking Association in Memphis in 1909.

Although its acronym, TOBA, was said to stand for "Tough On Black Asses", its nationwide circuit of gigs was central to the economy of black entertainment, sustaining and spreading the succeeding styles of music, dance and comedy for decades.

O n national television, during his 1968 Christmas show, the so-called "Comeback Special", Elvis Presley set out to explain what had happened:

> I'd like to talk a little bit about music – [*chuckling*] a very little… There's been a big change in the music field in the last ten or twelve years. [*Someone whistles.*] You like that, huh? And I think everything's improved, the sounds have improved, the musicians have improved, the engineers have certainly improved. I like a lot of the new groups, you know – the Beatles and the Byrds… [*He pronounces it "the Beards", but no-one laughs: either no-one gets his joke, or they're afraid he's really been away so long that he doesn't understand psychedelic spelling.*] and the – whoever. But I really like a lot of the new music. But a lot of it is basically – our music is basically – rock'n'roll music is basically gospel or rhythm and blues, or it sprang from that, and people have been adding to it, adding instruments to it, experimenting with it…

By 1968, there was critical consensus that rock'n'roll was what happened when Country & Western met Rhythm & Blues. Gospel's part was not much mentioned at a time when the agenda of rock was sex, drugs, menace, revolution. Elvis's point seems partly to emphasise a purely black paternity for rock'n'roll, and mainly to claim that the crucial collusion – or collision – was not between white and black, country and blues, but across the wider gulf separating the saved from the damned, the factions of the sanctified and the sinful within black music.

Certainly the exuberance of a lot of Fifties R&B, pre-rock-'n'roll – especially that of the vocal groups – comes straight from church. Above all, the *joy* of rock'n'roll was not something it could have inherited from the post-war electric blues, which for all its pride and power kept a grain of grimness between its teeth. If we take it back through the big bang of the swing bands, right back through the Jazz Age to New Orleans and 'When the Saints Go Marching In', the jumping jive is grounded in the ecstasies of the holy rollers, while the flight of the doo-wop birds – the Swallows and the Orioles and so on – was inspired by the incredible excursions of the gospel quartets, like the Swan Silvertones and the Dixie Hummingbirds.

So before we leave, we should remember the Church of God in Christ, the biggest of all those Sanctified or Holiness Churches whose passionate pentecostalism gave rise to gospel music, founded by Reverend C.H. Mason in 1895 in the city of Memphis. Then, having honoured its contributions to integration, we should remember the terrible blow that the city dealt to the dream on 4th April 1968, when Martin Luther King was shot down at the Motel Lorraine.

And so into the Delta, and the Devil's Music.

> There ain't no heaven, ain't no burnin' hell.
> Where I'm going when I die, can't nobody tell.
> (Son House, 'My Black Mama')

The Mississippi Delta is a leaf-shaped alluvial plain some two hundred miles long and about fifty across at its broadest point, bounded on the east by the Tallahatchie and Yazoo rivers and on the west by the Mississippi, with Memphis at its northern extremity and Vicksburg at the southern. The main highway north and south through this region is Highway 61, which runs roughly parallel with the Mississippi. At its midpoint, the Delta is bisected by the east-west Highway 80. On its eastern flank, beyond the Tallahatchie, is Highway 51, also running north-south. Several lines of the Illinois Central railroad criss-cross the land.

The fertility of this floodplain, whose bed of black river mud is the thickest on the planet, up to a hundred and forty feet deep in places, made the Delta a centre of cotton-growing, and consequently one of the greatest concentrations of black people in the United States, originally brought as slaves to the plantations. Whatever the other factors, that is a simple reason for its incredible musical fecundity. Considering only those who were celebrated in the blues revival of the Sixties, these are some of the musicians who were born or raised in the Delta and the surrounding countryside:

Son House, Skip James, Bukka White, Mississippi John Hurt, Furry Lewis, Robert Wilkins, all of whom recorded in the 1920s and '30s and were rediscovered and played again to great acclaim, predominantly before young white audiences, in the 1960s;

Robert Johnson, whose long-posthumous LP, *King of the Delta Blues Singers*, released in 1961, was a touchstone of all blues enthusiasts;

Big Bill Broonzy, whose visits to Britain in the 1950s laid the foundations for the UK "Blues Boom";

John Lee Hooker, Muddy Waters (and his outstanding pianist Otis Spann), Jimmy Reed, Elmore James, Howlin' Wolf, Sonny Boy Williamson (the second), Willie Dixon, whose sounds and whose songs became the staples of all subsequent blues bands;

B.B. King, Albert King, Little Milton, Magic Sam, Pops Staples, modern hitmakers who brought their Delta roots into the era of Rock and Soul.

Heading south from Memphis, down Highway 61 into Mississippi, the first stop is the railway junction of Lake Cormorant, only a few miles outside the city, where Alan Lomax, scouting for the Library of Congress, recorded the country blues band of Son House, Willie Brown, Leroy Williams and Fiddlin' Joe Martin in 1941. (In the middle of Son House's solo performance of 'Shetland Pony Blues' you can hear a train rolling past on the Illinois Central line.) The following year, about ten miles further south in the settlement of Robinsonville, he recorded Son House again, on his own, in one of the finest of all Delta blues sessions. House had cut some sides commercially for Paramount in 1930, on a trip up to Wisconsin with his musical partner Willie Brown and his musical mentor Charley Patton. He'd assumed that some payment would also be due for his sessions with Lomax, but all that was forthcoming was a Coke. It was, he noted magnanimously, "a nice cold Coke".

It was while Son House and Willie Brown were based in Robinsonville in the late Twenties, ruling the roost along with Charley Patton, that they acquired the young Robert Johnson as a follower. A lot of House's music got into Johnson's (while Willie Brown, who travelled with him, was immortalised by being mentioned by name in two of his songs) but the older man avowed that he didn't teach the younger how to play. Johnson played some harmonica and watched the big men's fingers, but his attempts to imitate them on guitar met with derision. Then he is supposed to have disappeared for a while, and when he showed up again he was playing every bit as well as them, if not better.

From this sudden accomplishment sprang the legend that Johnson sold his soul to the devil in exchange for his musical abilities – a legend that he promulgated himself in songs like 'Me and the Devil Blues' and 'Hellhound on My Trail'. But talent, burning desire and a spell of intense application – the concentrated solitary practice that jazz musicians

called 'woodshedding' – might account for the rapid transformation.* After all, Son House himself had taken up guitar
only three years before he made his masterly Paramount sides
in 1930.

The legend of the demonic pact seems to have been popular in that country: it was also attached to, and may have
originated with, another, older Johnson – Tommy – who came

---

*Another abiding mystery about Robert Johnson is the rpm conundrum.
Is it true, as a Japanese musician told me it is widely held to be in Japan,
that Robert Johnson's records play way too fast? Should he actually sound
much more like his great mentor, Son House?

One guitar tutorial book, *Country Blues Bottleneck Guitar* by James
Ferguson and Richard Gellis (Walter Kane Publications, New York,
1976), proposes that Robert Johnson's 'Walking Blues' is played with the
guitar tuned to G (i.e. so that the open strings play a chord of G major –
D-G-D-G-B-D, from bass to treble) and with a capo on the fourth fret.
This means that the opening phrase, played an octave above the open
strings at the twelfth fret (relative to the capo), must be played, with that
capo position, at the sixteenth fret. On the kind of guitar which has the
neck joining the body at the twelfth fret – like the Gibson that Johnson
is holding in his long-sought-after photograph – this means playing
about two and a half inches beyond the end of the neck, a most uncom-
fortable position; indeed, for most guitarists, an impossible place to play
accurately with a slide.

There are four other Johnson tunes in the book; one, 'I Believe I'll
Dust My Broom', is given in an arrangement by Taj Mahal; the rest follow the original recordings, and all of these are supposed to be capoed at
the third fret. The only other piece in the book to be played with a capo
on the third is by the Georgia-born Tampa Red, who played a guitar with
the neck-body junction at the fourteenth fret. The pieces by the other
Mississippi Delta slide players in the book – Bukka White, Bobby Grant,
Mississippi Fred McDowell – are all played open or, in one case, with a
capo on the first.

Now if we turn to the song on which Robert Johnson's 'Walking Blues'
is based, namely 'My Black Mama' by Son House, we find that on his
recording of it in 1930, he plays in open G, capo on the first. What happens, then, if we slow Johnson's record until it is in the same key as the
song it's modelled on – and if we bring the rest of his records down likewise, so that those pieces that sound as though they're capoed on the
third would actually be played in the much more natural way, with open
strings? This means lowering the key by three semitones, a quarter of an
octave – which means slowing the records to 80 per cent of the speed that

from southern Mississippi, ran away for a couple of years as a teenager, up into the Delta around Rolling Fork, and came back a skilled musician. According to his own brother, Reverend LeDell Johnson, this was how Tommy accounted for his playing: that he had taken his guitar to a crossroads at midnight, where a big black man had taken it from him, played a piece on it and handed it back. Whether or not

they normally play, slowing a 33⅓rpm LP to 26⅔rpm. (I achieved this by turning the pitch control on my old Akai turntable as low as it would go, taping with the pitch control on my Sony cassette deck turned up as high as it would go, then playing it back with the pitch turned slightly slow and dubbing it again.) And what comes out of the speakers?

A music transformed: so that it is with trepidation that I suggest this might be the true sound of Robert Johnson.

The sound of a man: this dark-toned voice would no longer lend credence to the youth of seventeen or eighteen that Don Law, the only person to record him, thought he might be. Now, especially in the dip of his voice at the end of a line, we can hear the follower of Son House, and the precursor of Muddy Waters. Hear him pronounce his name in 'Kind Hearted Woman Blues' – now he sounds like "Mr Johnson", a man whose words are not half-swallowed, garbled or strangled, but clearly delivered, beautifully modulated; whose performances are not fleeting, harried or fragmented, but paced with the sense of space and drama that drew an audience in until people wept as they stood in the street around him. (The wordless last lines of 'Love in Vain', in this slowed form, are the work of one of the most heartbreaking and delicate of blues singers.)

This is a Steady Rolling Man, whose tempos and tonalities are much like those of other Delta bluesmen. Full-speed Johnson always struck me as a disembodied sound – befitting his wraith-like persona, the reticent, drifting youth, barely more than a boy, that Don Law spoke of: the Rimbaud of the blues. Johnson slowed down sounds to me like the person in the recently discovered studio portrait: a big-boned man, self-assured and worldly-wise.

It works for me, but try it for yourself. As for why and how it could have come about, I've no idea. But if all the recordings should really play at 80 per cent of their current speed, that wouldn't make them exceptionally long. The sixteen cuts of the first Robert Johnson LP, *King of the Delta Blues Singers*, have an average duration of two minutes 38 seconds – noticeably shorter than the just-over-three-minute average of the sixteen cuts on a collection of Leroy Carr's blues from 1932 to '34, and of the twelve cuts on a collection of Blind Willie McTell's blues from 1935 (about 80 per cent of the length, in fact). On the other hand, it matches,

Johnson met the Devil in the Delta, it is known that he met Charley Patton and his pupil Willie Brown.

Tommy Johnson was only recorded twice, in 1928 and 1930, but his music was very influential and widely imitated, because it was so beautiful. Robert Johnson certainly emulated its lyricism, adding the floating vocal line and the more delicate and intricate guitar accompaniment to those bedrock elements of his style that came from House and Brown and

---

almost to the second, the average duration of sixteen tracks recorded in May 1937 by Sonny Boy Williamson and Big Joe Williams, a month before "poor Bob's" last session. But this is up-tempo, good-time blues, as the title-track of the LP suggests – 'Throw a Boogie Woogie'. Two of its songs became rocking Blues Boom standards in the Sixties – 'Good Morning School Girl' and 'Please Don't Go'.

Similarly, on a two-CD set collecting all 42 masters that the rugged Delta musician Tommy McClennan cut between 1939 and '42, the average length is only a wee bit longer than Johnson's, around two minutes fifty – but McClennan is another purveyor of the boogie, a much simpler artist than our "Robert child", and when he was recommended for his first recording session by Big Bill Broonzy, the duke of pre-war Chicago blues, it was surely because, despite the rude country style, his ever-driving beat and bold personality could still cut it with the juke-joint dancers – something that 'Hellhound on My Trail' was never likely to do. If the theory I've advanced is not completely crazy, a possible reason for Johnson's records to be speeded up might have been to try to make them more exciting for an age in which the Delta tradition he came out of was already a thing of the past.

Maybe there are scientific tests that could be applied to the sound to establish its original frequencies – to the qualities of the voice, for example, like the vibrato, which at full speed sounds to me like an alien nasal flutter but at slower speeds like a proper musical ornament; or to the decay time of the guitar notes, perhaps. These sides are of unique historical importance for the influence they have had. They are universally acclaimed by critics: Greil Marcus, for example, the dean of rock writers, while he would not be so crass as to tag the first Robert Johnson LP The Greatest Album Of All Time, certainly regards it as An Album Than Which None Better Has Been Made. They are also of considerable continuing popularity: the 1990 issue of *The Complete Recordings*, with an expected sale of about twenty thousand, sold half a million. If they are in fact so wildly off-key, I think we should be told.

Or maybe it's just me. Anyway, I'm happy with my deep Johnson.

Charley Patton – the taut, declamatory vocals, the snapped-string descending riffs, slashing and rattling bottleneck strokes and high, singing slide phrases.

61 runs on through Tunica County, with the Coldwater River to the east, the railroad close by to the west, and the Mississippi beyond, defining what must be the most serpentine state boundary in the USA, where the edge of Arkansas tries to make sense out of the windings and loops of the river. A bit further south, where it has cut across one of its bends, Arkansas actually has some of the Mississippi's east bank, just below Friars Point, the landing place celebrated in Robert Johnson's 'Travelling Riverside Blues':

> If your man gets personal, want to have your fun…
> Just come on back to Friars Point, mama, an' barrelhouse
> all night long
>
> I got womens in Vicksburg, clean on into Tennessee…
> But my Friars Point rider, now, hops all over me
>
> I ain't gonna state no colour but her front teeth crowned
> with gold…
> She got a mortgage on my body, now, an' a lien on my soul

This is the country where the blues grew up, and where its Empress died. On 61, just north of Clarksdale, the car carrying Bessie Smith smashed into the back of a truck in the small hours of Sunday, 26th September 1937. She died in hospital in Clarksdale later that morning.

One of the longest-lived of the Delta bluesmen, John Lee Hooker, was born in Clarksdale in 1917, and was still proclaiming "blues a healer" in the 1990s, in a style that had stripped the Mississippi music down to the very bone. He was a key figure in the resurgence of the 'downhome' blues on the R&B charts of the late Forties and early Fifties, scoring first with 'Boogie Chillen' in 1949. Muddy Waters followed suit in 1950 with 'Rollin' Stone', though he'd been recording electrified Delta music, without great success, since 1947 – starting with 'I Can't Be Satisfied', as good a blues as any ever made.

Muddy also grew up and started to play in Clarksdale which, as the only sizeable town in the northern Delta, was a main venue for musicians. He modelled himself chiefly, he said, on Son House (who was born just outside the town, in Lyon), with a bit of Charley Patton and a bit of Robert Johnson. House can certainly be heard in his singing, but Muddy's uncanny, microtonal slide guitar is something unique. As for the band he formed in Chicago in the Fifties, which was the grandparent of all twin-guitar electric rock groups, none of its successors has ever bettered it.

Thirty miles south of Clarksdale, 61 reaches Cleveland, in Bolivar County (which I suppose is the reference of Thelonious Monk's tune 'Ba-lue Bolivar Ba-lues-are': Monk is the jazz composer who seems closest, in his angularity and tension, to the Delta blues). Five miles to the west, in Sunflower County on the banks of the Sunflower River, is Dockery's Plantation where Charley Patton lived in the nineteen-teens and -twenties. Patton is the Jesse out of which our whole tree of blues musicians rises, perhaps the most widely influential popular musician of the twentieth century. As well as those we've mentioned, his pupils included Howlin' Wolf and Pops Staples.

Every player cited in this passage through the Delta has mingled with Bob Dylan's music at some point, but Roebuck 'Pops' Staples is the only example of two-way traffic. He sang the lead on the Staple Singers' brooding version of Dylan's MASTERS OF WAR in 1964, done as a martial-sounding waltz, edited down by two verses, and with the line "And I hope that you die" softened to "One day you're gonna die".

Thirty miles further south, Highway 61 crosses Highway 82 at Leland. Fifteen miles to the west lies Indianola, B.B. King's birthplace. Another thirty-five miles on down 61 is

Rolling Fork, where Muddy Waters was born in 1915, a couple of years after Tommy Johnson stayed there. One of Dylan's favourite bluesmen, Tommy McClennan, grew up about thirty miles due west of here, in Yazoo City, midway between Highways 61 and 51.

McClennan recorded his 'New Highway 51' in Chicago in May 1940, a year before Robert Zimmerman was born. It's not even known for certain whether he was living or dead in November 1961, when Bob Dylan recorded a HIGHWAY 51, of similar rudimentary melody and using McClennan's first two verses, for his debut album. He doesn't use the great line about the bus – "Now yonder comes that Greyhound with his tongue hanging out on the side" – but in a verse of his own, Dylan claims: "I know that highway like I know the back of my hand". I wonder, then, if he's paying deliberate homage to his inspiration when he sings McClennan's opening line: "Highway 51 runs right past my baby's door". Highway 51, as it runs north, converges with Highway 61 in Memphis. In the suburb of Whitehaven to the south of the city, the stretch of 51 that runs right past the gate of a mansion called Graceland has been renamed Elvis Presley Boulevard.

Forty-odd miles further, and 61 enters Vicksburg and leaves the Delta behind. Here, in 1946, a raucous boogie ensemble, the Mississippi Misrulers, led by Previous Albert Brown (who played a concertina fashioned from a pair of shoes) and including Bedslats Ogilvie on imitation bass and the Rollins twins, Hiram and Peleg, known as Ham and Pickle, on guitar and triangle, recorded an anachronistic final echo of the jug-band tradition with their 'Sawdust in My Biscuits' and 'Mopbucket Stomp'.

The last stretch of this pilgrimage, as the road carries on, faithful to the river, down to the Gulf Coast, is not so populous with ghosts – in fact, not so populous at all – but in each of only two sizeable places that Highway 61 passes through, we can commemorate a living and tirelessly creative musician. Sixty miles southwest of Vicksburg is Natchez, the oldest post-Colombian settlement on the Mississippi River, where the adolescent Jerry Lee Lewis, sneaking across from his home in Ferriday, Louisiana, listened and pumped piano in the 'colored' juke-joints. Another 70 miles, down through the sparsely peopled southwestern corner of Mississippi and into Louisiana, and 61 reaches Baton Rouge, where Buddy Guy was born, brilliant torch-bearer of the Chicago blues.

And so to our last port of call, New Orleans, "the Home of the Blues" – according to James Brown, anyway, in his song 'Night Train'. I'd be loth to argue this point with the Godfather of Soul – and if we make "the Blues" subsume and stand for the whole movement of secular black music out into the world, then it is easy to agree, because that movement certainly began in the Crescent City.

Of the blues in a purer sense, the Big Easy has not produced a great deal, though the guitarist and singer Snooks Eaglin, who led an R&B band but also sang on the streets, did oblige with three LPs of solo pieces in the late Fifties and early Sixties, when collectors were most intent on catching the falling stars of the country blues tradition. I can vouch for the third of these – his eponymous album in the Prestige Bluesville series – as beautiful folk-blues. And almost as good is a recording of Eaglin in 1971 released in Sam Charters' Legacy of the Blues series.

To the golden age of the blues, New Orleans' main connection is Lonnie Johnson, one of those performers – Jimmie Rodgers is another, and so is Bessie Smith; and so, later, is T-Bone Walker – who effortlessly knot the ampersand in the old record-shop signs, 'Blues & Jazz'.

That's the city all over, spread across the neck of land between Lake Pontchartrain and Lake Borgne, like the big and little loops of an ampersand toppled over on its back, while the Mississippi winds past and, oblivious to the end of the land, like a cartoon character running over a cliff, flows out to sea for 40 miles on a branching spit of its own mud before it finally frays away.

New Orleans, of course, produced the first jazz: this early-established fact in the legend of American popular music stands indisputable, though the moment of birth itself remains tantalisingly just beyond the reach of historical record. Sometime in the last years of the nineteenth century, as a result of new segregation laws passed in the South – the so-called Jim Crow laws – the 'mixed race' musicians of Creole orchestras, schooled in the European musical system, were brought into closer contact with the 'Negro' musicians who had translated the largely vocal music of the slaves on fiddles, guitars, banjos, trumpets, fifes, drums, bones. An amalgam emerged that was called jass or jazz, for reasons that no-one has adequately explained. King Oliver, Louis Armstrong, Jelly Roll Morton, Sydney Bechet, Johnny Dodds – these are some of the New Orleans players who carried it out to the world at large.

As they did so, jazz turned out to be the name, not so much for a type of music, as for a capacity of assimilation and adaptation and an urge for growth that constantly pulled the past into the future. The history of jazz is so compelling and has such momentum, spanning in its recorded form from the 'traditional' sound of King Oliver to the 'modern' sound of John Coltrane and Ornette Coleman in barely forty years, that it is the most complete revenge of a people denied their history: sweet revenge, an act of love to enemies.

This capacity appears to have remained with the city, so that its music, right into the present – in the new-wave old-style bands like the Dirty Dozens Brass Band, for example – is an encyclopaedic compound with the most identifiable local character in the United States, a rhythmic suppleness and a colour all its own. In this, New Orleans seems more a northern outpost of Caribbean culture than a part of the Deep South. It's easy to see how qualities like these, almost obliterated by the music industry, would have drawn Dylan to make albums there in later days (*Oh Mercy* and *Time Out of Mind*).

As well as producing the one pre-rock'n'roll R&B star whose music flowed without a hitch into the new era – Fats Domino – New Orleans also produced the most explosive rock'n'roller of all – Little Richard. His records, his wild-eyed performance on film in *The Girl Can't Help It*, were the best evidence for that strange little sub-myth that has run through rock – that the music came from outer space. For the young Bobby Zimmerman, he was the one who dynamited the pass. After that, there was no going back. On his graduation, Bob wrote in his high school year-book that his ambition was "To join Little Richard". With *Highway 61 Revisited* he did, in those Hesperides where rock'n'roll heroes go when they live. And Highway 61, finally, does just that: it joins Bob Dylan with Little Richard.

Coming into the heart of the city, it ceases to be a highway, becomes Tulane Avenue, and then Common Street.

## · 11 ·

# My Name It Is Nothing

The name Dylan chose, he said in the early days, came from an uncle called Dillon who was a gambler in Las Vegas. He also denied quite vehemently that it had anything to do with Dylan Thomas. Both claims seem unlikely. Such was the Welshman's renown after his death in New York in 1953, that whether or not Bob knew a line of his work, he could hardly fail to associate the name Dylan with a poet. This reverberation, crossing that of Marshal Matt Dillon, the hero of the TV Western series *Gunsmoke*, struck the right chord: the cowboy champion of the good and the bad-boy poet.

The name had another resonance, though, that came from closer to home. If you leave Hibbing, going west on 31st Street, cross the tracks of the Duluth Missabe and Iron Range Railroad, pass the trailer park, and just keep straight on along County Highway 465, into the wasteland of mine-dumps that lies beyond the town, then take the first left just before the tailings pond, you're on Dillon Road. It's the back way to the Maple Hill Cemetery.

> Used to run in the cemetery,
> Dance and sing and run when I was a child,
> And it never seemed strange.
> Now I just pass mournfully
> By that place where the bones of life are piled.
> I know something has changed,
> I'm a stranger here
> And no-one sees me.
>
> (NOBODY 'CEPT YOU, 1973; released on *Biograph*, 1985)

It would certainly be fitting if the young wanderer, whose eponymous first LP was so concerned with death, should have named himself after the road to the graveyard. It seems fitting, too, that the spelling he chose for his name should make it, like that of his great hero, a Welsh one. Actually, that should be qualified: St Elvis was Irish, but his name is preserved in Wales.

About 30 miles west of Dylan Thomas's last home at Laugharne, on the south Pembrokeshire coast, the tiny port of Solva lies hidden up a narrow inlet where Vikings came to provision a thousand years ago (the name is Norse for 'samphire') and from which emigrants are known to have sailed for North America in the 17th century. Nearby is St Elvis Farm, the last remnant of the former parish of St Elvis, which was described in 1833, in *A Topographical Dictionary of Wales*, as:

> a parish in the hundred of Dewisland [i.e. David's land], county of Pembroke, South Wales, 4 miles (E by S) from St David's, containing 44 inhabitants. This parish, which is situated on the shore of St Bride's bay in St George's channel, and near the road from Haverfordwest to St David's, is one of the smallest in the principality, containing only two farms, which do not comprise together more than two hundred acres. ... The church, dedicated to St Teilaw, is a small edifice, possessing no architectural features deserving notice...

That church has now disappeared and St Elvis Farm stands on its site. About a hundred yards from the farmhouse, beside the path that leads to the clifftops, is St Elvis Cromlech, a neolithic burial chamber some five thousand years old.

So who was St Elvis? According to a manuscript of about 1080 (that is, about five hundred years after his time), Aelfyw, latinised to Elvis, was the Bishop of Munster, the southern kingdom of Ireland, and a cousin of St David, the patron saint of Wales, whom he baptised. This last fact probably accounts for his name being attached to the Stone Age monument: the St Teilaw who is mentioned above was a contemporary and sometime companion of St David, and the two are linked in legend; so an ancient site near to Teilaw's church might quite naturally have been Christianised by being ascribed to one of his generation's spiritual ancestors.

As for the most famous namesake of this sixth-century Irish bishop, his genealogy is sketchy. He got his unusual Christian name from his father, Vernon Elvis Presley, but it's not recorded among his forebears before that. The idea that Elvis's parents knew the source of the name is slightly supported by the naming of his still-born twin, Jesse Garon. Jesse was Vernon's father's name, so the two brothers were given the name of the paternal grandfather and the father's middle name, which is nothing unusual. However, the two are also linked in their origins, in that Jesse in the Bible is the father of King David, as Elvis was the spiritual father of St David. The webpage devoted to the Welsh Elvis theory (www2. prestel.co.uk/littleton/z0.htm) also reminds us that Garon bears some resemblance to the Welsh name Geraint, and that some 20 miles inland of St Elvis Farm are the Preseli Mountains, which give their name to this part of Wales, the Preseli Pembroke district (and from which, by means still unexplained, some of the blocks of Stonehenge were brought four thousand years ago – though the hills hold a building almost two thousand years older than that). Although the main connections are on Vernon Presley's side, we might also note the Welsh name of Elvis's mother, Gladys.

All in all, though the Scottish and Irish roots of American 'hillbilly' music are usually emphasised, names like these – Jimmie Rodgers, Hiram (Hank) Williams, George Jones, Waylon Jennings, and now Elvis Presley – seem to me to favour a Welsh ancestry for Country & Western.

The name Dylan chose means, in Welsh, 'the sea', as explained in the medieval collection of legends called the *Mabinogion*. A maiden who is promised in marriage is asked to prove her virginity by stepping over a hooped stick:

> Aranrhod stepped over the wand, and with that step she dropped a sturdy boy with thick yellow hair; the boy gave a loud cry, and with that cry she made her way for the door… "Well," said Math, "I will arrange for the baptism of this one… and I will call him Dylan." The boy was baptised, whereupon he immediately made for the sea, and when he came to the sea he took on its nature and swam as well as the best fish. He was called Dylan [sea] son of Ton [wave], for no wave ever broke beneath him.

Carl Jung, in his studies of what he termed the "collective unconscious", saw in the sea the image of the collective unconscious itself. He pointed, for example, to the book of Revelation, where an angel elucidates the vision of the Great Whore of Babylon, saying to St John: "The waters that thou sawest, where the whore sitteth, are peoples, and multitudes, and nations, and tongues."

Given all that was said earlier about folk and its Romantic-rooted connections to the unconscious, it is peculiarly apt that Dylan should alight upon this symbol when he came to rename himself as an Everyman, a voice of the people, a dream figure for the masses who would be "bigger than Elvis" (as he vowed to be in his youth). Given that he's unlikely to have known the name's meaning when he chose it, or to have connected it with Jung's or the New Testament's symbolism, this significance could not have been a reason for his choice – unless it was a reason beyond reason. Unless, in other words, as he sought intuitively for a name that would speak to the collective unconscious, the collective unconscious proposed one of its own names.

The sea, while not so common or persistent a symbol as the road in Dylan's lyrics, is a peculiarly important one. The second question that the world at large heard him ask, after "How many roads…?", was:

> Yes, 'n' how many seas must a white dove sail
> Before she sleeps in the sand?

The apocalyptic associations of the image are clear from this very first use, whether the dove's rest represents the eventual achievement of peace or, taking it closer to its origins in the story of Noah, a still greater deliverance.

The next important appearance of the sea is in A HARD RAIN'S A-GONNA FALL, which was crucial to Dylan's development. It appears at the end of the song – as it does several times in key pieces – after a long chain of images which seem to summarise a long, long journey, as the end of the road.

This was a spectre raised by Kerouac: while Whitman's "plain public road" could still seem, in a wild-frontiered America, to open into boundless possibility, for the twentieth-century wanderers of *On the Road*, their wild highway journeys must eventually come to a dead end, in one or the other ocean. The Beat solution was to turn round and do it again – to seek fulfilment in a perpetual if purposeless motion. For all his love of travelling, Dylan refused to accept this from an early age. So when he comes to the sea at the end of the highway, he confronts it; he recognises an absolute which the provisional resources of the road cannot carry him over. This is the conclusion of A HARD RAIN:

> I'll tell it and speak it and think it and breathe it
> And reflect from the mountains so all souls can see it,
> Then I'll stand on the ocean until I start sinkin'
> But I'll know my song well before I start singin',
> And it's a hard, it's a hard…

The swift transition from "all souls" to "the ocean" lends support to our equation of the waters with the mass of people, and if we unpack this image, we'll find more.

Someone who stands on the waters first of all evokes Jesus; then possibly that angel in Revelation

clothed with a cloud: and a rainbow was upon his head, and his face was as it were the sun, and his feet as pillars of fire:

And he had in his hand a little book open: and he set his right foot upon the sea, and his left foot on the earth,

And cried with a loud voice, as when a lion roareth: and when he had cried, seven thunders uttered their voices.

But then "until I start sinking" leads away from these images of divine power to one of human faith, and failure; not of Jesus but of Peter walking on the water. (Which goes to show that as a twenty-two-year-old Jew, Dylan had already absorbed more of the Gospels than many a nominal Christian.)

And in the fourth watch of the night, Jesus went unto them, walking on the sea.

And when the disciples saw him walking on the sea, they were troubled, saying, It is a spirit; and they cried out for fear.

But straightway Jesus spake unto them, saying, Be of good cheer; it is I; be not afraid.

And Peter answered him and said, Lord, if it be thou, bid me come unto thee on the water.

And he said, Come. And when Peter was come down out of the ship, he walked on the water, to go to Jesus.

But when he saw the wind boisterous, he was afraid; and beginning to sink, he cried, saying, Lord, save me.

And immediately Jesus stretched forth his hand, and caught him, and said unto him, O thou of little faith, wherefore didst thou doubt?

By placing that image at the end of his extraordinarily long song, with the suggestion that he stands on the ocean *before* he starts singing, Dylan holds all of its not-quite-seven-minutes in the moment of faith. Twenty years later, at the start of the album *Infidels*, the moment is still holding:

> Standing on the waters, casting your bread
> While the eyes of the idol with the iron head are glowing.
> Distant ships sailin' in through the mist...

"Cast your bread upon the waters," says the Preacher in the book of Ecclesiastes, "for thou shalt find it after many days."

By 1983, the faith that sustained him to sing had been codified in a particular brand of Christianity – and was now perhaps being decodified. In 1963, it clearly wasn't religious faith in that sense, though the tenor of Dylan's thought has always been religious. The only change that time has made in that is to reveal that he actually meant it when he sang on his first record:

> Meet me, Jesus, meet me,
> Meet me in the middle of the air.
> If these wings should fail me, Lord,
> Won't you meet me in the night I prayer.

But the faith by which Dylan stands at the end of HARD RAIN is not in Jesus – he is not enabled to walk on the waters by walking *towards his Lord* – but, I would suggest, in the waters themselves. By which I mean, returning to the sea's symbolism, the mass of people.

Dylan explains in the sleevenotes to *Freewheelin'* how HARD RAIN was written in the depths of the Cuban crisis: "Every line in it is actually the start of a whole song. But when I wrote it, I thought I wouldn't have enough time alive to write all those songs so I put all I could into this one." More parable than history, perhaps; yet he believed, in the face of that ultimate deterrent – the destruction not only of himself, but of all that might remember him or receive him, of all that might give meaning to what he wrote – that it was worthwhile casting his bread on the waters, that there was a purpose to writing the song; indeed, that it was all he could do.

The opening lines of JOKERMAN could be a snapshot of the moment when HARD RAIN was composed. The "idol with the iron head" suggests a war-god who is also a war-machine; in my mind's eye, an idol shaped something like a missile. And the "distant ships sailing in" recall the Russian freighters drawing closer to Cuba, drawing the superpowers to the brink.

The next lines, by this interpretation – "You were born with a snake in both your fists / While a hurricane was blowing" – say that the crisis saw the birth, not of Dylan as an artist, since he was born already, but of a certain power in his art: the 'jokerman' power, discovered in that disjunct style that bore some of his greatest songs; in which, throwing out logic, he spoke to the collective through association; in which he became a "dream-twister".

To revive the moment 20 years later is an act of assertion, an allegation of his continuing power as a figure of mass consciousness "standing on the waters". Yet it introduces a collection of songs deeply troubled by such figures. So the Jokerman, "manipulator of crowds", is mirrored, at the start of the other side, by the MAN OF PEACE, with "a sweet gift of the gab, a harmonious tongue, / He knows every song of love that ever has been sung", who can "ride down Niagara Falls in the barrels of your skull", and who could be an emissary of Satan. Likewise the invocation, "Jokerman dance to the nightingale tune", is countered right at the end of the record by a verse of typical and brilliant scorn:

> What about that millionaire
> With the drumsticks in his pants?
> He looked so baffled and so bewildered
> When he played and we didn't dance.

After *Infidels*, at the end of his next record, *Empire Burlesque*, he gave one more view of himself standing on the waters, and a clear indication that it was not enough:

> A million faces at my feet
> But all I see are dark eyes.

At the time of HARD RAIN, though, it was enough – to speak out to as many as would hear him. The question-and-answer form of the song – "Oh, where have you been, my blue-eyed son?", "And what did you see…?" and so on – is taken from the ballad 'Lord Randal'; but there the young man who answers is incurably poisoned and dying. Dylan takes this moment of imminent death and turns it into an affirmation of life, however temporary – "until I start sinking". And to give this message is the meaning of his life, as he understood it then. "The voice of honest indignation," wrote William Blake, "is the voice of God." And the voice of God, wrote Ezekiel, is "like a noise of many waters".

Let's glance aside at some lines, to see the condensation that Dylan achieved under the pressure to say all he had to say at once.

> I saw a black branch with blood that kept drippin'.
> I saw a room full of men with their hammers a-bleedin'.
> I saw a white ladder all covered in water.

The black branch evokes the bloody tree of Christian symbolism, the Cross; and the sufferings of the black 'branch' of humanity, and the trees of lynchings. The next line might make us look forward to the courtroom scene of THE LONESOME DEATH OF HATTIE CARROLL, and think of the law that colludes in bloodshed; or it might make us think back to John Henry, the black worker-hero who died with his hammer in his hand. If we are still thinking raciologically, the ladder, as contrasted with the branch, might stand for the artifice and hierarchy of 'whiteness' against a natural and rooted 'blackness'. But this image seems to me to be a condensation of one verse in Woody Guthrie's 'Grand Coulee Dam':

> Now at Bonneville on the river there's a green and beautiful
> sight:
> See the Bonneville Dam a-risin' in the sun so clear and
> white
> While the leaping salmon play along the ladder and the
> rocks
> And there's a steamboat full of gasoline a-whistlin' in the
> docks.

This harmony of Man and Nature, of past and present ("a steamboat full of gasoline") is Guthrie's vision of a socialist paradise, and Dylan's "white ladder all covered in water" fuses it into a single image of aspiration which also, in its supernaturality, reminds us of Jacob's Ladder, connecting earth and heaven.

The image is too mysterious to be a source of light in the song, but where almost every other resonates with either sorrow or menace, its ambivalence allows some sense of wonder. There is one, however, and only one, which is simply bright:

> I met a young girl, she gave me a rainbow.

The rainbow represents a promise: the covenant between God and the earth which was told to Noah, that "the waters shall no more become a flood to destroy all flesh". It is God's reminder to stop the rain, though here it appears, not as supernatural sign, but as a token of human love. Slight as this one shaft of light is, it counterbalances the whole of the rest of the song, for it is the assurance that the "hard rain" is not the end of the world.

The rainbow should be borne in mind wherever the sea, the flood, the waters appear in Dylan's songs as an eschatological emblem. ('Eschatology' the *Shorter Oxford* defines as "The science of 'the last four things: death, judgement, heaven, and hell'.") Because of the promise that the world will not be consumed by water but by "the fire next time", Dylan can speak with an apocalyptic urgency without coming under the condemnation Jesus levels at the false prophets who say, "The time draweth near".

In THE TIMES THEY ARE A-CHANGIN', for example – which was written purposely in the vein of HARD RAIN and BLOWIN' IN THE WIND, as a statement from what his manager, Albert Grossman, had dubbed "the voice of a generation" – the 'changes' are once again a flood:

> Come gather round, people, wherever you roam
> And admit that the waters around you have grown
> And accept it that soon you'll be drenched to the bone.
> If your time to you is worth savin'
> Then you better start swimmin' or you'll sink like a stone
> For the times they are a-changin'.

Changing but not – as later, in Dylan's explicitly Christian apocalypse – ending. In fact, the flood of THE TIMES seems as much a baptism as a catastrophe.

WHEN THE SHIP COMES IN, on the same LP, also sets its moment of final reckoning beside the sea, and so too does the 'first ending' of DESOLATION ROW, Dylan's largest and most concentrated apocalypse, which we'll look at in detail later. But perhaps more telling than these deliberate grand statements is the appearance of the sea in moments of what might be called personal eschatology. I mean, for example, the "heaven" at the end of MR TAMBOURINE MAN (though in view of 'where Dylan's head was at' in 1964, this liberation and enlightenment might better be described as nirvana or satori):

> Yes, to dance beneath the diamond sky with one hand
> > waving free,
> Silhouetted by the sea,
> Circled by the circus sands,
> With all memory and fate
> Driven deep beneath the waves.
> Let me forget about today until tomorrow.

As for "hell", there is the sinking volcanic island of BLACK DIAMOND BAY on *Desire* – a song which marks, behind its highly polished verse and glamorous fiction, a real turning point in Dylan's life – the first stirrings of his religious commitment. Also on *Desire*, SARA, the song that commemorated his marriage, and the death of his marriage, is set by the sea:

> Now the beach is deserted except for some kelp
> And a piece of an old ship that lies on the shore.
> You always responded when I needed your help...

And finally, to complete the tally of "four last things", judgement comes with the sea in EVERY GRAIN OF SAND (*Shot of Love*, 1981):

> I hear the ancient footsteps like the motion of the sea.
> Sometimes I turn there's someone there, other times it's
> > only me.
> I am hanging in the balance of the reality of man...

The colored rider was laughing and saying, "Man! Man! When th' good Lord was workin' makin' Minnesoty, He couldn' make up His mind whethah ta make anothah ocean or some mo' land, so He just got 'bout half done an' then he quit an' went home! Wowie!" He ducked his head and shook it and kept laughing...

(Woody Guthrie, *Bound for Glory*)


*... c'est comme si dans l'onde j'innovais
Mille sépulcres pour y vierge diparaître.*

... as though I founded in the wave
A thousand tombs in which to disappear, untouched.

(Mallarmé, 'Le Pitre Châtié' / 'The Clown Chastised')

•••••••••••••

# Interchapter

•••••••••••••

# Watching
# The River Flow

● ● ● ● ● ● ● ● ● ● ● ● ● ● ● ● ●

O n 2nd March 1927, in New York City, Bessie
Smith recorded four songs with a small band
drawn from the Fletcher Henderson Orchestra.
The choice of material was unusual. The singer was celebrated for her blues, a form which had emerged from the obscurity of its folk roots to enjoy a huge popular fad in the
Twenties. She was the most popular and most brilliant out of
the wave of black women singers who had followed in the
wake of Mamie Smith's 'Crazy Blues' in 1920. The songs
selected for this session were not blues, however, but pop hits
of varying age: 'After You've Gone', 'There'll Be a Hot Time
in the Old Town Tonight', 'Alexander's Ragtime Band' by
Irving Berlin, and 'Muddy Water (A Mississippi Moan)' by P.
DeRose/H. Richman/J. Trent.

These last three songs – 'pop' versions of black culture –
are in a tradition which stretched back over a hundred years,
through the "Ethiopian melodies" of Stephen Foster and
other minstrel songs of the mid-nineteenth century to some
of the very first popular songs to be published in the United
States, like 'Jim Crow' and 'Zip Coon' in the 1820s and '30s.
The most extreme of our three examples is 'Muddy Water',
which had been a hit in 1926. The lyrics begin in as clichéd a
way as can be imagined:

Dixie moonlight, Swanee shore –
Heading homebound just once more
To my Mississippi Delta home.

In among the minstrel-show pastiche, though, there are some
surprising snatches of reality:

Muddy water in my shoes
Reelin' and rockin' to them lowdown blues

The lyricist, Jo Trent, was no dullard – he was just willing
to use whatever came first to hand, whether it was second-
hand or new (unlike the overwhelming majority of pop lyri-
cists, who are only willing to use what has already been tried
many times). He had collaborated with Duke Ellington in
1923, and together they wrote (in one afternoon, supposedly!)
a show called *Chocolate Kiddies* which proved a huge success
in Berlin, where it ran for two years, starring the dancer
Josephine Baker and the singer Adelaide Hall.

Numbered among the works of Peter De Rose, the composer of 'Muddy Water', is a song called 'The Memphis Blues'
from 1931, but his preference for the romantic over the earthy
is revealed in the titles of later compositions such as 'Autumn
Serenade', 'A Marshmallow World', 'Lilacs in the Rain' and
'Deep Purple' (voted by *Sheet Music* magazine one of the ten
best songs of the twentieth century, incidentally). The third
claimant on the song's copyright – Harry Richman (born
Reichman) – was a vaudeville song-and-dance man who had
presumably secured a third of the royalties in exchange for
being the first to record the song. He also has a share in a tune
called 'Blue Bonnet – You Make Me Blue', for example, issued
in 1926 by Irving Berlin's own music publishing company.

Bessie Smith's was not the only attempt in 1927 to follow
up on Richman's success the previous year: an act trippingly
named 'Don Voorhees and his Earl Carroll's "Vanities"

Orchestra with Harold Yates' also recorded 'Muddy Water' in 1927. Here we are, then, in the very belly of that blatant, shameless beast which is branded Tin Pan Alley.

No-one represents the cheerful opportunism of pop song better than Irving Berlin, one of the best, most prolific and least pretentious of its practitioners, who was born Israel Baline in Russia in 1888 and lived to be a hundred and one on the proceeds of his thousand songs. 'Alexander's Ragtime Band', written in 1911, is only the most enduring of his cash-ins on that particular craze. We might also mention his appeal, in 1909, to the Yiddish-speaking immigrants to the United States, whose numbers had been swollen by vicious pogroms between 1903 and 1906: 'Yiddle, On Your Fiddle, Play Some Ragtime'. Then there was his monument to Bolshevism, 'That Revolutionary Rag' of 1919. Come the Twenties and Thirties and the word Blues takes the place of Rag in his titles, but long before that he'd been mining the same vein of Dixie nostalgia as 'Muddy Water', with songs like 'When That Midnight Choo-Choo Leaves for Alabam'' (1912) and 'When It's Night Time Down in Dixieland' (1914).

The race-relations of our song are already complex, then: a black lyricist in a northern city writes of nostalgia for south-ern black rural life in a sentimental commercial style largely shaped by white entertainers for white audiences, and the song is a hit for a Jewish performer before it is adopted by a black singer from the rural south, who has become popular with both black and white, North and South.

Undeflected by its conventional ornament, Bessie Smith seizes on the core of the song and turns 'Muddy Water' into a genuine cry of love, and a proud assertion of roots, testifying with the full broadside power of her voice: "That's God's own shelter, down on the Delta!" This has one resonance for those like herself who had left the South, and must have had anoth-er again for those who stayed – for whom Bessie Smith, as much as anyone, represented the opportunities offered by the

North. For all her pearls and Packards, she says, she misses the down-home ease of "muddy water in my shoes". Using that phrase to encapsulate the sensations of Delta life would prove prophetic; through it, Bessie's expression of solidarity with her southern audience would take on a weight that she couldn't have envisaged.

A few weeks before she cut 'Muddy Water' she had made one of her greatest records, 'Back Water Blues', her own song, accompanied by the king of the Harlem stride pianists, James P. Johnson. It recounted an experience she had had on tour in January 1927, when her company got caught in a flood somewhere near Cincinatti, in the Ohio River basin. 'Muddy Water' also refers glancingly to the flooding that was endemic to the Mississippi, combining its chaos with what I take to be an image of carefree play, of happy splashing about:

> Muddy water round my feet,
> Muddy water in the street.

Only a few months after these records came out, in June 1927, the Mississippi broke out in a flood that became a national disaster: the sombre 'Back Water Blues' and, in its more oblique way, 'Muddy Water' suddenly had a powerful topicality. In the last line of the latter, in the lyric's one flash of real genius, Bessie sings: "My heart cries out for muddy water!" She thirsts to taste that water again – even though it's poor, even though it's dirty – and at the same she cries out at what it has done. For black people in the Delta, the Empress of the Blues singing 'Muddy Water (A Mississippi Moan)' in the wake of the flood of 1927 must have been a powerful thing.

Near Clarksdale, a boy named McKinley Morganfield was being brought up by his grandmother, who had nicknamed him from an early age 'Muddy', "her little muddy baby", as he told Charles Shaar Murray in 1977, in an interview for the

*NME*. He recalled that by the time he was thirteen – which was in 1928 – he was already accomplished enough on harmonica to be playing on the streets for change: "I started to play the harp when I was seven. At nine I was really tryin' to play. At thirteen I thought I was good. The kids I used to sing to would call out 'Hey Muddy Waters play us a piece.'

"I didn't like that 'Muddy Water' thing, ya know… I didn't mind my grandmother calling me Muddy, but that whole Muddy Waters thing, I didn't like it. It just growed on me."

If it was indeed Bessie Smith's record that rounded out the name his grandmother had started, it could hardly be more apt, since Muddy Waters came to represent exactly what the phrase "muddy water" does in the song – an essence of the South remembered and revitalised in the North.

It has been said before that Muddy Waters, with his telepathic-sounding sidemen, took the music of Robert Johnson – which he knew from records – and orchestrated for a five- or six-piece ensemble what Johnson had played on one guitar. However, part of the reason, it seems to me, for the density and diversity of Johnson's compositions is that his style was not only an amalgam of various kinds of rural blues, but also of all sorts of other blues and blues-related music – like the orchestral, stage-influenced sounds of Bessie Smith – which he heard on disc.

> We played it on the sofa and we played it 'gainst the wall
> But now my needle's rusty and it will not play at all.

he sang in 'Phonograph Blues' – touching once again on his recurrent theme of impotence – and also suggesting that for him sex was something as good as listening to records.

In 'Muddy Water', the arrangement by Fletcher Henderson, played by two clarinets, cornet and trombone, banjo and piano, comes halfway to meet him. A strange sawing little figure on the reeds, punctuated by interjections from the brass, seems deliberately to echo the bass-and-treble alternations of a Delta slide guitar player.

One of the clarinet players is Coleman Hawkins, the man who is said, without much disputation, to have invented the saxophone as a serious jazz instrument. As a clarinettist he had joined Mamie Smith's Jazz Hounds in 1921, the year after she had sparked the blues craze with her 'Crazy Blues'. In 1924 he began a ten-year stint with the Fletcher Henderson Orchestra, during which he brought his second instrument, tenor saxophone, to the fore. In the first Jazz Age, the saxophone was regarded as something of a novelty instrument – and on 'Hello Lola!', recorded by the Mound City Blue Blowers in 1929, though he plays with great wit and agility, his tone is not so far from the "blue blowing" – i.e. kazoo – of the leader, Red McKenzie. By the mid-Thirties, however, he had advanced the saxophone to the stage where it was ready to take over as the leading voice of jazz, so that for the next thirty years each new wave would be spearheaded and symbolised by a saxophone player – Lester Young, Charlie Parker, John Coltrane, Ornette Coleman.

In 1927, the next wave of jazz was being shaped by Fletcher Henderson himself, who was pivotal in the development of Swing out of the earlier New Orleans-derived styles. He was an early model for Duke Ellington, the greatest bandleader of the Swing era (though he was much else besides). With Swing, a black musical style became for the first time the predominant sound of American popular music.

In 'Muddy Water', then, every current feeds into every other – folk, art and pop, blues, jazz and Tin Pan Alley – in a way that lent American music of the mid twentieth century its vigour. This eclecticism Bob Dylan has been devoted to emulating for the last forty years.

# Part II

# A Little
# Upside Down

● ● ● ● ● ● ● ● ● ● ● ● ● ● ● ● ●

On the night of 9th and 10th June 1964, in New York City, Bob Dylan recorded the eleven songs that would make up his fourth album, *Another Side of Bob Dylan*. Thirty-seven years on from that Bessie Smith session, pop, art and folk music were converging again, by different routes.

To record an entire LP in a single session is not a common feat, and not one that Dylan has repeated, but it is only an extreme example of his preferred method. Long after most people in his field stopped, he has carried on recording his songs as performances – segments of actual time, rather than assemblages of sound on tape. While other rock'n'roll stars settled into the habit of living in the studio for weeks on end, tunnelling into the strong-room, as it were, his *modus operandi* remained the smash-and-grab.

*Bringing It All Back Home*, his fifth album, was recorded in three days (15th-17th January 1965). All but one track of his seventh album, the double *Blonde on Blonde*, comes from two three-day bouts in Nashville, Tennessee, starting on Valentine's Day, 1966. Three brief sessions in the autumn of 1967, with gaps of a couple of weeks between them, sufficed for his eighth album, *John Wesley Harding*. In 1978, fronting a nine-piece band and three backing singers, Dylan stuck to live recording for *Street-Legal*, his sixteenth collection of songs, tracking it in five days.

To make an album in one go was still a novel thing for him in 1964, though. He had built up his third LP, *The Times They Are A-Changin'*, in a series of sessions spaced over three months; and for the one before that, *The Freewheelin' Bob Dylan*, he had a choice of tracks from eight sessions that spanned exactly a year, from 24th April 1962 to 24th April 1963. Obviously, there was no constraint on his access to the studio, if he wanted it, when he made *Another Side*. There must have been a certain eagerness on the part of Columbia Records to take delivery of more material, since he had become, if not the best-selling, certainly one of the most talked-about names on their roster. He had songs on the charts and he had not been in the studio for seven months, at a time when hitmakers like the Beatles released a single every three months. But he had already gained a degree of artistic freedom which contemporary pop musicians – even the Beatles – would have boggled at. The decision to make this record, *Another Side of Bob Dylan*, the record of a 'moment', then, was quite deliberate, and has something to do with the nature of the moment.

· 1 ·

# Something Is Happening Here

I n the USA, 1964 marked a watershed. In the previous year, the Civil Rights movement had seen one of its most glorious days, the March on Washington on 28th August; but the assassination of President Kennedy in November dealt a profound blow to hopes for peaceful change. The rumour that had been awoken by the terror of the Cuban crisis – that a society ready to contemplate thermonuclear war was not in need of modification but of dismantling – got louder. The big organisations of youth – like the Student Non-violent Coordinating Committee (SNCC or Snack), and Students for a Democratic Society (SDS) – became more radical. In the fall of 1964, the confrontation between the Free Speech Movement and the University of California at Berkeley set the spark for a series of campus revolts that would escalate throughout the decade. On 1st October, Mario Savio concluded his address to the crowd outside the administration block:

> There is a time when the operation of the machine becomes so odious, makes you so sick at heart, that you can't take part; you can't even passively take part, and you've got to put your bodies upon the gears and upon the wheels, upon the levers, upon all the apparatus, and you've got to make it stop. And you've got to indicate to the people who run it, to the people who own it, that unless you're free, the machine will be prevented from running at all.

Then he directed the students to move orderly into the hall they were to occupy, "Up on the left. I didn't mean the pun."

The spread of lysergic acid, which would influence much of the best and some of the worst deeds of the counterculture – the music of Jimi Hendrix, for example, and the murders of Charles Manson – also had its western epicentre at Berkeley. In the east, there was another LSD circle. Richard Alpert and Timothy Leary had been dismissed from lectureships at Harvard in the summer of 1963 for their psychedelic experiments. In July 1964, the Merry Pranksters, California's contingent of acid prophets, with prankster-in-chief Ken Kesey, crossed America by bus. Their destination plate read "Furthur". Their driver was Neal Cassady, the archetypal Beat and hero of Kerouac's *On the Road*, under the name of Dean Moriarty. (Moriarty was the nemesis of that superman of reason, Sherlock Holmes.) Apparently, the meeting of the two camps was not entirely harmonious, but the contact itself marked a turning point in the history of the Sixties and of hallucinogenic drugs.

Dylan undertook his own on-the-road adventure in the spring of '64, when he drove south in a camper with a bunch of friends to join the Mardi Gras in New Orleans. Their jaunt was fuelled with grass rather than acid, but it seems likely – on the evidence of his writing, above all – that he took a trip about the same time, perhaps through the agency of Allen Ginsberg, whom Dylan first met in 1963, and who had been taking acid since 1959.


While Dylan was on the road that spring, the year's great event in popular music made itself felt over the radio – a revolution which could be summed up in four words: John, Paul, George and Ringo. The Beatles' music, which had been released in the United States since the beginning of 1963, to zero response, made its first transatlantic impact with 'I Want to Hold Your Hand', which came out just after Christmas. By the beginning of February 1964 they were on *The Ed Sullivan Show*, and by early April they had all five of the top five singles on the US pop chart. Their first American tour in August marked perhaps the highest pitch of Beatlemania.

They were clearly the biggest thing since Elvis, and they rekindled a love of rock'n'roll in a lot of people who had lost interest after the King was drafted. The crucial difference was that their stardom affirmed the power of the collective. And partly just through the passage of time, because they drew back those young rock'n'roll fans who were now of college age, they forged a link between rock and the students, and student politics. Their acceptance among the intelligentsia was symbolised by Allen Ginsberg – to the astonishment of his party – jumping up to dance when 'I Want to Hold Your Hand' was played in a New York night-club.

Lyrically, they may not have been so far from the teen-idols that Dylan had mocked in TALKIN' WORLD WAR III BLUES: "It was Rock-a-day Johnny singing, 'Tell your ma, tell your pa, our love's a-gonna grow, ooh-wah, ooh-wah'." But his creative mishearing of their words shows that he took them to be close to his own wavelength. He thought they sang, in the bridge of 'I Want to Hold Your Hand', "It's such a feeling that, my love, I get high" – rather than "I can't hide" – and was amazed to discover, when he first met them in August and offered them some grass, that they had never smoked it before.

To state the Beatles' impact in a sentence, one could use the words of William Blake, one of the sacred elders of both Beat and psychedelic movements: they attested that "Energy is Eternal Delight."

American pop music was not quite the wasteland it's sometimes made out to be before the Fab Four came to save it. With the Righteous Brothers' 'You've Lost That Lovin' Feeling', produced by Phil Spector, and 'Pretty Woman' by Roy Orbison, the full-blown operatic pop of the early Sixties reached an apex in 1964. And while the compactness and freshness of the new groups put a stop to the escalatingly extravagant hits which Spector and Orbison had created, the big arrangement was soon resurgent in the productions of Motown. Berry Gordy's hope for "The Sound of Young America" began to be fulfilled in 1964 when his dream-team, the Supremes, crossed over with 'Where Did Our Love Go?' In the same year two more of Motown's biggest acts, the Temptations and the Four Tops, also emerged onto the pop charts.

The 'British invasion' of bands like the Beatles and the Rolling Stones, name-checking black artists as their favourites when they came over to America, and covering the songs, not only of the blues giants like Muddy Waters and Howlin' Wolf, but also of contemporary R&B hitmakers like Barrett Strong, Chuck Jackson, the Marvelettes, the Shirelles, Wilson Pickett, Solomon Burke, the Miracles, must have aided and encouraged the efforts of Berry Gordy and others to reach a wider, whiter audience. We should also note, though, Charlie Gillett's take on the same period, in *The Sound of the City*:

> With the advent of the British singers, it had become harder for rhythm and blues to make headway in the popular market, but at the same time pressure in the rhythm and blues market from pop records was reduced. A few producers took advantage of the changed conditions, orienting their product more directly to black tastes and interests than they had done for some time.

In 1964, 'soul' was not widely known as a musical term (except to describe a school of jazz players) – but its spirit of hope, pride and liberation was clearly abroad in records like 'Dancing in the Street' by Martha and the Vandellas, 'A Change Is Gonna Come' by Sam Cooke and 'People Get Ready' by the Impressions.

Otis Redding, arguably the greatest of the 'Southern soul' singers – and certainly the one who came to stand for the style as far as the pop audience was concerned – established his dominion in 1964 with a single that coupled 'That's How Strong My Love Is' and 'Mr Pitiful'. Joe Tex, arguably the most inventive of the Southern soul men, also established his name in late '64 with 'Hold What You've Got', the first of a string of brilliant gospel-and-rhythm-and-blues-and-country-

and-western sermonettes, embracing both comedy and pathos, and always imbued with compassion. That same year, in the summer, the style went to the country with a remarkable package tour which included Otis, Tex, Don Covay, Solomon Burke and Wilson Pickett.

Also in '64, Soul Brother Number One, James Brown, had his first record on the pop charts, 'Out of Sight'. Its pure funk style – an ingenious, muscular miracle sprung full-formed from the Godfather's brain like Minerva from the head of Jupiter – has had perhaps the strongest influence of any created in the Sixties

As influential as this new spirit in black music – and more perhaps than just an ancestral influence – was the old spirit of the blues. The rediscovery and re-recording of singers who had last been heard of in the 1930s had gathered pace over a number of years, but the 1964 Newport Folk Festival represented a peak moment for that movement. Perhaps the greatest of the rediscoveries – Son House and Skip James – performed there for the first time that July, along with an A-team of bluesmen who had already appeared in previous years – Mississippi John Hurt, Sleepy John Estes, Robert Pete Williams, Revd Robert Wilkins – and also the great, previously unheard Mississippi Fred McDowell. It was the *annus mirabilis* of the blues revival.

The Newport Folk Festival of 1963 had seen the high-water mark of 'protest', or more properly 'contemporary folk' music, and Bob Dylan had emerged from it as the "Crown Prince" of the folkies, to Joan Baez's "Queen". (It's odd that these phrases should have been used in America, especially with reference to a predominantly socialist movement, but they were.) The festival of 1965 was to be dominated by Dylan in a different way, of course. The controversy over his 'going electric' was a crossroads, where he divided his audience (and he was by that point the biggest name in folk music) between 'his' people and the 'folk' people – which meant, on the whole, dividing the young and old. In the history of that largely forgotten but potent thing, the Generation Gap, it marks a key moment, in which the rebel young turned from even their rebel elders.

Dylan's performance at Newport in 1964 had already caused unease, however, and prompted an Open Letter from Irwin Silber, one of the folk elders, which appeared in *Sing Out!* magazine in November. In a nutshell, he was accused of being too into himself, too aloof. Silber had a point: obviously there was something about that tribal gathering that brought out the young folksinger's antagonism. At the 1963 festival, he'd adopted a bullwhip as a fashion accesory, strolling the grounds with it coiled around his shoulder; while in '64 his protection was a beshaded minder, just like a presidential secret serviceman. On the main stage, more to the point, he eschewed the rallying songs and sang unfamiliar new material – introspective, visionary or oddly mocking – that had yet to appear on record: ALL I REALLY WANT TO DO, TO RAMONA, CHIMES OF FREEDOM and MR TAMBOURINE MAN. For an encore, he came back with Joan Baez to sing WITH GOD ON OUR SIDE – in retrospect, a rather poignant last bow for Dylan as the Great White Hope of the Folk Revival. The song comes from his then-current and most consistently 'protest' album, *The Times They Are A-Changin'*; but, as we shall see later, beneath its overt anti-nuclear and anti-war message it reveals a profound ambivalence.

The new songs of his set, with their complex, prolix lyrics, seem in their style to show Dylan diverging widely from the blues, but not in artistic spirit. He was seeking some intensely personal form, of existential rather than political content, of a kind which was exemplified by the blues. It was partly because the blues was not a medium for a 'message' that it lived such a protean second life in the rock of the Sixties. Like Dylan's, it was a music both immediate and mysterious, surrealistic in the non-continuous structure of its lyrics, plain-spoken yet puzzling (if only because of the colour bar and the lapse of time).

## · 2 ·

# Reels Of Rhyme

These, then, were some elements of the times in which Dylan chose to make his moment. How much of their climate can be read in the grain of the record?

The first thing that might strike the listener coming to it fresh from *The Times They Are A-Changin'*, is its refreshing, or lamentable, lack of freight. For example, the three opening songs of that predecessor had predicted, accurately enough, the advent of irreversible and violent social upheaval (THE TIMES THEY ARE A-CHANGIN'); then dramatised the grinding poverty that drives a man to murder his wife and five children before shooting himself (BALLAD OF HOLLIS BROWN), then summarised and satirised the history of American militarism (WITH GOD ON OUR SIDE). The first three songs of *Another Side* are ALL I REALLY WANT TO DO ("is, baby, be friends with you"), each verse of which relentlessly lists all the unfriendly things he doesn't want to do ("compete with you, beat or cheat or mistreat you") before tumbling into its falsetto-spiked refrain; then a raggy and sardonic blues on piano, BLACK CROW BLUES; then SPANISH HARLEM INCIDENT, a song about madly fancying a girl seen passing on the street.

Dylan insisted, in the notes that accompanied the retrospective triple CD *Biograph*, that he was dead-set against calling this record *Another Side of Bob Dylan*, and it was titled at the instigation of his producer, Tom Wilson. "I begged and pleaded with him… it was my feeling that it wasn't a good thing coming after *The Times They Are A-Changin'*, it just wasn't right. It seemed like a negation of the past which in no way was true… Tom meant well and he had control, so he had it his way. I guess in the long run, he might have been right to do what he did."

Something in this story doesn't ring true. I can well believe that Dylan capitulated to Wilson's earnest desire, but not that he can have been forced to accept it against his will. He was right, though – it is a drastic title. If this is 'Another', then its predecessor was 'One Side of Bob Dylan', which rather radically relativises its claim to universal significance. In fact, from the perspective of *Another Side*, the record before could have been called – and its sleeve can be read this way – *The Times They Are A-Changin' Bob Dylan*.

"In the long run", as Dylan allows, the title was accurate. What, then, is this other side?

It's not simply levity. He'd displayed plenty of that on his second album, *The Freewheelin' Bob Dylan*, though there was none on *The Times*. What distinguishes the humour of this fourth album is the way it blends with seriousness. Rather than an alternation of the funny, the sad, the angry – a succession of different facets, as on *Freewheelin'*, and going beyond the grim-subject-treated-humorously, as in TALKIN' WORLD WAR III BLUES – the comic parts on *Another Side* are melded with the non-comic in a single, overall mood. And the element in which they fuse is an air of intoxication.

The comedy routines – I SHALL BE FREE NO. 10 and MOTORPSYCHO NITEMARE lack the incisive wit of Dylan's earlier Talkin' Blues; they are more purely silly even than the first I SHALL BE FREE at the end of *Freewheelin'*, which kept a certain spikiness. (Was the jump in numbers intended to show how far he felt he'd come, or had Dylan decided to count in binary, 10 representing 2?) No. 10 begins with his Everyman persona expanded to the point of disintegration:

> Now I'm just average, common too,
> I'm just like him and the same as you,
> I'm everybody's brother and son,
> I ain't different than anyone.

Later on, we see the hobo sprouting into a proto-hippy:

> I'm gonna grow my hair down to my feet so strange
> Till I look like a walking mountain range,
> Then I'm gonna ride into Omaha on a horse,
> Out to the country club and the golf course,
> Carry the *New York Times*, shoot a few holes,
> > blow their minds.

This fool who clowns, though, is not so far from the romantic fool of SPANISH HARLEM INCIDENT and I DON'T BELIEVE YOU; the clever fool – his former self – that he holds up to mockery in MY BACK PAGES; or the holy fool of CHIMES OF FREEDOM who feels that a thunderstorm speaks of a power to redress the injuries of the whole world.

This 'other side' of Bob Dylan, then, we might call an undefended side. The artist of *The Times* is grave and very definite; here he is often irresolute, blurred at the edges, like a creature that has shed a skin. "Ah, but I was so much older then, I'm younger than that now" he sings in the chorus of MY BACK PAGES, and the idea that he is somehow less experienced than before is borne out by BALLAD IN PLAIN D. On *The Times* he had achieved a masterly love ballad, BOOTS OF SPANISH LEATHER, something delicate and accurate. Here he returns to the form and produces something maladroit and half-baked – if more honest to the bewilderment of broken love:

> With unknown consciousness I possessed in my grip
> A magnificent mantelpiece, though its heart being chipped,
> Noticing not that I'd already slipped
> To a sin of love's false security.

Quite what the first two lines of this verse signify would be utterly obscure, were it not for the photograph on the front of Dylan's next album, *Bringing It All Back Home*. This carefully-composed shot was taken in the apartment of Albert Grossman, Dylan's manager, and in the background is a magnificent stucco mantelpiece with two large (and roughly heart-shaped) chips out of its centre. Just below, tucked into the cushions of a chaise longue, behind the elegant form of a woman in scarlet who reclines there, can be seen the cover of this record, *Another Side*. What may have taken place in front of that hearth, or on that chaise longue, or with a woman, and which may have been the subject of "lies that I told her", as mentioned in BALLAD IN PLAIN D in the verse before the mantelpiece – I know not, and is beside the point. The point being, first, that Dylan's work – if we include in that the way he presents himself in photographs, films, interviews and such – is pretty much self-supporting. While he fights shy of explaining or giving biographical background, Dylan is quite willing to gloss, as he does in this picture, what would otherwise be an unavailable private reference.

The second point is that by linking this record with his next, he put a special emphasis on their continuity. *Bringing It All Back Home* obviously marks the beginning of his rock'n'roll career. (Though not obviously at the time: the outcry held off, due to the largely acoustic sound of the band on the record, until Dylan broke out the polka-dots and strapped on his Strat at Newport.) By referring back to the step before, he seems concerned that it should be understood, not as a break with the past, but a development out of it: to show that he had been influenced by himself, if you like, just as he had been influenced by those others – like the Impressions and Robert Johnson – whose LP sleeves he also has arranged around him in the cover shot.

One innovation of *Back Home* that is clearly foreshadowed on *Another Side* is the idea of new-found youth. When Dylan sang as "spokesman for a generation", he may have spoken *for* the young but he still spoke *to* the elders: "Come you masters of war"; "Come senators, congressman"; "Come mothers and fathers". On *Back Home* he speaks *to* the kids – "Look out, kid, they keep it all hid." He even gives his rejuvenated self a new superhero-type handle: "They asked me my name and I said, 'Captain Kidd'" (BOB DYLAN'S 115TH DREAM).

Of course, getting back to playing rock'n'roll was effectively a return to youth for Dylan, who had left it behind about six years before. *Another Side* doesn't really presage the rock beat, but there's certainly a new looseness and swing to a lot of it, bordering on the rhythmically chaotic in I DON'T BELIEVE YOU. Bringing this new physicality into his music, Dylan shows a fondness for triple time, rather than 4/4. TO RAMONA, for example, is fully a waltz, that "riotous and indecent German dance", whose name means 'the roll'.

A new youth and a new sensuality are conveyed by the sense of time on the record. *The Times* was concerned predominantly with history – with the past and the future. *Another Side* is preoccupied almost exclusively with immediate sensations. Hence that moment at the mantelpiece (admittedly not carried off with great distinction), which depicts the *setting* of a thought, although it's not really clear what the thought is.

SPANISH HARLEM INCIDENT is all about the instant when Eros's arrow strikes, which I DON'T BELIEVE YOU also vividly recreates:

... her skirt it swayed as the guitar played,
Her mouth was watery and wet.

– though that song's subject is the discrepancy between the moment, the night, and its aftermath next day.)

In the three verses of IT AIN'T ME, BABE, a single movement is split into three micro-movements:

Go 'way from my window...

Step lightly from the ledge...

Go melt back into the night...

And CHIMES OF FREEDOM stretches out a single event – in essence, the split-second of a lightning-flash – over more than seven minutes.

The precedence of the moment is shown in the images of being enraptured, mesmerised, and even engulfed by it:

Gypsy gal, you've got me swallowed,
I have fallen far beneath
Your pearly eyes so fast and flashin'...
     (SPANISH HARLEM INCIDENT)

Trapped by no track of hours for they hanged suspended...
Spellbound and swallowed till the tolling ended.
     (CHIMES OF FREEDOM)

Your magnetic movements still capture the minutes I'm in.
     (TO RAMONA)

I got to know, babe,
Will you surround me
So I can tell if I am really real.
     (SPANISH HARLEM INCIDENT)

The theme would be stronger still if some other songs, long associated with *Another Side*, had made it onto the LP. One of these is LAY DOWN YOUR WEARY TUNE (now available on *Biograph*), which was always ascribed, in its long years as a bootleg, to the session for *Another Side*, though it is actually a *Times* out-take. Another, also a candidate for inclusion on *The Times*, is ETERNAL CIRCLE (available on *The Bootleg Series, Vols 1-3*). This too, by dint of its tone and subject matter, used often to be assigned by collectors to 9th June 1964. What links these two is that they are both songs about song, and about a moment in which an eternity is glimpsed.

ETERNAL CIRCLE is a simple enough story: a singer becomes aware, as he sings, of a woman in the audience, and feels his connection with her; but when his number is over, she is gone, and so he begins another. So the "eternal circle" is song itself – or it could be that cycle of cause and effect wherein the performer, seeking to communicate with the audience, finding that performance itself is a form of isolation, feeds the desire for communication. To put it more strongly than the song suggests, this circle is more infernal than celestial – it is a circle of separation, a kind of trap.

There is also a circle of self-reference here, in that the song the singer is singing about becomes identified with the song he is actually singing; though, paradoxically, the song in the song is "long", and ETERNAL CIRCLE, by Dylan's standards, is pretty short – just over two and a half minutes.

The pull of the moment that Dylan surrenders to on *Another Side* is already here – again it is the moment of being smitten with a woman – but it is felt as a conflict of moments, of absorptions. His sensitivity to the room, in which the musician must try to draw out of himself the magic circle of another, self-sufficient world, a time out of time – nearly draws him away from its centre. But since it is the song around which the relationship revolves, the show must go on…

The same feeling that the song somehow keeps him from the moment is the seed of LAY DOWN YOUR WEARY TUNE. Here it is not the beauty of a woman which calls him away but the beauty of nature, which appears as a music greater than music:

> I stood unwound beneath the skies
> And clouds unbound by laws.
> The cryin' rain like a trumpet sang
> And asked for no applause.

In the earthly cycles – the day and night, the ocean, the river, the rain and wind, "the last of leaves" – he finds release from his eternal circle:

> Lay down your weary tune, lay down,
> Lay down the song you strum,
> And rest yourself 'neath the strength of strings
> No voice can hope to hum.

Again, there is a self-referential loop. The song is played with that strict cast-iron strum that characterises *The Times*, and sung with slow, deliberate emphasis, which does lend it a weary tone. But its steady rising and falling tune, its hymnal simplicity and the frank assurance of the singing unite it with the "strength of strings" that he feels embrace the world.

Concealed in that image is another circular figure: coming from a guitar-player, the place *beneath* "the strength of strings" suggests the guitar's generally round sound-hole. So we see the circle, the globe, giving out the sounds of the cosmos vibrating above it. It may not have been too early in his self-education for Dylan to have been thinking here of the Chinese figure of Heaven, the first of the hexagrams of the I Ching, formed of six unbroken lines like the strings of a guitar.

Now we come to a song that was first recorded in June '64, though its released version dates from six months later, January '65. In its richly atmospheric poetic style, MR TAMBOURINE MAN seems to outstrip any of the other lyrical innovations of *Another Side*, which suggests it is one of the latest compositions; too late, perhaps, to have been ready for inclusion. There is one circumstance though that weighs against this, which is the imagery it shares with LAY DOWN YOUR WEARY TUNE, of bare trees near the sea. That song moves from the "drums of dawn", through the ocean "like an organ" and the rain "like a trumpet", to the "branches bare like a banjo", and ends with the river "like a harp". In MR TAMBOURINE MAN the singer asks to be taken

> Far past the frozen leaves,
> The haunted, frightened trees,
> Out to the windy beach…

– unseasonal images for a song written in the spring or summer. On the other hand, LAY DOWN YOUR WEARY TUNE, recorded at the end of October 1963, was composed in Joan Baez's home in southern California – not noted for its wintry weather. Perhaps the "last of leaves" came later, back in New York. Whether or not the beach and the bare branches, juxtaposed, were originally drawn from nature, their reappearance in TAMBOURINE MAN shows that they mark a season in the soul.

From what has been said about the youthful, tender quality of *Another Side*, we might assign its season as spring. For reasons I shall go into later, I think it is winter, with the vigour of the old year withdrawn and the vigour of the new maybe just beginning to stir. MR TAMBOURINE MAN is such a leap in Dylan's art – a really new thing – that it might seem strange to link it with winter, usually seen as the natural analogy for stasis and death. What it means here, though, is the shedding of dead forms, and the possibility of a new beginning.

The song is not directly concerned with what comes next – "Let me forget about today until tomorrow" – but it does have a belief in the future. It starts at sundown, when "evening's empire has returned into sand", and it ends at midnight, "beneath the diamond sky"; yet its chorus is about the morning:

> Hey, Mr Tambourine Man, play a song for me
> In the jingle-jangle morning I'll come following you

In the verses he submits himself powerlessly to his mentor – "take me on a trip… my hands can't feel to grip", "take me disappearing" – while in the chorus he will be purposely "following". The relationship is like that of disciple to guru. Tonight, as a novice, he surrenders his will and undergoes a kind of ritual death, a loss of self; and tomorrow he will rise and follow as a matter of free choice, as an initiate.

Since many of the first wave of acid-trippers were introduced to it in a context like this, as an initiation, and since the intensity of the sensations it induces can lead to the kind of immobility Dylan describes, and for a number of other reasons, the song was widely believed to be about an LSD experience, which its writer has always denied. It would be more accurate to say it is about the kind of experience of which the acid trip may be an instance. We should not forget, however, that the song is literally about music – about a drummer – and could as well be said to celebrate a resurgent love of rock'n'roll as any hallucinogenic drug.

Beginning with a chorus, a very uncharacteristic feature for a Dylan song, was a device favoured by the Beatles in their early phase. (Oddly, another Dylan song that shares this rare structure is LAY DOWN YOUR WEARY TUNE, which was written before he was even aware of the Beatles.) The effect is to make the song circular in form – and the circle appears several times in its lyric: "reels of rhyme", "smoke-rings of my mind", "circled by the circus sands", and primarily in the tambourine itself. (The "jingle-jangle morning" also suggests an identification of the drum with the sun.)

The cover of *Bringing It All Back Home*, on which MR TAMBOURINE MAN eventually appeared, reiterates the circle in the lens effect that frames the front photograph, so that we seem to peer in through the smoke-ring of a mind at these symbolic objects, cryptically arranged. Or, to quote the LP's opening lines, down into the "basement" where Johnny's "mixing up the medicine". The significance of the circle and the joy of self-abandonment in MR TAMBOURINE MAN is that the artist had realised for the first time how his creative power could renew itself cyclically, so long as he let go of "whatever was" (as he put it once, in I AND I).

It's clear that by the end of *The Times They Are A-Changin'*, Dylan really was ready to lay down that weary tune. He had hitched his young art to duty, and if there was a strand of opportunism twisted into the rope, still it was composed mainly of fellow-feeling, of sincere wrath and sorrow, as anyone who listens to the best of his 'protest songs' can surely attest. But he could not haul the troubles of the world any further, and it seems to have got to the stage where he seriously thought of giving up altogether. In one of the most beautiful performances of the *Times* sessions, MOONSHINER (now released in *The Bootleg Series*), he sounds as old in spirit as he ever has in his life. The delight of MR TAMBOURINE MAN is the discovery that he could follow music – and particularly rhythm – to new life, on a new morning.

## · 3 ·

# Who Are You Anyway?

M R TAMBOURINE MAN clarifies another way in which *Another Side of Bob Dylan* gains in immediacy, which is by direct address. 'You' first appears early in Dylan's recordings, in the first track of his first LP, YOU'RE NO GOOD – and that would be the attitude of some of his best songs. The first of his songs on record (leaving aside the comic monologue, TALKIN' NEW YORK) is also in what might be called 'half-dialogue' form. It is not a song for or about, but a song *to* Woody, set dramatically by Woody's side, "a thousand miles from my home".

The lyric addressed to 'you' in popular music stems from the stage – the revue and the musical – which provides it with a dramatic context. Since the early period of popular music on record, dominated by the show-song, it has become such a universal convention that we tend to forget that it is one. But a second-person address is far from common in the folk song from which Dylan drew his first forms, and not much more so in the earlier blues, which seem to have acquired it as they mingled in the mainstream.

What is common in the folk ballad, and hardly used at all in pop song, is full dialogue, two voices rendered by one. This can achieve some surprising effects, as for example in the British ballad 'The White Cockade', a song about enlistment, which begins in the voice of the soldier, explaining how he came to be persuaded – with "a flowing bowl of grog" and an advance of "two guineas and a crown" – then skips to the complaint of the maid, who curses the man that enlisted her ploughboy "and sent him away from me", and then skips back to the soldier, who, it turns out, is not yet "away" but here listening to her:

> Then he took out a handkerchief and wiped a flowing eye:
> "Leave off your lamentations, likewise your mournful cries…"

He promises to marry her on his return, and the last verse skips again to her, now presumably singing her devotion in his absence:

> Oh yes, me love's enlisted and I for him will rove
> And carve his name in every tree that grows in yonder grove

Devices like this enable the folk ballads about love to be more rounded, to portray relationships better than almost all pop love-songs. (It is interesting that Country & Western, the form of popular music most closely related to the ballads, is also the one that deals most thoroughly with everyday relationships – not only boy-girl love, but marriage, divorce, childhood, parenthood, bereavement, employment and so on.) The pop song with its antecedents on the stage must be one-sided, insofar as it is conceived as a sung speech from a dialogue. This is not the only form it can take, of course: it might as well be a sung soliloquy, addressed to a 'her' or 'him', or a 'you' who is offstage. Still it is the complaint, the plea, the promise, the seduction or rejection of one party only.

Where it gains is in erotic intensity. It can dramatise in an immediate way our passions – our desire, sorrow, frustration or rapture under Eros' sway. Developed along this line, the pop song began to embrace intimacies that were never part of the musical show, perhaps under the influence of the movies with their bedroom scenes and close-up kisses. To cite an example I've already mentioned, 'Go Slow', as sung by Julie London, is musical pillow-talk, in which a woman advises her lover how most to please her. It can only be visualised as being sung in bed, or on the way there. The same is true of many of London's torch-songs, which transpose the sultry seductress-es of film to the microgroove. (She was a Hollywood actress as well as a singer.) The images they conjure are cinematic, and anyone who has seen enough movies of the period will know exactly how these scenes are costumed, staged and lit. They are far more libidinous, of course, than any movie equivalents; and, apart from occasional dance-as-seduction numbers, they allow the female to be far more forthcoming than the love-scenes of that era, or of this, generally.

These developments are pertinent, too, to the great male heart-throbs leading up to Elvis, like Sinatra and, at the beginning of the line, Bing Crosby, the king of the crooners. Crooning – singing softly, as to one other person, in front of an orchestra – was made possible by the electrical microphone. It meant that for every female fan, 'you' in the song could become *you*, the listener – hence that fervent, swooning adoration which Bing was the first pop singer to excite. For the male, *he*, with his assured sexual success, becomes the voice of your desires: you yourself say 'you'. In this vein, no-one has ever played the microphone as well as Elvis. Just as the thrill of his fast songs is the way you can hear him move, so his ballads are filled with the sensual presence of his mouth, in intense close-up, his breath, and the warm resonance of his chest.

Isn't Dylan as a singer the antithesis of this whole strain, though? In the main, yes. It's revealing that his early hero from the heart-throb era was Johnny Ray, whose voice, rising out of his deafness, always sounded like what his best-known record called it, a 'Cry', cried as though there were no-one else in the world, let alone in the room. Another early model from when Dylan first began to play, sing and write, was Hank Williams, whose voice hardly conveyed intimacy either, with its hard, broken edge. In fact, its honesty is often so cutting because it sings what has not been spoken. Do we really believe he says to his wife:

> Well, you start your jaws a-waggin' and they never stop.
> You never shut up until I blow my top...

– or is it just what he wants to say?

A telling example of how Williams uses 'you' is 'There'll Be No Teardrops Tonight', in which the groom on the night before his wedding addresses his bride-to-be, saying that he knows she has another lover:

> I'll pretend that you still love me
> When you wear your veil of white,
> Though I know you love another,
> Still there'll be no teardrops tonight.
>
> Shame, oh shame for what you're doing.
> Other arms will hold you tight,
> But you don't care who's life you ruin,
> So there'll be no teardrops tonight.

The catch is that – as he has decided to marry her anyway, and keep her secret as his secret, which is why "there'll be no teardrops tonight" – what the singer says to "you" in the song is precisely what he will not say.

Whether or not he absorbed the idea from Hank Williams, Dylan has certainly favoured this form of dissociated dialogue. There's an inkling of it already in SONG TO WOODY, which is addressed face-to-face, as it were, but to someone who cannot reply, or at least not in the same mode, since by the time Dylan came to see him, Guthrie was no longer able to sing and play, and had difficulty even speaking.

On *Freewheelin'* the dissociation of the 'you' song is much more apparent. GIRL OF THE NORTH COUNTRY, a love-song of uncommon gentleness, is also unusual in that its subject is a 'she', and 'you' is an intermediary:

> Please see for me if her hair hangs long,
> If it rolls and flows all down her breast.

So direct address is used to heighten the awareness of distance which is the song's theme.

MASTERS OF WAR has this element of distance, too, but to different effect. By directly addressing those who cannot be directly addressed ("You that hide behind walls / You that hide behind desks") it increases the power – the armour-piercing power, we might call it – of the lone voice crying out against them: "I just want you to know / I can see through your masks."

A HARD RAIN'S A-GONNA FALL is a rare example of the full dialogue form of folk song, though the answers of 'I' don't really seem to be addressed to 'you'. If one were to try to stage this scene, wouldn't the outpouring of images from the "blue-eyed son" be directed at a point in mid-air, in a fit of distraction, a trance almost, rather than to the mother directly?

A couple of years later, Dylan returned to the mother-and-son scenario for an equally large and bleak panorama, IT'S ALRIGHT, MA (I'M ONLY BLEEDING), whose subtitle surely evokes the scene of Jesus on the cross speaking to, and beyond, his mother. In that song, we have no real sense of her presence at all: it is more easily envisaged as a letter home than as direct speech. Yet there is a suggestion of her closeness – close enough to hear his breath – in the lines:

> So don't fear
> If you hear
> A foreign sound
> To your ear:
> It's alright, ma,
> I'm only sighing.

That closeness echoes the speech of Tom Joad to his mother towards the end of *The Grapes of Wrath*, the book that led

Dylan to discover Woody Guthrie. He tells her as he leaves her, a wanted man: "I'll be all aroun' in the dark. I'll be ever'where – wherever you look." In IT'S ALRIGHT, MA, we can see this reversed: the mother all around, as the young man surveys the life into which she has brought him. There is a characteristic paradox, though, and that twist of the absurd that marks it as Dylan's, in this huge catalogue of the world's ills couched in the form of reassuring his mother that he's fine, just fine.

The song that has the clearest dialogue form on *Freewheelin'* is DON'T THINK TWICE, IT'S ALL RIGHT, a companion to A HARD RAIN at the growing point of his art. This is where he plays most clearly upon the paradox, the dissociated nature of the dialogue; for this outspoken final settling of the account between two lovers is also explicitly *unheard*:

> It ain't no use in callin' out my name, gal,
> I can't hear you any more.

And she, presumably, cannot hear him.

If we were to stage this song, I think the result might well be something like a scene from an early Brecht play – from *Baal*, perhaps. There is that same tough, bruised persona that Brecht often wore in his early love lyrics. The time is before morning; there is a wall with a window, where the woman is sleeping, from which she will look out at dawn; and a road where her lover walks slowly away, singing his song. There's even a hint as to the lighting:

> It ain't no use in turnin' on your light, babe,
> I'm on the dark side of the road.

The comparison is not fanciful. Suze Rotolo, the young woman walking arm in arm with the artist on the front of the record, was involved in a fringe production of Brecht, and Dylan apparently attended rehearsals with interest.

It is his sense of drama, conveyed by the direct address and the evocation of a setting, that lends Dylan's songs in this mode their vividness. We hear them as soliloquy rather than inner monologue. In this case, the woman addressed is not so much absent as *offstage*. With this form, he can create a speaking character, and something of the character he is speaking to; and, in a subtle but involving way, a whole world that radiates out from this central relationship. DON'T THINK TWICE, sounding a note not heard before in popular song, is the first entrance into one of these 'Dylanesque' worlds, with its distinctive, melancholic atmosphere, its visionary starkness and variable weather.

The influence of Brecht is at its strongest on *The Times They Are A-Changin'* – perhaps even stronger than that of Woody Guthrie, though this is supposed to be Dylan at his most Guthriesque. Again, it is their dramatic quality that has kept these motivated, topical songs as vivid and forceful today as when they were recorded. The political nature of the record – political in the broadest sense, as concerned with the conditions and governance of society – means few songs of personal relation, but there are some interesting developments of the 'you' lyric.

One of these is BALLAD OF HOLLIS BROWN, which switches from "he" to "you" after the first verse. "Hollis Brown, he lived on the outside of town" it begins, with a characteristic compression of the common forms of speech – 'on the outskirts of town', 'the other side of town', 'outside of town' – into a new and fitting phrase, "*on the outside* of town", to portray social exclusion in a single offhand stroke. In the second verse both tense and pronoun shift, after an indeterminate line, to a definite second-person present:

You look for work and money and you walked a ragged mile.
Your children are so hungry that they don't know how
to smile.

This is a rhetorical device to make you, the listener, enact in imagination the terrible fortune and terrible deeds of a man whom despair leads to murder his entire family. Insofar as "you" is Hollis Brown himself, though, this is the most dissociated of all Dylan's songs in this mode, since it is addressed to a dead man.

The two love-songs on the record are both about separation. One, BOOTS OF SPANISH LEATHER, adopts the full dialogue of the ballad and represents the best marriage of Dylan's songwriting to traditional form. The other, ONE TOO MANY MORNINGS, is this record's furthest advance into a curt, modern idiom of his own. It grows out of DON'T THINK TWICE and presents the obverse situation: nightfall instead of predawn, a man standing on the threshold again, but now it is she who has gone:

From the crossroads of my doorstep my eyes begin to fade
As I turn my head back to the room where my love and
I have laid...

Only in the third and final verse does the address shift from "my love" to "you", whom we're inclined to assume is the same person

It's a restless hungry feeling and it don't mean no-one
no good
When everything that I'm saying, you could say it just
as good.
You are right from your side and I am right from mine,
We're both just one too many mornings and a thousand
miles behind.

That last line makes the song, as Dylan said of DON'T THINK TWICE in the sleevenotes to *Freewheelin'*, "a statement that maybe you can say to make yourself feel better". Now he is no longer the one left behind, the powerless one. Now they are both "behind"; both moving, in opposite directions. She has not left him; they have left each other.

Here's a good example of how Dylan typically wrests an upbeat out of the downbeat; of what he meant when he said that all his songs end with "Good luck, I hope you make it." This 'uplift' or 'optimism' is a bleaker, bluer thing than the intransigent grin of Woody Guthrie, and perhaps not so hard-won, but it remains through all sadness, a survivor's twist in every tale. It's not exactly comedy, but it's a comic principle, the Little Man always bouncing back.

There's another way to hear that last verse, however. That "you" could be you or me, the listener. In other words: you've been through this, too, that's why you understand this song; we're in this thing together – which is a different sort of comfort. (Notice how the thought in the second line is reinforced by the lame rhyme of "good" with "good": see, I'm not much of a poet. Even in very early songs – like MAN IN THE STREET, say – where he is still a genuinely naive lyricist, Dylan uses the naive in clever ways. And by the time of *Times* he was far from naive.)

There is one other song on *Times* that turns on the identity of "you", and this is THE LONESOME DEATH OF HATTIE CARROLL, its most powerful statement, which we will return to.

After *The Times*, the 'you' song comes into its own, gaining steadily in prominence on each successive album, until on *Blonde on Blonde* every song but one is addressed to a second person, to some degree. (The exception, contrarily, is VISIONS OF JOHANNA, which is the song most specifically about and for an actual and deducible second person.) *Another Side* doesn't have this preponderance of direct address, but it does occur at key points, namely the beginning, the middle and the end, in ALL I REALLY WANT TO DO, TO RAMONA and IT AIN'T ME, BABE.

Actually, the practice of bracketing a record with 'dialogue' of two contrasting types can be traced back to the first album, starting with the comic denouncement of YOU'RE NO GOOD and ending with the tragic plea of SEE THAT MY GRAVE IS KEPT CLEAN. *The Times*, likewise, opens with the bold and clear public announcement of the title song and closes with the obviously heartfelt but hesitant, circuitous and apparently drink-befuddled confession of RESTLESS FAREWELL.

On *Another Side*, the contrast of beginning and end could not be clearer: the amorous approach, ALL I REALLY WANT TO DO, against the flat rejection, IT AIN'T ME, BABE; the light against the sad tone. Midway between them stands TO RAMONA, upon which this opposition pivots, a richer and subtler song than either. Before saying more about it, though, I would like to turn aside to explain further the image of the pivot.

# · 4 ·

# I Plan It All And
# I Take My Place

I've never really understood how the Beatles could be credited with inventing the LP as an artistic unit. I can see
that *Sergeant Pepper* had the kind of impact that previously only pop singles had had. It was swallowed whole, as it
were; the entire LP being played repeatedly over and over on
the radio in the days of its first appearance. In that sense it
marks a definite turning point, a shift of focus from single to
album in the pop market. But there is no question of the
Beatles being the first to think of making a unified LP: what
was Miles Davis and Gil Evans's *Sketches of Spain* in 1960; or
Charles Mingus's *Tijuana Moods* in 1957; or Frank Sinatra
and Nelson Riddle's *In the Wee Small Hours* (1955) or *Come
Fly With Me* (1958)?

For that matter, Woody Guthrie's *Dust Bowl Ballads*,
released in 1935 as an actual 'album' (i.e. a package containing
several 78s; re-released for the first time on LP in 1964, coincidentally) was a pretty early example of the concept album.
The Beatles may have been the first to aim for larger form in
the amnesic context of rock, but even here, Dylan, who joined
them in that field in 1965, had been practising the art of
composing LPs ever since he recorded his first in 1961.

I don't know of anybody else emulating the specific form
which he developed over his first three LPs, though people
almost certainly have. It takes the long-playing record as a
physical object – two independent sequences of music of
roughly the same length, one stamped on the obverse of the
other, nominally 1 and 2, or A and B, but not actually fixed in

order – and works these material conditions into an artistic device.

The first step to understanding this form is to think of the two sides as *reflecting* each other in two parallel sequences, so that tracks 1, 2, 3, 4, 5 on one side are echoed somehow in tracks 1, 2, 3, 4, 5 on the other. Dylan's form takes this a step further by *fully reflecting* the two sequences, making one the reverse of the other, so that the themes that appear in the order A, B, C, D, E on one side appear in the songs on the other side in the order E, D, C, B, A. The linking of the paired songs is often by contrast as much as by similarity; for example, two diametrically opposed treatments of the same theme.

The first sketch of this design is on the first album, where the two original compositions, TALKIN' NEW YORK and SONG TO WOODY, are placed in corresponding, reversed positions, second on side 1, and second to last on side 2. On *Freewheelin'* the scheme is worked out in full:

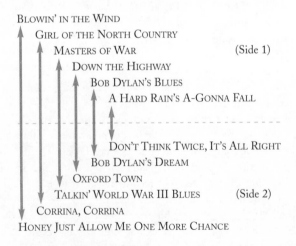

BLOWIN' IN THE WIND
  GIRL OF THE NORTH COUNTRY
    MASTERS OF WAR        (Side 1)
      DOWN THE HIGHWAY
        BOB DYLAN'S BLUES
          A HARD RAIN'S A-GONNA FALL

        DON'T THINK TWICE, IT'S ALL RIGHT
      BOB DYLAN'S DREAM
    OXFORD TOWN
  TALKIN' WORLD WAR III BLUES    (Side 2)
CORRINA, CORRINA
HONEY JUST ALLOW ME ONE MORE CHANCE

      I SHALL BE FREE

Some of the links are stronger than others. We can see, for example, that two gentle love songs correspond, GIRL OF THE NORTH COUNTRY and CORRINA, CORRINA; as do two songs about war, MASTERS OF WAR and TALKIN' WORLD WAR III BLUES; and two about Bob Dylan, BOB DYLAN'S BLUES and BOB DYLAN'S DREAM. The pairing of the BLUES and the DREAM, which is based on the English ballad 'Lord Franklin', gives a clue to the link between DOWN THE HIGHWAY and OXFORD TOWN, the album's purest evocations of blues and country traditions, respectively, black and white. As for the innermost couple, HARD RAIN and DON'T THINK TWICE, they are the growing point of this phase, pointing in different ways to the future of Dylan's songwriting. They are also paired by contrast: the departure, of lover from lover; and the homecoming, of son to mother.

The oddest and also most informative coupling is the outermost, of BLOWIN' IN THE WIND with HONEY JUST ALLOW ME ONE MORE CHANCE. The former was really the song that secured Dylan's position – it was the reason why everything had changed between the appearance of his first album and this one. ONE MORE CHANCE, on the other hand, is *Freewheelin's* one throwback to the gulping and frenetic comic blues style of *Bob Dylan*. He acknowledges BLOWIN' IN THE WIND's importance by leading off with it, but the pairing with ONE MORE CHANCE shows him symbolically consigning it to the past, already determined not to be contained by his own former achievements. Hence the 'freewheeling' tailpiece, I SHALL BE FREE, escaping the structure.

*Freewheelin'* is arranged around a fairly loose net of associations. On the next album, *Times*, that form is tightened up and made symmetrical. The 'argument' of the record is built up dialectically, as befits its maker's most political work. That this construction also relates to a sense of constraint felt by the artist – which he eventually broke out from, angrily – can be seen in the pairing of the first and the last songs:

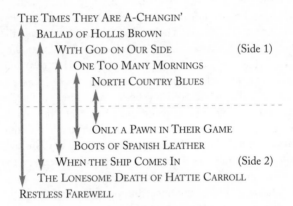

THE TIMES THEY ARE A-CHANGIN'
    BALLAD OF HOLLIS BROWN
        WITH GOD ON OUR SIDE                    (Side 1)
            ONE TOO MANY MORNINGS
                NORTH COUNTRY BLUES

                ONLY A PAWN IN THEIR GAME
        BOOTS OF SPANISH LEATHER
    WHEN THE SHIP COMES IN                       (Side 2)
THE LONESOME DEATH OF HATTIE CARROLL
RESTLESS FAREWELL

RESTLESS FAREWELL shares some points with I SHALL BE FREE. They're both 'moving on' songs to close out their respective records, and both inebriated:

> Oh you ask me why I'm drunk alla time,
> It levels my head and eases my mind.
> I just walk along and stroll and sing,
> I see better days and I do better things…

he chants tipsily at the end of I SHALL BE FREE. And RESTLESS FAREWELL is set in this boozy haze:

> … the bottles are done,
> We've killed each one,
> And the table's full and overflowed,
> And the corner sign
> Says it's closing time
> So I'll bid farewell and be down the road.

The difference is all in the tone, of course. RESTLESS FAREWELL can't just bounce out of the door to "catch dinosaurs" and "make love to Elizabeth Taylor" like I SHALL BE FREE. It has to stand on the threshold and explain itself away. Why? Because of what its partner on the other side of the record has proclaimed: a revolution, a battle, a 'flood' of change that overrides all other considerations. How, in the thick of this momentous event, can Dylan now be justifying his intention (as we can see it retrospectively) to go on and make a record like *Another Side*, wholly concerned with personal moments?

The explanation, foreshadowing the fuzzy logic of *Another Side*, is not easy to follow – though the sharp depiction of the end of a night of drinking gives good dramatic grounds for the thought to ramble. The topic that the singer's mind keeps circling is "time". The word is used five times, in different contexts, occurring in every verse but the third. In this, FAREWELL is already an antithesis to the title song. While that proposes "the times" – the movement of time itself – as a single, irresistible engine of change, this last song suggests that "time" is not such a straightforward idea, but has varying meanings; that there may be several different "times".

It is the third verse that confronts the challenge of THE TIMES THEY ARE A-CHANGIN' most directly. This is the middle verse, and the song seems to revolve around it. To paraphrase: the first verse says, I like to spend my money on showing my friends a good time, but now it's time to go. The second says, I don't have time for a committed relationship with a woman. And the third – switching from attachment to antagonism, but sticking with commitment, or lack of it – concerns fighting for a cause. Again, using the most basic symbol for the triumph of good over evil, which is the coming of light after darkness, day after night, time itself is seen as bringing inevitable victory in the struggle. The conclusion is peculiar, though:

> But the dark does die
> As the curtain is drawn
> And somebody's eyes must meet the dawn,
> And if I see the day
> I'd only have to stay
> So I'll bid farewell in the night and be gone.

He slips easily out of the logic of his political metaphor – that
the victory of a good cause is as inevitable as the rising of the
sun, so you don't really need *me* to help it, do you? – and into
the logic of the party-goer – that if you stay till morning, as
somebody surely will, you're bound to get caught up in the
next round. So he arrives at his desired conclusion – that it is
time for him to leave the party – by sleight of hand.

This is the pivotal point of the song – what it set out to
prove. The fourth verse turns back towards the second, dealing with music and self-expression and friendship whereas
that had dealt with love. And the last verse touches again,
like the first, on the artist as a social creature, and on the
effect of his success. Here we come to the final refutation of
THE TIMES:

> Oh a false clock tries to tick out my time,
> To disgrace, distract and bother me,
> And the dirt of gossip blows into my face
> And the dust of rumours covers me.

This "false clock" is surely, in this context, the time measured
by the media, the never-quite-present of the news and current
affairs, which he was no longer simply a commentator on, but
was becoming a subject of. How can I write on that basis, he
seems to say, when I know from experience how much of it is
gossip and rumours? Likewise, the first verse implies, how
long can I sing about poverty, when I have more money than
I know what to do with?

# · 5 ·

# The Arrow On
# The Doorway

t is because it contends so fiercely against itself that *The
Times* has lasted. The "quarrel with oneself", which W.B.
Yeats said was at the root of poetry, has made for good art,
if bad agitprop. I don't mean that the album is really just
another self-portrait: its contentions are *over the issues* that it
raises, but they are based in Dylan's own double-mindedness.
The dialectical symmetry of *The Times* is indeed so tight that
the sides do not just reflect on each other, but begin to turn in
on themselves.

The inner pair of songs, NORTH COUNTRY BLUES and
ONLY A PAWN IN THEIR GAME, are clearly counterparts. The
first takes the viewpoint of an individual – a woman of the
North – and, looking out through her eyes, creates a picture
of her whole society. ONLY A PAWN works the opposite way,
from a generalised view of a society, *inwards* towards an
unknown individual – a man of the South – whom it never
manages to identify.

At the same time, NORTH COUNTRY BLUES, at the end of
its side, is also a counterweight to THE TIMES THEY ARE A-
CHANGIN' at the beginning of it: for here is a very clear tale of
times that change but that don't thereby make the loser win, or
the first to be last. (This is the hardest irony of the record: that
it is mainly about things that time hasn't changed, like poverty, bigotry, exploitation and injustice; that Dylan could sing
BALLAD OF HOLLIS BROWN [badly] at Live Aid in 1983, with
*more* topicality than when he wrote it twenty years earlier.)

Likewise on the second side, ONLY A PAWN at the beginning finds its correspondent in RESTLESS FAREWELL at the end: in the obvious sense that the latter refuses to conform to the pressures of society as the "pawn" has done; and also because it draws its conclusion, albeit confusedly, from the unspoken view of politics that underpins ONLY A PAWN.

The chess metaphor lies sleeping for most of the song and is suddenly brought to life in the last verse:

> On the day Medgar Evers was buried from the bullet
> he caught
> They lowered him down as a king...

This is literally true, in that Evers – the Mississippi co-ordinator for the National Association for the Advancement of Colored People – received a state hero's funeral, with the President and the Attorney-General of the United States, John and Robert Kennedy, in attendance. But the comparison of Evers to a black "king" also casts the central symbol of the white "pawn" in a new light.

The simile does no dishonour to Evers' memory, since it breaks open the chess analogy even as it illuminates it. The king in chess cannot be taken, so this "king" transcends the metaphor. He appears as a kingly person, rather than as a piece. The resonance with the most widely known Civil Rights leader, Dr King, could not have been accidental.

Nevertheless, once we are alerted to the notion that there are *two sides* to this game of chess, and different ranks of pieces, the whole image becomes problematic. Are the black pieces black people and the white pieces white people? If that were the case, since Dylan is white, it would have to be 'Only a Pawn in *Our* Game'.

No: then the two sides must be *causes*, the cause of equality against the cause of racism. But surely, in this conflict, the pawn is condemned for something more than being 'theirs', i.e. not one of us; or for being "only" a pawn, i.e. not very important? If "their game" is the politics of racists, in opposition to 'our game' of campaigning for Civil Rights, then, within this metaphor, Dylan himself is also a piece, doing his bit. "He's only a pawn in their game" – whereas I'm a bishop in our game. Is that the moral of the story?

The key lies in the word "their", because chess is not a game of them and us, but of you and me; so "their game" is not one that you and I are playing but one we are watching. The pawn's crime is not to be a piece in the wrong hands, but to have been part of the game at all, to have surrendered his autonomy and been 'moved' by forces outside himself – which is what RESTLESS FAREWELL determines against.*

The two sides of *The Times* turn on themselves like two wheels. (I wonder, did their composer already have this form in mind when he evoked the bicycle in the title of *The*

---

* As it transpired, the pawn was not a cowed and uneducated "poor white man" at all, but an affluent one, Byron de la Beckwith, who was convicted in 1994 for the cold-blooded murder he had committed 30 years earlier. The story of his trial – which represented the longest delay between murder and conviction in US legal history – was made into a movie by Rob Reiner (the director of *This Is Spinal Tap*), starring Whoopi Goldberg as Evers' widow Myrlie and James Woods as de la Beckwith. It was released in America as *Ghosts of Mississippi* and retitled, with blinding blandness, *Ghosts of the Past* for the UK market.

In 1997, de la Beckwith made a four-part television series, *Redemption*, in which he got to explain his worldview. The programme's host, Richard Barrett, counsel for the white supremacist Nationalist Movement based in Learned (!), Mississippi, said: "That's all he ever wanted – to get his story out." The inscription that Dylan composed 38 years ago can now be engraved: "When the shadowy sun sets on the one / That fired the gun, / He'll see by his grave / On the stone that remains, / Carved next to his name, / His epitaph plain: / Only a pawn in their game." De la Beckwith died on 22nd January 2001, and an obituary of him can be read on the Nationalist Movement's website, www.nationalist.org. "I'll never quit or back down from standing up for freedom," he is quoted as saying in 1994, who had lain in hiding to shoot an unarmed man in the back in front of his wife and children. The obituary points out that the jury which con-

*Freewheelin' Bob Dylan*?) At the hub of each side is a song, not about politics, but about God and history. In the 'us and them' world that the record appears to inhabit, their messages are clear enough. WITH GOD ON OUR SIDE says God is not on their side, i.e. the side of nationalism or warmongering. And WHEN THE SHIP COMES IN says God is with us. Of course, their resonances are deeper than this.

WITH GOD ON OUR SIDE depicts the education of a young man who introduces himself much as Bob Dylan introduced himself to the world:

> Oh my name it is nothing,
> My age it means less.
> The country I come from
> Is called the Midwest.

It plots a succession of America's conflicts, from the Indian

---

victed him was made up of "eight minorities, three American women and one American man".

We might also note, as a phrase that Dylan had quite possibly read before he wrote his song, the reaction of Governor George Wallace of Alabama to the murder of Medgar Evers: "The state of Alabama does not have sufficient resources to be guarding every pawn of the NAACP." (This quote, and the story of de la Beckwith's TV series, is drawn from the Bob Dylan Who's Who at www.expectingrain.com.)

It is interesting to note, too, Martin Luther King's comment to *Life* magazine (November 1964), about the Oxford, Mississippi incident of September 1962 – the topic of Dylan's song OXFORD TOWN. Medgar Evers had been prominent in the campaign to enroll the first black student to enter the University of Mississippi, James Meredith, whose appearance on campus led to riots, quelled by the National Guard, in which six people died. The situation was so grave that President Kennedy made a televised appeal to the honour of the South to defuse the situation. (On the night that Medgar Evers was shot, nine months later, the President had again been speaking on television on the subject of Civil Rights.) Meanwhile both John and Robert Kennedy were meeting behind the scenes with Ross Barnett, the governor of Mississippi, trying to reach a compromise. Dr King's comment was that these secret meetings "made Negroes feel like pawns in a white man's political game".

Wars to the Cold War, and charts his growing up in parallel.
So the second verse has a primary school simplicity:

> The cavalry charged,
> The Indians fell.
> The cavalry charged,
> The Indians died.
> Oh the country was young
> With God on its side.

The third moves on to the Spanish-American and Civil wars,
and the rote-learning of history: "the names of the heroes I's
made to memorise / With guns in their hands / And God on
their side." The fourth verse takes us into the realm of the
exam question, as it might be, 'Discuss the political situation
in Europe in 1914':

> The First World War, boys,
> Came and it went.
> The reason for fighting
> I never did get.

There's hick humour here, of course: all that this rube's
historical lecture reveals is that he has learned nothing about
history, nor what any of these wars were about. 'We won and
we wuz right' is the sum of his knowledge.

The Second World War corresponds to college age, perhaps, in that it shows the first hint of questioning what he's
taught:

> Though they murdered six million,
> In the ovens they fried,
> The Germans now too have
> God on their side.

By the time we reach the Cold War, he is of military age himself, saying of the Russians:

> If another war comes,
> It's them we must fight.
> To hate them and fear them,
> To run and to hide…

Yet there has also been a suggestion all along that he has been *going through* these wars himself, that he is their survivor: so one war "had its day" and another "was soon laid away", and another again "came and it went", and yet another "came to an end". The boy who has been "taught and brought up" through the song is also all the boys who went to fight in these wars, believing they were right.

Dylan seems to have taken his cue for this from a Woody Guthrie song known variously as 'The Great Historical Bum' or 'The Biggest Thing That Man Has Ever Done'. The song doesn't have a final form: the published version is a collection of optional verses which show Woody adapting his original idea – a celebration of the migrant worker and the casual labourer as the true creators of the world's monuments – to different ends. One version makes the war against Hitler "the biggest thing that man has ever done", and another makes it the building of the Grand Coulee Dam. From this source, Dylan adopts the narrative form – a quick, offhand summary of history – and the central character, an immortal Everyman:

> I'm just a lonesome traveller, the Great Historical Bum.
> Highly educated, from history I have come.
> I built the Rock of Ages, 'twas in the year of One…

Among the branching paths of Guthrie's song, one points to the United States as "the biggest thing", in a beautiful verse where the Bum, having divorced Madam Slavery, says:

> I'm living with my freedom wife in this big land we built.
> It takes all forty-eight States for me to spread my quilt.
> Our kids are several millions now, they run from sun to sun,
> And that's about the biggest thing that man has ever done.

Another ending has an even broader final goal: "The people are building a peaceful world, and when the job is done / That'll be the biggest thing…" And yet another brings the song round in a circle so that this Bum who "built the Rock of Ages" and "signed the contract to raise the rising sun" is both the Logos of St John's Gospel, the Word of God who "was in the beginning with God" and by whom "all things were made"; and also creative, collective humanity, as its own best creation:

> I better quit my talking now, I told you all I know,
> But please remember, pardner, wherever you may go,
> I'm older than your old folks, and younger than the young
> And I'm about the biggest thing that man has ever done.

If WITH GOD ON OUR SIDE is a descendant of 'The Great Historical Bum', it is also a kind of answer-song, deriding the idea of a divinely-anointed United States. And the religious undercurrent of Guthrie's lyric may account for the sharp twist away from satire in Dylan's penultimate verse:

> Through many dark hours
> I've been thinkin' 'bout this,
> That Jesus Christ was
> Betrayed by a kiss
> But I can't think for ya,
> You'll have to decide
> Whether Judas Iscariot
> Had God on his side.

Why this sudden appearance of Judas? Dramatically, it is

because the speaker's gradually maturing awareness has reached a point of philosophical crisis, in which he questions himself and his assumptions. The crisis has been triggered, in the verse before, by the prospect of nuclear annihilation:

> One push of the button
> And a shot the world wide
> And you never ask questions
> When God's on your side.

The fact that the Judas verse does ask a question shows that he does not have God on his side; and it is these thoughts of infidelity to the God he was brought up with that provoke his contemplation of the traitor.

What is the answer to his question? No: in that "Then entered Satan into Judas surnamed Iscariot. And he went his way, and communed with the chief priests and captains, how he might betray him unto them." (Luke, 22:3-4). Yes: in that Jesus, having openly announced to the disciples that one of them will betray him, appoints Judas to his role by giving him a piece of bread soaked in wine, which he has already privately told John will indicate the traitor: "And after the sop Satan entered into him. Then said Jesus unto him, That thou doest, do quickly." (John, 13:27) The proclamation of his imminent betrayal is surely a self-fulfilling prophecy. In the Gospel account, Jesus is intent on the death he feels must befall him, and so Judas is a necessary agent of the work of God.

In its context, the question has further ramifications. Did Judas have "on his side" the same "God" whom the speaker was raised to believe in, but who he now thinks is false? Could this "God", in other words, actually be Satan?

The question is clearly meant to hang unresolved, to trouble our minds. It makes a live issue of the word "God" which has lain inert for most of the song, as we saw happen earlier with the word "pawn"; and I'm sure the memory of this sudden and disturbing intrusion of religious feeling inspired the famous yell of "Judas!" that Dylan faced down at the Free Trade Hall in Manchester a couple of years later.

The figure of Judas carries over into the last verse, where the image of the speaker's overspilling words recalls the death of the lost disciple as described in Acts: "falling headlong, he burst asunder in the midst, and all his bowels gushed out".

> And now as I'm leavin'
> I'm weary as hell.
> The confusion I'm feelin'
> Ain't no tongue can tell.
> The words fill my head
> And they fall to the floor,
> That if God's on our side
> He'll stop the next war.

Of course we've always known that our young hero was heading for a fall: he was set up for this very purpose, to 'betray' the God of militarism and nationalism. Where Dylan reaches beyond what we expect is in making the collapse of his beliefs arise from a change of heart, the outcome of self-development and self-examination. We had expected this guy to be knocked down, rather than to come to life. And we had expected the twist to be: God doesn't take sides; God doesn't want wars; you can't use God to justify them. While these things are conveyed, the ending actually twists a bit further than might be thought desirable.

From the point of view of anti-war campaigning, that "he" should have been 'we' – 'we'll stop the next war'. The socialist milieu of protest folk in America may have been imbued with more Nonconformist Protestantism than Marxist atheism, but it was still not quite kosher to be calling on God for aid.

The quiet surprise lurking in this verse however, is the word "our", which is actually used here for the first time.

Despite the title, the refrains have always spoken of "its", "their" or "your" side. Rather like the "their" of ONLY A PAWN IN THEIR GAME, the "our" of WITH GOD ON OUR SIDE becomes an open question. It seems unlikely to be the nation, since that has been 'it' before. It could be the anti-war or the anti-nuclear movement; or it could be the whole of humanity, under threat of eradication: a "side", in other words, transcending all sides.

WHEN THE SHIP COMES IN, the partner to WITH GOD ON OUR SIDE, also twists away from its apparent line at the end, albeit subtly. This is the plainest piece of 'us and them' rhetoric on the record. According to Joan Baez, it was inspired by an incident on the West Coast when Dylan was touring with her as a guest artist. He went into a hotel ahead of her and asked about her reservation. The desk-clerk, taking him for an intrusive fan, refused to confirm that she had a booking. After she had straightened things out, he wrote the song in the hotel that night.

To demand the Last Judgment as recompense for a minor slight might seem a bit excessive – evidence of what has been called Dylan's vast reservoir of "free-floating rage". But if the artist's vision is to see the universe in a grain of sand, and heaven in a wild flower, it can also be to see history in a single scene.

The paradox of the lyric is that its dream of vengeance is sheathed in such a benignly anthropomorphic world: having been belittled, he adopts a childlike view where friendly fishes laugh and seagulls smile. A somewhat darker source, though, lies beneath. The song's precedent is 'Pirate Jenny's Song' from Brecht and Weill's *Threepenny Opera*, in which a prostitute fantasises a fairy-tale retribution on all the men who have used her. A ship comes into the harbour and shells the whole town flat, apart from the cheap hotel which serves as her bordello. Then her clients are rounded up and executed.

The ship of death in Dylan's version, however, is also a ship of salvation that comes from the gospel music tradition. The more common vehicle to represent the coming of the kingdom of God has been the train, of course – as in 'This Train Is Bound for Glory' or Dylan's own SLOW TRAIN COMING. There has also been at least one 'Heavenly Aeroplane', as recorded by the Watersons on their 1977 album *Sound, Sound Your Instruments of Joy*, the notes for which also mention 'The Christian Automobile'.) The idea of the kingdom as a vehicle befits the Christian belief in it as both eternal – self-contained, with a population of the elect separated from the world as are the passengers of a ship or train – and also as something historical, coming *in time*: like the train, moving on an undeviating line; like the ship, enduring the forces of the world in its crossing.

The train was a potent symbol of release, of possibility to the black people of America, of course; in fact, it is so potent a symbol that it can become anything – death, sex, heaven, hell, freedom, fate. The ship may be rarer, but its memory reaches farther back, so that 'The Old Ship of Zion' is surely a spiritual reversal of "the ghosts of slavery ships". The symbol was made urgent again by Marcus Garvey's plans for the Black Star Line, a shipping fleet to return the New World's black people to Africa, and thus it lives on in the music of Rastafari:

> Black man, meekly wait and murmur not,
> Meekly wait and murmur not,
> For the Black Star Liner shall come.
> (Culture, 'Black Star Liner', *Two Sevens Clash*, 1977)

The biblical sources for this symbolism of a *travelling heaven* I think are twofold: the chariot of God seen by Ezekiel; and the mobile city, the New Jerusalem in Revelation, "coming down from God out of heaven, prepared as a bride adorned for her husband." (Steven Spielberg, a man who thinks best in myths, recreated the latter vision to the letter for the extrater-restrial Mothership in *Close Encounters of the Third Kind*.)

WHEN THE SHIP COMES IN is about God taking a side, then, if not in so many words. In the end the "foes" are stricken down like the enemies of Israel, the Egyptians and the Philistines:

> And like Pharaoh's tribe
> They'll be drownded in the tide
> And like Goliath they'll be conquered.

The twist comes in the final word. While harmonically most of the song is painted in simple, primary colours, at the end of each verse there is a touch of minor as the voice holds out the last word: "breaking", "ocean", "watching", evoking a sense of openness or mystery.* With the word "conquered", where we would expect a triumphal note, the voice instead wavers and falls in sympathetic movement with the enemy. In the end, almost in spite of himself, Dylan still turns away from identifying with the overdog.

---

* The "ocean" lines, incidentally, make the only allusion to Dylan Thomas's poetry that I have come across in Bob Dylan's lyrics. By instinct, I would guess, in composing his child-like world, he alights on Thomas's childhood vision, 'Fern Hill', which ends: "Oh as I was young and easy in the mercy of his means, / Time held me green and dying / Though I sang in my chains like the sea." Dylan sings:

> And the words that are used
> For to get the ship confused
> Will not be understood as they're spoken
> For the chains of the sea
> Will have busted in the night
> And be buried at the bottom of the ocean.

It is Thomas's lines that provide the link between the sea, language and chains which is otherwise missing.

Note the cunning use of "busted", which breaks with the half-expected internal rhyme-word, 'broken', and also breaks away from the poetic tone of the lines – a small but definite busting of the chains of language.

WHEN THE SHIP COMES IN is the closest thing to a straightforward "finger-pointing song" (as he himself called them) that Dylan had done. It is followed on the record by his best piece of topical protest, which points a far sharper finger, but in a most unexpected direction. THE LONESOME DEATH OF HATTIE CARROLL has its obvious villain – William Zantzinger, a wealthy young white man who casually killed a middle-aged black maid – but the song's refrain is not addressed to him:

> Ah but you who philosophise disgrace
> And criticise all fears,
> Take the rag away from your face:
> Now ain't the time for your tears.

Who are "you"? The "philosophise" and "criticise" suggest the intelligentsia – that educated liberal class that was Dylan's constituency, by and large. And so does the "rag", if that means a newspaper – such as he took the story from – as well as a handkerchief.

After each verse, recounting the killing, then the callousness and privilege of the perpetrator, then the innocence and hardships of his victim, Dylan repeats his command. It is not for any of these things that "you" should cry. (Again, direct address lends immediacy to a narrative that is not in itself dramatically formed, being laid out as a kind of legal deposition of the facts.) The fourth and final verse is the courtroom scene, and here, having held back the tears for three verses, and having steadily raised the tension of that restraint by gradually increasing the length of the verses, till the last is almost twice as long as the first, he finally relents, after the judge "handed down strongly for penalty and repentance / William Zanzinger with a six-month sentence... *Now is the time for your tears.*"

Why now? Because this is the worst thing that has happened in the song? Not necessarily. To say "now ain't the time" can mean 'not yet', or 'not for this', and also 'it's too late'. It's not that the murder, the killer's remorselessness or the victim's blameless life were not cause for grief, but that "you" could not have done anything about them; you bear no responsibility, so they are not cause for *your* tears. But the formulation of laws and the administration of justice are, or should be, the responsibility of those who "philosophise" and "criticise", who discriminate nicely. Dylan makes us *feel* that that "sentence" is too short by the sheer length of his own. Each verse is a single sentence – the longest sentences in any of his songs. And then he turns and points the finger at *us*, at the people he's supposed to be spokesman for, and says: The law is what you educated people make and apply; this is your doing.

And why not 'our' tears? What separates the singer from this "you"? It must be that he does not "philosophise disgrace and criticise all fears". And what are the fears and the disgrace? The disgrace, I would say, is indicated by a pun in the penultimate verse:

> Got killed by a blow, lay slain by a cane…
> Doomed and determined to destroy all the gentle

It is our ancestral propensity to murder, represented by Cain. To "philosophise" this might be to apportion blame, to say it is 'their' fault, without acknowledging in the heart a common disgrace, that belongs to us as a species for our violence.

The "fears", then, would be that such evils are ineradicable, which is the kind of fear represented in HOLLIS BROWN, the partner song to HATTIE CARROLL. The farmer's suffering, while its root is shown to be poverty, is not depicted as a social fact, but as an existential curse. In the moment of killing, "Seven shots rang out like the ocean's poundin' roar"; but the waves of the ocean break forever. The rising waters, which are bringing in a new age in THE TIMES THEY ARE A-CHANGIN' and WHEN THE SHIP COMES IN, are pitilessly destructive here, and the changing of time just a relentless cycle. The song ends baldly:

> There's seven people dead on a South Dakota farm…
> Somewhere in the distance there's seven new people born

There is no call for tears. But in HATTIE CARROLL there is; because, if human evils are ameliorable, as "you" maintain – I am abstracting an argument where Dylan gives none – then it must be through the operations of justice, for which "you" are responsible.

The unease that we have found underlying so much of the writing – rooted in the fact that Dylan did not really share the faith in political action which he supposedly 'spoke for' – comes to a head in HATTIE CARROLL, where he rounds on his audience. It's not surprising that what follows is a RESTLESS FAREWELL.

Clinton Heylin argues plausibly that LAY DOWN YOUR WEARY TUNE was intended to end the record, and that RESTLESS FAREWELL was a late afterthought. Certainly the latter is a lesser song, and the former would have made a profound resolution of the album. But would it not have been too resolved? To say, after HATTIE CARROLL – 'therefore resign your human effort' would have been the wrong conclusion to the record's argument, and it would also have distorted the meaning of WEARY TUNE.

On its own, the song points only to itself. The "weary tune" is contrasted with the music of nature, and in that sense it stands for all human music; but it is also only one tune, or kind of tune, perhaps only *this* tune. Whereas, attached as a summary to a body of songs, it could not help but be heard as gathering all of them under the head of 'tunes to be laid down': the "tune" would become a collective term for Dylan's music. And he was not yet ready to lay that down. His actual resolve, as in RESTLESS FAREWELL, was to go on somewhere else with his art "and not give a damn". (Which is, I suppose, a backhanded form of blessing.)

Actually, LAY DOWN YOUR WEARY TUNE does allow for this continuation, in that to 'lay down' does not only mean to put aside or cease, but also, in musical terms, to record. The chorus, then –

> Lay down the song you strum
> And rest yourself…

can be taken to mean and *then* rest yourself. Complete your song, and when you have done that, you can take comfort from it – like a hobo when he lays down his blanket.

As a counter-statement to THE TIMES THEY ARE A-CHANGIN', WEARY TUNE would say, yes they are, but these things remain: the wind, the rain, the trees, the ocean – and music. RESTLESS FAREWELL says something rather smaller, but more immediate: yes they are, and so am I. Except that, being Dylan, he actually says the opposite:

> So I'll take my stand
> *And remain as I am*
> And say farewell and not give a damn.

There's a hint here of that travelling-by-standing-still that we saw at the end of ONE TOO MANY MORNINGS, where she is a thousand miles "behind" him, simply by virtue of him turning his back on her. To "take my stand" can be read just as standing up to go, but it also implies that he is not going anywhere. If he is saying farewell, it is because 'we' are leaving him.

And when it came to the folk/rock rift, that turned out to be pretty much the case. The artist didn't go anywhere – he carried on doing just what he'd always done, writing songs and laying them down and putting them out. Despite the accusations that he had 'left' his old audience, in practice it was they, a portion of them, who turned their backs on him. He may no longer have done what they first liked him for, but they were still as free as ever to put down their bucks to hear him sing and play. No-one was *excluded* from listening if they wanted to, as no-one was obliged to if they didn't.

# · 6 ·

# Talking To The Folks

One of Dylan's roles is prophetic, although he has often denied that he has any 'message'. This is tricky. He is surely right, as an artist, to defend his work from paraphrase and to refuse to provide his own abstracts or summaries, even supposing that he could. Nevertheless, in some of his songs we clearly hear the voice of the preacher: not just in the so-called 'protest' songs (which are still a live part of his work today) but obviously in many of those from his Christian albums, and in later work like DISEASE OF CONCEIT. He doesn't necessarily make his 'commentary' in this mode, of course: MAN OF PEACE or CLEAN-CUT KID are teachings in the form of satirical portraits. So, too, is LICENCE TO KILL; but we can hardly mistake the preacher's tone in its opening lines:

> Man thinks
> Cause he rules the earth
> He can do with it as he please
> And if things don't
> Change soon
> He will.

He has also contained 'his' preaching in a satirical narrative, as in TALKING TV, where he reports the words of a speaker in Hyde Park.

'Preachy' is now such a derogatory term – conveying something dour, simplistic, obvious, humourless – that it is worth emphasising that the preacher can be both artist and entertainer, though neither primarily. In Britain we are not much exposed through our mainstream media to preaching. In America, things are different, of course, what with its huge industry of broadcast evangelism; and in recent interviews Dylan has spoken of his love of listening to preachers on the radio. Near where I live, at the Elephant & Castle, in south London, there is a large reminder that sermons need not be 'worthy but dull'. Facing the shopping centre, an imposing Corinthian facade is the last remnant of the Metropolitan Tabernacle, built in 1861. It was dubbed "the cathedral of the south London Baptists", but it was commonly known as "Spurgeon's tabernacle", after the preacher whose huge following it was built to accommodate. It held a congregation of six thousand, of whom three and a half thousand could be seated. Often it was packed, and Charles Spurgeon might address the gathering for a matter of hours at a time. Clearly these people did not come to be bored.

After *The Times*, Dylan let drop his prophetic role, or at least its outward appearance. He was no longer involved with political campaigns, such as the voter registration drives in the South, and no longer wrote on topics of obvious social import. The underlying issues of *The Times* did not just go away, however. They were transmuted into a different kind of politics, and a different conception of 'us and them'.

The moment of this mutation can be seen on *Another Side of Bob Dylan* in MY BACK PAGES and its companion song, CHIMES OF FREEDOM. The former openly repudiates Dylan's own political thought (if a text so opaque can be said to do anything openly):

> Lies that life is black and white
> Spoke from my skull. I dreamed
> Romantic facts of musketeers
> Foundationed deep somehow.

Ah, but I was so much older then,
I'm younger than that now.

We've already seen, in part, how that paradox is true of *Another Side*: that the singer really does seem to have grown younger. The common sort of phrases which he has reversed – Ah, but I was young then, I know better now – are usually in the nature of an excuse; but turned around like this it amounts to something more sweeping than a self-exculpation: it means he has *unlived* these things, they no longer happened.

The paradoxical nature of the song goes deeper still, because much of the terminology that he accuses himself of spouting, he had never actually used before. He depicts himself as a deluded intellectual, and in the process gives his poetry access to a whole new vocabulary of concepts and abstractions: "liberty", "equality", "prejudice", "politics", "serious", "ideas", "abstract threats", "romantic facts", "self-ordained professor", "define these terms". This is the tone of the talk which surrounded his protest songs, of the milieu they moved in, which by turning and attacking he incorporates into the subject matter of his art.

In this respect, the song is crucial in the transition from the archaic diction of folk song to a style open to modern speech, to words and phrases like:

| | | |
|---|---|---|
| amphetamine | binoculars | businesslike |
| coincidence | compromise | concise |
| cyanide | diplomat | disillusioned |
| escapades | geometry | headache |
| heart attack | housing project | hysterical |
| immaculately | infinity | lifelessness |
| preoccupied | primitive | repetition |
| security | situations | superhuman |
| tax deductible charity organisations | | vacuum |

The other strain of language that runs through MY BACK PAGES is the imagery of war: "in a soldier's stance I aimed my hand", "rolling high and mighty traps" (i.e. snare drums), "musketeers", "mutiny", "corpse", "skull", "pounced with fire", "threats", "protect", "my enemy", "my guard". Entwining this with the abstract vocabulary gives an effect as of a man wrestling tortuously with thin air, sustained in the higher register of the verse, before he drops it with a shrug: "Ah, but…" A comic effect, for all the weighty tone of the lyric, "too serious to fool".

It is another paradox of the song that its stilted poetry, depicting an overheated intellectuality that he claims to be putting behind him, is in fact the beginning of a new phase of his writing. Likewise, the accusatory attitude he accuses himself of once having taken actually rises here to a level of vituperation never heard before – "corpse evangelists", "mongrel dogs who teach" – presaging the monumental scorn of the songs he would be writing in a year or so, with their "genocide fools" and "the finest school, alright, Miss Lonely" and "just what do you do anyway?" and "how does it feel to be such a freak?" It's a paradox accounted for in the paradoxical chorus, of course: if he's "younger than that now", then these things he describes are indeed *yet to come*.


CHIMES OF FREEDOM, the partner to MY BACK PAGES, reflects it in the way we have come to expect: the promise of a millennial future to correspond with a renunciation of the recent past. The lyrics also point to a new verbal density in Dylan's songs, but here, rather than the difficult birth of new means, we have the furthest development of the old. While the metre owes something to an external source, to be sure – the cumulative, long-breathed lines of Beat poetry, of Ginsberg's 'Howl' particularly – the lyric remains rooted in the word-rich late style of Woody

Guthrie. It is still contained – just – within the ambit of folk song.

Without wishing to reduce art to a symptom, there may be a sign of the loosening of mental control that is one effect of Guthrie's genetic disorder, Huntington's chorea, in the almost-overflowing lines of his Columbia River songs. 'Grand Coulee Dam', for instance, shows how he adorned the plain style of folk, building it up to a new speed and complexity. He has taken the Carter Family's train-song 'Wabash Cannonball' – "From the lakes of Minnesota where the rippling waters fall" – as the model for his river-song: "She heads up the Canadian mountains where the rippling waters glide".

There's an interesting sexual ambiguity about 'her', though – the King Columbia River:

> She winds down the granite canyon then she bends across
> the lea
> Like a prancing, dancing stallion on her seaway to the sea…

An ambiguity which comes to the full in the final lines:

> And the roaring Flying Fortress wings her way for
> Uncle Sam,
> Spawned upon the King Columbia by the big Grand
> Coulee Dam.

In common usage, offspring are engendered *by* the father *upon* the mother, but here the mother is a "King" while the father is a "Dam" – an archaic term for mother. Though Guthrie was a wholehearted propagandist for the war against Hitler, in which he served in the Merchant Marine, there is (unconsciously perhaps – though it is not wise to underestimate the wiles of Woody), a taint of monstrosity about the 'spawning' of the warplane.

Guthrie, even more than Dylan, is the one-without-whom

in the poetical transformation of popular music last century. He established a breadth of subject matter and form, a distinctive persona, and a verbal inventiveness in folk song that were truly unprecedented, whereas Dylan had him to start from.

There were elements of "wild mercury" for him to gather from his forerunners, however. For example, the Carter Family, in the first verse of their great hit of 1928, 'Wildwood Flower', sang:

> Oh, I'll twine with my mingles and waving black hair,
> With the roses so red and the lilies so fair,
> And the myrtle so bright of the emerald hue,
> The pale and the leader, and eyes look like blue.

This, like the whole of the lyric, is actually an approximate remembering of a much older song, 'I'll Twine 'Mid The Ringlets' by Maud Irving and J.P. Webster, from 1859:

> I'll twine mid the ringlets of raven-black hair
> The lilies so pale and the roses so fair,
> The myrtle so bright with an emerald hue
> And pale aronatus with eyes of bright blue.

("Aronatus", oddly – as a seed for the verbal virus that later transformed these lines – is a word unknown to dictionaries and flora alike.) The intriguing thing is that the Carters preferred to stick to nonsense that sounded like the memory than to replace it with new sense. The result is not so far from what James Joyce was doing across the Atlantic, writing his dream-epic *Finnegans Wake*, named after a comic ballad and crammed with allusions to popular song: "*You won't need be lonesome, Lizzy my love, when your beau gets his glut of cold meat and hos soldiering*"

Following this strange principle of consonance, time and again the Carters arrive at far more piercing lines than those they imitate. "I'll charm every heart, and the crowd I will sway" becomes "I will charm every heart, in his crown I will sway". "Another has won him, ah misery to tell" becomes "How my heart now is wondering, no misery can tell". The tendency of their changes is always towards simpler syntax and more direct emotion, and at the same time to greater mystery: an atmosphere of dream pervades the whole song. How much more poetic is their version of these lines:

> I'll live yet to see him regret the dark hour
> When he won, then neglected, the frail wildwood flower.

which they took from the middle of the song and moved to the end:

> Oh I long to see him and regret the dark hour
> He's gone and neglected this pale wildwood flower.


In one line – "Through the mad mystic hammering of the wild ripping hail" – CHIMES OF FREEDOM clearly echoes 'Grand Coulee Dam' – "In the misty crystal glitter of that wild and windward spray" – elaborating on Guthrie's lyric as he had on the Carters' 'Wabash Cannonball'. Dylan seems to have decided to give full rein to the ornate alliterative style of later Guthrie; to release a dynamic which had been suspended by the untimely demise of Woody's faculties.

Although his mid-Sixties work is often thought of as characterised by word-drunken streams of consciousness, he soon developed a sparse, laconic diction, and the period of his getting in *all* the words he could think of was only brief. Nevertheless, it was important in the broadening of his vocabulary, and CHIMES OF FREEDOM, a celebration of the release of energy, opens a door in this respect. For all its sense of promise, though, its eye on the future, I hear in the song a kind of farewell – a final, *ne plus ultra* expansion of the tradition from which it arose. It's apt that it should be a giant hymn of hope, then, "that simple hope" which he said in the Sixties that he was lacking and which Guthrie is so rich in. (Not that Dylan's alternative is despair; as he said, "All my songs kind of end with 'Good luck, I hope you make it'.") It's apt, too, that it should be a hymn to *electricity*, since that is what the Columbia River songs are at root (and especially so since electricity was to be the force that divided him from his folk roots).

It is nowhere clearer than in CHIMES, however, that Dylan's hope is not political or materialist, as Woody's was. In what way is the power of a thunderstorm *for* all these downtrodden or rejected people that he claims it for?

> In the city's melted furnace unexpectedly we watched,
> With faces hidden as the walls were tightening,
> As the echo of the wedding bells before the blowing rain
> Dissolved into the bells of the lightning,
> Tolling for the rebel, tolling for the rake,
> Tolling for the luckless, the abandoned and forsaked,
> Tolling for the outcast, burning constantly at stake,
> And we gazed upon the chimes of freedom flashing.

The only way to connect a thunderstorm, a wedding, and the salvation of "the abandoned and forsaked" is through the *parousia* – the second coming of Christ, who says of it: "For as the lightning cometh out of the east, and shineth even unto the west; so shall also the coming of the Son of man be." The kingdom is compared by Jesus to a wedding and to the arrival of a bridegroom, and we have already seen the New Jerusalem compared to a bride in Revelation. The closing cadence of the Christian Bible begins: "And the Spirit and the bride say, Come. And let him that heareth say, Come. And let him that is athirst come. And whosoever will, let him take the water of life freely." CHIMES OF FREEDOM combines these images with the

Beatitudes of the Sermon on the Mount: "And he opened his mouth, and taught them, saying, Blessed are the poor in spirit: for theirs is the kingdom of heaven. Blessed are they that mourn: for they shall be comforted. Blessed are the meek: for they shall inherit the earth." The lightning and thunder *in themselves* can do nothing for the oppressed, but they are taken by the poet as the token of this new covenant, as the rainbow was the sign of Noah's. They *proclaim* liberation, as bells proclaim a wedding, and the proclamation itself liberates, rousing the strength of hope.

In this theme of inward release and of a burden discharged, CHIMES OF FREEDOM joins MR TAMBOURINE MAN and LAY DOWN YOUR WEARY TUNE, and in its last lines he links, with a pun, the cosmic and the personal dimensions of the song:

> Tolling for the aching ones whose wounds cannot be nursed,
> For the countless confused, accused, misused, strung-out
> ones and worse,
> And for every hung-up person in the whole wide universe,
> And we gazed upon the chimes of freedom flashing.

An emphatic pause between the "every" and the "hung-up" creates a second meaning in the line. The 'trivial' personal suffering of the hang-up has superimposed upon it a cosmic image of the Crucified, of a person "hung-up… in the whole wide universe". Dylan articulates, in religious form, a key credo of the Sixties – that the battle with oppression began (and all too often ended) with a liberation of the individual from repression, inhibition, conditioning. He also articulates a key element of the Christian creed: that Jesus died "for our sins", and the suffering of the crucifixion reaches down to and atones for even the most inward of our own.

It is the shifting of the 'protest' impulse from the social to the personal that links CHIMES OF FREEDOM to MY BACK PAGES. The oppressed whom these chimes are "for" are suffering primarily from isolation, through being misunderstood. So both songs are concerned in the end with the struggle against wrong thinking, which was to be the key 'protest' of Dylan's rock work.

Now we should turn again to the form in which that partnership takes place.

· 7 ·

# The Springtime Turned

The two sides of *Another Side* reflect each other in the way that we know. The pairings are quite close, but they don't generate much of a dialectic. The 'Ballad' and the 'Blues' meet, as do the instant-love songs I DON'T BELIEVE YOU and SPANISH HARLEM INCIDENT; and the last-of-protest songs, CHIMES and PAGES; and the comedies, I SHALL BE FREE NO. 10 and MOTORPSYCHO NITEMARE:

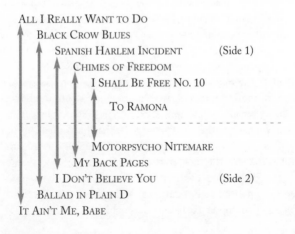

ALL I REALLY WANT TO DO
  BLACK CROW BLUES
    SPANISH HARLEM INCIDENT    (Side 1)
      CHIMES OF FREEDOM
        I SHALL BE FREE NO. 10

          TO RAMONA

- - - - - - - - - - - - - - - - - - - - - - - - - - - - - - - - - -

        MOTORPSYCHO NITEMARE
      MY BACK PAGES
    I DON'T BELIEVE YOU    (Side 2)
  BALLAD IN PLAIN D
IT AIN'T ME, BABE

What characterises *Another Side* is the overall contrast of the two sides. There was a hint of this on *The Times*, which has a northern first side, with the stories of Hollis Brown in South Dakota, the boy from the Midwest in WITH GOD ON OUR SIDE and the woman in NORTH COUNTRY BLUES, and a southern second, with the stories of Medgar Evers in Mississippi and Hattie Carroll in Maryland. Here, the poles might best be called the positive and negative, or the bright and dark. The titles on the second side are as grim – Don't, Back, Ain't, Plain, Nitemare – as those on the first are full of Incident and Freedom.

*Another Side* we might say has a rotation rather than a reflection from one side to the other. And in turning from bright to dark, it proved to indicate the direction of Dylan's whole work. Not that his folk music is exactly cheerful, in the main; but of straightforward songs of hope like CHIMES OF FREEDOM, of tenderness like GIRL OF THE NORTH COUNTRY, of conviction like THE TIMES THEY ARE A-CHANGIN', or of liberation like MR TAMBOURINE MAN, there would be no more. The rock albums to follow are a wonderful artistic flowering, but the world they depict is largely one of broken connections, where all communication is problematic; of bewilderment and ennui; of veiled violence; of loss and isolation.

I f Dylan's music ended with *Blonde On Blonde*, if he had died in his motorcycle accident, it would have had a certain sufficiency. The first seven albums unfold a continuous and self-consistent drama, which concludes in a single giant close-up, with our hero gazing into the face of a woman for the eleven minutes of SAD-EYED LADY OF THE LOWLANDS and asking "should I wait?" As a myth, it has fullness; but it would have been less lasting, I think, without the critique which he gave it afterwards in *John Wesley Harding*, which speaks of such things as forgiveness, tolerance, co-operation and, finally, intimacy. Because of that, and the many other dimensions of experience that Dylan went on to show in the thirty-five years after *Blonde on Blonde*, we can see what is still partial in that first period, as well as its completeness.

*Another Side*, fourth of the seven records, is the centre of the cycle, and at its centre is the song on which the whole thing revolves, To Ramona. Not that it has any appearance of a grand central statement; on the contrary, it is a quiet, intimate moment, a still point. Along with It Ain't Me, Babe, it's the most focused song on the record. Its lyric stands midway between the folk and rock styles, having the former's plain speech, stripped of the archaic, and the latter's sense of immediacy.

Here the 'you' song comes into its own. The warm, flowing sound of guitar and voice create a space and time in which the story unfolds. The lovers are quietly alone together in a room in a metropolitan city; the light is dimming; the traffic can be heard outside. She is crying. He says:

> Ramona, come closer,
> Shut softly your watery eyes.
> The pangs of your sadness will pass
> As your senses will rise.

Again, liberation is to be found inwardly; and again there is the attack on wrong thinking, and the emphasis on the illusory quality of the "smoke-rings" of the mind:

> It grieves my heart, love,
> To see you tryin' to be a part of
> A world that just don't exist.
> It's all just a dream, babe,
> A vacuum, a scheme, babe,
> That sucks you into feelin' like this.

The song turns gently upon itself, as the whole record turns more fiercely around it, from ALL I REALLY WANT TO DO to its flat opposite, IT AIN'T ME, BABE. If the opening lines say in effect "all I really want to do is, baby, be friends with you" (perhaps a little more than friends), the final verse, while it is far from a rejection, sounds to my ears a note of farewell:

> I'd forever talk to you
> But soon my words
> Would turn into a meaningless ring.
> For deep in my heart I know
> There is no help I can bring.
> Everything passes, everything changes.
> Just do what you think you should do.
> And someday maybe,
> Who knows, baby,
> I'll come and be crying to you.

In a much kinder tone, this says something similar to IT AIN'T ME, BABE – "I'm not the one you need".

TO RAMONA is in a long tradition of 'persuasions to love', of which John Donne is perhaps the best-known proponent. The paradox here is that Dylan, arguing against thought and for sensation, appears to end up persuading himself out of love, rather than her into it. The movement of the lyric, beginning "closer" and ending further away, foretells the movement carried on in the 'you' songs to follow. They become steadily more prevalent until, by *Blonde on Blonde*, they take up every corner. But by then 'you' is hardly ever present. In fact, in this respect, TO RAMONA is almost unique.

When Dylan sang the song in July 1964 at the Newport Folk Festival, he made a point of saying, "This is called To RAMONA. It's just a name." Which suggests that it is not just a name.

There has been a good deal of cryptological interpretation of Dylan over the years, and much of it may be wide of the target, but there is no doubt that from time to time he is a deliberately cryptic artist. For example, when he composed the title SAD-EYED LADY OF THE LOWLANDS from a jumble of the letters of his name and his wife's name, Dylan/Lownds*. Or when he took as the title for an LP the name of an outlaw whose initials are almost those of God – *John Wesley Harding*, JWH. (The tetragrammaton, the four Hebrew letters which indicate the name of God, is usually transliterated in English as JHWH – and commonly pronounced Jehovah.)

So I think it is no coincidence that the first half of To RAMONA, the four letters TORA, should be those that appear in Waite's Tarot pack on the High Priestess card, on the scroll which lies in her lap, partly concealed by her sleeve. Waite explains that this is the Torah, the Jewish law, corresponding to the first five books of the Bible, and that the last little bit of the word which is hidden indicates the small amount of God's mystery which has not been openly proclaimed. The same four letters appear on the Wheel of Fortune card, in the four quarters of the wheel, so that they can be read T-O-R-A again, or T-A-R-O-T, or R-O-T-A (which is to say, in Latin, a wheel).

Dylan deliberately placed this song at the centre of *Another Side*, when he clearly felt that he was at a turning point. What he could not have known was that the back wheel of his motorbike was going to lock and wreak a deci-

---

*Strangely, this works even better when Sara's name is misspelt Lowndes, which for many years it was cited as being, due to an urban myth that, after being a Playboy Bunny, she had married Victor Lowndes, one of the chief executives of the Playboy organisation.

sive break in his career, so that this would also be the hub of the whole first phase of his work.

The resulting pattern even has that reflective symmetry we've seen in individual LPs. At either end are the two self-portraits, *Bob Dylan* and *Blonde on Blonde* (whose title spells out BOB). But 'self' is perhaps a misleading term. The first record, as we have seen, is more concerned with negation of the self and the creation of an archetype in its place. (Perhaps that is why, at his birth, there is so much of death in the music; as Robert Zimmerman dies to make way for Bob Dylan.) *Blonde on Blonde*, likewise, while it is a peculiarly self-centred work, is less a portrait than a looking-glass, in which many people have seen themselves reflected, becoming at the time (and still from time to time, for some) a new pair of eyes through which to see the world.

I say self-centred because, although there are other records almost as preoccupied with 'I' and 'you', there is none where the 'I' is so thoroughly stuck with itself. Yet its self-expression is perpetually enigmatic and teasing; its pictures all suggestion without presentation. And it is because of this indeterminacy, autobiographical yet non-specific, that we can identify with this 'I'. At the same time, we also become this 'you'. For when 'you' is not there, in the setting of the song, to be spoken to, the song itself, the recording, becomes the message – a form of communication more direct than the speech it contains. And therefore *you*, the listener, are as much the one addressed as any other. The meltdown of pronouns is surely what the blurry portrait of a squinting artist on the outer sleeve illustrates: we see him as he myopically sees us, our viewpoints becoming interchangeable.

However, bearing in mind Eliot's dictum, "poetry is not an expression of personality but an escape from personality", should we call this mind we meld with 'his'? After all, the person who wrote these songs about separation, isolation and the frustration of communication was himself just three months married. Similarly, interviewers were surprised to find, on meeting the man who had just released the thoroughly heart-broken, lonesome and world-weary *Time Out of Mind*, that he was thoroughly fit, vigorous and happy in his work – as he had every right to be, given its quality. As Rimbaud wrote, "I is another." And as Dylan wrote in his note to *Highway 61 Revisited*, "there is no eye – there is only a series of mouths".

On a point of biographical speculation, Sara Lownds, whom he married on 22nd November 1965, seems likely to be the woman who appears in the song (apparently never record-ed by him) LOVE IS JUST A FOUR-LETTER WORD:

> Seems like only yesterday
> I left my mind behind,
> Down in the Gypsy Café
> With a friend of a friend of mine.
> She sat with a baby heavy on her knee…

(Sara already had a child from her first marriage when Dylan met her.) This is the song that Joan Baez, clearly suspecting his attachment, rather pointedly sings in the backstage docu-mentary *Dont Look Back*. To which Dylan shoots back, "I never finished that song, did I?" In another scene, Baez sings to Sally Grossman (the sphinx of the *Bringing It All Back Home* cover, through whom the soon-to-be-Dylans met): "Sally go round the roses, Sally don't tell your secret." The point being that if, as Joan Baez appears to tell us, FOUR-LETTER WORD is about Sara, it is apt that it should also con-tain this perfect description of the poetic of *Blonde on Blonde*:

> Searching for my double, looking for
> Complete evaporation to the core…

Yet the song also shows how, with her, he may already have passed through the whole embroilment in which *Blonde on Blonde* is caught:

After waking enough times to think I see
The Holy Kiss that's supposed to last eternity
Blow up in smoke, its destiny
Falls on strangers, travels free,
Yes I know now, traps are only set by me,
And I do not really need to be
Assured
That love is just a four-letter word.

When he stepped into the control-room to hear the play-back of ONE OF US MUST KNOW (SOONER OR LATER), which he sings with the passion of a man in whom the bitterness and the tenderness of an unrequited love are at each other's throats – were these Bob Dylan's overriding emotions, or was he more interested in the organ part? "Aesthetic emotion", as Eliot called it, is not the same thing as the emotion of everyday life.

Again, after he'd signed the contract to record his first album, which would be full of premonitions of death and an abiding sense of one who "ain't got no home in this world any more", did he wander off down the lonesome road with his head bowed down and crying? "I was like on a cloud," he told Cameron Crowe for the *Biograph* booklet. "It was up on 7th Avenue and when I left I was happening to be walking by a record store. It was one of the most thrilling moments in my life. I couldn't believe that I was staring at all the records in the window. Frankie Laine, Frank Sinatra, Patti Page, Mitch Miller, Tony Bennett and so on and soon I, myself, would be among them in the window."

Which brings me, by the long way round, to say again that both *Blonde on Blonde* and that first record may be about Bob Dylan, but this Bob Dylan is not identical with the one who carries a passport under that name.

On *Bob Dylan* we see the Little Tramp who is Everyman "hard travellin'" in the wilderness, a figure made small by the

immensity of the land and the dark clouds gathering over-
head. On *Blonde on Blonde*, our Everyman is an everywhere:
we are effectively inside him, and we cannot see so far as the
edge of him, let alone beyond, to what may really be going
on outside. Yet while he has expanded, his horizon has
shrunk, to the dimensions of a room, or a succession of
rooms – for almost every scene of *Blonde on Blonde* is an
interior; and his travelling has become stasis, stuckness and
waiting.

The most extreme form of this contrast is between the
first song of the cycle and the last; between YOU'RE NO
GOOD, a minute-and-a-half burst of frantic, comic denun-
ciation, and the seven-times-as-long SAD-EYED LADY OF
THE LOWLANDS – eleven hypnotically-slow minutes which
say nothing but 'you're wonderful', or even 'there is no good
but you'.

That the sequence of seven records should have a beginning and an ending is not astonishing, but that it should
have a middle is, since that implies a foreknowledge of the
end. Knowledge is perhaps the wrong word. Whether or not
Dylan is subject to conscious premonitions or clairvoyance, I
have no idea, but he does often exhibit an uncanny, intuitive
feel for the changing of the times.

The disease which struck him down in 1997, between
the recording and the release of *Time Out of Mind*, is a case
in point. He has shrugged off any suggestion of a connection between the songs and his sickness, which was an air-
borne infection picked up months after the recordings were
done. Nevertheless it is striking that the lyrics of that record
are so studded with images of physiological affliction, of a
kind that have not appeared in his work before, and that
shortly afterwards he should suffer, by chance, a potentially
fatal illness. Consider:

… heat rising in my eyes …

… hearts a-beatin' like pendulums swinging on chains …

… clouds of blood …

… your heart torn away …

… my nerves are exploding and my body's tense …

… my eyes feel like they're falling off my face, sweat

falling down …

… my brain is so wired …

… every nerve in my body is so vacant and numb …

… got ice-water in my veins …

… even if the flesh falls off of my face …

… my heart can't go on beating without you …

… I'm breathing hard …

… until my eyes begin to bleed …

… nothing can heal me now but your touch …

… if I'm still among the living …

… I feel like I'm coming to the end of my way …

… I'm love sick …

… I'll die here against my will …

… maybe in the next life …

For the how and why of such phenomena one might appeal to Jung's theory of synchronicity, or to the prophetic element of poetic inspiration, but these are explanations that do not explain. For myself, before we leave this region of thin air, I would just like to point out an astrological fact, which seems to me to represent, to a nicety, something in the nature of Dylan's gift.

His natal chart has an extraordinary clump of planets in the fifth and sixth houses, in the signs of Taurus and Gemini. Seven out of the ten planets of modern astrology are clustered here, within a segment of just over thirty degrees. The nucleus of this group, concentrated within a fourteen-degree segment, are the Sun, Moon, Jupiter, Saturn, and Uranus, which lies in the middle of the five, conjunct with all of the other four. This suggests to me that the effect of the prodigious multiple conjunction is focused through that planet.

The first of the modern planets – discovered by Hershel on 13th March 1781 – Uranus is said by astrologers to represent the changing of times and movements of the mass psyche. Since my astrological learning is sketchy, I will quote from one of the many websites on the subject:

> As Uranus takes 84 years to go around the Sun, it will be in any one sign for 7 years – therefore its effect is on a collective level, influencing successive generations. Uranus is often associated with revolutions and its sign position shows in what psychological area of humanity revolutionary changes will take place. It is the harbinger of sudden and unpredictable events and electric and lightning in its effect.

Uranus was assigned as the ruling planet of the sign of Aquarius. The symbolism suggests Dylan, the Gemini, ruled by Mercury, as a herald of the age of Aquarius. In artistic terms, I would suggest that it symbolises his intimate and vital connection with the Zeitgeist.

He is often spoken of as a maverick, a stubbornly independent genius who will not bow to the expectations of his audience. It is true that he has withstood pressures and distractions of fame and popular demand that have thrown many an artist from the track. But he is not a Blake or a Van Gogh or a Cézanne, one of those artists who have gone on undaunted even while the public that they burned to reach has shunned them. (Though to be fair, he has not had his lifelong ally, his Catherine or Theo or Hortense 'The Cannonball', to keep him going, either.) Dylan has had his share of hostility and ridicule, but he has always had an audience, and it was in the period when his relations with his public were most afflicted, in the 1980s, when the general trend of popular music was against everything he stood for, that his art faltered. Even with his creativity undimmed, as in the lyric writing of *Infidels* (some of the most potent of his entire career) when it came to presenting the work to the world his sureness of touch failed him without that connection to the current of the times. He remains a popular artist in the best sense, for whom both words are of equal weight.

# Interchapter

|  | I<br>Spring | II<br>Summer | III<br>Autumn | IV<br>Winter |
|---|---|---|---|---|
| 1962<br>–64 | Bob Dylan | The Freewheelin'<br>Bob Dylan | The Times They<br>Are A-Changin' | Another Side<br>of Bob Dylan |
| 1965<br>–66 | Bringing It All<br>Back Home | Highway 61<br>Revisited | Blonde on Blonde | |
| 1967<br>–70 | The Basement<br>Tapes | John Wesley<br>Harding | Nashville Skyline | Self-Portrait |
| 1970 | New Morning | | | |
| 1973<br>–76 | Planet Waves | Blood on<br>the Tracks | Desire | |
| 1978<br>–80 | Street-Legal | Slow Train<br>Coming | Saved | |
| 1981<br>–86 | Shot of Love | Infidels | Empire Burlesque | Knocked Out<br>Loaded |
| 1988<br>–90 | Down in<br>the Groove | Oh Mercy | Under the<br>Red Sky | |
| 1992<br>–95 | Good As I Been<br>to You | World Gone<br>Wrong | Unplugged | |
| 1997– | Time Out<br>of Mind | Love and Theft | | |

# Upon The Steps
# Of Time

• • • • • • • • • • • • • • • • • •

I
n the table opposite, Dylan's principal recordings are arranged chronologically according to a scheme of four phases, which I have named after the four temperate seasons. The compilations, the *Pat Garrett* soundtrack and the live albums are excluded, apart from one, 1995's *Unplugged*, for reasons I'll come to.

There is nothing very arcane about this scheme. The underlying idea is just that Dylan's creativity is periodic, and that each cycle has the natural structure of a beginning, a middle and an end, followed by quiescence and a new beginning. The quiescent stage, which I call winter, rarely produces new songs. This is part of the special quality of *Another Side*: it is the most complete expression of this 'underground' phase, where the artist sheds the confining, conscious skills he has acquired to let a new kind of art emerge, as yet unknown. Other winters coincide with his road accident and recuperation in 1966-67; and the period in 1977 which he shared between divorce proceedings and the editing of a five-hour film about marriage.

The major anomaly of the scheme is *New Morning*, which I have placed at the beginning of a new phase, but which was followed only by three years of near-silence. It seems that here a cycle died a-bornin'. Either that, or it was a quantum of creative energy small enough to have beginning, middle and end all within one LP, which is the explanation that I favour. The record has a unique abundance of natural imagery, including a menagerie dogs, pigeons and mules; rabbit, groundhog and rooster; robin and weasel, locusts and rainbow trout – along with sun and moon and rainbow; sky, stars, winds and clouds; hills, mountains, rivers and streams; rain, sleet and snow; apple, rose and daisy; sea and ocean, wood and swamp, grass and trees, wheat and corn, summer, winter and spring. In this sense at least it contains all four seasons in one.

How do these seasons normally manifest themselves? The easiest way to describe them is by looking first at the mid-point of each cycle, which I have called the summer. In that column we find a number of the records that are widely regarded as Dylan's best: *Freewheelin'*, *Highway 61*, *John Wesley Harding*, *Blood on the Tracks*, *Oh Mercy*. If there was one quality that all these could be said to have in common, compared with their neighbours, it is a sense of focus.

In the records of the first phase, of spring, there is a feeling of emergence. The idea of something erupting or coming up from underground occurs in several of the titles – *Planet Waves*, *New Morning*, *Shot of Love*, with its Pop Art explosion on the cover, *The Basement Tapes*. The basement also appears in the first lines of *Bringing It All Back Home*, – "Johnny's in the basement / Mixin' up the medicine" – whose cover shot does indeed appear to peer down into a subterranean space full of medicine-objects. There's often a restless and exhilarating energy to these records, and a slight fuzziness of outline, a kind of vibrational blur to the picture. Think of how *Planet Waves* foreshadows the subject matter and lyric style of *Blood On The Tracks*, but how much sharper and clearer are the scenes and images of the latter. Nevertheless there's a freedom and vivacity to *Waves* that makes it a distinct pleasure.

A way to show this pattern of energy released and then channelled and consolidated is through the change in vocabulary from *Bringing It All Back Home* to *Highway 61 Revisited*. The former is crammed with verbs: to run, jump, chase, duck, dodge, startle, stumble, ramble, ride, hop, skip, leap and crawl;

to weep, squint, peek, laugh and wink; to moan, yell, howl, wail, whisper, sigh, roar, scream, gargle, bark and bay; to scrub, shovel, haul and slam; to grab, pet, push, stick, rap, knock, bend, strip, strike and bust; to collide, explode, boil, break, flip, rip, tear and crash; to dangle, crumble, tremble, wave, fade and vanish; to swirl, swing, fly, spin, dance, twist and glide.

On *Highway 61* there is instead a wealth of *actors*. The energy of invention condenses into figures with definite outlines: Abraham and T.S. Eliot, Gypsy Davy and Cinderella, Ophelia and Queen Jane, the king of the Philistines, the Phantom of the Opera, and so on.

In the third phase, which I call an autumn, the controlling element comes to the fore: self-consciousness predominates, as intuition did in the first. The records are not less rewarding for that, but they are often more enigmatic. The subject matter becomes problematic, paradoxical or dichotomous, as we've seen in *The Times They Are A-Changin'* and *Blonde on Blonde*, and shall see later in *Desire*. To pursue the seasonal metaphor further, this is the time of seeding: in the questions which are raised here lies the nub of the material that will fill the next cycle. Under the surface of *Desire*, for example, run the religious concerns that would break out in the open with the brimstone and salvation sequence of *Street-Legal*, *Slow Train Coming* and *Saved*.

The reason I have included *Unplugged*, alone of the live albums, is partly because it is different anyway from the rest, having been set up primarily as a recording; and mainly because it seems to me to complete the folk cycle of *Good As I Been to You* and *World Gone Wrong*. Here, Dylan handles his own songs in the same spirit as he had the traditional material in the earlier sessions. It's an underrated record, in my view.

The trend over the whole of Dylan's career has been for the cycles to be completed more slowly. If we discount any winter records or silences and measure the span of recording sessions (rather than release dates) between spring and autumn, then the first or 'folk' cycle took just under two years, the second or 'rock' cycle took 15 months, and the third or 'country' cycle about 18. If the cycles are measured like wavelengths, however, from the beginning of one to the beginning of the next, including any intervening silences, we see bursts of creativity occuring within a steadier rhythm.

The first cycle covers 38 months, the second 29, and the third 33. The fourth cycle – the anomalous one, containing only *New Morning* – lasted 44 months, and the fifth lasted 53, although its new musical works – *Planet Waves*, *Blood on the Tracks* and *Desire* – were all made within two years. Similarly, in the sixth or religious cycle, which spans three years, the new work was actually done in less than two.

The interval of the seventh or 'pop' cycle, beginning with *Shot of Love*, was six years; and the eighth or 'back to basics' cycle, beginning with *Down in the Groove*, lasted five. The ninth, or 'new folk', cycle shows the greatest discrepancy between the overall 'wavelength' and the productive outburst: although it covers just over four and a half years altogether, its work – *Good As I Been to You*, *World Gone Wrong* and *Unplugged* – was done in less than 18 months.

The tenth and current cycle, if I am right in putting *Time Out of Mind* as its beginning, has already been going on for nearly five years. I have placed the latest record, *Love and Theft*, as a continuation of it, but this is just hunchwork. The scheme is not meant to be predictive and its patterns are discernible only with long hindsight. Nevertheless, my early impression is that the new record does have the qualities of breadth and focus that characterise the summer.

I originally took this pattern, traced over the whole course of Dylan's work, to show some unconscious, organic fluctuation of his creativity. But it may also have had some conscious element: the artist may, more or less clearly, have foreseen such distinct phases of composition, each with its beginning, middle and end.

••••••••••••

# Part III

••••••••••••

# In The Final End

● ● ● ● ● ● ● ● ● ● ● ● ● ● ● ● ● ● ●

Ever since his first LP, where death was so prominent, the end has loomed large in Dylan's art. Consider the number of key songs that turn on the ending of something, whether a way of life or a love affair or the world: DON'T THINK TWICE and HARD RAIN; LAY DOWN YOUR WEARY TUNE and MY BACK PAGES; IT'S ALL OVER NOW and LIKE A ROLLING STONE; DESOLATION ROW and VISIONS OF JOHANNA; I SHALL BE RELEASED and ALL ALONG THE WATCHTOWER; KNOCKIN' ON HEAVEN'S DOOR and IDIOT WIND.

Apart from his brief and anomalous country period, where he treated of life as a day-to-day matter (and which ended by petering out in silence), Dylan's drama has played as a succession of last acts. Not that his writing cannot deal with the ordinary: it's rich in touches of mundane reality, but they tend to shine in the shadow of finality. BROWNSVILLE GIRL, for example, with its brilliant cinematic immediacy, is set, as the last lines reveal, "a long time ago, long before the stars were torn down" – which is an image straight out of Revelation.

It's a reminiscence of this image, I suppose, that leads to the sudden incursion of doom in the middle eight of SHOOTING STAR, an otherwise gentle love ballad, recorded three years later for *Oh Mercy*. The body of the song is built on the two obvious facts of a shooting star – that it is short-lived, and that it represents a wish. So the verses meditate on the wishes of two former lovers and the fact that their affair has irretrievably passed. (Perhaps buried among these more common associations is a third, deriving from John Donne's famous opening line, "Go and catch a falling star" – which makes it a symbol also of impossibility.) Into this atmosphere of nostalgic tenderness, the middle-eight brings a startling whiff of sulphur. The single star falling, with its romantic connotations, has set off at least three biblical resonances: the tail of the great dragon in Revelation sweeping down the stars, as recalled in BROWNSVILLE GIRL; also from Revelation, the falling of the star called Wormwood into the sea, which turns the water bitter; and Jesus's prophecy, "the stars of heaven shall fall".

> Listen to the engine, listen to the bell,
> As the last fire-truck from hell
> Goes rolling by
> All good people are praying.
> It's the last temptation, the last account,
> Last time you might hear
> The Sermon on the Mount,
> Last radio's playing.

From which doomsday scenario the last verse returns with:

> Seen a shooting star tonight
> Slip away.
> Tomorrow will be
> Another day.

It's the same balance – or collision, perhaps – of the quotidian and the apocalyptic as in these striking lines from I AND I, half a dozen years earlier:

> The world could come to an end tonight but that's alright.
> She should still be there sleeping when I get back.

About twenty-five years ago, if we'd looked back over Dylan's work of the previous decade, including *Blonde on Blonde, Nashville Skyline, New Morning, Planet Waves* and *Blood on the Tracks*, and asked what was his largest theme, the answer would have seemed fairly obviously to be love or, more accurately, the relationship of man and woman. But the work of the last couple of decades, bolstered by a good deal of what went before, has brought apocalypse to the fore. At the very least we would have to say that his abiding concerns are two: love and the end.

There is another general trend of endings in Dylan's songs to which SHOOTING STAR and *Oh Mercy* generally make an interesting exception. This is the use of final refrains, often the same as the title: IT'S ALL OVER NOW, BABY BLUE; DESOLATION ROW; DON'T THINK TWICE, IT'S ALL RIGHT; TANGLED UP IN BLUE; BLOWIN' IN THE WIND; EVERY GRAIN OF SAND, and so on. There are many variations, and many songs with fully fledged and independent choruses, but there is a characteristic movement, which cascades down through each verse and comes to resolution in the same few words at the end. If we look for a source for this form, the prime candidate would be Hank Williams. His refrains have very much the same effect as a lot of Dylan's: they nail the sense of the verse with a single laconic phrase.

Of course there are any number of ways that refrains and choruses work, and Dylan has used a lot of them. To get another view of this characteristic movement I am trying to define, with the verse tumbling down to land on a point of balance in the refrain, think of the character of early Beatles choruses like 'Please Please Me' or 'She Loves You', where the verse builds up to them as to an explosion. Their choruses seem to burst into the open, radiating out from their verses, while Dylan's verses seem to focus down into his refrains.

MR TAMBOURINE MAN is perhaps the most Beatlesque of his choruses in this respect, with its feeling of taking off, created in part by the unpredictable, 'anti-gravitational' fall of the accents on the words. The "is" of the second line, for example, is the last word we'd expect to be emphasised: "there is *no* place I'm going to" perhaps, or "there is no *place* I'm going to"; but "there *is* no place" is an odd assertion to make. Odd but fitting, since it *is* a no-place that Dylan is going to, "through the smoke-rings" of his mind.

These refrains, if they are also titles, are words that we may know, as record-listeners, before we even hear the song. Since they are the name we know it by, they are generally the words we first remember of it. This is to say, one way or another, we quickly come to anticipate the arrival of the refrain. We sense it as the destination of each verse, reached by a route which Dylan nearly always makes interesting, often surprising, and sometimes astonishing.

In this sense, the refrain, this first phrase we come to know, seems also to be the *beginning* of the song – which in the history of the composition it may be; but I mean that the refrain, carrying the nub of the meaning, may seem not only the conclusion but also the seed out of which the song unfolds. It has to have some such quality to work, of course, because it must give a launch into the next verse as well as provide a landing for the last.

*Oh Mercy* is unusual because it has a preponderance of songs which either start with refrains – POLITICAL WORLD, RING THEM BELLS, WHAT WAS IT YOU WANTED – or both begin and end with refrains – MOST OF THE TIME, DISEASE OF CONCEIT, WHAT GOOD AM I?, SHOOTING STAR. The refrain-first song ruled on the next record, *Under the Red Sky* – in WIGGLE WIGGLE and HANDY DANDY, 10,000 MEN and 2 x 2, UNBELIEVABLE and CAT'S IN THE WELL and GOD KNOWS. Then, having turned his usual style upside down, Dylan shut up as a songwriter for seven years.

But to go back to his earlier and more common practice, the refrain at the end of the verse, like the dialogue or half-dialogue, can be seen as a basic form of duality. In this, as in other things, BLOWIN' IN THE WIND is the foundation, with verse and refrain as the simplest kind of counterparted speech – question and answer. Except that "The answer, my friend, is blowin' in the wind" is no kind of answer to the three questions of each verse: it's an illogical content for a logical form.

The question and answer recurs in A HARD RAIN'S A-GONNA FALL, though the refrain is not the answer to the question, but what appears to be a conclusion to the answer. By biblical analogy, we take the flood to be a judgment upon all the things that have been listed in the verse: 'and therefore a hard rain's a-gonna fall'. But there is only an "and", and no therefore. The logical connection of the refrain to the verse is as indeterminate as it is in BLOWIN' IN THE WIND.

The refrain as a 'logical' but paradoxical counterpart to the rest can be seen in a number of songs. In ALL I REALLY WANT TO DO and IT'S ALRIGHT, MA and DON'T THINK TWICE the refrain is a single positive counterbalance to the much larger body of negatives in the verse. The result is a tense and dynamic, unbalanced balance – the most extreme example being IT'S ALRIGHT, MA (I'M ONLY BLEEDING), where a huge mass of negativity in each verse is set spinning on the single affirmative point: "But it's alright, ma, I can make it." According to his mother, the song 'Accentuate the Positive' was her son's party piece when he was a small child. IT'S ALRIGHT, MA certainly shows one way of doing that – by surrounding the positive with reams of grimness.

**B**oth of these ideas – of the refrain as the positive counter-weight in a 'negative' song and of a seemingly logical but actually paradoxical or elusive connection between the refrain and the rest – will play their part now we come to look at DESOLATION ROW, Dylan's most concentrated and extended song of the end.

At first glance, however, neither of these things would seem to be so. How could such a bleak-sounding phrase as "Desolation Row", repeated at the end of every verse, have cheerful connotations? And what ambiguity can there be about its relation to the rest of the verse? Isn't it just the sign on the street whose strange, multifarious life the song describes?

Let's look first at the resonances of the name. One, which becomes more apparent towards the end of the song, is that it's a kind of street-talk translation of *The Waste Land*.

Poetry, especially the poetry of the Beats, had been a part of Dylan's inspiration, at least in terms of attitude, since his college days in Minneapolis. But his songs from about the end of 1963 start to show a strong literary influence. There's the broadening and modernising of his vocabulary that we noted on *Another Side*, for one thing. Easier to trace as a steady development is the change in his metre.

The terms of literary prosody don't apply directly to song lyrics: a metrical sequence that trips over itself on the page may be perfectly apt in its musical place. It makes a huge dif-ference that the accents of the words are not making the beat on their own but are playing along with and against another beat. Thus an emphasis that would be clumsy and false in a poetic line, like that "is" in MR TAMBOURINE MAN, can be spot on in a song. Nevertheless I shall use some conventional prosodic terms just for convenience.

In Dylan's early lyrics, the distinctive metrical foot is the anapaest, a cluster of two lightly stressed syllables followed by a heavy one. This is a verbal match for his trademark acoustic strum, with its constant lightly hurrying beats punctuated with heavier strokes. So we have:

Yes 'n' how many years can some people exist

But I see through your eyes
And I see through your brain
Like I see through the water
That runs down my drain

Heard the roar of a wave that could drown the whole world

(Bear in mind, though, that I have picked regular lines from songs that have plenty of irregular ones.)

By the time of *The Times They Are A-Changin'*, Dylan was experimenting with metre. Reversing the anapaest for THE LONESOME DEATH OF HATTIE CARROLL, he writes in dactyls, a pattern of one strong followed by two light syllables. (The Greek name means 'finger', after the resemblance to the three bones, one long and two short, of our fingers.)

William Zanzinger killed poor Hattie Carroll
With a cane that he twirled round his diamond-ring finger

(Note how the metre, by crushing together 'diamond ring' and 'ring finger', helps to create a suggestive new compound, 'diamond–finger', to convey both Zantzinger's hardness and the 'worth' which he's regarded as having, above his victim.)

What particularly suggests the growing influence of page-poetry from here on, however, is the increasing use of iambs, a straight alternation of light syllable and heavy syllable, the most common metre of English verse.

> Lay down your weary tune, lay down
> Lay down the song you strum

There are also examples of the reverse of this foot, known as the trochee:

> Gypsy gal, the hands of Harlem
> Cannot hold you to its heat

We can see that his grasp of this beat is still not firm from the example above, and *Another Side* generally shows different metres jostling each other for the lead. By the time of *Bringing It All Back Home*, though, a very definite iambic line has been established:

> Of war and peace the truth just twists
> Its curfew gull it glides

In fact it's a somewhat over-definite line. But within a few months he had arrived at a fluent and supple iambic beat, which he could hold consistently without syntactic contortions and which he could vary freely without confusion.

By the time of DESOLATION ROW, he was ready for a concerted attempt on the citadel of modernist literature. The song's allusions to *The Waste Land* – and to Eliot's earlier poem 'The Love Song of J. Alfred Prufrock' – are concentrated in the last two verses, but there is some common imagery scattered throughout. "The fortune-telling lady" recalls "Madame Sosostris, famous clairvoyante". "Ophelia" could be a compilation of the opulent lady and the neurotic lover of *The Waste Land*'s second section, 'A Game of Chess'; while the street-wise Cinderella and the degraded "moaning" Romeo have elements of Eliot's barmaid and "the young man carbuncular" who seduces the typist. Eliot's "Unreal City" is a port, where "fishmen lounge at noon" and "The river sweats / Oil and tar", and so too is Dylan's, to judge by the seaside references of the first verse. The impending shipwreck of Dylan's penultimate verse (the first of his song's two endings) recalls "Phlebas the Phoenician, a fortnight dead", the drowned sailor of *The Waste Land*'s briefest and most lyrical section, 'Death by Water'.

Nearer and grimmer echoes of Desolation Row are, first, Death Row, and second, "the abomination of desolation", the sign which Jesus, quoting the prophet Daniel, gives as the last warning of the destruction of Jerusalem. As we shall see later, THE BALLAD OF FRANKIE LEE AND JUDAS PRIEST on *John Wesley Harding* makes a seemingly casual reference to this gospel passage which suggests that Dylan had meditated quite deeply on it.

To counteract these bleak allusions there are also two warmer resonances from Dylan's own Beat background. One is Kerouac's novel *Desolation Angels*, and the other is John Steinbeck's *Cannery Row*, which was a crucial book for him. According to his first biographer, Antony Scaduto, he was bowled over when he read it as a teenager in Hibbing. It's not surprising that its depiction of life in a decaying single-industry town struck a chord. Perhaps more important, though, was its portrayal of the outsiders and the losers as heroes, in which *Cannery Row*, published in 1945, is a clear precursor of Beat literature.

"Mack and the boys", the down-and-outs who occupy centre-stage in Steinbeck's novel, are the free, who "avoid the trap, walk around the poison, step over the noose while a generation of trapped, poisoned, and trussed-up men scream at them and call them no-goods, come-to-bad-ends, blots-on-the-town, thieves, rascals, bums."

The population of DESOLATION ROW, and of *Highway 61 Revisited* as a whole, is divided cleanly into Steinbeck's two types, the insiders and the outsiders, 'straights' and 'freaks'. On the one hand, there are the authority figures – diplomat, doctor, city father, cop, professor, promoter, adviser, sergeant-at-arms and lawyer; and on the other hand there are the tramp, clown, juggler, geek, thief, leper, crook, sword-swallower, fortune-teller, flower-lady, bandit and gambler. As the song progresses it becomes clear that Desolation Row is the place for this latter class. And as it darkens, from carnival evening to murderous midnight, the thought of Desolation Row itself becomes brighter. It comes to seem, like Cannery Row, a place of refuge from the trap, the noose and the poison.

After reading *Cannery Row*, the young Dylan sought out more of Steinbeck, and thus came to *The Grapes of Wrath*, for which his enthusiasm was even greater. This led to his being lent *Bound for Glory*, as an eye-witness account of the same Dust Bowl exodus that Steinbeck's novel describes; and so began his absorption in Woody Guthrie.

The relation of Cannery Row to DESOLATION ROW is not only ancestral, however, as can be seen in the form. The novel is composed as a mosaic of brief, discrete episodes, and the song, with its reference to "postcards" in the opening line, is likewise a series of disparate scenes, of about the length, in fact, that one could write on a postcard. The disorderly seaside setting of the novel also seems to carry over into the opening shots of the song:

> They're selling postcards of the hanging,
> They're painting the passports brown,
> The beauty-parlour is filled with sailors,
> The circus is in town…

That first line makes a bizarre connection with the end of the song before, JUST LIKE TOM THUMB'S BLUES, which starts

"When you're lost in the rain in Juarez" and finishes: "I'm going back to New York City / I do believe I've had enough".

There used to be one road that ran from El Paso, lying across the Rio Grande from Juarez, all the way to Buffalo, New York, and the connection with the New York State Thruway. That was Highway 62, passing en route through Lubbock, Texas, birthplace of Buddy Holly, and Okemah, Oklahoma, birthplace of Woody Guthrie. According to Woody's biographer, Joe Klein, in 1911, the year before he was born, his father Charlie Guthrie took part in the lynching of a thirteen-year-old boy, Lawrence Nelson, and his mother. They were hanged from a bridge over the North Canadian River after a deputy sheriff had been shot and bled to death in their yard. Mrs Nelson's baby was left exposed at the roadside. The local newspaper, the *Okemah Ledger*, says Klein, "published a grisly photo of the lynched bodies which later was reprinted as a postcard and became a popular novelty item in local stores."

Recently it has emerged that a similar thing happened in Dylan's own birthplace, Duluth, twenty years before he was born. The events have come to light because the city, to its credit, chose to commemorate their eightieth anniversary this year. Six black performers with a visiting circus, which had come to take part in the city's fiftieth anniversary celebrations, were falsely accused of raping a white girl. On 14th June 1921, three of them were sprung from jail and hanged. A postcard of that lynching was also put on sale.

The remembrance of this story, received from his relatives (who quite possibly felt that the Jews were liable to be next after the Negroes) seems to attach to several elements of Dylan's opening lines: the circus, the port (whose iron-ore shipping might account for those brown passports), the "tightrope" and bound hands which occur later in the verse. Whether he might also have discovered in 1964, when he swung across the country in his van, the parallel events in

Okemah and their connection with his hero, I can only guess. Perhaps they sparked off each other and both are present among the layers of association in which the images of the song are built up. The history of skin-colour (did I mention that the Nelsons were black?) may lie behind the painting of the passports; but the idea of changed identity, as in the beauty parlour filled with sailors, also links the beginning of the song with the ending, and the lines of the last verse, "I had to rearrange their faces / And give them all another name."

If Dylan did discover less-than-saintly antecedents and a grim shared heritage for the man whom he called, when he first met him, the "holiest, godliest one in the world", one can see how fittingly that fact would introduce a song in which the Open Road he learned through Woody is renamed as a desperate dead-end.

Without those layers, though, what is the bare meaning of the opening image? It points to Dylan himself, in his pop vision of destruction and oppression, selling his own "postcards of the hanging".

## · 1 ·

# Savage  Rose  &  Fixable

Though the ten verses of DESOLATION ROW are discrete, they are not unconnected. They have a pattern which is best understood through the sort of doubling that we looked at in Part II. The same architectural form can be traced in a single verse as in the song as a whole. The lines are arranged syntactically in pairs:

> Now the moon is almost hidden,
> The stars are beginning to hide.

And these are joined into fours by rhyme:

> The fortune-telling lady
> Has even taken all her things inside.

There are two groups of four lines to each verse, capped off with the final group that rhymes on the title phrase:

> And the Good Samaritan, he's dressing,
> He's getting ready for the show.
> He's going to the carnival tonight
> On Desolation Row.

Similarly, the ten verses of the song fall into two groups of four, each arranged as two pairs, followed by a final pair, verses 9 and 10, which are two alternative endings. The pattern is easier to see when the sequence of verses is laid out as below, with summary descriptions:

1. The evening parade
2. Cinderella
3. The fall of night
4. Ophelia

5. Einstein
6. Dr Filth
7. Getting ready for the feast
8. The midnight round-up

9. The *Titanic* at dawn

10. Alone in the room, signing off

The first four verses alternate scene-setting with character-study. No. 1 is a lively, if absurd and vaguely disturbing crowd-scene, while No. 2 focuses on an individual, Cinderella, who is similarly full of life and movement. No. 3 is a scene again, but now the streets are empty, and the single figure in verse No. 4, Ophelia, is correspondingly still and (almost) inert. She and Cinderella illustrate to perfection the two camps of *Highway 61*, insider and outsider, square and hip, straight and freak, or whatever you want to call them.

The pattern is altered in the next set of four verses, and the two individuals, now two males, are grouped together, followed by the two broader scenes. The same alternation of movement and fixity, and of straight and freak, can still be traced, though. So the weird genius-outlaw, "Einstein disguised as Robin Hood", is followed by the sinister and repressive "Dr Filth". What appears to be a theatre, in verse 7, with the actors backstage preparing for "the feast", is followed in verse 8 by the "Factory" and the "castle".

In the first verse there is an emblem of this yoking of opposites which is the governing principle of the song's form:

> And here comes the blind commissioner,
> They've got him in a trance.
> One hand is tied to the tightrope-walker,
> The other is in his pants.

The man in charge is helpless and the outsider is in control. The "commissioner" may not be commissioner of police, though. He could be the commissioner of this work of art; in which case he would stand for Dylan's will, the high ambition that has led him to attempt an epic composition and to base it on the central work of modernist literature in English.

In his interview with Paul Zollo for *Song Talk* magazine in 1991, Dylan spoke of the importance for him of keeping the conscious mind at bay when he writes. The commissioner, if he represents the conscious mind, certainly shows it to have been switched off – unseeing, unthinking, turned in on himself, self-pleasing. By this interpretation, the "tightrope-walker", who moves by feel, would be the unconscious or the intuition, which takes the lead.

Although it has a great deal of patterning and symbolic intricacy, there is still an air of spontaneity to the writing of DESOLATION ROW which suggests that its order is associative, a structure established in the unconscious mind rather than purposely designed. There is none of the cunning contrivance that is displayed in IT'S ALRIGHT, MA, for example, which was his previous shot at a world-summarising song. Nor is there the studiedly surrealist invention of GATES OF EDEN, nor the poetical effusion of MR TAMBOURINE MAN. Its speech is for the most part so fluent and direct that one could *almost* believe Dylan's claim that the song was written straight out "in fifteen minutes in the back of a cab in New York".

Note, though, that the tightrope-walker in this image cannot carry out his proper task any more than the commissioner can. He has the upper hand in this relationship, but he is earthbound by it, who should be destined for higher things.

If you will grant that Dylan has projected into the beginning of the song an image of the state of mind which produced it, proving what he promised in MR TAMBOURINE MAN – "I'm ready for to fade / Into my own parade" – you may also see him at the end of this first verse as a pair of spectators:

> As Lady and I look out tonight
> On Desolation Row.

As he sings it, "Lady 'n' I" is actually an anagram of I, Dylan. The full significance of the observer of DESOLATION ROW being split or doubled like this will appear in the final verse.

For the first half of the song, its menace is all in hints – the absurdity of the beauty parlour filled with sailors; the sinister postcards; the cruel edge to the treatment of the blind commissioner, seemingly displayed for public amusement; and the danger of a "restless" riot squad. In the second verse, some incident of violence appears to have been elided by a sudden jump-cut, when someone says to Romeo:

> … "You're in the wrong place, my friend,
> You'd better leave."
> And the only sound that's left
> After the ambulances go…

At the beginning of the third verse, there is a suggestion of a more general threat in the strange behaviour of the stars and the diviner:

> The stars are beginning to hide.
> The fortune-telling lady
> Has even taken all her things inside.

The stars are not hidden but *hiding*, as though no longer willing to look down on our fate. Whether the fortune-teller can no longer predict the future, as a result, or it is just that she doesn't want to say any more what it holds, her deed seems not to bode well.

From about midway, the action of the song gets steadily worse, and at the same time the prospect of Desolation Row itself becomes progressively brighter. "As Lady and I look out tonight on…": the natural assumption is that the song will be describing life as lived on the Row, and the events of the first verse have been happening there as "Lady and I" watch them. But it doesn't say that in so many words. Likewise in the second verse, after the ambulances go, we are left with "Cinderella sweeping up on Desolation Row", and again we assume that the whole encounter was set there. Yet there could be a shift of scene as well as of time when, after the Romeo incident, the verse jump-cuts. It could be that the "easy", off-duty Cinderella who seems so out of character, with "her hands in her back-pockets, Bette Davis-style", is not on Desolation Row at all, and it is only the Cinderella at the end who is there, doing her traditional dirty work.

At the end of the third verse, the Good Samaritan "going to the carnival tonight on Desolation Row" needn't mean that he's not on that street already, but it does make it sound as though he's heading off *somewhere else* to party. There can be no doubt that the fourth verse is *not* set on Desolation Row. Here we see Ophelia "'neath the window" – which is where the Romeo of verse 2 belonged. She is the diametrical opposite to Cinderella, whom we saw moving, speaking, smiling, and changing over time. Ophelia is placed at the outset and remains static. Her character is portrayed only through attributes and abstractions, without action: "She wears an iron vest. / Her profession is her religion, / Her sin is her lifelessness."

From this immobility she breaks just once, right at the end:

And though her eyes are fixed upon
Noah's great rainbow,
She spends her time peeking in-
To Desolation Row.

Obviously you cannot really have your eyes "fixed" on one thing
and also be "peeking" at another. She is *supposedly* intent on the
rainbow, but the temptation to look into Desolation Row is too
great for her; hence the surreptitious flicker of the eyes enacted
by the little word "into" darting across the line break.

But why is she tempted to peek? The rainbow is a divine
assurance against catastrophe – of a certain kind – and it is this
that Ophelia clings to (though it is surely absurd to be "fixed"
upon something so fleeting as a rainbow; and doubly so for a
woman whose fate, if her name is anything to go by, is to
drown). Perhaps when she looks into Desolation Row she sees
another kind of catastrophe already unfolding, against which
the rainbow is no defence; or perhaps she sees a different kind
of promise there. Either way, she is clearly not *on* Desolation
Row herself. At the same time, that one sign of life that it
brings to her, that human frailty, makes of it a sign of hope.

The next verse is the strangest of the lot. What are we to
make of "Einstein disguised as Robin Hood, with his
memories in a trunk"? Is there a joke about elephants in there
– trunks and never forgetting? That would fit with Einstein,
the twentieth century's icon of an intellectual, since the
Hindu god of wisdom and knowledge, Ganesh, has the head
of an elephant. But this is a genius who behaves like an idiot:
"Then he went off sniffing drainpipes / And reciting the
alphabet." Around Cinderella and Ophelia there is an emotional colour which you get at once, despite their puzzles; but
Einstein remains perfectly enigmatic. Is he a sad and broken
has-been, a lunatic, a clown, an enlightened Zen fool?

One way to understand the image of the travelling out-law-genius, with the devoted following ("his friend, a jealous monk") and the dada habits, might be to project onto it the documentary film of Dylan on tour in England, *Dont Look Back*, which was shot a few months before the song was recorded, in April and May 1965. It's possible that he'd seen some of the rushes already, though the film was not released until 1967, after painstaking editing by the maker, D.A. Pennebaker. Or perhaps certain moments were etched on his memory anyway, like the scene at the end of the film, when the limo is speeding away from the fans after the tour's final concert at the Royal Albert Hall.

Albert Grossman tells him that the English press have dubbed him "an anarchist", because he doesn't offer any answers.

Dylan gazes distractedly at the London streets, and says: "Hm. Gimme a cigarette. Give the anarchist a cigarette." And indeed, as our verse puts it, "he looked so immaculately frightful / As he bummed a cigarette".

He says, "I feel like I've been through some kind of *thing*, man."

"You have," says a voice, which is Pennebaker's.

The thing he has been through, as much as anything, is the film itself. *Dont Look Back* is more than a record of Dylan's transformation, as one latterday reviewer put it, "from nice folkie to nasty rock'n'roller": it's a catalyst of that change. The presence of the camera prompts him to extend his performance off the stage and into the press-call and the party and his 'private' life. In the famous scene towards the end where he is interviewed by a journalist from *Time* magazine, as he fences and turns to the attack, Dylan shines with a hard light that makes the wacky beatnik landing at Heathrow at the beginning look positively fuzzy. The process of filming demonstrated, after a fashion, the postu-late of Einsteinian physics, that observation alters what it observes. Indeed, that appears to have been the aim. Pennebaker recalled in 1997 that "Albert [Grossman] came to see me... I think he wanted to have Dylan go through the experience... He kind of wanted to see if Dylan could handle it."

The self-distancing effect of the film can be deduced from the lines at the end of verse 5,

> he was famous long ago
> For playing the electric violin
> On Desolation Row.

This "long ago" was written within a week or so of the notorious events at the Newport Folk Festival which made Dylan renowned for his use of electric instruments. The fact that it is the only verse in the past tense supports the idea of it as a kind of wrong-end-of-the-telescope self-image, where the telescope is a movie projector. The comparison of himself with Einstein may seem inflated, but conjure the vision of the great scientist in green tights and feathered cap: such a thoroughly ridiculous image is hardly self-aggrandising.

The imagery of *Dont Look Back* crops up again in verse 7, preserving that linkage of the alternate verses that we saw in the first group of four. From verse 5 to verse 6, though, we move between two contrasted male figures, like the contrasted females of verses 2 and 4.

Dr Filth, like Ophelia, is another example of fixity and containment: "he keeps his world / Inside of a leather cup / But all his sexless patients / They are trying to blow it up." I wonder if anyone will follow me in finding in these lines, coming hard on the heels of Einstein, a suggestion of his contemporary, Dr Freud, who revolutionised and relativised our inner world as the physicist did the outer universe. Does that "leather cup" chime with the bald dome of Sigmund's skull? Many people certainly regarded him as a "Dr Filth" and would gladly have exploded his theories of the sexual motivation of our dreams and thoughts.

In the lines that follow, though, this figure metamorphoses into something a deal more horrible.

> Now his nurse, some local loser,
> She's in charge of the cyanide hole
> And she also keeps the cards that read
> 'Have Mercy On His Soul'.

The "cyanide hole" immediately recalls the vents above the sealed chambers of Auschwitz where the crystals of Zyklon B, potassium cyanide, were poured in. And the cards evoke the postcards, preprinted with messages of reassurance, which the prisoners were given to send home before they were gassed.

Casting its shadow backwards, this imagery makes of the "sexless patients" the emaciated inmates of the concentration camps; of the "leather cup", perhaps, an artefact of human skin such as were made for some Nazis' homes; and of Dr Filth one of the medical men who performed appalling experiments in torture and lent their expertise to the Final Solution.

But why should these coincide, even implicitly, with Freud? I don't believe a moral comparison is intended. There is a convergence, however, of Freudian psychology with Nazism, in the sense that the Third Reich, which manipulated the mass unconscious so effectively, appears to confirm the psychoanalyst's view of the mind as primarily charged, along with guilty sexual urges, with fear, vengefulness and violence. It would not be surprising for Freud to occur as a negative figure in this song, given its creative dependence on the unconscious, since he stands as a minatory guardian at the gates, warning that what lies beneath consciousness is properly suppressed. At the same time, he illuminates the psychology of Nazism, which projected the Jews as a social id to the Aryan superego. They were simultaneously, in the propaganda of antisemitism, a dirty, bestial, rapacious, 'degenerate' race, and the hidden controllers of the world's history for their own ends. It's not too hard to see how, by making a people into the external focus for our fear of our own unconscious minds, a term and a practice like 'ethnic cleansing' is born.

Verse 6 points straight to the explicit vision of totalitarianism and industrialised murder which follows in verse 8. Before that, following the linkage of alternate verses, there is a smaller murder taking place in verse 7, which is again illuminated by the memory of *Dont Look Back*. It may seem grotesque to juxtapose the Holocaust with the trivia of a backstage pop documentary, but I think that Dylan is simply dealing with two aspects of history that weigh heaviest for him: his own life, as turned into instant history by the film, and the immediate history of his own people, which is also the inescapable event of the twentieth century.

As the atmosphere of the song darkens now, the role of Desolation Row as a refuge becomes clearer. So at the end of verse 6:

> They all play on the penny whistle,
> You can hear them blow
> If you lean your head out far enough
> From Desolation Row.

"You" are on Desolation Row, where these sinister characters are not.

Why the penny whistle, when the vagabond of the previous verse had played the last word in musical technology? Perhaps Dylan had understood how the ideology of folk studies and the Nazi ideology of *ein Volk* shared a common ancestry. Anyway there is something both absurd and eminently plausible about these oppressors enthusiastically embracing the art of the people. "They all" would seem to include doctor, nurse and patients in one concert: the cheerful connotation of the penny whistle in such a setting reminds me of those little bands of prisoners which played tunes from Mozart and light operetta on the well-groomed lawn above the gas chambers as the cattle-trucks unloaded.

Verse 7 begins:

> Across the street they've nailed the curtains,
> They're getting ready for the feast,
> The Phantom of the Opera
> In the perfect image of a priest.

This feast in preparation seems part makeshift theatrical performance – hence the nailed curtain – and part religious ritual, which turns out to be a human sacrifice. A viewing of *Dont Look Back* puts flesh on these images of backstage sycophancy:

> They are spoonfeeding Casanova
> To get him to feel more assured
> Then they'll kill him with self-confidence
> After poisoning him with words.

Along with the ritual killing, the nailed curtain may recall, for the biblically minded, St Paul's comparison of Christ's body on the cross to the veil of the temple, which hid the Holy of Holies and which tore in two when he died.

To see a pop star as a sacrificial victim may seem hyperbolic to us now, but Dylan was already being referred to in the press as a "singing Messiah", so the hyperbole is not entirely of his own making. Casanova, however, is not a spotless sacrifice like Christ, but a transgressor. As the Phantom explains to the "skinny girls", he is "just being punished for going to Desolation Row". Why should this be a capital offence? The implication is that Desolation Row offers something dangerous to law and order, and this is finally made explicit in verse 8, where the darkness of the song reaches the full:

> Now at midnight all the agents
> And the superhuman crew
> Come out and round up everyone
> Who knows more than they do,
> Then they bring them to the Factory
> Where the heart-attack machine
> Is strapped across their shoulders
> And then the kerosene
> Is brought down from the castles
> By insurance men who go
> Check to see that nobody is escaping to
> Desolation Row

The parallels with the Final Solution are clear in the "superhuman crew", like the Nazi *Übermensch*; in the mechanical method of murder; and in the hint at cremation with the kerosene. The cross is in there too, with the means of death strapped across the shoulders. But who is this "who knows more than they do"?

In the frame of the Holocaust, it may be the Jews, given the tradition of learning exemplified by the two Jewish thinkers just mentioned, Einstein and Freud, and by Dylan himself – while in the Nazi perspective the Jews 'knew too much' because of their supposed international conspiracy. Apart from the genocidal motivation, a multitude also died in the camps for various intolerable forms of knowledge – Communist, Christian, humanist; and perhaps, for Hitler, the Jews' faith in God was their ultimate crime.

In the framework of *Highway 61 Revisited*, this verse is the grisly culmination of the division into outsiders and insiders, or freak and straight. The options are two: either to go down and hang with "Mack and the boys" on Desolation Row, or to be brought in among the "trapped, poisoned, and trussed-up men". The burden of the record all along has been that the freaks *know something*. That is the message of LIKE A ROLLING STONE:

> You said you'd never compromise
> With the mystery tramp but now you realise
> He's not selling any alibis
> As you stare into the vacuum of his eyes
> And say, 'Do you want to make a deal?'

It's the message of BALLAD OF A THIN MAN: "Something is happening here, but you don't know what it is, do you, Mr Jones?" Mr Jones stands for the height of straightdom hitting an all-time low. With his pencil in his hand, his eyes in his pocket and his nose to the ground, he might be one of the "insurance men" himself.

> You hand in your ticket
> And you go watch the geek
> Who immediately walks up to you
> When he hears you speak
> And says, 'How does it feel to
> Be such a freak?'
> And you say 'Impossible!' as he hands you a bone.

But 'the Joneses' are just our neighbours, whom we are enjoined to love *as ourselves*. Do any of us know what is happening in this absurd tale, where the average man finds himself the complete outsider? No. So who is Mr Jones? Mr Jones is you, obviously.

As the last eight (and possibly all twelve) lines of verse 8 move implacably on as a single sentence, the conclusion they drive to is that Desolation Row is a place of refuge from the horrors of the Factory. But where are we, what is our viewpoint? Are we there? Or are we just safe because we don't try to know too much, or at least not more than "the agents"? In verse 9, the most intricate and allusive of the song, Dylan tries to resolve the question of where to be.

"Praise be to Nero's Neptune," he begins, "The *Titanic* sails at dawn." Have we jumped forward from the "midnight" of the verse before – or backward? History suggests the latter. The catastrophe of the *Titanic* in 1912 has come to seem the dawning moment of the twentieth century, the wreck of the greatest and most sumptuous creation of the age foreshadowing by a few short years the carnage that would bury the assurance of Western civilisation in the mud of the Western Front. The "midnight" of the previous verse, then, insofar as it refers to the Holocaust, follows rather than precedes this dawn.

From the Classical reference, though, we can see that the *Titanic* is only quasi-historical. Her freight is now the whole of Western civilisation from Rome on. "Nero's Neptune" is a rich phrase: a reminder of the orchestra playing on as the ship sank, and of the fatal nonchalance of those in command, just as that emperor is supposed to have fiddled while Rome burned. At the same time it encapsulates in two words a basic tension of Dylan's catastrophe theory, between flame and flood. This tension underlies HARD RAIN too, where Dylan promised water while the world was in fear of fire falling from the sky. In the sinking of the *Titanic* we have another instance of death by water, which as a general doom is what "Noah's great rainbow" insures against. But placing it under the aegis not just of Neptune, god of the sea, but also of Nero, the overseer of conflagration, allows for the possibility of truly eschatological events, of "the fire next time".

> Everybody's shouting
> 'Which Side Are You On?'

That question, the title of a miners' strike song of the 1930s, seems a meaningless one to ask about the coming collision of Man and Nature, the ship and the iceberg, but about the only meaningful question there is if it refers to the quayside – i.e. are you aboard or ashore?

> And Ezra Pound and T.S. Eliot
> Fighting in the captain's tower
> While calypso singers laugh at them
> And fishermen hold flowers

The fighting, like the question in the previous lines, is enigmatic. It could be pointless or it could be vital. The laughter of the calypso singers inclines us to see it as a ridiculous scrap between two poetic egos for pride of place on this doomed venture. But it doesn't actually say that they are fighting each other: they could be fighting side by side to seize the "captain's tower", i.e. the bridge of the *Titanic*. That's a more biographically accurate image, at least.

Eliot and Pound, while they differed widely in social theory, held similar ideas about the social responsibility of poetry. It is ideally through its influence on the sensibility of a ruling elite that poetry contributes to the general well-being of a culture. W.B. Yeats, whose views were similar in some respects, used the tower specifically as an emblem of governance, and of its current shortcomings, in 'Blood and the Moon':

> Are all modern nations like the tower,
> Half-dead at the top?

Pound himself called artists the "antennae of the race". If such 'feelers' could be alert to the ice ahead and change course, disaster would be averted. This fight for the helm, then, could be the salvation of the ship: for if the *Titanic* were better steered, then she need not sink.

All three of these poets, it may not be omitted, flirted with Fascism in the Thirties, to varying degrees. Pound's dalliance, of course, became a full-blown though largely unrequited infatuation. If Dylan's image of Ezra Pound and T.S. Eliot is to be interpreted in the generous way I have suggested, it is a mark of magnanimity in him, given the antisemitism which poisons much of the writing of one and degrades the poetry of the other.

Which Side Are You On? The *Titanic* is bound to sink – that is part of her meaning as a symbol – but she's also bound not to have Pound and Eliot on board. If her history can be that much changed, then we can't say her fate is inevitable or that their fight is pointless. Listening to our rock'n'roll record, though, we are naturally inclined to align ourselves with the folk, the calypsonians and fishermen, rather than the mandarins of high culture. This certainly seems to be the safer side. I picture them as onlookers, the islanders and sailors waving the great ship off from the harbourside, holding garlands of flowers for the travellers. Their humbler lives and daily intimacy with the sea preserve them from the vainglory that will send the *Titanic* to the bottom.

Can we be so sure that we are standing with them, though? By entering into a song as complex and allusive as this, by hearing it on a gramophone record, by even registering the reference to Ezra Pound and T.S. Eliot, we show that we are 'in the same boat' with them, a part of the modern, mechanical culture which the *Titanic* represents.

And it is here that Dylan leaves us, in the midst of this conundrum. The fishermen with their flowers, like the young girl with the rainbow in A HARD RAIN, make the song's one spot of unalloyed brightness; or almost unalloyed, since the flowers they are are holding may not be garlands for voyagers after all, but wreaths for the soon-to-be-drowned.

In *The Waste Land*, the fisherman is a key figure, since the mythic form underlying the poem is the Grail legend of the Fisher King. He appears, for example, to introduce the poem's coda of fragments: "I sat upon the shore / Fishing, with the arid plain behind me…".

The image of flowers in the poem is fleeting but of vital importance, since it is this one ecstatic moment near the beginning that opens the way to Eliot's final vision, the *Four Quartets*:

> …when we came back, late, from the hyacinth garden,
> Your arms full, and your hair wet, I could not
> Speak, and my eyes failed, I was neither
> Living nor dead, and I knew nothing,
> Looking into the heart of light, the silence.
> *Oed' und leer das Meer.*

(The German, quoted from Wagner, means "Barren and empty the sea".)

With a similar kind of blissful vision, the ninth verse of DESOLATION ROW breaks off:

> And fishermen hold flowers
> Between the windows of the sea
> Where lovely mermaids flow
> And nobody has to think too much
> About Desolation Row.

On paper, these lines appear to run on as one sentence to the end of the verse, but the voice clearly makes "Between" the beginning of a new sentence, which trails off unfinished. Or it could circle back to the harbour town at the beginning of the song: "Between the windows of the sea – they're selling postcards of the hanging." DESOLATION ROW may not only be a nightmare but a recurring one, perpetually left hanging.

If all the other allusions to Eliot which I have adduced seem tenuous, I think it will be allowed that there is an incontrovertible one here. It is not to *The Waste Land*, however, but to the final lines of its predecessor, 'The Love Song of J. Alfred Prufrock':

> We have lingered in the chambers of the sea
> By seagirls wreathed in seaweed red and brown
> Till human voices wake us, and we drown.

If we could live with the mermaids "between the windows of the sea", we would not have to worry about our ship sinking, or whether we're on board or off. But at the very mention of what we would then not have to think about, Desolation Row, we wake, and drown. And here Dylan's voice disappears beneath the waves, and he blows a long and urgent breather-apparatus solo.

When he surfaces again, he appears to be a different man. The voice that had been so poetic in the penultimate verse returns with a dry, scornful tone:

> Yes, I received your letter yesterday,
> About the time the doorknob broke.
> When you asked me how I was doing,
> Was that some kind of joke?

The syntactical arrangement of these lines is crafty. They come across as perfectly plain, and I have punctuated them according to the top layer of their sense. But consider the word "about": does it mean it was roughly at this time that the letter arrived, or that the letter was *about* the time the doorknob broke? Did the doorknob break when you asked me how I was doing? Was the breaking of the doorknob "some kind of joke"?

All these people that you mention,
Yes I know them, they're quite lame.
I had to rearrange their faces
And give them all another name.

Are we to understand that all of the nine preceding verses constitute this letter, written by "you" but rewritten by "I". And who are you and I? Is "you" the "I" who looked out in the first verse? Is it only the editing of this second "I" that has made the song so cryptic?

Even beneath this bare language there is still a cryptic level. As the first ending of the song alluded to the end of 'Prufrock', so this second ending alludes to the end of *The Waste Land*. The final section of the poem, 'What the Thunder Said', is based on a Hindu legend in which the thunder speaks the single syllable DA and the three orders of beings – gods, humans and demons – each interpret it according to their own nature. To the gods it is DA: *datta* (give). To the humans it is DA: *dayadhvam* (sympathise). And to the demons it is DA: *damyatta* (control).

These are parodied in turn in Dylan's lines, as give becomes "received"; sympathise "some kind of joke"; and control "to rearrange their faces". It is the middle one that he focuses on, however, for his "I" trapped in his room by a broken doorknob is a kind of burlesque of Eliot's passage on sympathy:

DA
*Dayadhvam*: I have heard the key
Turn in the door once and turn once only
We think of the key, each in his prison
Thinking of the key, each confirms a prison

Eliot's lines are themselves an allusion, to the death of Count Ugolino in Dante's *Divine Comedy*, who is locked in a tower to starve. So we are returned to the "captain's tower" of the previous verse, now as a symbol of the individual intellect rather than of political wisdom.

In the end, Desolation Row offers one ray of hope to break this isolation. It's a meagre hope, perhaps, compared with its earlier potential as an alternative society and a refuge from the agents and the superhuman crew. Now it just holds out the possibility of communication through the sharing of hardship:

> Right now I can't read too good,
> Don't send me no more letters, no,
> Not unless you mail them from
> Desolation Row.

Which makes the place more elusive than ever, since it implies that the "letter" we have just heard was not from Desolation Row at all – and nor presumably is this reply in the last verse. In the whole enormous song we may not in fact have seen its ostensible subject, Desolation Row, at all.

The lyric makes another circle with these closing words, from "letters" back to the "postcards" of verse 1 – a further instance of Dylan's fondness for tying beginnings and endings together. Even more characteristic, perhaps, is the contradiction of concluding his single most literary song with the statement, "Right now I can't read too good".

There is no resolution to DESOLATION ROW. Though there is much that may be unravelled in it, as I hope I have shown, the knot will not finally come undone, and its nested, interlocking enigmas remain such. The poetry of the song is not impenetrable – we can go into it, but we cannot come out on the other side, and in the end we are returned to the surface – to these scenes and characters which come at us so vividly, so economically drawn, and so dreamlike. For the renaming and rearranging of everybody is very much like the dream process as described by Freud. Perhaps this is another double image of the mind like that I posited in the first verse, with "I" as the conscious mind receiving but censoring the imagery of the unconscious "you". Everything in the lyric is *just there*, but everything in it also troubles us with an insistent sense that it means *something else*; and this combination of the immediate and the mysterious is of the essence of Dylan's poetry.

# · 2 ·

# The Dark Is
# Just Beginning

Impending catastrophe, which had been so prevalent a subject before, fades into the background after DESOLATION ROW. Yet it was still *in* the background, in that powerful aura of personal doom which was perceived and described around Dylan in the relatively brief moment of his rock apotheosis (really only a year, from mid-'65 to mid-'66). He was seen and said to be burning too brightly – or too darkly – to last, to be threatening to explode or disintegrate. So the songs of I-and-you that followed *Highway 61* did seem to be letters from Desolation Row.

Those songs radiate out from the conclusion of DESOLATION ROW in rather surprising ways. They don't pick up the discourse of the song at all. The very large questions it raises – is Western civilisation doomed? is it redeemable? can an alternative society exist in between its cracks? – appear to just disappear. Instead of following them up, Dylan takes off at right angles, as it were, from other, seemingly minor points. It is dramatic rather than logical continuity that he maintains.

What makes this continuity remarkable is that the two songs which provide the bridge between *Highway 61* and *Blonde on Blonde* were recorded and quite likely written before DESOLATION ROW. They are POSITIVELY 4TH STREET and CAN YOU PLEASE CRAWL OUT YOUR WINDOW?, released as singles in September and December 1965 respectively, but recorded in July at the *Highway 61* sessions. They make such a perfect one-two sequence of stepping-stones between the two albums that it's hard to believe that Dylan didn't conceive them as such in the first place.

There is even, to tie them together, the little reference back, at the end of CRAWL, to the first line of 4TH STREET: "You've got a lot of nerve to say you are my friend if you won't crawl out your window." I think this kind of self-quotation would just seem silly or be confusing between two tracks on an album: to work, it needs to be reference *backwards*. The charming thing about it is that the line in CRAWL is so friendly and playful-sounding, when what it quotes is so savage first time round – the opening cut of an absolutely merciless sabring.

It's a pity that these two didn't enjoy more success (by the measure of LIKE A ROLLING STONE, at least, they were not hits), since Dylan appears to have been geared up to run a string of singles alongside and in between his chain of albums. Songs like IF YOU GOTTA GO, GO NOW, I WANNA BE YOUR LOVER and perhaps even SHE'S YOUR LOVER NOW seem to have been recorded with this in mind. On the other hand, it's not surprising that it didn't happen. CRAWL and 4TH STREET are two of the finest 45s of the Sixties, I reckon, but neither has the universal appeal of ROLLING STONE. The conjunction of "vomitific" personal release and a particular moment of mass consciousness simply could not be replicated deliberately.

POSITIVELY 4TH STREET must have been quite a shocker at the time – remember that Dylan on the radio in the summer of '65 meant primarily LIKE A ROLLING STONE and the Byrds' version of MR TAMBOURINE MAN, which was Dylan as the Pied Piper. These opened out into a world of possibility that was both scary and exhilarating. After all, what could have been cooler or wilder in those days than to be like a Rolling Stone? Both songs are about losing everything, about shedding a personality, and thereby becoming free. LIKE A ROLLING STONE may be scornful and sarcastic, but the obvious answer to its insistent question "How does it *feel*?" is yes, it feels *good*.

In terms of pop music, POSITIVELY 4TH STREET is no less revolutionary, but it is a good deal less inviting. No-one had put a nerve so naked nor allowed anything so ugly onto a pop record before. This came from a dimension beyond scorn; more than just a put-down or a getting-even, it's an expression of enmity so pure and focused as to be almost sanctified, like the more terrifying of the Psalms.

Its bare-bone diction, and its treatment of song as a private letter, are picked up from the last verse of DESOLATION ROW. Indeed, we might speculate that it is a reply to that verse:

> You've got a lot of nerve to say you are my friend.
> When I was down you just stood there grinning.

The "I" at the end of DESOLATION ROW could be this "you", and that "you" this "I". After all, you've got a lot of nerve to treat my friendliness as "some kind of joke", when all the sympathy you can offer is to take my nightmare and "rearrange" it.

In fact, the end of POSITIVELY 4TH STREET does make "you" and "I" interchangeable:

> I wish that for just one time you could stand inside
> my shoes
> And just for that one moment I could be you.
> Yes I wish that for just one time you could stand inside
> my shoes:
> You'd know what a drag it is to see you.

Except of course that you wouldn't: you'd know what a drag it is to see *me*, who is now in your place.

The self-castigating subtext here is picked up again in CAN YOU PLEASE CRAWL OUT YOUR WINDOW?, in that this "he" is very much like the "I" both of POSITIVELY 4TH STREET and of the final verse of DESOLATION ROW:

> He sits in your room, his tomb, with a fistful of tacks,
> Preoccupied with his vengeance,
> Cursing the dead who can't answer him back.

The slight return of a previous spirit makes CRAWL something of an overlooked gem. Although the attack on "him" is one of the nastiest in this nasty phase of Dylan's writing, the song overall conveys just that liberation which it invites "you" into. Its falling night – "Come on out, the dark is just beginning" – seems as alive with possibility as MR TAMBOURINE MAN's. I suppose, since nothing is actually said about what lies beyond the room, it must be because the playing is such a shared joy, full of fierce-yet-comic angularities, and with that magical quality that so often attends on the recordings of Dylan and the Band together. The sound itself is the utter contrary to the oppressive room.

The funny particularity of the movement, too, is another flashback to *Bringing It All Back Home*, like all the running and jumping on that album:

> Please crawl out your window,
> Use your arms and legs, it won't ruin you.

While Miss Lonely falls from a height and unwillingly into liberation, this woman is invited and seems to *swim* out into hers. (I assume the crawl was known to Dylan as the name of a stroke.)

The repressive thinker in the room with no working door (it seems, since "you" must leave by the window), rolls the monstrosities of *Highway 61* – Ophelia, Dr Filth, Mr Jones – into one glorious, hateful ball. There is no satire quite as imaginative as this on the LP:

> He looks so truthful – is this how he feels?
> Trying to peel the moon and expose it.

With his businesslike anger and his bloodhounds that kneel,
If he needs a third eye he just grows it.

Yet the conclusion of the refrain has an unusual even-handedness:

How can you say he will haunt you?
You can go back to him any time that you want to.

Who in their right mind would want to, we might ask. But if she *did* want to, it may be because he is not as bad as he's been made out to be, or 'I' may not prove so much of an improvement. (There is a hint in that "haunt", and in "his tomb" – and perhaps also in the "grinning" person of 4TH STREET – that these figures are themselves "the dead who can't answer... back".)

The room which someone can't get out of or can't get into; stuckness and stasis; the song as a personal communication (though broadcast to the world): these are the things that carry over from the end of *Highway 61*, through the singles, to *Blonde on Blonde*. They make a continuity, as I said, but hardly the one we would expect. There have, however, been a few other instances of this right-angled linkage.

Because of it, *Desire*, for example, was first received with a certain amount of suspicion. Instead of keeping on at the "open heart university" that had informed the bulk of *Blood on the Tracks*, the new record was devoted to the fictional narrative mode that had appeared in SIMPLE TWIST OF FATE and LILY, ROSEMARY AND THE JACK OF HEARTS. So it was felt that Dylan had retreated from his honesty behind a screen of artifice. Odder yet was the way that *Street-Legal* followed *Desire*, turning its underlying mythic symbolism into a shuffled deck of cards.

It is astonishing, and exciting, and sometimes frustrating, how quickly Dylan can exhaust what seems to be a newly discovered mode and move on to the next. The great cast of historical and literary characters that fills *Highway 61*, for example – Napoleon and Beethoven, John the Baptist and Einstein, F. Scott Fitzgerald and Bo Diddley, Delilah and Bette Davis and Belle Starr – are reduced to three on *Blonde on Blonde*. Mind you, they could hardly be a more quintessential trio: Achilles, the hero of the first poem in Western literature; Mona Lisa; and Shakespeare.

Similarly, the aphoristic wisdom-sayings which Dylan was celebrated for – "There's no success like failure", "When you ain't got nothing you got nothing to lose", "Money doesn't talk, it swears" – have come down to one:

> But to live outside the law you must be honest
> (I know you always say that you agree).

Again, though, the one is a pretty essential one – a kind of hip distillation of the teaching of St Paul. (To be fair to him, 'faithful' should really be substituted for "honest".)

This is very much in the nature of the whole collection: though the language is generally simpler, the effect is not to make the songs clearer but to make them more enigmatic, laconic and riddling. *Highway 61* has its share of inquiries – "How does it feel?", "Won't you come see me?", "Do you, Mr Jones?", "Was that some kind of joke?" – but *Blonde on Blonde* has many more:

> Ain't it just like the night…?
> Won't you come with me…?
> Where are you tonight…?
> How can I explain?
> Can I jump on it sometime?
> Ain't it clear?

What else you got left?
I wasn't very cute to him, now was I?

I'd ask him what the matter was
I asked him why he dressed
I asked the doctor if I could see you
I asked her how come
I asked her for some
asked me if I was leaving with you or her
ask me to open up the gate
ask himself if it's him or them that's insane
Now don't ask for mine

'Name me someone that's not a parasite…'

'You can't look at much, can you, man?'

Is your heart made out of stone, or is it lime,
Or is just solid rock?

How come you don't send me no regards?
You know I want your loving,
Honey, why are you so hard?

Who among them do they think could bury you?
[and nine other similar questions]

Should I leave them by your gate
Or, sad-eyed lady, should I wait?

The overall indeterminacy, the strange combination of the personal and the unspecific, helped these recordings to entwine with their listeners' minds and become part of the fabric of their times. This was the beginning of an era of LP-listening as a small-scale but universal social ritual – of sitting around together getting stoned (i.e. sensorily amplified, perceptive of hitherto-hidden meanings, mildly bewildered and perhaps a little paranoid) and playing rock albums. So *Blonde on Blonde* blended seamlessly into the world in which it was heard, with its preponderance of interior settings, its finely detailed sound, its puzzled and puzzling tone, and its fragmentary conversations. This is one of its peculiarities: while almost all the songs are addressed to a "you" who is not present – so that in a sense there is no direct speech on the record – there is a lot of talking in them.

The comparison with *Highway 61* is illuminating. There is also quite a lot of reported speech there, but it tends to be declamatory or theatrical:

> Screaming she moans...
>
> 'Death to all those – !'
>
> 'Stop all this weeping!'
>
> Shouting the word 'Now!'
>
> Shouting to skinny girls
>
> Shouting 'Which Side Are You On?'

Often the speakers make dramatic gestures to accompany their words:

> Dropping a barbell he points to the sky...
>
> He walks with a swagger and he says to the bride...
>
> He crosses himself and then he clicks his high heels...
>
> Lay down their bandanas and complain...

The exchanges of *Blonde on Blonde* are casual, slangy, often ambiguous, and often misunderstood, like those of real life. In all of these respects they clearly have their antecedents in the last verse of DESOLATION ROW.

# · 3 ·

# The First Lesson
# In Chinese

There are three big songs on *Blonde on Blonde* that each follow on from DESOLATION ROW in a different way. They are, in order of appearance, VISIONS OF JOHANNA, STUCK INSIDE OF MOBILE WITH THE MEMPHIS BLUES AGAIN and SAD-EYED LADY OF THE LOWLANDS. The first expands on the poetic achievement; it is the artistic heir and the album's lyrical *pièce de resistance*. The second takes up the outward form; and the third has the same structural role as the large-scale finale.

The middle one first. STUCK INSIDE OF MOBILE has a similar two-step movement to DESOLATION ROW. Each verse is formed of two groups of four lines, each group of four made up of two pairs. The metre is similar too – generally three stresses to a line, heavier at the beginning and end and lighter in the middle, and the lines alternating feminine and masculine endings. Thus in DESOLATION ROW we have:

> Now the moon is almost hidden,
>> the stars are beginning to hide.
> The fortune-telling lady
>> has even taken all her things inside.

And in MEMPHIS BLUES:

> Shakespeare, he's in the alley
>> with his pointed shoes and his bells,
> Speaking to some French girl
>> who says she knows me well.
> And I would send a message
>> to find out if she's talked,
> But the post office has been stolen
>> and the mailbox is locked.

Even in this early and relatively regular verse, you can see the liberties that are taken with the metre, and over the course of the whole track the singing is so full of subtle variations on this basic scheme that one would have to say that Dylan has effectively arrived at a free-verse song-form. Indeed it is purely inventiveness of phrasing that carries us along, since there is no inherent progression to the lyric.

The steady sardonic tone of voice and the gallery of eccentric characters are familiar from DESOLATION ROW, but the breaking up of the verses into discrete "postcards" has been taken further. There is no pattern of contrasts or gradual intensification such as informs us, however subliminally, that a drama is unfolding in the earlier song. The ten verses of MEMPHIS BLUES could, we feel, come in any order – as befits its subject of stuckness. The scenes could be outtakes from DESOLATION ROW, but the absurdity and danger which there seemed to spring from a world teetering on the brink of cataclysm have just become everyday life here.

That this *here* should be called Mobile shows that Dylan had appreciated Henry Miller's book *The Air-Conditioned Nightmare* – a bilious account of his return to America after long years abroad, published in 1945. Dylan's refrain is surely drawn from the chapter entitled 'My Dream of Mobile', a magical piece of associative prose in which Miller builds up a picture of a place he had never visited, from the resonances of its name. The fact that Dylan is stuck "inside of" rather than just stuck *in* Mobile suggests it is more a state of mind than a city.

A passage from 'My Dream of Mobile' evokes the atmosphere, sound and imagery not only of the song but of the whole of *Blonde on Blonde*:

> Mobile is a deceptive word. It sounds quick and yet it suggests immobility – glassiness. It is a fluid mirror which reflects sheet lightning as well as somnolent trees and drugged serpents. It is a name which suggests water, music, light and torpor. It also sounds remote, securely pocketed, faintly exotic and, if it has any colour, is definitely white. Musically I would designate it as guitarish. Perhaps not even that resonant – perhaps mandolinish. Anyway, pluckable music – accompanied by bursting fruit and thin light columns of smoke. No dancing, except the dancing of mote-beams, the evanescent beat of ascension and evaporation. The skin always dry, despite the excessive humidity. The slap-slap of carpet slippers, and figures silhouetted against half-drawn blinds. Corrugated silhouettes.
>
> I have never once thought of work in connection with the word Mobile. Not anybody working. A city surrounded with shells, the empty shells of bygone fiestas. Burning everywhere and the friable relics of yesterday's carnival. Gaiety always in retreat, always vanishing, like clouds brushing a mirror. In the center of this glissando Mobile itself, very prim, very proper, Southern and not Southern, listless but upright, slatternly yet respectable, bright but not wicked. Mozart for the mandolin. Not Segovia feathering Bach. Not grace and delicacy so much as anaemia. Fever-coolth. Musk. Fragrant ashes.

At the end of the chapter, having meandered away, Miller returns to his main theme and improvises a coda:

Take the milk of aloes, mix clove and brandywine, and you have the spiritual elixir of Mobile. There is no hour when things are different, no day which is not the same. It lies in a pocket, is honeycombed with light, and flutters like a plucked cat-gut. It is mobile, fluid, fixed, but not glued. It gives forth no answers, neither does it question. It is mildly, pleasantly bewildering, like the first lesson in Chinese or the first round with a hypnotist. Events transpire in all declensions at once; they are never conjugated. What is not Gog is Magog...

STUCK INSIDE OF MOBILE is one of the two songs on *Blonde on Blonde* not addressed to "you". (It is nominally addressed to "mama" – "Oh mama, can this really be the end?" – and is, like the earlier 'mother' songs A HARD RAIN and IT'S ALRIGHT, MA, a summary report on experience. Oddly, the song was listed on the original LP sleeve and label as 'Stuck Inside of Mobile With Thee', though you'd be hard-pressed to say who in the song could be "thee". Not mama, surely? I suppose it must be you again, the listener.) And the other non-you song is VISIONS OF JOHANNA – which is paradoxical, since it obsessively circles its single 'significant other'.

It shows its descent from DESOLATION ROW, firstly, in its beginning, with the narrator "stranded" in a room and, secondly, in that its ostensible subject does not appear. Not only is there no sight of Johanna, there is no imagining of her either. We never see "these visions of Johanna that conquer my mind" – unless, of course, they are everything that we see.

The overall trend of the lyric is the contrary to DESOLATION ROW. Here we begin with a plain-spoken naturalism which gradually dissolves into strangeness. The seed of dissolution is the one non-naturalistic image of the first verse: "Louise holds a handful of rain, tempting you to defy it". By the final lines, this rain has flooded out all other sense:

The harmonicas play the skeleton keys in the rain
And these visions of Johanna are now all that remain.

The biggest mystery of this mysterious song is how it con-
jures grandeur out of seeming triviality, since its subject matter
is but a set of inconclusive and ill-defined personal exchanges.
Part of the answer is the momentum of the performance.
Starting from a sound that foreshadows *John Wesley Harding* –
just the bass and drums of Charlie McCoy and Kenny Buttrey
and Dylan's own acoustic guitar, adorned with faint strands of
organ – as the clear, habitable space of the first verse gradually disintegrates and dissolves, the music becomes steadily richer, fuller and more solid, rolling irresistibly into the last verse
where "we see this empty cage now corrode".

The end of a world is unfolding here as surely as in
DESOLATION ROW, but it is not 'the world' in the biblical
sense of the social order; rather it is the fabric of space and
time itself that seems to be coming apart at the seams. A
broader reference for this disintegration of dimensions is art-
fully given in verse 4, where its analogue is found "inside the
museums". As "infinity goes up on trial", we move from the
Mona Lisa, in her sound frame of perspective, to "the jelly-
faced women" – of Picasso's post-Cubist portraits, for example – to the wonderful and inexplicable Surrealist image,
"Jewels and binoculars hang from the head of the mule",
which one can easily visualise in a painting by Dalì, or
Chagall perhaps, or as the title of one by Miró.

While the visual and tactile world comes undone, though,
the auditory world is preternaturally sharpened. We can hear
"in this room, the heat-pipes just cough"; and just as clearly
"we can hear the night-watchman click his flashlight" and
"the all-night girls whisper" in the empty lot, and "voices
echo" in the museums, and Little Boy Lost "muttering small
talk at the wall while I'm in the hall". That sounds should be
so vivid in a song called 'Visions' is a characteristic paradox,

like the use of the very uncharacteristic word "we" in a piece about overwhelming isolation.

The foundation for the eventual corrosion and explosion of the perceived world lies in the splitting and fusing and dissolving of persons. In the beginning – since "we sit here stranded though *we're all* doing our best to deny it" – there appear to be at least three: namely, the narrator and "Louise and her lover so entwined". But from the next verse it seems possible that the narrator and "her lover" are one and the same, since "Louise is alright, she's just near, / She's delicate and seems like the mirror", which suggests that "she" and 'I' are "entwined".

Then in the third verse we hear of "Little Boy Lost", who speaks "to me". This is an odd conversation, however, with him "muttering small talk at the wall while I'm in the hall". Perhaps the narrator is not "in this room" at all. Or perhaps "in the hall" is a sexual metaphor and "Little Boy Lost" is a reflection that the 'I' finds in the "mirror" of Louise even as he enters her, a portion of the self that is "bringing her name up", and "speaks" (internally) "of a farewell kiss to me". His similarity to 'I' is quite marked: "he takes himself so seriously./ He brags of his misery, he likes to live dangerously". That could certainly be said of this singer – a lover whose pining spirals into global collapse, and whose expression is 'dangerous' in one of its older senses, which is difficult or chary.

So when we come to the fifth verse and find another male-female conversation – "The peddler now speaks to the countess who's pretending to care for him" – the suspicion arises that this is actually the same encounter between the same people that has been going on all along, and only the names have been changed. A suspicion that is heightened by the sudden reversion to Louise – "but like Louise always says". Likewise, when we hear no more of "the peddler" but are suddenly introduced to "the fiddler", we may feel that there is definitely a fiddle going on, and that the count in this song – despite the appearance of the "countess" and so on – has never risen above two.

We were warned from the start, though: "Ain't it just like the night to play tricks…?" And again: "We sit here stranded". To be stranded, as well as meaning to be stuck, also means to be twisted together of separate strands, like a rope: a metaphor picked up at the end of the verse in the word "entwined". So the different characters may all just be different strands of the same two personalities.

It has been mooted that Johanna, as well as being the heavenly woman, the "Madonna" who "still has not showed", also echoes the Hebrew name for the pit, Gehenna, which became the punitive Christian Hell, but which was originally just the abode of the dead, the place of oblivion. The sense of loss of more than a lover, a loss of soul, is heightened by the reference to Blake's poem 'The Little Boy Lost' in the *Songs of Experience*:

> 'Father! Father! Where are you going?
> 'Oh do not walk so fast.
> 'Speak, father, speak to your little boy,
> 'Or else I shall be lost.'
>
> The night was dark, no father was there;
> The child was wet with dew;
> The mire was deep, & the child did weep,
> And away the vapour flew.

Here is an analogy for the song's conversations with apparitions, figments and absences. More importantly, it illuminates the sense of desolation which outstrips the initial mood of romantic melancholy and in the end overwhelms even the self: "And these visions of Johanna are now all that remain."

I shan't ask you to believe, if you do not wish to, that the artist could have sensed in making it that this record was to bring a cycle of his work to a close. Nevertheless there is a peculiar aptness to its ending. SAD-EYED LADY OF THE LOWLANDS, its last and largest song, is without any parallel in Dylan's writing. And unlike the endings of the earlier chapters in our wanderer's story, this suggests no further for him to go. "Should I wait?" are the final words.

Again there is the curious absence of the main subject, as in VISIONS OF JOHANNA. The vision of the sad-eyed lady fills every corner of her song, but for all the apparent closeness – the recurrent images of eyes, face, mouth, fingers – it still appears that "I" is not with her and cannot get to her: hence, "My warehouse eyes, my Arabian drums, / Should I leave them by your gate…?" Where SAD-EYED LADY differs is that the whole song is static. The verses of STUCK INSIDE OF MOBILE may seem arbitrary in their order, but each one is still an incident in itself, moving forward in time. This finale has no progression at all, no narrative thread, no underlying dramatic development. Its large, slow and stately melody, pitched unusually low, seems set to revolve for ever.

What makes it hypnotic instead of dull is the brilliance of its mouth-sculpture. Dylan draws our focus to the mouth with the first line – "With your mercury mouth in the missionary times" – the stretched-out first syllable of "*mer-rr*cury" pursing the lips as if to kiss. In his sleevenote to *Highway 61 Revisited*, he had written, "the songs on this specific record are not so much songs as exercises in tonal breath control": from that point of view, SAD-EYED LADY is indeed a culmination.

The first six months of 1966 were probably the speediest of his life, during which Dylan recorded *Blonde on Blonde* in the gaps between his American concerts, then embarked on a species of rock world tour that had only just been created, baiting and dividing audiences wherever he went, filling his spare time with a fractured novel, *Tarantula*, and an equally fractured documentary film, *Eat the Document*, and fuelling the whole schedule on a diet of hazardous chemicals. In true Einsteinian fashion, the nearer he approached the speed of light, the more that time, in his songs, appears to come to a standstill.

# · 4 ·

# Scald Like Molten Lead

As he came round from his accident, he seems to have reflected on the life he had left behind as a form of madness. In the refrain of THIS WHEEL'S ON FIRE, he alludes to King Lear, awaking from his dementia on the blasted heath to see the face of Cordelia:

> You do me wrong to take me out o' the grave.
> Thou art a soul in bliss, but I am bound
> Upon a wheel of fire, that mine own tears
> Do scald like molten lead.

And the echo of this speech, and of Lear and Cordelia, recurs in TEARS OF RAGE:

> Oh what dear daughter 'neath the sun
> Would treat a father so,
> To wait upon him hand and foot
> Yet always tell him 'No'?
> Tears of rage, tears of grief…

Whether it was the vanity of the earlier life, or the close brush with oblivion that had brought it to an end, the post-crash songs of the Basement Tapes are full of the idea of naught: NOTHING WAS DELIVERED, TOO MUCH OF NOTHING, YOU AIN'T GOIN' NOWHERE, I'M NOT THERE.

The most peculiar evocation of madness and the void is CLOTHES LINE SAGA, which on its first level is a parody of Bobbie Gentry's 'Ode to Billy Joe'. Taking the same form – an everyday family scene sown with hints of some terrible secret

– it empties out the portents and offers instead a completely mundane mundanity:

> After a while we took in the clothes.
> Nobody said very much.
> Just some old wild shirts and a couple pairs of pants
> Which nobody really wanted to touch.
> Mama came in and picked up a book
> And Papa asked her what it was...

It was *Bound for Glory*.

Perhaps it was because Dylan was living a small-town life such as he had not known since he was a boy, and such as Guthrie evokes so strongly in the childhood chapters of his autobiography. And perhaps because Woody Guthrie himself had begun his final decline, and would die on 3rd October 1967. About that time, Dylan released a demo disc of four-teen of the Basement Tapes songs through his music publish-er – songs in which his mentor's spritely, quizzical voice and his comic spirit are resurgent. However the passage came back – whether he remembered it, or reread the crucial book in trying to piece together what had happened to him – the connection is clear.

Woody is with his mother in the yard of their new home, which is being fumigated. In her mind, the smoking house triggers a memory of the oldest child, his sister, who burnt to death when her dress caught fire, and this precipitates her into her final madness. As the child realises that his mother is reverting to her mania, "I was popping out with smoky sweat," he writes, "and my eyes saw hopes piled like silky pictures on celluloid film curling away into some kind of a fiery hole that turns everything into nothing." At the end of this chapter, 'A Fast-Running Train Whistles Down', after she has tried to burn down the house, Woody's older broth-er reveals her fate:

"She's on the westbound passenger train." Roy slid down on the floor beside me and fumbled with a burner on the wreck of a stove. "On her way to the insane asylum."

Nobody said very much.

Away off somewhere we heard a long gone howl of a fast-running train whistling down.

Oddly, the opening sentence of the same chapter, broken into lines, might easily be a verse from the Basement Tapes:

> I was standing up in the truck
> With my feet on our old sofa,
> Waving my hands in the air,
> When we hit the city limits of Okemah.

It's a shame that the original acetate LP of the Basement Tapes, which founded the underground and supposedly parasitic subculture of bootlegging within the music industry, has never been reissued officially. Of the various contenders for the title of The Great Lost Dylan Album, this is easily the champion: a masterpiece entire to equal those either side of it, *Blonde on Blonde* and *John Wesley Harding*. The double LP version released in 1975 – a forerunner of the current rock-historical box-set, with previously unheard rarities, etc – sadly distorts the shape of the original, and I suppose now it will have to wait until copyrights expire for a future editor to recreate it.

The three-in-a-row – *Blonde on Blonde*, the Basement Tapes, *John Wesley Harding* – are a bolder hat-trick even than the famous trio *Back Home*, *Highway 61*, *Blonde on Blonde*, because they vary so widely from each other, and each is so complete of its kind.

The Basement Tapes pick up on the mouth-music of their predecessor, taking it further into the realm of pure association and patterns of arbitrary word-sound. There's an analogy to this in Henry Miller's 'Dream of Mobile', in the coda quoted from above, where he passes from rhyming images into soundscape:

> Events transpire in all declensions at once; they are never conjugated. What is not Gog is Magog – and at nine *punkt* Gabriel always blows his horn. But is it music? Who cares? The duck is plucked, the air is moist, the tide's out and the goat's securely tethered. The wind is from the bay, the oysters are from the muck. Nothing is too exciting to drown the pluck-pluck of the mandolins. The slugs move from slat to slat; their little hearts beat fast, their brains fill with swill. By evening it's all moonlight on the bay. The lions are still affably baffled and whatever snorts, spits, fumes and hisses is properly snaffled. *C'est la mort du carrousel, la mort douce des choux-bruxelles.*

Where Dylan and the Band's collaborations of 1967 break from *Blonde on Blonde* is in their openness of feeling. It is this that marks them as the beginning of a new cycle. The riddling songs of '66 had used language to feint and fence around emotion, whereas the enigmas of these '67 songs seem to spring from emotion overflowing and outstripping the normal forms of articulation. Hence a song like I'M NOT THERE, with its haunting vocal hovering at the border of speech, now on the near side, now on the far.

Among the words there are, though, we find such passionate terms as "grief" and "rage", "shame" and "anger", "joy" and "despair", and it is in this respect that the Basement Tapes make way for *John Wesley Harding*. On that LP, there is a vocabulary of morality and sentiment none of which could have been heard on *Blonde on Blonde* without a twist of sarcasm: "shame" and "joy" and "anger" again, and "honest" and "foolish", "good" and "bad", "true" and "falsely", "please" and "sorry", "sad" and "glad"; "guilt", "misery", "mercy" and "relief"; "evil" and "wicked", "weakness" and "jealousies", "hates" and "fears", "regret" and "worry", "trust" and "pity"; "panicked", "trembled", "suffered" and "cried"; "understand", "in love" and "true love".

## · 5 ·

# Standing Where
# It Ought Not

The sense that some things "needed straightening out" that Dylan spoke of at the time; repentance and deliverance, judgement and forbearance: these define the emotional tenor of *John Wesley Harding*. The characteristic movement of the record is from the closed to the open. The condensed stories that these ten songs tell are every bit as enigmatic as the Basement Tapes, though their language is simple and pellucid. What is clear is that many of them are about states of bondage and subsequent release; that while imagery of the law abounds – trial, imprisonment, execution, crimes and contracts – the common closing note is one of relenting or letting go:

> And while everybody knelt to pray
> The drifter did escape.

> I put my fingers against the glass
> And bowed my head and cried.

> 'I'm sorry, sir,' he said to me,
> 'I'm sorry for what she's done.'

Even the doom that gathers at the end of the miniature apocalypse ALL ALONG THE WATCHTOWER is the foreshadowing of liberation. It echoes these verses from Isaiah, 21:8-10, where the catastrophe of the fall of Babylon means the end of the captivity of Israel:

And he cried, A lion: My lord, I stand continually upon the watchtower in the daytime, and I am set in my ward whole nights: And, behold, here cometh a chariot of men, with a couple of horsemen. And he answered and said, Babylon is fallen, is fallen...

The transition from closed to open – or the journey to freedom, put more simply – is enacted over the course of the whole record by the gradual change of tense. Side 1 is couched entirely in the past tense. The period is never clearly defined, but from the Old West evocation of the front cover photograph and the opening song, and the fact that Tom Paine is still alive in the second song, we know that it is an earlier, frontier America. The latest technologies to be mentioned are "the telegraph" and a "steamboat whistle".

Side 2 begins with three songs in the present tense, DEAR LANDLORD, I AM A LONESOME HOBO and I PITY THE POOR IMMIGRANT, each of which ends with a conditional future:

> ...if you don't underestimate me
> I won't underestimate you.

> ... hold your judgment for yourself
> Lest you wind up on this road.

> I pity the poor immigrant
> When his gladness comes to pass.

The fourth song, THE WICKED MESSENGER, returns to the past tense and in effect summarises the judgment of the whole record, as we shall see. This also ends with a prescription for the future: "If ye cannot bring good news then don't bring any."

The album closes with two simple love songs, quite different in tone from the rest. DOWN ALONG THE COVE moves from past – "I spied my true love coming my way" – to present – "We walk together hand in hand"; and then the last song moves from the present to a confidently predicted future – "I'll be your baby tonight."

In keeping with the progression of tenses, there is a sense in which the sequence of songs is also chronological, a loose re-enactment of Bob Dylan's course from 1961 to 1966. The parallel is approximate, and is closest at the beginning and end. I don't find a precise point-to-point mapping, such as would make each song correspond to a given moment in time. Still the sequence can be read reasonably closely as revisiting Dylan's career up to that point.

It begins with the creation of the western wanderer persona, parodied in the hollow paean of the title song. John Wesley Hardin was one of the least heroic or appealing of the outlaws of the Wild West. In an 'autobiography' which appeared posthumously – after he had been shot in the back of the head while sitting at the card table – he claimed a total of thirty-seven killings, though he didn't include Mexicans in his count. By adjusting the spelling with a final 'g', Dylan signals that the hero of his song need not bear any resemblance to his historical near-namesake; and perhaps also makes a comic restitution for all those dropped 'g's of the past – a-changin', blowin', talkin' and so on – by adding one where none was required.

The satiric nature of the tale is revealed in the word "known" at the end of each verse:

> But he was never known
> To hurt an honest man.
>
> For he was always known
> To lend a helping hand.
>
> He was never known
> To make a foolish move.

He was chivalrous, charitable and wise, it would seem. But the emphasis falls by repetition on the "known", and this is reinforced by other references to what was said about the hero: "all across the telegraph / His name it did resound" and "It was down in Chaynee County, / A time they talk about". The ballad is less concerned with Harding's doings than with his reputation and how it was noised abroad.

When it comes to heroic actions, the song sidesteps: "… he took his stand / And soon the situation there / Was all but straightened out". What he may have done remains unclear, and there's something suspiciously evasive in that "all but". And other holes start to show when you look more closely. That "he was never known to hurt an honest man", for example, puts his victims in a double-bind: if he only hurt the dishonest, any claim they make to have been wrongfully injured is therefore a lie. Likewise, "he was always known / To lend a helping hand": but we are supposed to help without being known to do it, to perform acts of charity without even letting the left hand know what the right hand is doing.

The image of our hero taking his stand "with his lady by his side" in a 'chainy' county evokes the images of Joan Baez and Bob Dylan together on Civil Rights platforms, which lends bitterness to that "all but straightened out". I am reminded of the "dark does die" argument of RESTLESS FAREWELL: oh well, this problem's almost fixed, so I'll be moving along. The charge that Dylan lays against this wanderer is that he was more concerned with the fame of his good works (if they were such) than with their effectiveness.

The second song, AS I WENT OUT ONE MORNING, tells the story of the helping hand and the chains from a different angle:

> I spied the fairest damsel
> Who ever did walk in chains.
> I offered her my hand,
> She took me by the arm.
> I knew that very instant
> She meant to do me harm.

In this scenario, our hero is ensnared, we may say, by Liberty herself: an image of him finding his muse in bondage to good causes. The title phrase, one of the favourite opening lines of English folk song, shows that we are still in the earliest period of Dylan's writing. (Just as the first song, which has quite a close parallel in Woody Guthrie's outlaw ballad 'Pretty Boy Floyd', shows us the Woody interpreter and not-yet-singer-songwriter who first emerged as Bob Dylan.)

The third song reflects on the prophetic role that he then adopted, and contrasts it with that of the true prophet who is willing to be martyred:

> I dreamed I saw St Augustine,
> Alive with fiery breath,
> And I dreamed I was among the ones
> Who put him out to death.

The last line is not quite so strong as 'put him to death': it connotes rejection more than violence. To put someone out is to eject them, and his subsequent death may not have been a direct act. It also suggests the putting out of his "fiery breath" – the refusal of his message.

Neither of the famous pair of Saints Augustine was martyred, but both were men whose breath was breathed into Dylan's nostrils. One, Augustine of Hippo, provided a cornerstone of western Christian theology, while the second, the evangelist of the English, was, symbolically at least, begetter of the King James Bible, which has been one of the deepest sources of Dylan's poetry. When, at the end of the song, he puts his fingers "against the glass" and cries, we might think of the glass through which St Paul says we see God "darkly". In other words, it is the separation of God and man and of man from man which, in resisting the pentecostal fire of Augustine, he has accepted instead.

In the short story that Dylan wrote for the sleevenote (the most satisfying and coherent of his small corpus of prose works), the character Frank is described as "the key" to this record, and when the three kings ask him to open it up for them, "just far enough so's we can say that we've been there", the last act of the bizarre performance he gives as an exegesis is to take a deep breath, moan, and punch "his fist through the plate glass window". Part of the key to these songs, then, seems to lie in getting beyond that barrier – whether mirror or window we cannot tell – against which he cries in I DREAMED I SAW ST AUGUSTINE.

With the fourth song, ALL ALONG THE WATCHTOWER, we move from the prophet to the prophecy. This micro-vision corresponds to Dylan's intensifying apocalypses of the mid-Sixties, here rendered with a degree of irony, in that the joker complains to the thief about people taking things from him, and the thief complains to the joker about people not taking things seriously.

I wonder if Frankie the gambler in the fifth song, THE BALLAD OF FRANKIE LEE AND JUDAS PRIEST, is the same as

Frank the key. It suggests itself as a central statement simply by virtue of its size – eleven verses, when the rest of the songs are only three. It seems to tell the story of Dylan's 'selling-out', when he leapt at his chance of rock'n'roll stardom. In the end "Frankie Lee, the gambler, whose father's deceased", stands transfixed at the sight of a house which his friend Judas Priest has told him is Paradise :

> …that big house as bright as any sun
> With four-and-twenty-windows
> And a woman's face in every one.

The sun may remind us of the label on those records that were the first that Dylan heard of Elvis, his model of stardom. It surely recalls too the HOUSE OF THE RISING SUN – the New Orleans bordello immortalised in a song which he sang on his first record. When he found his arrangement of it transformed into a rock'n'roll hit by the Animals in 1964, it inspired him to attempt the transition himself, in his twenty-fourth year.

Frankie Lee, magnetised by this apparition of power and glory, plunges in and is destroyed by it. Dylan escaped that fate, and as the dreamer of this dream we may say he is transformed in the end into "the little neighbour boy" who carries Frankie to rest. Little boys are not very numerous in Dylan's lyrics and it's intriguing that this one, like "Little Boy Lost" in VISIONS OF JOHANNA, should also be "muttering":

> And he just walked along alone
> With his guilt so well concealed,
> And muttered underneath his breath,
> 'Nothing is revealed.'

That could mean there has been no revelation, or it could mean that there has been a revelation of nothingness, like the void or the vanity (literally, emptiness) that Dylan awoke to in the Basement Tapes songs.

If this little boy is anything like the one in the earlier song, he may prove to be the *doppelgänger* of another character, just as Little Boy Lost turned out to be closely related to "me". That he has guilt to conceal implies that he might actually be Judas, who engineered Frankie's destruction. At the time it would not have been so obvious, but now, for anyone who's heard that famous concert, "Judas" instantly evokes Dylan on the rock'n'roll heights. The metamorphosis of Judas Priest into a little boy, if that were indeed him, is reminiscent of Melville's Confidence-Man in one of his more uncanny changes of persona. That he may be – or may also be – a reincarnation of Frankie the gambler is suggested by the earlier mention of his father, who is "deceased". Little Boy Lost in Blake's poem, you may remember, was calling after a father who is not there.

This is not quite the end of the song, for there is an odd, platitudinous moral tacked on the end, which we shall come back to look at later, in the light of THE WICKED MESSENGER.

The last song on Side 1, DRIFTER'S ESCAPE, can also be linked to the period of Dylan's 'selling out' and specifically to the strange experiences of those first electric concerts in late '65 and early '66, which are here converted into a Kafkaesque trial-by-entertainment where "the jury cried for more". The "bolt of lightning" that "struck the courthouse out of shape" is a good image of what Dylan's use of electricity did in concert. It's also, of course, a good image of the sudden blow that enabled that worldwide drifter to escape.

I should say again that the gist of these songs is not an encrypted autobiography, but that they establish by fleeting and oblique reference a dialogue with the events that led up to them, as one level of their meaning.

In reviewing his former life, Dylan has also revived, in a

more ghostly form, the mirror-image structure that we saw in his early albums:

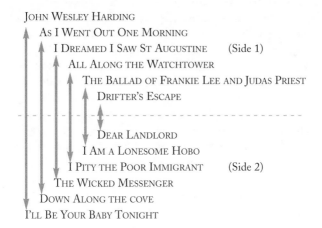

JOHN WESLEY HARDING
 AS I WENT OUT ONE MORNING
  I DREAMED I SAW ST AUGUSTINE       (Side 1)
   ALL ALONG THE WATCHTOWER
    THE BALLAD OF FRANKIE LEE AND JUDAS PRIEST
     DRIFTER'S ESCAPE

      DEAR LANDLORD
     I AM A LONESOME HOBO
    I PITY THE POOR IMMIGRANT       (Side 2)
   THE WICKED MESSENGER
  DOWN ALONG THE COVE
 I'LL BE YOUR BABY TONIGHT

In the middle, DRIFTER'S ESCAPE and DEAR LANDLORD are linked by the law – "Dear Landlord, / Please don't dismiss my case" – and both open with a plea:

> 'Oh help me in my weakness,'
> I heard the drifter say…

> Dear Landlord,
> Please don't put a price on my soul.

I AM A LONESOME HOBO and the BALLAD both end on the same word – "road" – while WATCHTOWER and I PITY THE POOR IMMIGRANT both concern the "final end" of an iniquitous regime, Babylon in one and in the other a town built "with blood".

More substantial than these threads between the individual songs is the balancing of the group of three 'I' songs at the beginning of Side 2 against the three dialogue songs at the end of the first side, each with its central pair of speakers – joker and thief, gambler and priest, drifter and judge – which suggests that those pairs may all be translatable into aspects of 'I'.

The wicked messenger is the counterpart to the holy messenger, St Augustine. Both, it turns out, are itinerants, the saint "with a blanket underneath his arm" and the messenger making his bed "behind the assembly hall". (In fact, most of the men on this record are of no fixed abode – the outlaw who "travelled with a gun in every hand", the drifter, the gambler, the hobo, the immigrant, the insecure tenant.) Our messenger, for all his supposed wickedness, seems a harmless and even rather pathetic character, ill-equipped for his task, which he performs with a combination of puzzling gestures and written notes. His master is "Eli", who may be God. This is the name that Jesus, quoting the 22nd Psalm, calls on from the cross: "Eli, eli, lama sabachthani? that is to say, My God, my God, why hast thou forsaken me?" It is also, however, the name of a man: the high priest who appears at the beginning of the first book of Samuel. This is worth looking at in detail.

Samuel, like a number of the heroes of the Old Testament, is the child of a woman, Hannah, who had hitherto been barren. She prays for a son at the tabernacle in Shiloh and Eli adds his prayer to hers, so that when the boy is born she brings him to the priest to be his servant.

Here is one possible analogue for our messenger, then. But Samuel is not wicked; he is a true prophet, who is chosen by God to take over the priesthood from the sons of Eli, Hophni and Phinehas. These last, who 'come from' Eli in one sense at least, are indeed wicked – "sons of Belial", it is said. Their great sin is to appropriate holy things for themselves: "Also before they burnt the fat, the priest's servant came, and said to the man that sacrificed, Give flesh to roast for the priest…" For this simony, the blessing is taken away from the house of Eli and Samuel is appointed by the Lord in their stead.

Still a child, he hears a voice calling his name as he lies in bed, and rushes to Eli's side, thinking it is him. This happens three times, until Eli advises Samuel to speak back to the voice, and on the fourth time of asking, God tells Samuel that he will destroy Eli's sons. Next day, understandably, the child doesn't want to tell his mentor God's word, but the old man insists on hearing and, when he does, bows to the divine will.

Two aspects of this story reflect on the present song. "When questioned who had sent for him / He answered with his thumb / For his tongue it could not speak but only flatter." This is curious: a messenger is sent; he is not normally sent *for*. Samuel is, however. He thinks he has been "sent for" by Eli the man, though actually it is the other Eli who is calling him.

It remains ambiguous whether Dylan's character is the anti-Samuel: that thumb could point either down or up. For that matter, it could be the gesture of a hitch-hiker, meaning: no-one sent for me, I just happened along. In at least one respect, though, we can see that he is the opposite of Samuel: if that child could not at first speak the truth to Eli, it was because he *would not* flatter.

One further link between the song and the book of Samuel should be explained. When his mother brings him to the tabernacle for the first time, she speaks a great psalm of praise, proclaiming the belief which would be so central to Jesus's faith: that the high shall be brought down and the low exalted, the proud humbled and the downtrodden raised up. What makes this psalm so fitting at this point, at the moment at which Samuel is "lent to God", is that he will grow up to anoint the first king of Israel, Saul, who – in a replay of the story of Samuel and Eli and his sons – will be succeeded not by his natural heir but by his young protégé, David, the Psalmist.

Among the lines of Hannah's magnificent poem (the equal of David's later ones), are these:

He will keep the feet of his saints, and the wicked shall be silent, in darkness; for by strength shall no man prevail.

Our wicked messenger, who is silent, appears one day "with a note in his hand that read, / 'The souls of my feet, I swear they're burning.'" Here is the strongest indication that he is not of the saints, like his counterpart on the other side, Augustine, but is indeed an anti-Samuel.

Unlike Frankie Lee, however, or Augustine for that matter, the messenger is not destroyed, but redeemed:

> Oh the leaves began to falling
> And the seas began to part
> And the people who confronted him were many,
> And he was told with these few words
> Which opened up his heart,
> 'If ye cannot bring good news, then don't bring any.'

This is the crux of what "needed straightening out" on *John Wesley Harding*: that Dylan had sought to prevail as a prophet "by strength".

The opening lines of the verse allude to the passage in Revelation which is the source of the title – *Eat the Document* – that Dylan gave to the film of his 1966 world tour, when he was confronted by the many. The verses in question (10:8-11) concern the same angel that we saw in the first chapter, in connection with A HARD RAIN'S A-GONNA FALL, "clothed with a cloud: and a rainbow was upon his head, and his face was as it were the sun, and his feet as pillars of fire: and he had in his hand a little book open: and he set his right foot upon the sea, and his left foot on the earth, and cried with a loud voice"; the angel who proclaims "that there should be time no longer". The Revelator goes on:

And the voice which I heard from heaven spake unto me again, and said, Go and take the little book which is open in the hand of the angel which standeth upon the sea, and upon the earth. And I went unto the angel, and said unto him, Give me the little book. And he said unto me, Take it, and eat it up; and it shall make thy belly bitter, but it shall be in thy mouth sweet as honey. And I took the little book out of the angel's hand, and ate it up; and it was in my mouth sweet as honey: and as soon as I had eaten it, my belly was bitter. And he said unto me, Thou must prophesy again before many peoples, and nations, and tongues, and kings.

It's not too hard to see, from the songs themselves, what was sweet as honey to the artist at first taste turning his insides bitter. Call it fame and fortune if you will: the achievement he had dreamed, yearned and laboured for since boyhood. I think it was something bigger. The glow that hangs around the folk-rock turning point, the thrill that abides in those songs, is not due to them being hits or making him a star. It's the excitement of discovery – of a young man opening hitherto-unsuspected possibilities, both in himself and the form he works in, having believed constantly, however unlikely it might have seemed to those around him, that it was his destiny to do so.

His realisation on *John Wesley Harding* is that he mistook the attainment of this personal summit for the possession of God's final secret – the little book that reveals the last things. The correction he applies to himself is quite severe. By one interpretation, since "good news" is the translation of the Greek word 'gospel', the wisdom that opens the messenger's heart is that the only true mission is the preaching of God's word.

However, there is another reverse image from the book of Samuel to consider here. A ragged messenger somewhat like our itinerant, with torn clothes and dirt on his head, runs to

Eli to tell him just about the worst news he possibly can: that the Philistines have captured the ark of the covenant and killed his sons; on hearing which intelligence, Eli keels over and dies.

These fatal bad tidings that fulfil God's word remind us that the righteous messenger need not always bring good news. The final scene of THE WICKED MESSENGER, then, may not present Dylan's own verdict, after the fact, on his mission – or not only that. It might depict the rejection he faced at the time, the calls for him to bring back the good news of protest – of faith in The People and progress. One could hardly accuse Dylan in performance in 1966 of not opening up his heart, and opposition to the dark and brilliant newness of his electric music seems only to have energised him further. The harmonisation of the two divergent readings might be that Dylan allows the Judas-shouters had a point, but not the point they thought they had.

His error had been to take the apocalyptic strain of the gospel – the warning of impending catastrophe and the vanity of worldly things – and to neglect the good news of the kingdom, which causes Jesus, in St Luke's Gospel, to conclude his teaching on the end of the world with the saying: "And when these things begin to come to pass, then look up, and lift up your heads; for your redemption draweth nigh."

The resulting brew of self-importance and knowledge-as-power is exactly how Jesus characterises the false prophets of the end times, starting the Lucan version of his apocalypse: "Take heed that ye be not deceived: for many shall come in my name, saying, I am Christ; and the time draweth near…" (There is a paradox in this teaching: the false prophets saying the end is nigh are the first sign that the end *is* nigh.)

In Dylan's defence, he behaved more in keeping with Zechariah's description of the true prophet: "And it shall come to pass in that day, that the prophets shall be ashamed every one of his vision, when he hath prophesied; neither shall they wear a rough garment to deceive: But he shall say, I am no prophet…" (More paradox: the truth-teller falsely denies that he is one.)

In a rather devastating sixtieth birthday salute published in the magazine *Uncut*, Ian MacDonald suggested that the positive purpose behind the negative assault of the '66 tour was, as Henry Miller defined the function of the artist, "to inoculate the world with disillusionment". It is well to remember, however, that to inoculate is not the same as to infect: the idea, if we take Miller at his word, is not to *make* people disillusioned but to *prevent them* from becoming disillusioned. Dylan's songs portrayed a world where meaning and understanding are hard to come by; it does not necessarily follow that he hoped to persuade his audience that their lives were meaningless or incomprehensible. And this was not the effect his music had.

The revolution of the Sixties, whose rumblings we still try to decipher, was fuelled by a belief that much of what society held to be of value was empty or pernicious. Its lasting significance has been the supposedly naive quest for new understanding, new relation and new social forms. Aided by the over-signifying effects of various drugs, many people felt that Dylan himself had already arrived in this "Furthur" world and was beckoning them into it, albeit with enigmatic gestures. The darkening subject-matter of his songs showed the light in silhouette, as it were: not the kingdom but the kingdom's suffering in the world. Hence the solidarity-in-isolation that he makes the keynote of *Blonde on Blonde* with the opening song, RAINY DAY WOMEN #12 & 35 (reprising the major terms of his previous hit, stone, feel and alone):

> They'll stone ya when you're tryin' to be so good,
> They'll stone ya just a-like they said they would…
> But I would not feel so all alone:
> Everybody must get stoned.

Stoning in the Old Testament is particularly the punish-
ment of the infidel: those of Israel who worship idols or
preach other gods (a Jewish Christian would be subject to this
death according to Deuteronomy); a rebellious son, especially
one who is a drunkard (Dylan carefully rendered the whole
band drunk when they cut this track); an adulterous wife
(hence the hers-indoors of the title, presumably); wizards or
those with familiar spirits. It's on the last grounds that the
people of Nazareth try to stone Jesus. There is only one actual incident of stoning to death reported in the Bible, which is
the killing of St Stephen, the first Christian martyr. Stoning
is thus a sign of fidelity, too.


The most telling sign of *John Wesley Harding*'s maturity is
that it aims to redeem rather than to repudiate, as the
earlier Dylan would have done. As a critique of the first dou-
ble-cycle of his work, it lends those seven records completeness. By showing us where they lack, it makes them more
appreciable than if they stood alone.

Equally, *John Wesley Harding* is important for the door it
opens into the future. It became commonplace to use Dylan's
early work as a stick with which to beat his later, but I think
we would value it less if it led nowhere. Whatever his misgivings about the course he had taken, *John Wesley Harding*
attests his belief in his gift, by summong all the artistic
resources he had acquired in the previous seven years.

Nothing shows better the sanity and moderation of this
work (it's almost impossible to recapture now how eccentric,
at the time, this sanity and moderation were) than the quiet
tone in which its most damning judgment is delivered. THE
BALLAD OF FRANKIE LEE AND JUDAS PRIEST has a moral:

> The moral of this story,
> The moral of this song,

Is simply that one should never be
Where one does not belong.
So if you see your neighbour carrying something,
Help him with his load,
And don't go mistaking Paradise
For that home across the road.

That first judgment, mild as it sounds, has a terrible resonance. It echoes the words of Jesus, in St Mark's Gospel,
describing the final sign of the end: "But when ye shall see
the abomination of desolation, spoken of by Daniel the
prophet, standing where it ought not, (let him that readeth
understand,) then let them that be in Judaea flee into the
mountains…" This abomination is usually understood to
mean a person who sets himself up to be worshipped in the
place of God: one standing where the One belongs.
Revelation elaborates the vision, identifying the abomination with "the image of the beast" who is served by a false
prophet.

To end this discussion of prophets, true and false, let me
quote a story rather like the one we have been unravelling. It
was told by someone who was close to Dylan both immediately before and immediately after his crash. Robbie
Robertson's song 'Daniel and the Sacred Harp', which the
Band recorded for their third album, *Stage Fright*, suggests its
reference to their former employer both in the similarity of
names and in the choice of instrument: Dylan's mouth-harp
remains, somehow, the very essence of his presence, and still
receives the loudest cheers at his performances. In 1970, when
the song was cut, Dylan was the country clown of *New
Morning*, perhaps the only period in which we might picture
him dancing through the clover:

Daniel, Daniel and the sacred harp,
Dancing through the clover.
Daniel, Daniel, would you mind
If I looked it over?

I heard of this famous harp years ago,
Back in my home town,
But I sure never thought ol' Daniel'd be the one
To come and bring it around.
Tell me, Daniel, how's the harp?
It came into your possession:
Are you one of the chosen few
Who will march in the procession?
And Daniel said:

'This sacred harp was handed down
From father on to son
And me not being related
I could never be the one.
So I saved up all my silver
And took it to a man
Who said he could deliver the harp
Straight into my hand.

'Three years I waited patiently
Till he returned with the harp from the sea of Galilee
He said, There is one more thing I must ask
But not of personal greed.
But I wouldn't listen, I just grabbed the harp
And said, Take what you may need.'

Now Daniel looked quite satisfied
And the harp it seemed to glow
But the price that Daniel had really paid
He did not even know.

Back to his brother he took his troubled mind
And he said, 'Dear brother, I'm in a bind.'
But the brother would not hear his tale.
He said, 'Ol' Daniel's gonna land in jail.'
So to his father Daniel did run
And he said, 'Oh father, what have I done?'
His father said, 'Son, you've given in.
You know you won your harp but you lost in sin.'

Then Daniel took the harp and went high on a hill
And he blew across the meadow like a whippoorwill.
He played out his heart just the time to pass
But as he looked to the ground he noticed
No shadow did he cast.

Daniel, Daniel and the sacred harp
Dancing through the clover.
Daniel, Daniel, would you mind
If I look it over?

## · 6 ·

# A Key To Your Door

Jo*hn Wesley Harding*, as a replay of Dylan's story up to that point, ends with a pair of love songs that correspond to *Blonde on Blonde*, the richer palette of that record reflected in a slightly augmented instrumentation. While some air had been let into the mix at the beginning of Side 2, with Dylan's switch from guitar to piano for DEAR LANDLORD, still his spritely pianism on DOWN ALONG THE COVE, and the introduction of Pete Drake on pedal steel for this and I'LL BE YOUR BABY TONIGHT seem positively luxurious after the austerity of the rest. The appearance of a middle eight in the last number also reflects the writing on *Blonde on Blonde*, where this quintessential pop-song device was prevalent for the first time. Such is the record's economy of means that these lightest of touches have an effect as distinct as though a sepia print were suddenly flooded with full colour.

Looking back to the first side, the correspondence of tracks appears in the repeated phrase "I spied" in DOWN ALONG THE COVE and AS I WENT OUT ONE MORNING. In that second track on Side 1,

> I spied the fairest damsel
> Who ever did walk in chains.
> I offered her my hand,
> She took me by the arm.

And in this penultimate track on Side 2 (where the sea again coincides with the moment of fulfilment):

> Down along the cove, I spied my true love comin' my way
> I said, 'Lord have mercy, mama, it sure is good to see you
> comin' today.'

The contrast of the two encounters is clear when the hand appears again in the last verse: "Down along the cove, we walk together hand in hand."

The directness of speech, the simplicity and reciprocity of feeling, and the buoyant voice are the antithesis of *Blonde on Blonde* in a nutshell.

Likewise the closeness and emotional resolution of I'LL BE YOUR BABY TONIGHT finally put paid to the alienation and anxiety of the love-songs of '66. The depth which plain words can attain in Dylan's writing, by their place in a larger drama, can be seen in the deliberately corny lyric of the middle eight:

> That mockingbird's gonna sail away,
> We're gonna forget it.

The disappearing bird can't help but remind us of the master of mockery that Dylan had so recently been and who now, after he has done his straightening out, can be forgotten.

In the tradition of opposites, the 'I' of I'LL BE YOUR BABY TONIGHT is a plain contrary to John Wesley Harding – the one stopping still and letting his guard down while the other is at all times on the move and on the defensive; one closing while the other opens a door.

This last pair of contraries is surprising, given what was said earlier about the general movement of the record from closed to open. The first verse of JOHN WESLEY HARDING says:

> All along this countryside
> He opened many a door

while the last song begins:

> Close your eyes, close the door.
> You don't have to worry any more.
> I'll be your baby tonight.

The odd order of that advice – you would surely shut the door and then shut your eyes – suggests that this door is inside the head. Similarly, the hero opening doors – not in itself a particularly heroic action – alerts us to the relation between him and the hero who sings about him. Dylan's heroic status had a great deal to do with opening doors: the doors of perception, to quote a phrase.

He had used the metaphor in 1964, in 'Some Other Kinds of Songs', the poems published on the sleeve of *Another Side*, and presumably acquired it from Aldous Huxley's essay on psychedelics, *The Doors of Perception*. The poem can be read as a remarkably prescient history-before-the-fact of the psychedelic movement:

> first of all two people get
> together an' they want their doors
> enlarged. second of all, more
> people see what's happenin' an'
> come t' help with the door
> enlargement. the ones that arrive
> however have nothin' more than
> 'let's get these doors enlarged'
> t' say t' the ones who were
> there in the first place. it follows then that
> the whole thing revolves around
> nothing but this door enlargement idea.
> third of all, there's a group now existin'
> an' the only thing that keeps them friends
> is that they all want the doors enlarged.
> obviously, the doors're then enlarged
> fourth of all,

after this enlargement
the group has t' find
something else t' keep
them together or
else the door enlargement
will prove t' be
embarrassing

In asking for the door to be closed, and in turning from the hip vocabulary of his mind-expanding rock to the old-fashioned codes of country music, was Dylan, as some felt at the time, aligning himself with the consciousness-contractors?

Yes, the contrast of the closed and open door signals a change of heart, as had the oppositional endings of *The Times They Are A-Changin'* or *Another Side*; but it is not an antagonistic contrast. After all, a door should of its nature be sometimes open, sometimes closed. And if we look back to the source of Huxley's title, in an aphorism of William Blake's, we see that his call was neither for opening nor enlarging but for cleansing: "If the doors of perception were cleansed every thing would appear to man as it is, infinite." This purgation is *John Wesley Harding*'s main concern.

## · 7 ·

# By Golly, What
# More Can I Say?

W hat follows is intriguing. The clearest common trait of those records that the chart on page 194 assigns to autumn is duality. On the surface, *Nashville Skyline* shows none of the dialectical wrangling of *The Times They Are A-Changin'* or the ironic doublespeak of *Blonde on Blonde*. Yet it has a 'second mind' beneath its seeming straightforwardness. It aims to withdraw and advance at the same time, to be absent and present.

The desire for absence is expressed in a strange reluctance to begin. Dylan's albums before had always kicked off with a bang. This opens with a hesitant duet with Johnny Cash on GIRL OF THE NORTH COUNTRY, a six-year-old song that was almost archaic by the standards of the day, with the changes that had intervened. Next up is an instrumental, and then at last the first new words on the new album from the electric poet of rock.

TO BE ALONE WITH YOU, one of the slightest songs of a fairly insubstantial collection, embraces just about everything Dylan as a songwriter was supposed to be the antidote to. The lyric rhymes "your charms" with "in your arms"; it wants "To hold each other tight / The whole night through" because "They say that nighttime is the right time / To be with the one you love". The tune is not very distinguished, either.

The track begins with the famous line "Is it rollin', Bob?" – which is presumably the singer asking the producer, Bob Johnston, if the tape's running. (According to the first Dylanologist, A.J. Weberman – if my memory serves me well – it's somebody asking Dylan if the heroin which he's just injected into his vein is beginning to work. [Frank Zappa skewered the two scenarios together neatly with a line in 'Flakes', his yet-to-be-bettered Dylan parody: "Wanna buy some mandies, Bob?" {That's Mandrax, a popular tranquilliser.}]) Anyway, by this stage the answer really is, well, no, it's not.

If you look at the lyric of TO BE ALONE WITH YOU on paper, his new poetry of syllables rather than words can be heard as you read. It's something he'd shown in I'LL BE YOUR BABY TONIGHT, where the refrain has no direct rhymes, but the verses chime with different bits of it: "eyes... door... I'll be your"; and "light... shade... afraid... baby tonight"; and "bring that bottle... be your baby". So here we have "alone... won't... hold... whole... alone" and other nice assonances. But the take doesn't have the poise and space or the tight focus on the voice that could carry the song off purely as syllabic dancing.

Then he hauls off and hits you with the sucker punch. I THREW IT ALL AWAY is perhaps the most perfect pop song he's made. The glimpses beforehand hardly prepare you for the snake-smooth new voice that uncoils here; a gliding, knowing voice that has learnt from the sophisticated hillbillies the art of precise, unexpected nuance.

One quick throwaway more, PEGGY DAY, and the first side is over. It's parsimonious as many a Nashville LP has been, but as Dylan never had before. More particularly, it reminds me of later Elvis product, with diamonds scattered sparingly, if not among dung, at least among beads of clay and plastic.

To say it's deliberately lightweight might be misleading: it would imply a handful of earth-shaking songs that he somehow held to his chest while he laid down these, pulling out the occasional high trump to keep us guessing. He does do just enough, however, to win the trick. The second side has only two big numbers, at beginning and end, but they are both absolute beauties – LAY LADY LAY and TONIGHT I'LL BE STAYING HERE WITH YOU. In between are three more featherweights, but each perfectly formed.

If the record takes a long time to get going, it may be because it doesn't have anywhere in particular to go. It ends exactly where *John Wesley Harding* ended – TONIGHT I'LL BE STAYING HERE WITH YOU rewriting the same scene as I'LL BE YOUR BABY TONIGHT. This was something new. Before, Dylan had always been pushing on; his records didn't end in the same place that they started, let alone in the same place as their predecessors. One explanation is straightforward. The artist had hit a bare patch, he'd lost it – 'it' being drive, purpose, or anything particular to say. But obviously he still had some motive to make records, unless it was just force of habit, greed or contractual obligation.

*Nashville Skyline* served to distance Dylan from his own reputation, and that appears quite deliberate. The well-established production of country music in Nashville was a milieu in which he could be, or pretend to be, 'just another' player; where the writer and singer practised as craftsperson first and foremost. Here was a role in which he might honour his commitment to music and yet escape the mountingly hysterical overtones that surrounded the rock star as prophet, phenomenon or freak. A buried but stubborn purpose underlies this strangely evasive period: to persist as a music-maker while trying to liberate his gift from the distorting grip of its fame. He could have withdrawn into silence, but that would only have intensified the fascination; so on *Nashville Skyline* he said next to nothing – a minimal sufficiency, carefully lowering expectations while stopping short of total disappointment.

Evidently that was not enough, and so his next step was to confound utterly, and to un-be all that he was supposed to be, with *Self Portrait*, on which in 1970 a double helping of too much of nothing was delivered.

Country in the late Sixties was an antidote to the confrontational militancy abroad in the counterculture and in rock music – for which, of course, Dylan himself was a prime inspiration. While would-be revolutionaries took a name, the Weathermen, from one of his songs, he crooned to the barricades and tear-gas:

> Love is all there is,
> It makes the world go round,
> Love and only love, it can't be denied.
> No matter what you think about it,
> You won't be able to do without it.
> Take a tip from one who's tried.

Country, politically speaking, was the enemy of the underground: opposed to the use of drugs, supportive of the war in Vietnam, and so on. In that the radicalism of the late Sixties was originally fired by the non-violent direct action of the Civil Rights campaigns, country as music of the white southerner also represented a hereditary foe. It was still produced almost exclusively by white artists (whereas one of the greatest 'black music' groups of the day, Booker T and the MGs, was evenly integrated, with two black and two white members). Where it made direct contact with politics, it was generally on the Right. I don't say this is how country was entirely – there were black artists like Charley Pride and non-conservatives like Johnny Cash, while singers like Merle Haggard and Loretta Lynn knew and sang more about the much-discussed working class than any rock revolutionaries. Nevertheless, that was how it was perceived from the furthur side.

Bewilderment at Dylan aligning himself with the Establishment caused A.J. Weberman to speculate – if I remember his theory right – that our hero had been brought into bondage to  corporate Amerika, probably through drug addiction, and was being held in some deadly pact, unwillingly or willingly (the sell-out again, already), from which the Dylan Liberation Front was supposed to spring him. Dylan was surprisingly gracious and accommodating to Weberman and his theories and the parties of liberators-cum-sightseers who were brought to hang around the star's home in New York – perhaps appreciating that this Dylanologist's interpretation at least had a suitably imaginative wildness. (Eventually Dylan snapped and knocked Weberman to the ground. Still, by the measure of a Mark Chapman, Dylan obsessives have proved a relatively benign tribe of the mad.)

The sense of tradition in country music must have had a strong appeal for Dylan: not the 'heritage' of folk but a creative continuity running through a thoroughly modern branch of the music business. (Hence the visual joke of the record sleeve, where the Nashville skyline is shown to be, not rural greens and blues, but a smoggy panorama of tower blocks.) Country songwriting also offered a form where the circumstances of his life – marriage, home, children – were prime themes. As it turned out, he didn't get into the domestic drama or 'You-know-the-other-day-my-little-girl-came-home-from-school' school of composition, and by the time he made a record about someone with a home and a past and a family, which was *New Morning*, country was only one ingredient of the musical mix.

However, for all its stability, contemporary country was not static. From one side, the 'countrypolitan' or 'Nashville sound' that developed in the second half of the Sixties – particularly the brilliant productions of Billy Sherrill – was bringing it closer to pop and soul. From the other side, there was a distinct reaction in the rock avant-garde in the late Sixties against the candied or over-sauced sounds of psychedelia. The Stones' *Beggars Banquet* in 1968 epitomised the rootsier style: plenty of steely blues guitar, plenty of woody acoustic too, and some overt, though parodic, Country & Western.

While the heaviositising of the blues continued apace –

and the years around the turn of the decade were the heyday of heavy blues, what with Cream, Free, Led Zeppelin, Ten Years After, Fleetwood Mac, Canned Heat and so on – there was also a new emphasis on the other side of the equation: blues + country = rock'n'roll. In this respect, the country field when Dylan entered it was similar to the folk revival. It stood outside the mainstream, yet it would soon affect it profoundly. In fact, the country-rock amalgam, in which Dylan was, again, a prime mover, would not only prove a distinguished genre in its own right – in the work of the later Byrds and Gram Parsons and his protégé Emmylou Harris and so on – but it would come to *be* the mainstream. For out of it hatched the Eagles, whose *Greatest Hits 1971-1975* was the best-selling album of the twentieth century, shifting twenty-six million units to date.

· 8 ·

# Builder of Rainbows

Acombination of oddness, wilfulness and wobble makes *Self Portrait* the definitive fourth-stage or 'winter' record. Which makes of *New Morning*, as I said before, something of an anomaly. There's plenty of the rough and ready energy of a spring record, but there are also summer-like tracks that are perfectly poised and complete, and stand on their own in Dylan's work, like IF DOGS RUN FREE, THREE ANGELS and WENT TO SEE THE GYPSY. Then there's the autumnal doubt of SIGN ON THE WINDOW, undermining the domestic content which prevails elsewhere. The record's single moment of strongest feeling is a statement that sounds more like a plea:

> Have a bunch of kids who call me Pa:
> *That must be what it's all about.*

There's even a dash of that oh-come-on-now-you-can-not-be-seriousness that is a sign of winter:

> Winterlude, Winterlude, my little apple,
> Winterlude by the corn in the field,
> Winterlude, let's go down to the chapel
> Then come back and cook up a meal.

The last line of this song is surely the pinnacle of cheese in Dylan's writing: "Winterlude, this dude thinks you're grand." The verses of la-la-las in THE MAN IN ME also have that unique kind of grace that your uncle Bill, full of bubbly, demonstrates when dancing to the wedding reception disco.


I f it weren't for the three-year gap, *New Morning* wouldn't be hard to place as the direct precursor to *Planet Waves*. The ebullient, loose-limbed rock of ONE MORE WEEKEND and NEW MORNING re-emerges in things like TOUGH MAMA and YOU ANGEL YOU (though the later melodies are stronger). Lyrically, the outdoor imagery persists as well, and particularly the memories of a rural youth. This integration of his real past, by then well known, into the 'I' of 'Bob Dylan' lends an air of frankness and of trust to *Planet Waves* especially which has made it a niche in the hearts of many fans.

*New Morning* does not have this frankness. The rough-edged, open-throated voice, and the forthright sentiments of songs like IF NOT FOR YOU may convey simplicity and lack of guile, but the puzzling nature of others hangs a question-mark over their straightforward-seeming. WENT TO SEE THE GYPSY, for example, if it is an anecdote of a private encounter with Elvis Presley, as seems plausible on internal evidence, folds away its meaning under the guise of a non-event:

> He smiled when he saw me comin'
> An' he said, 'Well, well, well.'

We are left to surmise whether the gypsy is quoting a favourite vocal kick-off:

> Well, that's alright now mama…     ('That's Alright, Mama)
>
> Well, I don't care if the sun don't shine…
>                         ('I Don't Care If the Sun Don't Shine')
>
> We-ell, I heard the news…     ('Good Rockin' Tonight')
>
> Oh well, I woke up this mornin'
> An' I looked out my door…     ('Milkcow Blues Boogie')
>
> Well, since my baby left me…     ('Heartbreak Hotel')
>
> Well, it's a one for the money…     ('Blue Suede Shoes')
>
> Well, bless-a my soul…          ('All Shook Up')

And at the end, when

> The gypsy's door was open wide
> But the gypsy was gone,
> And that pretty dancing girl,
> She could not be found,
> So I watched that sun come rising
> From that little Minnesota town,
> From that little Minnesota town.

we have to put together for ourselves the reference back to the open door as a metaphor for expanded consciousness. And to the Fifties' hipster slang use of 'gone' (who could be more solid gone than Elvis?) – roughly equivalent to the Sixties' 'far out'.

(Though Dylan gives us a nudge this way in ONE MORE WEEKEND: "You're the sweetest gone mama that this boy's ever gonna get".) And to the Sun label of Elvis's early singles, the first of which, 'That's Alright, Mama', is echoed in the repeated thats: "that… girl", "that sun", "that… town". From which mesh of hints we sense how that 'son' may have felt and reflected upon meeting his musical progenitor.

The effect is not of insincerity but of caution and reticence. As he sings himself, "The man in me will hide sometimes to keep from being seen" – which is a pretty unrevealing, because tautological, explanation of why you are hiding. Overall, in the oblique plainness of the lyrics, I don't hear intellect transcended in Zen-like directness, but rather a complex man playing the part of a simple one.

This is nowhere truer than in the last song, FATHER OF NIGHT. It's couched in an inconsistent biblical idiom where the verbs keep getting conjugated wrongly, the subject slipping between 'thou', 'he' and 'they'. He taketh, thou takest, but Dylan sings "Father who taketh the darkness away", and even "who *build* the mountain so high". It is the voice of the plain, untutored man a little awkward in his Sabbath best, and also reflects (as the serious student of the Bible would well know, who plays this plain man) the indeterminacy of the Creator in Genesis, where he is sometimes plural, sometimes singular.

Among the other solecisms, the grammatical quirk of the last line is easily passed over: "Father of whom we most solemnly praise." It should be just 'Father whom' – unless it is saying, in condensed form, "Father of [him] whom we most solemnly praise", that is to say, Father of the Son.

At the time it was reported that Dylan had been studying the faith of his fathers among the Hasidim in New York, and this song has even been cited to evince his reborn Judaism. But Father is not a Jewish appellation of God, and it is not even a common simile. There are two references to God being like a father in the Psalms: "A father of the fatherless, and a judge of the widows, is God in his holy habitation", and "Like as a father pitieth his children, so the Lord pitieth them that fear him." There may possibly be one in Malachi, the latest book of the Old Testament – "Have we not all one father? hath not one God created us?" – but that could as well refer to the Jews as children of Abraham.

It may be that calling God by the colloquial name Abba, equivalent to Dad, was not Jesus's personal innovation; yet there is no evidence of it anywhere else, and as far as all sub-sequent generations are concerned it is he who teaches us to call God our father.

At the end of THREE ANGELS, the musical poem *cum* Christmas song which precedes FATHER OF NIGHT, he asks about the model angels with their horns,

> Does anyone hear the music they play?
> Does anyone even try?

A paradox, since only a crazy person would try to hear the music made by figurines. (It's apt that this song about silent music should have no tune.) But what is the music that we should *imagine* they are playing? It is a fanfare for the birth of the Messiah.

The end of *New Morning* – as perhaps befits its nature as four seasons in one day, a whole cycle condensed into one record – points a bit further than usual, beyond the next cycle to the one after that, and Dylan's startling embrace of Christianity. Yet in their reticent way, the last two pieces on this record are perfectly clear confessions of Christ – which, like the angels' music, no-one seems to have heard.

# · 9 ·

# The Gone World

D ylan is not naturally a poet of the everyday and his country or family-man period is often regarded as an unfortunate blip. A blip it has certainly proved to be in the long view of his work, where he has been over-whelmingly a poet of endings, and of new beginnings. The country period did contribute something vital to his art, however, which is the natural imagery that refreshes *Planet Waves* and opens up and enriches the intimate matter of *Blood on the Tracks*.

Like the one urban image of *New Morning*, the rainy Main Street of SIGN ON THE WINDOW, the city only appears once on *Planet Waves*, and as a place of sorrow:

> I went out on Lower Broadway and I felt that place within,
> That hollow place where martyrs weep and angels play
> with sin.

Just from that, one can see how he had left behind the lacon-ic style and was starting to let his imagination freewheel. The image may be a bit 'painted' but it's instantly recognisable, and he is making the words spin against each other again. The "hollow" picks up the "Lower", so that the "place" is both within and on the street itself, and the "martyrs", "angels" and "sin" awake from "Lower Broadway" an echo of Jesus's metaphor of the broad road that goes down to hell.

Apart from that, *Planet Waves* is all about the country. Not, however, the picture-book idyll of *New Morning*, but real open places, any of which could be in the Minnesota hills of Dylan's boyhood. "Back to the Starting Point!" as he says in his charming scrawly sleevenote. (Perhaps charming is not the adjective for phrases like "Furious gals with garters & smeared lips on bar-stools that stank from sweating pussy". Lively, anyway.)

Before, nature had represented innocence; here it is highly eroticised: "Today on the countryside it was a-hotter than a crotch." Half of the songs are to women, none of whom seems to be a wife, but any of whom could be the spirit of those hills. There is something more than erotic promise about them, though. They are bringing Dylan once again to the edge, an end and beginning:

> Meet me at the border late tonight…
>
> You're going somewhere and so am I…
>
> My hand's on the sabre and you've picked up the baton…

The last quote suggests that they're about to march together – which is interesting given the lines in WEDDING SONG at the end of the record:

> It's never been my duty to remake the world at large
> Nor is it my intention to sound a battle charge.

The words seem to have migrated between the two lines. 'It's never been my intention' is the common construction, while "duty" goes with the military vocabulary below. By *avoiding* saying "intention" above, and by the shift of tenses, he leaves another sense hanging: although it's never been his duty [before], nor is it [now] his intention to do it by violence, yet it is his intention to remake the world. What else can an artist do, after all?

In his sleevenote, Dylan casts "a backward glance o'er travelled roads" and depicts the Sixties as they were in the Fifties, when he first discovered them. He calls it "the gone world" – the beginnings of that outsider community that would mushroom so spectacularly and almost as suddenly collapse, leaving Dylan here – and other songwriters of the early Seventies like Joni Mitchell on *Blue* or Jackson Browne on his early albums – pondering what had happened to it and them.

> Space guys off duty with big dicks & ducktails all wired up & voting for Eisenhower, waving flags & jumping off of fire engines, getting killed on motorcycles whatever – we sensed each other beneath the mask, pitched a tent in the street & joined the traveling circus, love at first sight! History became a lie! the sideshow took over – what a sight… the threshold of the Modern Bomb, …

(The threshold of the modern bomb I suppose was Bikini Atoll, the first hydrogen bomb test in 1954. Eisenhower was president from 1953 to 1961.)

It's intriguing that the Rolling Thunder Revue of 1976, culminating the creative resurgence launched with *Planet Waves*, and described by Dylan as rekindling the fire of the Sixties, should fit so precisely the imagery of the underground here – "we sensed each other beneath the mask" and so on. This was the resolve of his sleevenote, which circles back around to "Duluth! Duluth – where Baudelaire lived", in other words "Back to the Starting Point!", implying that now may be another one, another chance for the sideshow to take over.

The sensation of being on the verge of Something Big is pinpointed in GOING, GOING, GONE:

> I've been hangin' on threads,
> I've been playin' it straight,
> Now I've just got to cut loose
> Before it gets late,
> So I'm going,
> I'm going,
> I'm gone.

(Maybe cutting loose is another use for that "sabre" in SOMETHING THERE IS ABOUT YOU?)

Special mention must be made here of the playing of the Band, of which GOING, GOING, GONE is perhaps the most exquisite example. There are many great group performances scattered across Dylan's albums – tracks where, as Paul Williams puts it, the voice seems to be playing the music as well as singing; where every musician becomes an accompanist to the voice. This is the rationale of his preferred method of recording: to catch the songs early, before the musicians get too familiar, so that they have to focus on him instead of playing among themselves to a form they already know. On *Planet Waves*, though, Dylan is a member of the Band rather than the band being members of Dylan. It's a perfect marriage of material and method – it might not have worked with songs that were more lyrically elaborate – and the result is the best collective performance of all his records.

Shortly afterwards, Dylan and the Band turned this newly rekindled collectivity into a national event, with a US tour that attracted twelve million requests, reportedly, for about six hundred thousand tickets. The event was commemorated on the first of Dylan's live albums, *Before the Flood*.

# · 10 ·

# Iron Gates Of Life

There are now eight live collections, counting the recent snappily titled *Live 1961–2000: 39 Years of Great Performances*. They're a motley bunch. Two of them, *Real Live* (1984) and *Dylan and the Dead* (1988) are mostly in the thanks-but-really-you-shouldn't-have-bothered category, though I'm happy to have the three acoustic songs on *Real Live*, IT AIN'T ME, BABE, with Dylan huffing and puffing his harmonica until he finally blows some life into Wembley Stadium, a touching GIRL OF THE NORTH COUNTRY, and the recast TANGLED UP IN BLUE.

The new verses don't lock into the refrain with the satisfying snick of the old ones, but I think that's the point. The added lines are like a set of notes that has overwritten the original text, or like a subtext that has emerged on the surface. They depend for their effect on the audience knowing the words that aren't there, whose memory moves under the new ones. The un-neat cuts back to the refrain reinforce the ghost-presence of the original, better-fitted lyric:

> And when it all came crashing down
> I was already south.
> I didn't know if the world was flat or round,
> I had the worst taste in my mouth
> That I ever knew,
> Tangled up in blue.

There is no apparent connection between the "taste" and the tangling, apart perhaps from the thought that, as Peter Astor's song has it, 'No Food Is Blue'.

*At Budokan* (1978) is an odd album, a fulsome document of a completely uncharacteristic bit of Dylan's career, as the leader of a big ol' band, performing tightly arranged versions of his greatest hits. In fact that seems to have worked spectacularly well later on, when the same band came to Europe. Part of the problem with the album may just be that it caught the show too early in its run.

The four remaining live records are all good; their rankings will vary according to taste. The oldest set, *Live 1966*, released in 1998, is most valuable for its acoustic half, which is astonishing and hypnotic. The much-vaunted electric half, perhaps because it's so much vaunted, I'm not so drawn to. However fascinating, historic, exciting and brilliantly played the set is, it's not something I want to re-enact in the living room on a weekly basis. Invite your friends around, maybe: make it a party. Have half of them booing and half of them cheering your stereo.

To my mind the raw and ragged proto-punk, or metal-and-western-with-a-Jackson-Pollock-paint-job of *Hard Rain* (1976) is every bit as good as the Band recordings of '66 and a good deal more varied in tone. I'm with Paul Williams on this one – a neglected masterpiece. I feel the same about *Unplugged* (1995), which I've seen described as lacklustre and which I think may be the best all-round live release so far. If it hadn't been made under the auspices of MTV and hadn't been officially released, this recording would be legendary.

Which brings me, briefly, to the strange omissions – the official live recordings which languish in the vaults. These include the projected *Bob Dylan in Concert* LP of 1963, bits of which have been released on compilations (*Greatest Hits 2*, *The Bootleg Series 1-3*); the recordings of the first Rolling Thunder Revue, as excerpted in *Renaldo & Clara*, of which there must be enough to fill a CD; the 1986 Australian concert with Tom Petty and the Heartbreakers shown on TV and released on video as *Hard to Handle*, but not available on CD;

and the brilliant Supper Club sets which were filmed and recorded the year before *Unplugged* (I predict an eventual DVD-only release for this one, to entice us into the new format). I imagine there's a great deal more live material stockpiled, to be doled out gradually. Along with many hundreds of hours of unauthorised concert recordings that will take even longer to compile into readily available form, this will eventually make Dylan's legacy ten times the size of what I deal with in this book.

It would be a shame if Sony, after milking Dylan's present prominence and the critical success of his concerts with the *39 Years* miscellany, couldn't put out a proper document of the current and brilliant touring band. For the time being, to make good this omission, I recommend you apply for membership of the Unofficial Bob Dylan Free Tape Library (www.freelib.org) of Claremont, California, which provides an excellent service through the singlehanded dedication of Simon Campbell-Main. For the price of blank cassettes and two-way postage you can take your pick from a near-definitive collection of the bootleg material.

I can recommend Towson, Maryland, 19th November 2000, a whole show available in a high-quality audience recording. For some of the concert, two talkative young women near to the microphone give a disheartening demonstration of how modern listeners – encouraged by modern amplification, of course, and by the omnipresence of recorded music in public places – have forgotten that it's destructive to talk while music is actually being played, both for people who want to hear, and in smaller places for the musicians themselves; that silence is the canvas on which music is painted. Would you scribble on an artist's blank sheet before they started work on a painting you'd commissioned? Compare and contrast with the rapt attention which surrounds the acoustic set of *Live 1966*, and which enables Dylan to produce these extraordinary performances.

Anyway, this tape is the equal of any of the live albums, and it doesn't appear to be an exceptional show. I selected it because the librarian gave it a good write-up, but mainly because it was the most recent performance in the library. I trust that this vintage season of the Never-Ending Tour is being officially archived, to be enjoyed in the vast box-sets of the future, which will take more than a lifetime to listen to. (Despite Dylan's cavilling and the alternative tour-titles he proposes in the *World Gone Wrong* sleevenotes, the Never-Ending Tour seems to be how this decade-and-more of continual performing will go down in history.)

The title that Dylan (I assume) chose for his first live album, *Before the Flood*, shows that his millennial nerve reawoke about this time, though the idea that a rock'n'roll tour might be something more than just a business proposition is hard to recapture now. And of course Dylan and the Band in 1974 was a very large business. In fact, *Planet Waves* marks the beginning of Dylan's period of greatest commercial success. Between 1974 and 1976 he released three studio collections, *Planet Waves*, *Blood on the Tracks* and *Desire*, each successively America's No. 1 album; two live sets; and the retrospective *Basement Tapes* double. Apart from the last, these records all went gold (half a million copies sold, half that for double sets) within a year of release. *Desire* went gold before it was released, on the strength of advance orders, and went platinum (a million copies sold) a few weeks after it came out – far and away the most immediately popular of his records, and one of the four most popular altogether, along with *Blood on the Tracks* and the first two volumes of *Greatest Hits*. These are his only albums to date to sell more than two million (multi-platinum).

This run of success continued to the end of the decade, up to and including *Slow Train Coming*, which also sold a million within a year of release. After 1980, Dylan's popularity waned dramatically. Neither *Saved* (1980) nor *Shot of Love* (1981) has yet sold half a million; nor have *Empire Burlesque*, *Knocked Out Loaded*, *Down in the Groove*, *Oh Mercy*, *Under the Red Sky*, *Good As I Been to You* or *World Gone Wrong*. Apart from com-pilations, only *Infidels* in this period earned a gold record. (Mind you, *Another Side* didn't go gold for thirty-five years.) *Time Out of Mind* in 1997 finally reversed his fortunes, again going gold within a few weeks and platinum within a year of its release.

As I was saying before I digressed into statistics, Dylan's missionary zeal seems to have been rekindled when he undertook his US tour with the Band in 1974 (which makes it all the more ironic that the record that seems to have bro-ken his hotline to his audience, *Saved*, should be the one where missionary zeal emerged most nakedly).

To recall the era when rock musicians, as well as wanting to sell lots of records, felt that the music itself could still change things, read the booklet with the CD reissue of *Who's Next*, where Pete Townshend writes the history of his grand Lifehouse project: "I was selling a simple credo: whatever happens in the future, rock and roll will save the world." He described his goal at the time as "a piece of music which will enable each person present to get a better understanding of the fundamentals of their own personality"; and as "the finest music that rock is capable of", as "something that will come from everyone". This would be ridiculous were it not for the power of the stuff on the little silver disc.

Another example that happens to be to hand is the CD reissue of Janis Joplin's *Pearl*, with added live tracks, which reminds you how much of a preacher she was, trying to ignite and liberate and educate her audience, sexually and romanti-cally. These were the last and highest gasps of the Sixties. But the same millennial fervour, now turned ironic, underlies David Bowie's early LPs, which seem to be set in a narrowly impending science-fiction future, oscillating all the time between a number of well-established scenarios – grim collapse, scientific brave new world, technocratic totalitarianism, cosmic catastrophe, benign extraterrestrial salvation.

The imaginative world of glam-rock generally was a peculiar time-warp: a strain of Fifties revivalism cross-bred with space-age stylings to produce a nostalgic futurism, re-enacting the shape of things to come as seen in vintage pulp fiction and cult movies. The music was all in inverted commas – it didn't purport to change the world, but it belonged to a world already changed, that had become alien (yet somehow comfortingly so).

Although punk, according to the accepted history, revitalised rock, it proved to be a last hurrah for the belief that the music would save, or at any rate change the world. Perhaps for that reason, the overall quality of popular song, to my mind, declined drastically in the years immediately following the arrival of the 'New Wave'. Take your pick of the twenty best popular music LPs from 1977 to '83, and match it against a similar list chosen from the seven years from 1970 to '76: I think the latter will be the better by an extensive piece of calcium carbonate.

The millennial spirit of *Before the Flood* is in the nature of a revival – a reminder of something that was already widely regarded as over. Perhaps, as history would prove, it was already understood as a farewell to it. (Certainly the next time Dylan took the stage with the Band, on Thanksgiving Day 1977 for *The Last Waltz*, the collective valediction was being spelled out.)

The title may be a quote from Jesus, describing his Second Coming: "For as in the days that were before the flood they were eating and drinking, marrying and giving in marriage, and knew not until the flood came and took them all away; so shall also the coming of the Son of man be." Thus Dylan presents himself both as conscious of the advent of the kingdom, by his choice of title, and as unconscious of it, since the grand celebration of the tour is exactly the kind of unwitting festivity that Jesus describes.

The front cover picture of the crowd with lighters aloft – a rock'n'roll tradition which apparently began with this tour – reminds us also of the "waters" as representative of the mass of people, and the extraordinary tidal surge of feeling that greets the final songs on the LP, LIKE A ROLLING STONE and BLOWIN' IN THE WIND, shows another sense in which Dylan found himself standing before the flood.

The title could also be a quote, though, from Andrew Marvell, which would soon prove prophetic, with the breakdown of the Dylans' ten-year marriage, hastened by this tour, and subsequent events:

> I would
> Love you ten years before the Flood,
> And you should, if you please, refuse
> Till the conversion of the Jews.

Certainly the music itself is best described in the conclusion of this poem, 'To His Coy Mistress':

> Let us roll all our strength and all
> Our sweetness up into one ball,
> And tear our pleasures with rough strife
> Through the iron gates of life.

## · 11 ·

# I Do It For You

**B**lood on the Tracks is widely regarded as Dylan's single greatest work, and its greatness is often ascribed to the depth of personal anguish that provoked it. This is not what makes it a masterpiece, though. As Dylan sings in NOT DARK YET, on *Time Out of Mind*:

> Behind every beautiful thing there's been some kind of pain.
> She wrote me a letter and she wrote it so kind.
> She put down in writing what she had in her mind.

– which is a good example of the 'wandering mind' in these recent songs. The clearest channel linking the first to the second line of the quote is that one *depends on* the next, that the "letter" is the cause of the pain that lies behind the "beautiful thing", this work of art. But the two statements are also balanced *against* each other by contrast: the letter is an open declaration of "what she had in her mind"; whereas the pain is "behind" the art. In other words, the lines point out that art is *not* a letter, whose virtue is to be as straightforward an expression as possible, and that, in effect, beauty is a *concealment* of pain.

*Blood on the Tracks* is beautiful not because we can feel the suffering of the artist when he made it but because of what his suffering – and his joy – caused him to do. He brought together in song, at a moment when the course of his life was again in question, all the aspects of the art he had devoted most of that life to. By gathering in one place the virtues he had accumulated, the songs affirm a purpose to his course which the fracturing of his marriage cast in the shadow of failure. What we get is actually the obverse of his distress, which is why it can thrill and delight us, whereas the feelings aroused by estrangement and divorce would surely mortify us. Dylan's saying that he couldn't understand the popularity of *Blood on the Tracks*, "people relating to that kind of pain", shows that the record for him evokes too strongly his life at the time he made it. We don't have those associations, and what painful associations of loss or bewilderment or betrayal we identify in the songs are sublimated by them into beauty. The appeal of the art, in short, is not our attraction to affliction but to healing.

The lyrics of *Blood on the Tracks* draw on every style he had ever used: the plangent simplicity of folk and blues; symbolist tableaux and moments of surrealist pantomime; rapid-flowing narrative; recalcitrant invective; and moving through it all the feeling for the elements and the open air that came with his country records. In emotional range it's matched only by *Freewheelin'*: it doesn't extend to slapstick comedy, but it embraces bitterness and tenderness, rage and regret, stoic acceptance, exultant rebellion, adoration and contempt.

Part of the beauty of the record for me is that it is one half of a joint masterpiece. Bob commented not long afterwards that Joni Mitchell's song 'Blue' had been on his mind when he was writing *Blood on the Tracks*. Her album *Blue*, made in 1971, is likewise a sequence of bare-hearted songs about love, of friends, family and lovers; of rueful reminiscence and an embattled idealism, set to a stripped-back and atmospheric form of mountain music, with only the slightest touches of contemporary rock sound. Together the two, though separated by four years, make a profound elegy for the optimistic spirit of the Sixties, sinking in a mire of death, drugs, brutality and cynicism.

It's interesting that Joni – who wrote the theme song for the decade's grand finale, 'Woodstock' – should have reflected on this so soon. Jackson Browne too in the early Seventies sang as a seeker who had set foot on the Love Generation's rainbow bridge and found himself lost. He perfected his farewell to an era in 1974, with the sombre and lucid *Late for the Sky* (two of whose songs, 'Fountain of Sorrow' and 'Before the Deluge', Dylan alludes to in his sleevenote for *Desire*: "Meeting the queen angel in the reeds of Babylon and then to the fountain of sorrow to drift away in the hot mass of the deluge…") Dylan's resurgence of the mid-Seventies was really the last rose of that particular summer – fittingly, since he was also the first to appear of the Sixties' fecund generation of popular musicians.

## · 12 ·

# To Grasp And Let Go
# In A Heavenly Way

His Seventies trilogy ends with *Desire*. Like the other autumnal records we've looked at, *The Times They Are A-Changin'* and *Blonde on Blonde*, it is governed by duality. This is apparent both in the writing – mostly done in collaboration with Jacques Levy, a psychologist and theatre director – and in the singing, mostly harmonised by Emmylou Harris (and on HURRICANE, Ronee Blakely).

The subtler aspects of duality can be traced in the self-division that we see in those earlier records, and even in the seemingly breezy *Nashville Skyline*: an element of exaggeration and of ambivalence; a new self-consciousness in the public persona; a more deliberate artistry and a consequent sense of distance compared with the productions of a spring or summer phase, extending even to an air of elusiveness or riddling.

Perhaps by now we shouldn't be surprised to find Dylan following his most intimate and confessional work with his most theatrical, dominated by cinematically styled fictions and heavily fictionalised reportage. At the time, the contrast disappointed some critics and even awakened a mistrust of the artist's sincerity. While *Desire* is the most glamorous of Dylan's records, with its exotic locations and colourful imagery, its glamour is uneasy and deeply shadowed, with violence and sudden death a recurring motif of the stories. In the circumstances that's understandable: this was the moment of his greatest popular success and, in private, of his deepest trauma. 'Desires' might be the more accurate title, since his life was being carved slowly in two by his conflicting needs for his wife and family and security, and for his art and public and freedom (and the love of other women).

The stardom that he was resuming was of a different nature from the one he had left behind in 1966, however. He was a leader then, seen as being out on his own ahead of the field, yet his music was bound tightly, by threads of mutual influence, within the nexus of contemporaries like the Beatles, the Rolling Stones, the Byrds, Jimi Hendrix and so on. By 1976, there was no wider movement he belonged in, to charge him up with competition or bring in innovations and suggestions of the future. There was a school of singer-songwriters of which he was founder, but by definition that was a collection of isolated voices. Now he was really out on his own, and his artistic choices were sustained only by his own will, without the resonance of community.

*Desire* achieves the challenge with great panache. The music seems to come to us from off a stage, rather than the intimate informal place of *Blood on the Tracks*, and Dylan's singing is more flamboyant and idiosyncratic whereas before it had appeared natural and transparent. The sound is unconventional, if not unique, and the little band that fell into place – Rob Stoner on bass, Howie Wyeth on drums, Scarlet Rivera on violin, Dylan on acoustic guitar or piano, Emmylou Harris singing harmony – shows an inspired lack of choice on the leader's part. If he was navigating by any contemporary reference points, it could have been the gypsy-funk that Van Morrison made with the Caledonia Soul Orchestra on *Veedon Fleece* in 1974 and on the live album *It's Too Late to Stop Now*. The presence of the English funk band Kokomo along with mariachi musicians at the chaotic first session for *Desire*, where dozens of players were called in to get in each other's way, suggests he may have had something like that in mind.

SIS, the first of the Dylan and Levy collaborations to be written, is not unnaturally about a partnership that begins with a chance encounter and becomes a joint venture of an initially mysterious nature. It is also about a man who leaves his wife behind and heads off for the north – the traditional direction of isolation and ordeal – on a "reckless" quest for we know not what. As he rides with his companion through the "devilish cold", he dreams of jewels and "the world's biggest necklace", but the prize turns out to be emptiness and death.

The mythical references are given plenty of room to resonate: "We came to the pyramids all embedded in ice" evokes both the deepest circle of Dante's Hell, where Satan is embedded waist-deep in a frozen lake, and Egypt, where Israel was in bondage. Though drug references are uncommon in his writing, it's hard to avoid the *double entendre* in these lines, after reading the accounts of how much cocaine was around Dylan at this time:

> The wind it was howling and the *snow* was outrageous.
> We *chopped* through the night and we *chopped* through
>                                                   the dawn.
> When he died I was hoping that it wasn't contagious
> But I made up my mind that I had to go on.

What he finds there – "I broke into the tomb but the casket was empty" – clearly evokes the empty tomb of the Resurrection, before which Jesus is said to have descended into and returned from hell, and of which the redemption of Israel from Egypt is regarded as an Old Testament 'type'. With the kind of dark twist which is typical of the religious imagery on *Desire*, the narrator ends up putting a corpse *into* the empty tomb: his dead partner, who had said "There's a body I'm tryin' to find", becomes the body. There's still a redemptive promise behind this imagery however, in that through the resurrected Christ the Christian undergoes the death of the 'old man' and a new birth.

Dylan's theme though is not a unique Incarnation and Resurrection, but the cycle of death and rebirth as an eternal recurrence, of which Isis is the source. "The principal goddess of ancient Egypt," says *Brewer's Dictionary of Phrase and Fable*, "sister and wife of Osiris and mother of Horus, she typified the faithful wife and devoted mother. ... Proclus mentions a statue of her which bore the inscription: 'I am that which is, has been, and shall be. My veil no one has lifted. The fruit I bore was the Sun.' ... She was worshipped as a nature goddess throughout the Roman world and... in due course became an embodiment of the universal goddess." Her brother-husband, Osiris, was the Egyptians' dying-and-reviving god – murdered, dismembered and brought back to life.

The nub of the story is not the quest or its goal but the fact that he will go *and return*. Hence the little back-and-forth pun: "I said, 'Where are we going?' He said, 'We'll be back by the fourth.'" (The song begins, for no reason which I can discern, "I married Isis on the fifth day of May". Returning by the fourth presumably means he will be back in time for "the next time we wed".) In its dream-form, I suppose the song is quite close to Dylan's desire – to establish a cycle whereby he could go out on his quest, however pointless and profitless it might be accounted, and return and "wed" his wife again. And it's sad that the reconciliation didn't come about that he creates so beautifully in the last verse, where the two voices in their stand-offish, desultory exchange, suddenly rush together to speak the last word simultaneously:

> She said, You been gone. I said, That's only natural.
> She said, You gonna stay? I said, If you want me to – *Yes*!

This biographical interpretation, identifying Isis with his wife Sara, is not unreasonable, given that she appears in a picture on the LP's back cover wearing what does indeed appear to be "the world's biggest necklace", which he had hoped to find in the song.

There is, however, another lady on the sleeve who also wears a sizeable necklace and who could also be identified with Isis: the Empress of the Tarot. The card is from the Rider pack, conceived by A.E. Waite, who described the Empress as representing "all that is meant by the visible house of man" – a goddess of nature, in other words. Hers is one of three extraneous images set in the collage of snapshots on the back sleeve. Another is a portrait drawing of Joseph Conrad, whose dark tales set in bright places have a general bearing on the narratives of *Desire*, and whose novel *Victory* is a direct source for one of the songs, BLACK DIAMOND BAY. The third is a photograph of the giant bronze Buddha of Kamakura in Japan.

Buddha and Empress between them represent the duality of the record. There are obvious points of contrast – East and West, male and female – but the focal point of their difference is that title-word. The Empress, according to Waite, symbolises "in some aspects... Desire, and the wings thereof". She stands for the way of fullness and engagement with the world, while the Buddha taught the way of detachment and self-emptying. His Four Noble Truths turn on the idea of desire: 1. that to live is to suffer; 2. that the root of suffering is desire; 3. that the way to escape suffering is to eliminate desire; 4. that Nirvana, or the extinction of passion, is to be obtained by following the Eightfold Path, beginning with right understanding. Buddhism teaches that our physical being, rightly understood, is *maya* – illusion.

The quarrel of *Desire* is not immediately a religious one: the Buddha and the Empress represent issues of detachment and engagement, and of the real and the illusory, which are worked out in the songs in aesthetic terms. Nevertheless the representation of the record's argument in religious symbols points the way in which Dylan would eventually find his res-

olution. He may also have had in mind William Blake's identification of Desire with the Holy Ghost in *The Marriage of
Heaven and Hell*, where Christ "prays to the Father to send the
comforter, or Desire, that Reason may have Ideas to build on".

# · 13 ·

# Here Comes The Story

**D**esire reprieves the double-sequence as found on *The
Times They Are A-Changin'* and elsewhere, but with
the two sides running parallel rather than in
reverse. Each side follows the same course: beginning in the
objective world of public fact with a real-life story, and passing
through a series of fictions to the subjectivity or 'private fact'
of the love songs at the end. The Empress and the Buddha
shed an interesting light on this interplay of fact and fiction.
The former stands for "the visible house of man", the plenitude
and splendour of the material world we engage in, yet she is
herself a figment of imagination; while the Buddha, an actual
person, taught that the world itself is ultimately unreal.

The record begins with the most engaged of Dylan's protest
songs – the only one, in fact, with a concrete political objective,
to secure the release of a man wrongfully imprisoned. None of
those famous songs from his earlier protest period – THE
TIMES THEY ARE A-CHANGIN', THE LONESOME DEATH OF
HATTIE CARROLL, WITH GOD ON OUR SIDE and so on – had
been a call to action. In fact they all quite strongly suggest that
there is nothing to be done. (Though at the end of A HARD
RAIN'S A-GONNA FALL, Dylan does resolve to do something –
which is to sing A HARD RAIN'S A-GONNA FALL.) The arms
trade, rural poverty, racial injustice and violence go on despite

MASTERS OF WAR and BALLAD OF HOLLIS BROWN and ONLY A PAWN IN THEIR GAME, but Rubin 'Hurricane' Carter was eventually acquitted ten years after the song HURRICANE was released as a single, and after twenty years' imprisonment. The first retrial, which Dylan's involvement certainly helped to provoke, reconvicted Carter; a further retrial in 1985 finally saw the convictions quashed.

Dylan and Levy's lyric tells a complex story with consummate skill, concisely and grippingly, and the impetus of the performance is irresistible; after quarter of a century it still sounds urgent. (Whether this account is accurate is another question. The case does not appear to be quite as black and white as either the song or the recent Hollywood film which takes its title and its viewpoint makes out.) Interestingly, in a song whose *raison d'être* is to convince people that it conveys facts, it advertises its fictional quality right from the outset:

> Pistol shots ring out in the bar-room night.
> Enter Patty Valentine from the upper hall.
> She sees a bartender in a pool of blood,
> Cries out 'My God, they've killed them all!'
> Here comes the story of Hurricane…

This so clearly follows cinematic form – a dramatic pre-title sequence, followed by the opening credits – that it immediately alerts us to the artifice of what follows.

The tough-talk – "What kind of shit was about to go down", "The trial was a pig-circus", "The crime was murder one" – may seem to smack of gritty reality, but it gives the story the atmosphere of a particular kind of fiction – the gangster movie. In this version, the gangsters are the cops, and like many of Hollywood's mobsters, before *The Godfather*, they are mean, tough, cunning characters, but somehow, with their bluster, also a bit dimwitted and thick-skulled. Their questioning of a witness is convincingly aggressive, yet there is caricature in the vigour with which they condemn themselves out of their own mouths:

> 'You'll be doin' society a favour.
> That sonofabitch is brave an' gettin' braver.
> We wanna put his ass in stir.
> We wanna pin this triple murder on him.
> He ain't no Gentleman Jim!'

In the end, as at the beginning, the song again reminds us not to take it as pure reportage and to be aware that it is a work of imagination, by pushing beyond the practical into the realm of impossibility. The goal of publicising and raising support for Carter was admirably met, but the demand made in the closing lines could never be achieved:

> Yes that's the story of Hurricane
> But it won't be over till they clear his name
> And give him back the time he's done…

While it doesn't blunt the protest, that final paradox does ask us to think for ourselves and consider, since the time cannot be given back, what would constitute justice. Finally, the song appears more trustworthy and scrupulous for showing clearly its 'unreality' and the degree of artifice that went into it.

It is HURRICANE, the most worldly song on the record, which also contains the only overt reference to Buddha:

> Now all the criminals in their coats and their ties
> Are free to drink Martinis and watch the sunrise
> While Rubin sits like Buddha in a ten-foot cell,
> An innocent man in a living hell.

Whether Rubin is "like Buddha" or simply "sits like" him, in the lotus position, the implication is that he's attained a degree of detachment both from his own "hell" and from the "ties" of the hedonistic "free" life outside. (For me, the word Martini will always evoke the falsely-happy party-people of the vermouth ads I saw on TV as a child, with couples in evening dress drifting about in hot air balloons and the like. I don't know if that's a widespread association.)

From HURRICANE to the next song, ISIS, we're plunged from one extreme to the other, from the pressing concern of the present day into a timeless mythical zone. And yet ISIS is Dylan's most compelling delivery on the record – the deepest fiction somehow truer than fact.

The principle of maximum contrast seems to govern the placing of MOZAMBIQUE as well – the slightest and most trivial-sounding song after the most profound and intense. It takes its cue from the sunny exoticism of some of Paul Simon's early solo work – particularly 'Was a Sunny Day' on *There Goes Rhymin' Simon* (1973), though without that pellucid and detailed sound that makes the lightest of his songs pleasing. Dylan's choice of location must have been influenced by the fact that Mozambique gained independence from Portugal, after a long war, in June 1975; that is presumably "why it's so unique to be / Among the lovely people living free / Upon the beach of sunny Mozambique". It was effectively a beachhead of African self-government, cutting Rhodesia off from the sea. Independent Mozambique provided a base for the forces of the Zimbabwe African National Union who five years later formed the first Zimbabwean government under Robert Mugabe.

MOZAMBIQUE could be called filler, but since the album is only a whisker short of an hour long – about the maximum length for an LP and half as long again as what most artists provided – it hardly needed this little three-minute ditty as a makeweight. Spacer might be a better description. Like the tropical holiday it evokes, it serves as an untaxing moment of relaxation, a bright spell before the short, melancholic songs, ONE MORE CUP OF COFFEE and OH SISTER, that close out the side. If they'd followed straight on from ISIS, it would have made a rather sombre sequence after the energetic curtain-raiser of HURRICANE.

This little song, then, can give us quite a large insight into Dylan's art, and the degree to which his best albums have been composed as such: both after the fact, in the sequencing of the tracks once they have been recorded, and also in the writing, with individual pieces, as I suppose, not simply accreted until there is a sufficient heap, but growing out of and in response to each other.

The sequencing of MOZAMBIQUE shows a painterly touch, like a contrasting dab which changes the tonal balance and brings light into a whole area of a canvas. The afterimage of *Desire* is of something colourful and exotic, yet most of the first side is quite dark. MOZAMBIQUE relieves it with a brief, breezy foretaste of the tropical settings which fill the middle of the second side, and makes their brightness seem more general. Followed by ONE MORE CUP OF COFFEE, it also makes us aware of the album's high contrast; for as well as a work of bright surfaces, it is deeply shadowed. The relentless sunshine of MOZAMBIQUE turns suddenly to obscurity, as the traveller who asks for "one more cup of coffee for the road" sets out under cover of darkness – the most likely reason being that he is a fugitive, like a number of the characters on the second side.

The extreme contrast of the two songs, from festive noon to fearful midnight, reminds me of a scene in ISIS:

> I came to a high place of darkness and light.
> The dividing line ran through the centre of town.

The dreamlike image arises of a town divided down the middle of the main street into dark and bright sides. The "line" of course is more likely a boundary of some kind. I'm reminded of the hill town of Bristol, with the state line running through it, which the dead or dying Hank Williams passed through on his midwinter journey across the mountains.

The progression by opposites continues as we pass from ONE MORE CUP OF COFFEE to OH SISTER, which are speeches of departure and return respectively. But in both there is already more than physical distance between the man and woman:

> But I don't sense affection,
> No gratitude or love.
> Your loyalty is not to me
> But to the stars above.

> Oh sister, when I come to lie in your arms,
> You should not treat me like a stranger.

In ISIS his expedition led to a new wedding; here his coming or going make no difference.

The ending of OH SISTER and of the first side is a striking example of how Dylan composes songs to go together on records, as well as to stand alone, or be reconvened in different sets, in performance. The last verse of Side 1 is a mirror reflection of the last verse of SARA which ends Side 2:

> Oh Sister, when I come to knock on your door,
> *You gave me a map and a key to your door*
> Don't turn away, you'll create sorrow.
> *You always responded when I needed your help*
> Time is an ocean but it ends at the shore,
> *And a piece of an old ship that lies on the shore*
> You may not see me tomorrow.
> *Now the beach is deserted except for some kelp*

# · 14 ·

# King Of The Streets

The second side of *Desire* begins with reportage again – another true-crime story about a heroic free spirit who falls foul of society. (One of my favourite secondhand bookshops, now defunct, used to rack True Crime alongside Poetry, hoping to promote the least visited shelves by proximity to the most popular – or perhaps sensing a basic affinity between a taste for verse and an interest in gangsters and serial killers.) Again the opening lines alert us to the degree of artifice in what follows:

> Born in Red Hook, Brooklyn in the year of who-knows-
> when?
> Opened up his eyes to the tune of an accordi-en…

At which strained rhyme, on cue, an accordian enters.

As HURRICANE forcefully reasserted Dylan's role as denouncing prophet, the public truth-teller and "champion" of social justice, this eleven-minute epic, JOEY, immediately caused misgivings about his trustworthiness. And that appears to have been its purpose. It was soon reported that the song was about a senior mafioso, Joey Gallo, who had been gunned down in a restaurant in New York in 1972. Dylan portrays him as an advocate of non-violence, a student of psychology and philosophy whose closest friendships when he was in prison were with black men. Lester Bangs, for one, averred that this was all rubbish. Why should Dylan glamourise or make a tragic hero of such a man?

In fact JOEY is both an example of outlaw mythology and a critique of it. Even without other information, we're bound to be wary when someone tries to cast the mantle of Robin Hood over the practitioners of modern organised crime. And yet the appetite for romantic outlaws – outlaws as heroes or victims, as the uncorrupted outsiders who remain true to themselves in a dishonest society – persists unfailingly. If the evidence of contemporary professional criminals is anything to go by, the glamour that attaches to the names of Jesse James or Dick Turpin, or for that matter Robin Hood, is most probably misplaced: yet their allure remains.

Dylan had had a stab at the outlaw myth before, in JOHN WESLEY HARDING. In fact, JOEY may be the song he never got round to writing then. As he told Jann Wenner of *Rolling Stone* in 1969, JOHN WESLEY HARDING was going to be "a real long ballad. But in the middle of the second verse I got tired." As we saw, that song also reflects on Dylan's own outlaw legend.

Apart from his sometime taste in stimulants, it seems that Dylan has lived almost entirely inside the law. His habits may be irregular, but in many ways he has been a model citizen, making allowance for normal human failings and highly abnormal personal circumstances: an example of individual initiative, hard work and acumen, financial probity, responsible parenthood and so on. And yet the role of the outlaw still seems to fit him like a (fingerless leather) glove: it fits his elusiveness and now near-perpetual wandering, and it fits from time to time with his relation with his audience, which on more than one occasion has seemed less like a gathering of appreciative listeners and more like a posse banding together to run him out of town. The dubious glorification of JOEY cannot help but reflect on the glory of the singer, then at the height of his popularity.

Like JOHN WESLEY HARDING, as it turns out, the song is marked by a singular lack of evidence for its hero's heroism, and what there is comes apart in our hands as we look at it. The crucial verse in this respect is the second, since it contains the one definitely noble deed ascribed to Joey:

There was talk they killed their rivals but the truth was
                                          far from that.
No-one ever knew for sure where they were really at.
When they tried to strangle Larry, Joey almost hit the roof.
He went out that night to seek revenge thinking he was
                                          bulletproof.
When the war broke out at the break of dawn it emptied
                                          out the streets.
Joey and his brothers suffered terrible defeats,
Till they ventured out behind the lines and took five
                                          prisoners,
Stashed them away in a basement, called them 'amateurs'.
The hostages were trembling when they heard a man
                                          exclaim,
'Let's blow this place to kingdom come, let Con Edison
                                          take the blame.'
But Joey stepped up and he raised his hands, said 'We're not
                                          those kind of men.
'It's peace and quiet that we need to go back to work again.'

Dylan asserts what the truth was not, and then admits that no-one knows what it was. He denies they killed their rivals, and within a few lines Joey is setting out to do just that. That they call their prisoners "amateurs" suggests what kind of "work" it is they're anxious to get back to, in which they regard themselves as professionals. In the last line, the voice squeezes upwards in a mock protestation of innocence – "It's peace and quiet – that we need" – before dropping with menacing finality, "to go back to work again".

Dylan and Levy didn't count on pure misgivings or this kind of analysis to open up the ambivalence of their legendary tale. They chose an outlaw whose life was readily available in another countervailing version. *Joey*, a biography by Donald Goddard, came out a few months before *Desire*, and extracts were published in *Harpers & Queen* magazine. In fact, in his first line, Dylan prods us to check the facts for ourselves: "in the year of who-knows-when" sounds like 'no-one knows', but Gallo's exact age was actually well-publicised. His headline-making murder, in the small hours of 7th April 1972, followed a night spent celebrating his forty-third birthday.

If we compare Goddard's version of events with the second verse of JOEY, it's intriguing to see that the song has inverted just about every pertinent circumstance. Since Dylan heard about Gallo from Jacques Levy who heard about him through what Goddard calls his "latterday showbiz friends", it seems likely that the ultimate source of JOEY's disinformation is the self-mythologising of Joey himself.

According to Goddard's book, Joey and his brothers were indeed professionals – the "elite enforcers" for the Profaci family, New York's reigning mafiosi. Chafing under the tight control and high levies imposed by Joseph Profaci, the old-guard Sicilian Don, the Gallos launched a coup in February 1961. They took four important members of the ruling faction prisoner but failed, fatally, to snatch the Don himself.

> Profaci's obvious countermove now would be to ask the other New York families for help in putting down this mutiny, and no-one knew better than Joey that he would probably get it... He flew back from Florida with every intention of killing one of the hostages and demanding $100,000 in cash from Profaci as an earnest of good faith before sitting down to negotiate. But his brother [Larry] wouldn't hear of it.

Larry let the hostages go as a prelude to peace negotiations that never materialised. Instead Profaci struck back. In August, Larry Gallo was ambushed and garotted almost to death, surviving only through the chance arrival of a policeman. "Now vindicated by the turn of events," writes Goddard, "exhilarated by the prospect of action and bent on revenge, to the exclusion of almost everything else, [Joey] could hardly contain his high spirits."

From that account it seems this Profaci-Gallo feud is also the central action of *The Godfather*, where it is seen from the other side. The ambivalent glamour of Coppola's film is the cinematic reference point for JOEY as the older hard-boiled gangster movies are for HURRICANE. The idea of glamourising this particular story doesn't start there, though. After the failed coup, the Gallos were virtually besieged in their headquarters on President Street, and Goddard writes: "With the sugar-coated worldliness that characterises so much New York journalism, even at its most censorious, the tabloids and television were soon depicting the Gallos as a gallant band of Runyonesque folk heroes returning their enemies' superior firepower with volleys of wisecracks."

This was, remember, 1961, towards the end of the young Bob Dylan's first year in New York, when newspapers were an important source of material for his songs. There perhaps lies the first germ of the song. Goddard's phrase "sugar-coated worldliness" is certainly a fine description of JOEY's flavour. (In its sweetened guise the Gallos' story was also turned into a comedy crime film, *The Gang That Couldn't Shoot Straight*, which came out in 1971: this was how Joey came to have showbiz friends towards the end of his life.)

I don't think the motive for Dylan and Levy's song was to take someone they thought was a real bad guy, a complete parentpoker, and try and convey him as a good guy. It was the ambiguity surrounding Gallo that probably drew Dylan in particular. This character sketch from Goddard's book shows how he might have seen something of himself in the dead gangster:

Possessed of demonic energy, Joey was a man of action… He enjoyed risky enterprises. He loved tumult and conflict and trials of manhood, especially against the odds. Everything

had to be acted out, every idea and fantasy, without constraint… Given the standards most people live by, there was
nothing commendable in this, unless consistency is a virtue
even in wilfulness. Though he possessed many of the qualities that make for success in the 'straight' world – intelligence,
imagination, intuition, charm, determination, drive, concentration and a persuasive tongue – to suppose, as some of his
latter-day showbiz friends have hinted, that there, but for a
quirk of fate, went the Italian John Kennedy is sentimental-
ity. Joey carried the cult of individualism to its ultimate anti-
social degree… The primacy of self was absolute. And yet he
was also capable of great tenderness and compassion.

The idea that JOEY depicts a kind of shadow-self is lent
credence by some lines on Dylan's next record, *Street-Legal* –
the beginning of the last verse of the last song, WHERE ARE
YOU TONIGHT?:

> I fought with my twin,
> That enemy within,
> Till both of us fell by the way.

*The Enemy Within* was the title of Senator Robert Kennedy's
book on the Mafia, and it was Kennedy, as Attorney General,
who dubbed Joey Gallo "Public Enemy No. 1". According to
Goddard, when Gallo was shot in Umberto's Clam Bar in
New York, he should have died instantly of the bullet-
wounds. But he summoned a last burst of strength and stag-
gered out of the restaurant into the street where he "fell by the
way", dying in the gutter between two parked cars.

# · 15 ·

# Serpent  Eyes

Dylan's self-image on *Street-Legal* is not far removed from Goddard's summary of Gallo: wilful, demonic and self-centred fits the character of the record quite well. It's powerful but with a strength that shades into brutality. Images of conflict and betrayal abound. The 'I' here is cynical about the prospects of love, callused on his heart, determined, ruthless even. Under the hard carapace, the true ground-note is one of weariness and disgust.

This was a descent into the belly of the Old Adam, the natural unredeemed man, from which Dylan emerged a convert; an infernal experience leading to the divine. "This weekend in hell," he sings, "is making me sweat." The "weekend", with its associations of leisure and choice, suggests he deliberately entered this realm, for artistic purposes. It also recalls Christ's time in hell, from the Friday night of his entombment to the Sunday morning of his resurrection. Somewhere in the back of the mind of *Street-Legal* there moves this assurance of release.

Dylan has said that his conversion experience was as much of a surprise to him as it was to everyone else. But he had been referring to Christ for some time – on and off, of course, since his first record, but with notable frequency on *Blood on the Tracks*: "a lone soldier on the cross", "my crown of thorns", "they gamble for my clothes". Identifying himself with Jesus like this shows typical audacity, but it doesn't strike me as fundamentally sacreligious. Rather than proclaiming 'I am Christ', it seems to pose the question: 'How Christ-like am I?'

It's striking that the next image of Jesus should be found

imprinted faintly over the ending of JOEY. Juxtaposing and to some extent fusing an ideal and a shadow-self shows his question gaining in weight and intensity, if still buried.

> Sister Jacqueline and Carmella and mother Mary all did
> weep.
> I heard his best friend Frankie say, 'He ain't dead, he's
> just asleep,'
> And I saw the old man's limousine head back towards
> the grave.
> I guess he had to say one last goodbye to the son that he
> could not save.
> The sun turned cold over President Street and the town of
> Brooklyn mourned.
> They said a mass in the old church near the house where
> he was born.
> Some day if God's in heaven, overlooking His preserve,
> I know the men who shot him down will get what they
> deserve.

The parallels with the Passion of Christ are clear – "mother Mary" and the weeping women, the cold sun like the darkness over Calvary, and the bizarre analogy between "the old man" with "the son that he could not save" and God like a gangster "overlooking his preserve". Yet this final and most outrageous glorification of Joey is the one that the singer attests to personally – "I heard", "I saw" and "I know". Since it's extremely unlikely that Bob Dylan was at the funeral, we should understand from this that the narrative is not his account at all, but is sung in the character of one of the Gallos' friends.

The image of the deity as a vengeful *capo di capi* establishes a theme that runs through the next two songs – of divine retribution and, implicitly, of its obverse, salvation. This theme is hardly in hiding elsewhere on *Desire*. The single most strongly stressed word on the record was later the title of Dylan's second Christian album, and it's striking that it should receive such strong emphasis four years beforehand. In OH SISTER, Emmylou Harris and he draw the word out on a long unaccompanied note:

> We grew up together from the cradle to the grave.
> We died and were reborn and yet mysteriously *s–a–v–e–d*.

Before we follow the thread of vengeance and redemption through the next songs, though, consider the implications for JOEY. The refrain is:

> Joey, Joey,
> King of the streets, child of clay.
> Joey, Joey,
> What made them want to come and blow you away?

The answer that the song itself finally provides is: the judgment of a God who gives men "what they deserve".

The impending vengeance that is left over from JOEY is picked up in the next song, ROMANCE IN DURANGO. At first this seems to be in the same sunny mood as MOZAMBIQUE:

> Hot chilli peppers in the blistering sun,
> Dust on my boots and on my cape.
> Me and Magdalena on the run,
> I think this time we shall escape.

The Spanish chorus, though, harks back to that "overlooking" God of JOEY: *"No llores mi querida, / Dios nos vigila"* – 'Don't cry, my darling, / God is watching over us.' And when we hear what it is they are running from, we may be sure that the blood-debt of the previous song has still to be paid:

> At night I dream of bells in the village steeple
> And I see the bloody face of Ramon.
> Was it me that shot him down in the cantina?
> Was it my hand that held the gun?

The shooting parallels the killing of Joey, and the God who is watching here seems no more disposed to mercy than his predecessor:

> The way is long but the end is near,
> Already the fiesta has begun.
> The face of God will appear
> With serpent eyes of obsidian.

And the doom that finally strikes might well be from on high:

> Was that the thunder that I heard?
> My head is vibrating, I feel a sharp pain.
> Come sit by me, don't say a word.
> Oh can it be that I am slain?
> Quick, Magdalena, take my gun:
> Look up in the hills, that flash of light.
> Aim well, my little one.
> We may not make it through the night.

But do they? Or does Magdalena in her turn avenge this death? And if she does, must another link in the chain of vengeance now close on her?

## · 16 ·

# The Righteous
# With The Wicked

The continuity which emerges between JOEY and
ROMANCE IN DURANGO is made actual in a segue
from ROMANCE to BLACK DIAMOND BAY. Again
the opening is bright and sunny:

> Upon the white verandah
> She wears a necktie and a
> Panama hat.
> Her passport shows a face from
> Another time and place –
> She looks nothing like that,
> And all of the remnants of her recent past are
> Scattered in the wild wind.

There are no overt links in the sequence of narratives on
this side of *Desire*. The connection between the characters is
like a series of reincarnations, the same souls appearing in
new settings and guises, carrying over the karmic burden
from one to the next. In point of time, though, they could all
be chapters of one story. Despite the apparent shift from
modern New York to a Wild West scenario, if the protago-
nists of ROMANCE IN DURANGO had grandfathers who
"rode with Villa" then they are actually close contemporaries
of Joey Gallo. Could this mysterious woman, then, also
seemingly "on the run", be the Magdalena of the previous
song? And if so, what judgment awaits her? This turns out
to be the central question of BLACK DIAMOND BAY, but only

after we have been bewildered by the mesh of other destinies crossing hers.

The cinematic reference-points for the song seem to be the romantic thrillers of the 30s and 40s – *Casablanca*, for example, and Hitchcock's *Notorious*, and *To Have and Have Not*. There is a port, a hotel full of assorted foreigners doing deals, making contacts. Why does our mystery woman mistake "the Greek", who is bent on committing suicide, for "the Soviet ambassador"; and why does she want to speak with him? Neither this nor any of the other hinted sub-plots is resolved. For the structure of the song, as opposed to its atmosphere, is drawn from another film genre altogether: the disaster movie, which was hugely popular in the Seventies, with hits like *Airport* (1970), *The Poseidon Adventure* (1972), *Earthquake* and *The Towering Inferno* (1974), *Airport '75* and *Airport '77*. The plot of BLACK DIAMOND BAY, though, is a travesty of the form. In a disaster movie the interest, apart from the spectacle of destruction, lies in seeing which of the large cast of sketchy characters will survive. Here, the volcano erupts, the island sinks, and everybody dies. (Or perhaps not everybody…)

Because of the general air of shadiness about this hotel, its destruction by fire and brimstone evokes an act of divine retribution, falling on the whole nefarious population rather than one individual. In other words, behind the movie analogue, there is a basic biblical model for the story – the fall of Sodom and Gomorrah.

But what of our 'woman in white'? She "walks the other way" from the gambling room, and refuses the soldier who tries to buy her with a ring that "cost a grand". She tries to pack her bags and make a last-minute escape. Is she an innocent? Or does she bear the karmic debt of Magdalena? And if she is righteous, and there is a God who gives people "what they deserve", should she not be saved?

This is the question that Abraham asks of the Lord: "Wilt

thou also destroy the righteous with the wicked?... Shall not the Judge of all the earth do right? And the Lord said, If I find in Sodom fifty righteous within the city, then I will spare all the place for their sakes." Then, in one of the most touching passages in Genesis, Abraham haggles with God, bringing him down from fifty to forty-five, to thirty, to twenty and finally ten righteous. As it turns out, only Lot and his family are accounted righteous, so Jehovah destroys the city, but removes them first.

The idea that "she" may be the one righteous person to be found in Black Diamond Bay – "an innocent... in a living hell", as Dylan says of Rubin Carter – is supported by another source. The song takes its title, and a number of details, from Joseph Conrad's novel *Victory*, which is set around a Black Diamond Bay. There is also a sordid hotel full of Europeans, and a volcano, and a woman redeemed. She is a violinist, appropriately, given the defining presence of the fiddler Scarlet Rivera on *Desire*. Conrad's heroine is called Lena by her lover, Axel Heyst, but when he first asks her name she says: "They call me Alma. I don't know why. Silly name! Magdalena too. It doesn't matter; you can call me by whatever name you choose."

Heyst rescues Lena from the clutches of the hotel manager, a foul man called Schomberg. This redemption leads to her personal fulfilment and to love, but also eventually to her death in an act of self-sacrifice for her lover. The novel broaches questions of suffering innocence, of redemption, of true victory which lie beyond the ambit of *Desire* itself, but point the direction in which it is heading. What matters here is that Lena – or Alma, meaning "soul" – though a 'fallen woman' like Mary Magdalen by the standards of her day, is poor and innocent. In the context of the Sodom judgement, in other words, she deserves to be saved as Lot is.

There is a counter-allusion, however, which implies that she is not saved. As well as Conrad's novel, the song also echoes a recorded sermon from the 1920s called 'The Black Diamond Express to Hell' by the Reverend Gates, which describes the sinners on their last, inescapable ride. And certainly if she is to be saved, since "the last boat sailed", it must be by a miracle.

In the story of Lot, there is nothing explicitly miraculous about his escape, but there is a suggestion that the two angels who rescue him somehow remove him and his family with more-than-human speed, carrying them off, it seems, in the wink of an eye: "And while he lingered, the men laid hold upon his hand, and upon the hand of his wife, and upon the hand of his two daughters; the Lord being merciful unto him: and they brought him forth, and set him without the city."

How does our anonymous heroine fare, then? Here is the evidence:

> The tiny man bit the soldier's ear
> As the floor caved in and the boiler in the basement blew,
> While she's out on the balcony
> Where a stranger tells her 'My darling,
> > *je vous aime beaucoup.*'
> She sheds a tear and then begins to pray
> As the fire burns on and the smoke fades away
> From Black Diamond Bay.

A hopeful sign is the shift in tense, from past, for the soldier and the tiny man, to present for the woman and the stranger. The last lines are encouraging too, recalling Abraham's view on the morning *after* the Cities of the Plain have been destroyed: "behold, and lo, the smoke of the country went up as the smoke of a furnace".

And what of this stranger who emerges out of nowhere to declare that he loves her? His bilingual speech sounds familiar from earlier in the song:

As the morning light breaks open,
The Greek comes down and he asks for a rope an'
A pen that will write.
'*Pardon, monsieur,*' the desk clerk says,
Carefully removes his fez,
'Am I hearin' ya right?'

In Proust's novel *Remembrance of Things Past,* so I'm told, the hero, Swann, dreams of a party where he sees a mysterious young man in a fez, who turns out to be himself. If the "stranger" is the desk clerk, and the desk clerk is the double of the dreamer – the double dreamer in this case, Dylan and Levy – then the darling in the Panama hat has met her maker, as Lot did.

The stranger's double nature recalls the chapters of Genesis, the eighteenth and nineteenth, that tell the story of Abraham's visitation and of the Cities of the Plain. There's a persistent ambiguity as to whether the Lord here is singular or plural. Chapter 18 begins: "And the Lord appeared unto him in the plains of Mamre…" God has come to tell Abraham that his wife Sarah will finally bear a child. But here is what Abraham sees: "And he lift up his eyes and looked, and, lo, three men stood by him…" Throughout this encounter the Lord's voice is singular: "And he said…" When the visit is over, "the men rose up from thence and looked toward Sodom: and Abraham went with them to bring them on the way." God reveals his intention, again in a singular voice: "I will go down now, and see whether they have done altogether according to the cry of it, which is come unto me; and if not, I will know. And the men turned their faces from thence, and went toward Sodom: but Abraham stood yet before the Lord."

Now the three men and the one God appear to have separated. At the beginning of Chapter 19 these three travellers who are also one have become two, and now explicitly angels and not men: "And there came two angels to Sodom at even; and Lot sat in the gate of Sodom; and Lot seeing them rose up to meet them; and he bowed himself with his face toward the ground."

This repeats, with variations, Abraham's greeting of the three men that he sees from his tent door in the heat of the day. In what follows, the two are sometimes called angels and sometimes men; but when they have rescued Lot and his family they merge again in a single person: "And it came to pass, when *they* had brought him forth abroad, that *he* said, Escape for thy life…"

The family of Lot provides an intriguing link with ONE MORE CUP OF COFFEE, the corresponding moment on the first side of the record. Like Lot's, the family in the song is father, mother and two daughters. Lot's wife, of course, met a proverbial fate. Afterwards the father and two daughters go to live in the mountains – hence "the valley below" of the song. The two daughters decide to preserve their father's line by making him drunk and lying with him, and there's an odd connection here with ONE MORE CUP. The father

> … oversees his kingdom
> So no stranger does intrude.
> His voice it trembles as he calls out
> For another plate of food.

Dylan sings the song with a marked cantillation, or oscillation between notes on a single syllable, so that it is the voice of "I", who lies with the daughter, that is heard to tremble. There might also be a memory of the Bible story in his insistence on drinking coffee at night, rather than the wine with which Lot's daughters intoxicate him.

A buried allusion to Lot's unconscious incest would not

be surprising on *Desire*, which reaches back to the mytho-
logical roots where all male-female relationships tend to
meld together, father-brother-husband and mother-sister-
wife. The marriage of Isis and her brother Osiris is also
reflected in OH SISTER (a title in which their names seem
blended together):

> Oh sister, when I come to lie in your arms,
> You should not treat me like a stranger.
> Our father would not like the way that you act
> And you must realise the danger.

There's another "stranger", and another dominant father who
"oversees his kingdom". We don't know how close are the
"you" and the "I", the trembling-voiced singer, in ONE MORE
CUP, but we can deduce that he is no stranger, at least to the
father. Indeed he is a kind of reflection of him, who is also "an
outlaw and a wanderer by trade".

In our final glimpse of our "Magdalena", then, our "Alma",
or soul, is she saved? All we can say, as "the smoke drifts
away", is that she appears to be still alive, accompanied by a
'double' of her dreamer or creator – or 'father' – who tells her
that he loves her, and there the matter is left hanging. In the
final verse, the creator doubles himself again, in a brilliant
narrative trick:

> I was sitting home alone one night
> In LA watching old Kronkite
> On the seven o'clock news.
> It seems there was an earthquake that
> Left nothing but a Panama hat
> And a pair of old Greek shoes.
> Didn't seem like much was happening
> So I turned if off and went to grab another beer.
> Seems like every time you turn around

There's another hard luck story that you're gonna hear.
And there's really nothing anyone can say
And I never did plan to go anyway
To Black Diamond Bay.

It's like channel surfing from fiction to reality, from an old movie to the news – with the twist that the movie we've been watching *was* the news, the fable becoming fact in the same moment that it is consigned to oblivion. The self-portrait here is a unique moment in Dylan's songs, which perhaps could not have been achieved without the distancing of collaboration. The glimpse of the rock-myth-as-ordinary-bloke is scuzzily convincing – except that it contradicts the one thing that we as listeners know for sure about him, which is the song he has just been singing.

This is an ironic variant on James Joyce's description of the ideal artist in *A Portrait of the Artist as a Young Man*: "like the God of creation... within or behind or beyond or above his handiwork, invisible, refined out of existence, indifferent, paring his fingernails." Here he is so far beyond his handiwork that he claims no knowledge of it. The cycle of karma we've been following through these songs comes to a sudden standstill in this revelation of a creator who isn't "overlooking his preserve" to give his creatures "what they deserve", but is completely indifferent to it and them.

The blasé tone echoes Dylan's double in the story – "But the desk-clerk said 'It happens every day' / As the stars fell down and the moon split away" – and it foreshadows the blear-eyed cynicism of *Street-Legal*. He may have learned the lesson of Sodom and Gomorrah as exemplified by Lot's wife – i.e. don't look back ("seems like every time you turn around...") – but his world-weariness is implicitly judged by the zeal of Abraham. Here is a man who neither cares nor expects that "the Judge of all the earth" should "do right" – the counter image to the "champion" who began the record. From there, from HURRICANE, to "another hard luck story that you're gonna hear" is another of our journeys between opposites. With this ploy the record pushes its dualities of detachment and engagement, illusion and reality, to the limit.

# · 17 ·

# Another Hard-Luck Story

The closing of that circle consigns the record's last "hard-luck story" to a kind of limbo, though this should be the moment of most direct engagement. SARA promises, as the finale, a complete soul-baring. Following the sudden appearance of the everyday man at the end of the previous song, we anticipate more of the personal revelation that made *Blood on the Tracks* so gripping, but now in trumps – naming of names, the full confession.

Partly because of that expectation, the song was uneasily received by some critics, who found it mannered and even dishonest. It was pointed out, for instance, that the only glimpse that SARA allows into the connection between private life and public art seems to be a falsehood:

> I can still hear the sound of those Methodist bells.
> I'd taken the cure and had just gotten through.
> Staying up for days in the Chelsea Hotel
> Writing 'Sad-Eyed Lady of the Lowlands' for you.

This flies in the face of what any fan knows. Dylan admits to taking the cure, which implies some sort of drug problem, but that must surely have been after his motorbike accident, and well after the wasted, laced and wired work of *Blonde on Blonde*. Is he claiming to have straightened out *before* he wrote SAD-EYED LADY, that most opiate of songs? And his tale of days and nights spent on it in the Chelsea Hotel flatly contradicts his earlier account of writing it – finishing it, anyway – at the first of his Nashville recording sessions, a story corroborated by the musicians who had to hang around all night to play on it.

It seems to me that, rather like the rhetorical-seeming question at the beginning of JOEY which suggests we check our facts, we are deliberately offered a seeming inconsistency in SARA. Anyone who cares enough about the life and work to spot it may be prompted to look further, and find an alternative true meaning beneath the misleading revelation on the surface. The trouble is that the trail that was laid in the original form of the song (as I take it to be) was covered over in the recorded version.

SARA begins with the recollection of a family day on the beach. At the end of the second verse, Dylan shows us this home movie of his children:

> I can still see the shells falling out of their hands
> As they follow each other back up the hill.

The next three verses "follow each other back up the hill", working backwards in time through the history of a marriage to its origin and, as they go, scattering an assortment of "shells" – beautiful mementoes, but still only the relics of a life. The first of these verses, however, verse 3, is a particularly hollow collection of images, a disconcerting and disjointed collage of more or less banal family snaps:

> Sleeping in the woods by a fire in the night,
> Drinking white rum in a Portugal bar,
> Them playing leapfrog and hearing about Snow White,
> You in a marketplace in Savanna-la-Mar.

This is where the framework of the song is distorted. There is no story or connection for us between these disparate and not especially vivid scenes.

In Dylan's film *Renaldo & Clara* there is a shot of him on stage singing a single verse of SARA, which is an alternative form of this third verse. (I remember seeing it in the two-hour edition shown on British television but not, oddly, in the full-length cinema version.)

> Sleeping in the woods by a fire in the night,
> When you fought for my soul and went up against the odds.
> I was too young to know you were doing it right
> And you did it with a strength that belonged to the gods.

From "the woods" I see this as an image of their first unbroken spell together in Woodstock and the period of profound change that resulted in *John Wesley Harding*. From which point we move backwards in time and into that contentious fourth verse, which depicts a moment of awakening, immediately after his accident, I would guess, to "those Methodist bells" that echo with *John Wesley*'s title.

Look back at those four lines I first quoted. Because each of the four lines of verse 3 was a discrete phrase, we're inclined to hear these too as being punctuated in the same way, as four distinct but simultaneous images – a newly straightened-out Dylan, listening to church bells outside the Chelsea Hotel in New York while he works day and night on SAD-EYED LADY OF THE LOWLANDS. But if we remove a mental full-stop after "through", it turns out not to be "the cure" that he'd "just gotten through" but the "staying up for days" – comma – *and* the writing of SAD-EYED LADY. I would say we were still moving backwards in time here: I'd place the first as an image of Dylan back from his world tour, in say June or July 1966, in the apartment he shared with Sara, still speeding from his months on the road, doing ninety miles an hour down a dead-end street; while the second takes us back to those Nashville sessions that began on Valentine's Day '66. (SAD-EYED LADY was recorded on 15th February.)

As he re-orients himself after his "cure" (I don't know how literally to take that; his doctor at the time of his road accident told Howard Sounes there was no detoxification

involved in his recuperation) he retraces the steps that led him
there, and finds the thread of continuity that was Sara. So in
verse five we go back logically enough to:

> How did I meet you? I don't know.
> A messenger sent me in a tropical storm.
> You were there in the winter, moonlight on the snow,
> And on Lily Pond Lane when the weather was warm.

(We can date their meeting fairly accurately: New York was
hit by the tail end of two tropical storms in September 1964,
Hurricane Dora on the 14th and Hurricane Gladys on the
24th.) The two scenes that follow may be fleeting but they
carry feeling, with their sense of constancy through the seasons, and the persisting images of purity and whiteness, the
snow and the lily. But unfortunately these have been blighted
by the similar and shallower images in verse two – where the
same colour predominates in "Snow White" and "white rum".

Lily Pond Lane, we learn from the latest biography, was
the address of the Dylans' summer house on Long Island. So
the song returns for its last verse to the beach where it began,
but in the present tense. It's as if the landscape is completely
empty now and not even "I" is there. The place where he lay
in the first verse has been taken by wrack and flotsam, and all
that remains is the cine-camera of *Desire* still running on:

> Now the beach is deserted except for some kelp
> And the piece of an old ship that lies on the shore.
> You always responded when I needed your help,
> You gave me a map and a key to your door.

The wrecked ship and the striking rhyme on "help" suddenly illuminate the code that Dylan's been singing throughout in the choruses: "Sara O Sara" – S.O.S. – Save Our Souls.
This is the final duality: Dylan to the rescue in HURRICANE,

which wraps its public truth in visible artifice, in order to make it more immediate and accessible; and calling out to be saved in SARA, whose artifice disguises and deflects us from its private truth.

In its way, SARA too is a 'protest' song, but the simple demand of its last line – "Don't ever leave me, don't ever go" – was not to be met. It rhymes with "Glamorous nymph with an arrow and bow", a closing couplet that ties together two extremes of the 'real' and the 'artificial' – here distilled into contrasting forms of language – that have played themselves out over the whole record.

# Afterword

• • • • • • • • • • • • • • • • • • • • •

# A Diamond Voice

• • • • • • • • • • • • • • • • • • •

**D**ivorce not surprisingly brought confusion to Dylan's art. The 'S' albums, *Street-Legal* (1978), *Slow Train Coming* (1979) and *Saved* (1980), certainly make some double bends. All that survives from *Desire* on *Street-Legal* is the painted epithets of SARA – "Radiant jewel, a mystical wife" and "Glamorous nymph with an arrow and bow" become "a beloved maid / Whose heavenly face is beyond communication" and so on. This, and the dark undercurrent, which comes to the surface, and the preoccupation with esoteric and mythical symbolism. The vivid cinematic style and taut narrative structures disappear, and so does the organic quality of the music.

*Street-Legal* is the first of a series of records on which a shadow of doubt falls between the composition and the execution. Before, Dylan had so unfailingly matched great performance to great song that it came to seem inevitable. But in the early Eighties there are a number of songs, including most of those on *Saved*, and things like GROOM STILL WAITING AT THE ALTAR and CARIBBEAN WIND, where the canonic version seems less than definitive.

The murky sound, and the somewhat strained, formal way Dylan's voice relates to the accompaniment, befits the grimly determined material of *Street-Legal*, but it is less than fully satisfying. There were no such flaws on *Slow Train Coming*, where the lyric manner of its predecessor vanished without a trace, showing perhaps how willed and artificial it had been. The big, polished sound – with tight arrangements, hard-driving rhythm section, horns and backing singers – is so clearly what *Street-Legal* aimed for that one can't help but speculate what that record might have been if it too had been made with Jerry Wexler at Muscle Shoals. Magnificent is my guess.

The kind of musical drilling that went into these two – and which was quite contrary to Dylan's practice up to that point – seems to have sunk *Saved*. I can well believe Paul Williams' report, that the same numbers played by the same band were unsurpassed in concert. On the record, tired from a strenuous stretch of gigging, and with their leader perhaps letting his anger at the hostility of some audiences get the better of him, the ensemble is either doggedly plodding or straining for fervour. The songs of exhortation come across as hectoring, and the songs of faith a bit sour where they would be sweet or salty.

*Shot of Love*, the fourth 'S' album, is sometimes described as the third of a Christian trilogy with *Slow Train Coming* and *Saved*. The impulse behind it is something new, though. Dylan seems to have believed instantly that he should devote his gift and the platform of his fame to his new religion. But the gift has to do with imaginative freedom and the platform arose from his ability to touch a large public deeply. What I think of as the pop trilogy – *Shot of Love*, *Infidels*, *Empire Burlesque* – is concerned with reopening those channels, because that was who God had made him to be. In the year after John Lennon was gunned down by a fan, Dylan could hardly have called to his fans more openly:

> I need
> I need
> I need
> I need a shot of love.

Though there are a few wonderful things on each of these records, and some that come from the same period and were hidden, by and large Dylan was baffled in his attempts to find again a public voice befitting the times. The original *Infidels*, which was to have included BLIND WILLIE MCTELL and FOOT OF PRIDE, would have been as powerful and troubling a record as he'd ever put out, but he opted for controversy over contrariety and the linear over the labyrinthine. At the root of this choice there seems to be a failing confidence in his public's ability to follow what he was on about. A judicious CD edition of *Infidels* that restored some of the first cuts might still prove a belated masterpiece.

The music on *Infidels* is sometimes a bit mechanical; on *Empire Burlesque* is mostly sounds automatic, and the fact that it aims for parody doesn't rescue it. Thick, sickly icing overwhelms the flavour of the cake. The influence of later Randy Newman records like *Born Again* and *Trouble in Paradise* may be at work here, which tackle the falsity and bombast of modern America by absorbing them into the production. Yet building his songs on models he laughed at instead of ones he loved was not so good for the life of Newman's music either. For all their hard brilliance, neither of those records is as endlessly inviting as *Sail Away* or *Good Old Boys*.

*Empire Burlesque* earns its keep with its opening song, TIGHT CONNECTION TO MY HEART, which achieves the goal of being funny, schmaltzy, ridiculous and poignant all at once. The next song, I'LL REMEMBER YOU, is touching. Thereafter the rock doesn't rock and the love-songs are not less cloying for being self-consciously kitsch. Yet on the live tape from Towson, Maryland that I mentioned earlier Dylan produces a coruscating version of SEEING THE REAL YOU AT LAST which shows that the songs themselves may not be entirely at fault. The wiry, angular DARK EYES at the end of the record gains a great deal from the sheer relief of its simplicity.

As he sings elsewhere on *Empire Burlesque*, "I know it was

all a big joke, whatever it was all about", and "I'm gonna quit this baby-talk now". It's not so surprising that this cycle was well below his standard: the Zeit did not have that much Geist to connect with. In the Eighties, broadly speaking, the heart went out of popular music.

His hit-and-miss experiments with the preposterous sounds of the era were justified by the epical-historical tragi-comedy that is BROWNSVILLE GIRL on *Knocked Out Loaded* – otherwise an undistinguished and shapeless collection, another of those What-is-this-shit? winter productions.

*Down in the Groove*, scrappy as it is, set out to find a more organic kind of music-making, and *Oh Mercy* found it. His practice with writing stream-of-cliché hadn't gone to waste; witness the great lines:

> Roses are red, violets are blue
> An' time is beginning to crawl.
>     (WHERE TEARDROPS FALL)

The atmosphere is spooky: we think of time slowing down, getting old, coming to a standstill. But "beginning to crawl" is also an image of a baby. While he stresses that the times are out of joint, that "the world's on its side / And time is running backwards and so is the bride" (RING THEM BELLS), he clearly still believes that the world is racked ultimately with pangs of birth and not death.

*Under the Red Sky* was maligned on its release, yet it's a rounder record than *Oh Mercy*. The brambly R&B makes sense of the stuff he'd tried earlier like TROUBLE on *Shot of Love* or CLEAN CUT KID on *Empire Burlesque*. A back-to-the-roots mood had come over rock, newfangle had gone out of favour, and musicians weren't afraid to sound old-fashioned any more. Even what seems disposable on first hearing gradually takes a place in the scheme of things. 10,000 MEN has a perverse life of its own; 2X2 pulls off its special trick of being cute-as-pie and sad-as-fuck at the same time.

And so on. Since 1989 his records have all been good – few but good, odd but good. *Good As I Been to You*, the first of his latterday folk offerings, shows him effortlessly retaining all the rough edges he'd had thirty years earlier. It's a slower grower than its follower, *World Gone Wrong*, because it's in black and white while the latter is in colour. This record, recently listed in the buyer's guide on a glossy music magazine's website as for "Collectors Only", is one of the best he's ever made.

What Dylan finally acknowledged, I think, in the phase after the pop phase, the ragged-but-right phase, was that his records couldn't be part of a consensus any more, so they might as well have laws unto themselves. He was a bit quick off the mark with his folk albums, though – Chapter 64 of the Folk Revival didn't really get going till the second half of the Nineties.

In the wake of the justly acclaimed *Time Out of Mind*, Dylan has taken his place as beloved grandfather of the rocking folk. At sixty he looks like the one most likely to be producing worthwhile and surprising records at eighty.

# When We Were Made Of Dreams

And thereafter? Why should the reckoning of posterity be a concern of ours? Can the enjoyment of people born when we are dead in any way add to our own?

The reason I think that we appeal to posterity for a testimonial of what we approve, saying so-and-so will still be heard in a hundred years when such-and-such is forgotten, is that it is important to us as ancestors to feel we will be honoured by our descendants. When, in summing up the critical case for the defence, we claim that this will *last*, we are saying first that it sets well with the time-sifted art of the past, and also that it expresses the truest part of ourselves, what we would like our children's children's children to know of us. For it is through our art that they will understand us, if at all, as we understand our ancestors through theirs.

There can be little doubt that the chapter in popular music that was ushered in by Elvis Presley and flourished in the Sixties will remain of interest historically if on no other grounds; and Bob Dylan is one of the figures in the foreground of that story. In a longer and wider perspective, however, sound recordings of popular music – indeed, of all forms of music – were a development and a major artistic form of the whole twentieth century.

In this art-form (which would never have existed without commercial interests, though it includes many invaluable disinterested documents), opportunistic rubbish of a thousand flavours has an unassailable majority. It also contains the work of an array of gifted and prolific musicians, many of whom were also fascinating, colourful or tragic individuals. I find it hard to imagine a future in which people are not interested in Duke Ellington, Louis Armstrong or Charlie Parker; Billie Holliday, Woody Guthrie or Jimi Hendrix; Howlin' Wolf, Elvis Presley or Aretha Franklin.

The legacy of American music on record is at the heart of this treasurehouse, by virtue of sheer size if nothing else, but the industry was already established all over the globe before the Second World War, so that there are also long legacies of other forms like the chanson of France, calypso, tango, rembetika, son, flamenco, etc. There can hardly be a form of music on the planet now – from the Baka's in the Congo jungle to the Mongolian nomads' – that has not been touched by the recording industry.

Within this vast museum of sound, and especially in the American wing, Dylan still appears as a large and unique contributor. The comparison becomes difficult, though, when we try and measure his work against art outside the twentieth century, or the twentieth century's contribution to established arts like literature or painting. The achievements of a Joyce or Picasso take their place in centuries-old traditions – which Dylan's does as well, of course, but while we know him above all as singer and performer, the ancient predecessors of his art are all silent and largely lost to history.

Nor can we compare him directly with the composers of the past, nor with the poets. He composes primarily for himself as a performer and he writes words to be sung. Even if we encapsulate his work in his legacy of recordings (eventually including the masses of concert tapes and so on), there is nothing outside the last century to set it beside. To ask whether he is as good as Keats is like asking whether Keats is as good as Wren: the two are incommensurable.

As far as the poets are concerned, all we can say is that Dylan works words brilliantly for the requirements of his art, which do not include being read in books. In this he is unlike the other surviving poets of his language apart from Shakespeare, and I do not think his words will live the double life that Shakespeare's have, both as literature and performance. His lyrics can be enjoyed on the page, but as reminders of the songs.

The same problem of comparison applies to the future. People have been reading books for more than two millennia and despite the incursions of other media they continue to do so. The fortunes of literature may wax and wane but we can be fairly sure that it will remain an important part of our civilisation as long as there is one. Recordings have been a popular form of domestic – and, later, public – entertainment for about eighty years, and already their function seems to be changing. Music is more widespread than ever, but perhaps less a focus of attention than ever, as it becomes part of the environment in which we do other things – drive, eat and drink, talk, walk, shop or operate a computer. Who knows whether people will still turn to records in the future, as they read books, for a distinct aesthetic experience?

My guess actually is that they will. And as long as they do, I believe Dylan will be heard, and that his name can and will be mentioned in the same breath as William Blake, or Milton, or Walt Whitman.

# Just Like Old Saxophone Joe

And yet Dylan's art resists canonisation, because his compositions live lives of their own. Quite a few have entered that common stream out of which he, as a distinctive composer, so anomalously emerged. Even when all his own multiple interpretations have been compiled, the work will not be finalised. I SHALL BE RELEASED and THE TIMES THEY ARE A-CHANGIN' don't live only so long as someone listens to a memento of one of Dylan's performances, but so long as somebody somewhere is picking up their banjo and singing them. In this respect he has accorded with Bertolt Brecht's advice 'About the Way to Construct Enduring Works':

> How long
> Do works endure? As long
> As they are not completed.
> Since as long as they demand effort
> They do not decay.
>
> Inviting further work
> Repaying participation
> Their being lasts as long as
> They invite and reward.
>
> Useful works
> *Require people*
> Artistic works
> Have room for art
> Wise works
> Require wisdom
> Those devised for completeness
> Show gaps
> The long-lasting
> Are always about to crumble

Those planned on a really big scale
Are unfinished.

*(Translated by Frank Jellinek)*

(Hence the title of this epilogue, based on someone else's variation on a Dylan lyric. When the *NME* published an interview with him just after the release of *Shot of Love*, someone had heard a different line in EVERY GRAIN OF SAND, in place of "There's a dying voice within me", and the article was headlined "The Diamond Voice Within".)

And now? In the world of commerce Dylan is a middle-to-upper ranking property. His wealth and income are obviously fabulous by the standards of the average working musician, but there is also a large discrepancy in economic terms between his standing and those of the artists he is likely to be bracketed with – Elvis or the Beatles or the Stones, say. His particular success has been to evade the gigantism of the industry he works in, while securing a cachet that will permit him to do what he likes artistically for the rest of his life.

It has been suggested that his perpetual travelling is a perpetual flight from his personal isolation, as revealed in the desolate tone of *Time Out of Mind*. Consider, though, as C.S. Lewis said, "the man who writes a good love sonnet needs not only to be enamoured of a woman, but also to be enamoured of the sonnet." Likewise, when someone who loves the blues decides to write in true old blues fashion – that is to say, an assemblage of lines and phrases stolen from older songs, twisted and nailed together seemingly anyhow – then it's likely, since blues are predominantly sad, to be a sad work.

From day to day, there is reason to believe he loves the life he lives and lives the life he loves, the life he invented for himself forty years ago. The evidence for that is the perennial enthusiasm with which he performs.

It is a sad irony that the music industry which is largely founded on the global success of the popular music of the Sixties and the independent spirit it expressed should now be controlled by a handful of monolithic corporations. Within that market, Dylan's personal economy embodies some of the abiding and still vital ideals that were seeded in the Sixties. It is sustainable, relatively small-scale, and open to creative innovation and improvisation.

For example, in the first half of 2001 he played thirty-six concerts, twenty-two in Japan and Australia between 25th February and 31st March, and after a two week break, a further fourteen in the United States from 18th April to 6th May. His American itinerary included such infrequently mentioned destinations as Asheville, North Carolina; Blacksburg, Virginia (where he played the smallest venue on this leg of the Never-Ending Tour, a 2,800-seater); Kearney, Nebraska; and Dalton, Georgia. Certain elements of the show were fixed – namely the encore, which invariably included LIKE A ROLLING STONE and HIGHWAY 61 REVISITED, and almost always ALL ALONG THE WATCHTOWER, BLOWIN' IN THE WIND and, in a splendid bit of trickery, the seldom-if-ever-requested IF DOGS RUN FREE. Another fixture of the encores was a song chosen from his latest record, most commonly LOVE SICK. Over the whole course of these concerts, he played nine out of the eleven songs on *Time Out of Mind*.

On the back of this simple formula, he managed to work ninety-two different songs into his sets, including nine covers. The majority, fifty-odd, were from his Sixties albums. Everything from *Bob Dylan* to *Nashville Skyline* was represented; the latter – in keeping with the western garb that Dylan has favoured of late – contributing five songs. Five songs were also taken from *Blood on the Tracks*, but thereafter the coverage was sparse: ten songs altogether from the two decades from 1976 to 1997; none from *Desire*, *Street-Legal*, *Slow Train Coming*, *Infidels*, or *Under the Red Sky*.

To be fair, though, we should cast the net a bit wider. In the one hundred and eighty shows that Dylan played between March 2000 and May 2001, the repertoire rises to one hundred and thirty-one different songs, twenty of them previously unrecorded covers. All of his albums with the exceptions of *Self Portrait*, *Knocked Out Loaded* and *Good As I Been to You* are represented. And now *Under the Red Sky* contributes five songs, and *Oh Mercy* outstrips *Blood on the Tracks*, contributing six. In 2000, the most-performed song was TANGLED UP IN BLUE, followed by LIKE A ROLLING STONE, of course – which tied for second place with COUNTRY PIE.

His setlists show him happy by and large to follow the consensus on his records. Still they are full of surprise and an eagerness to keep the whole range of his work alive. The fact is, he could draw only on his thinnest decade, do an entire Eighties show, and still make it a mind-boggling set of songs: BROWNSVILLE GIRL, JOKERMAN, EVERY GRAIN OF SAND, TIGHT CONNECTION TO MY HEART, MOST OF THE TIME, SHOT OF LOVE, I AND I, ANGELINA, SERIES OF DREAMS, BLIND WILLIE MCTELL, FOOT OF PRIDE, HEART OF MINE, DARK EYES, SWEETHEART LIKE YOU, WHAT CAN I DO FOR YOU?, WHAT WAS IT YOU WANTED, DIGNITY... And who would mind if he had to have UGLIEST GIRL IN THE WORLD as well?

For those who didn't get this far, for those who gave out before they gave in – Otis, Elvis, Janis, Jimi and the rest – in that spirit, Dylan goes out night by night with heart and soul and imagination, to show that the way from one moment to the next is still an open road.

# For What

I bought my copy of *Love and Theft* on Monday, 10th September, the day of its UK release, and, having given it two or three listens, began to write in the small hours that I couldn't have made a happier ending for this book. Twenty years ago, when I took up the subject, it was partly because Dylan seemed most likely, of his generation of popular musicians, to carry his art on into old age and continue to be creative. It's a distinction of a number of the greatest painters and sculptors – Michelangelo, Titian, Rembrandt, Monet, Cézanne, Matisse and Picasso, to name a few – but far rarer among poets, particularly the moderns. (The shining example for me at that time was Yeats.) It's not a common trait among the Romantics, nor in American literature, and especially not in American popular music. In that field, the only figure to be lauded, as Dylan has been for his new record, for still producing work at sixty worthy of his first maturity, is Duke Ellington.

The chorus of praise, whatever the record was like, would be a story in itself. Across the Atlantic, the critics ranged from Vit Wagner of the *Toronto Star*, calling it a "crackerjack", more accessible than *Time Out of Mind*, though not so great; through Larry Katz in the *Boston Herald* rating it as "probably" better than its predecessor; to Robert Hilburn giving it four out of four stars in the *LA Times*, breezily comparing it to *Highway 61 Revisited*, and Rob Sheffield in *Rolling Stone* awarding it the first five-star score in nearly a decade (since REM's *Automatic for the People*) and describing the singer as: "Relaxed, magisterial, utterly confident in every musical idiom he touches…"

In the *New York Daily Post*, Jim Farber suggested that another summit had been reached: "Vocally, Dylan has never sounded more wonderfully wrecked. He's full of dust and gravel, like he just got run over by a truck and lived to sing about it. … It's not just the way Dylan addressed complicated emotions in these songs that impresses, it's also the flow and density of his words. He hasn't penned a lyric sheet this thick since his psychedelic days."

In fact, all the American reviews to be found online were glowing, and the European ones, as far as I could guess, seemed to be too: "Mesterværk fra Dylan", "Highlight der Woche", "Mesterligt skrammel", "renacimiento creativo". In the Parisian paper *Libération*, Nick Kent (I assume in translation) spoke of plenty of songs on the record that could easily rival the best of Dylan's entire career; of his having been miraculously reconnected with the blues "avec une intensité à couper le souffle"; and summed up by saying of the album: "Seuls les imbéciles se risqueront à l'ignorer."

If there was a risk of appearing imbecilic, gentlemen of Her Majesty's Press would of course be ready to sink to the challenge. David Sinclair of *The Times* depicted "a formerly distinguished performer cheerfully sliding into an advanced state of decrepitude", and Alexis Petridis of *The Guardian*, in his first week on the job, spent the first half of his review deriding anyone who takes Bob Dylan at all seriously as a bad case of arrested development, before allowing "some moments of genuine inspiration" among the "leaden and overlong... filler".

By Tuesday, 11th September, the day of its US release, what anyone thought of the new Bob Dylan album didn't seem that important. The music itself, though, still made sense. Only now, where it's exuberance and vaudevillean humour had sprung out at first, there were grimness and violence. After watching the plane on the screen slice into the South Tower again and again, until you couldn't watch it any more, the opening lines were a shock:

> Tweedle Dum and Tweedle Dee,
> They're throwing knives into the tree.
> Two big bags of dead men's bones...

The fantasia of Lewis Carroll from which this first song is drawn seemed to have as many rogue resonances as were sparked from the flinty lyrics of the record itself, in the aftershock of the destruction of the twin towers. We come across that tree again straightaway, as Alice takes the two brothers' hands and dances with them in a ring: "This seemed quite natural (she remembered afterwards), and she was not even surprised to hear music playing: it seemed to come from the tree under which they were dancing, and it was done (as well as she could make it out) by the branches rubbing one across the other, like fiddles and fiddlesticks." When the twins have agreed to do battle – "Let's fight till six, and then have dinner" – the death of those trees which are also art seems assured: "Tweedledum looked round him with a satisfied smile. 'I don't suppose,' he said, 'there'll be a tree left standing, for ever so far around, by the time we've finished!'" And the sense of something coming that recurs in the record – "You always got to be prepared, but you never know for what" – has its echo here too:

> It was getting dark so suddenly that Alice thought there must be a thunderstorm coming on. "What a thick black cloud that is!" she said. "And how fast it comes! Why, I do believe it's got wings!"
> "It's the crow!" Tweedledum cried out...

In the shadow of these deaths, and the horror, grief and fear, the rage and hatred that accompany them, a record of popular music may seem to belong in another dimension which it would be an impertinence or irreverence to introduce. (On Thursday 13th, I switched on to find that ITN's reporter in New York was called Harry Smith.) But among the few antidotes to the destruction of the 11th must be counted the creative and collective spirit in which good music lives. Conversely, it is a test of art that it is not rendered irrelevant by reality even at its least tolerable. Dylan's art has never shied from the worst, and the new and much uglier world into which we stepped does not seem strange to the songs of *Love and Theft*. This world had long been his preoccupation, as THE TIMES THEY ARE A-CHANGIN' reminds us. A bonus disc with the first edition of *Love and Theft* includes an alternative take of that song from the 1963 album sessions:

> There's a battle outside and it's ragin'.
> It'll soon shake your windows and vibrate your walls
> For the times they are a-changin'.

(The second of these bonus tracks is uncanny. In 1961, at twenty, Dylan sounds infinitely older and wearier singing I WAS YOUNG WHEN I LEFT HOME than he does now at sixty.)

It's too early for *Love and Theft* to have revealed much of itself. You don't really get the shape of a whole record until you start to anticipate the opening notes of the next song, till your breathing and heartrate attune to it: then you begin to understand how it flows from one to the next. (I do miss the frame provided by the sides of a record, too.) But already the new CD seems more fully formed than *Time Out of Mind*, with its foggy atmosphere and sustained melancholic mood.

Certain recurrences are obvious, the family especially: mother, father, brother, sister, uncle, aunt, grandmother, grandfather, second cousin, and even the closest relatives of all, siamese twins. Beyond these, a web of other roles and relations appears – of workers and bosses, soldiers and officers, buyers and sellers, fugitives and lawmen, duck trappers and undertakers. For the first time for what seems a long time, the world of this new record is a society. There are collective disasters and celebrations, a constant stream of contacts and encounters.

The contrast is particularly stark with *Time Out of Mind*, which was largely inhabited only by You and Me – minus You. The one notable social exchange – with the waitress in HIGHLANDS – is a model of crossed lines and disconnection. Back in the days of *Infidels*, when Dylan painted a world picture, 'I' wandered through it in splendid isolation, and doom-laden scenarios like LICENCE TO KILL and MAN OF PEACE were seen as from above. On *Love and Theft*, 'I' is down on a level with everyone else. "She's lookin' into my eyes, she's holdin' my hand": simple as it is, there hasn't been this much mutual presence in Dylan's songs for years.

When we speak of 'I' on this record, however, I think we'll have to see it as it was described on *Highway 61*: "there is no eye, there is only a series of mouths". Dylan has resurrected the persona of Everyman: where once he was a kind of cypher though, a wandering *anyone*, here he's become a streetful, a whole townful of people at once – the corner ranter, the local dandy, the life of the party and the cantankerous barfly, the village idiot and the preacher, the romancer and the diehard union man. Again the closest comparison I can find for this cross-sectional impression of a populous world, kaleidoscopic and panoramic, familiar and strange, is with *Highway 61*. Such breadth of vision is part of the appeal of others among Dylan's best works, though, like *Blood on the Tracks*, the Basement Tapes and, in a miniature way, *John Wesley Harding*.

The musical diversity of the songs on *Love and Theft* gives the scenes they describe more scope than those of *Time Out of Mind*: there the music seemed to embody physiological states rather than characters, landscapes and townscapes. Indeed, the network of allusions that we looked at in the lyrics of earlier records is here largely supplanted by skeins of musical reference. There are quite a few quotes from Dylan's own records – the Mardi Gras lurch of RAINY DAY WOMEN behind LONESOME DAY BLUES, the snatches of guitar lines from *Highway 61*, the building of HIGH WATER on the foundation of JOHN BROWN from *Unplugged*. There are also echoes from many of the names we've touched on in earlier chapters – of Muddy Waters and Howlin' Wolf in LONESOME DAY; of Charley Patton, Son House and Robert Johnson in CRY AWHILE; of Jimmie Rodgers in MOONLIGHT and Woody Guthrie in PO' BOY, and every roots music fan will hear dozens of others I'm sure. A number of reviewers saw in *Love and Theft* a window into history. At the moment, though, my favourite word in the lyrics is "beyond" –

Po' boy in a red-hot town, out beyond the twinklin' stars

– which sends our archaic world into outer space, as a number of science-fiction films have done with the frontier town of the Western.

For the *News & Observer* of Raleigh, North Carolina, David Menconi writes, in the light of current events, of how *Love and Theft* has taken on a compelling and uniquely consoling timeliness. The 11th didn't impinge on its author only through the ghastly timing of the release. One of Dylan's oldest friends and first musical companions, Larry Kegan, died of a heart attack on the same day that so many thousands of others were bereaved. Furthermore, as a rich and conspicuous American Jewish Christian, the artist would surely have considered that he is exactly the kind of person the attackers would have been happiest to kill.

On Sunday, 9th September, the day before I got *Love and Theft*, I saw two things that became entwined with my first listening. One was Werner Herzog's film *The Enigma of Kaspar Hauser* (or "Every Man for Himself and God Against All" as Herzog's German title has it). Bruno S. as Kaspar, in a performance of uncanny timing and poignancy and presence, seemed to speak the same language as I soon heard on this record, with its mélange of jokes, twisted pastoral and catastrophe.

Before we went to the National Film Theatre, we'd called in at the Tate Modern. There was a late Picasso there, a nude with a necklace, painted when he was eighty-seven, whose vitality was magnetic from across the crowded room. Some of the same spirit seemed to be in Dylan's voice as in this painting: the elements that coalesce and never quite crystallise, oscillating at the boundary between fragmentation and form, as each song of *Love and Theft* tells its story yet has no narrative; the quick, smeary, decisive brushwork; the freedom of shape and colour, like the singer's lines that appear as impossible clumps and tangles of language at first and unfold as unpredictable and perfectly balanced constructions in sound. People are talking of Dylan as old now – our first old rock star – but Picasso had more than quarter of a century on him when he made that picture. We can hope to hear plenty more from those golden cords yet.

The notice next to the Picasso nude offered the visitor an official explanation of it as a kind of sexual assault in paint. After last week, the metaphor seems pernicious: it's suddenly very clear how different is the nature of art from an assault. On Wednesday, 12th September, the Queen altered the Changing of the Guard ceremony for the first time in its history, and had her band play 'The Star-Spangled Banner'. In a moment when we couldn't do anything, and couldn't do nothing, a piece of popular music provided as true a condolence as one nation could send to another.

There are felicities of every kind – vocal, lyrical, instrumental, compositional – appearing in *Love and Theft* every day, that I have no more space or time to discuss here. They only require that the listener listen. Meanwhile, for their curacy of the past, their bequest to the future and most of all for their aliveness and alertness in the moment, I think we should thank Mr Dylan and his band. *Monday, 17th September 2001*

# Index

Titles of Bob Dylan albums are given in ***bold italic***; titles of Bob Dylan songs and performances on record are given in CAPITALS. Titles of other minor works (songs and poems) are in inverted commas, and of major works in *italic*.

2 x 2, 204, 346-7
'11 Outlined Epitaphs', 39
10,000 MEN, 204, 346

**A**bout the Way to Construct Enduring Works' (Brecht), 351-2
Abraham 42, 197, 290, 329-30, 331, 332, 333, 335
'Accentuate the Positive', 205
Achilles, 4, 240
Acts of the Apostles, 162
*Adventures of Huckleberry Finn, The* (Twain), 41-2, 69
'After You've Gone', 109
'Ain't That Loving You Baby' (Presley), 74
*Air-Conditioned Nightmare, The* (Miller), 245-7, 256
*Airport, Airport '75, Airport '77*, 329
'Alexander's Ragtime Band' (Berlin), 109, 111
ALL ALONG THE WATCHTOWER, 201, 258, 262, 265, 353
ALL I REALLY WANT TO DO, 124, 125, 146, 180, 183
'All Shook Up' (Presley), 288
Alpert, Richard, 119
American Studio, Memphis, 78
Ananse, 44
*Ancient Mariner, The* (Coleridge), 8
ANGELINA, 45, 354
Animals, 34, 69, 263
*Another Side of Bob Dylan*, 117-8, 124-31, 133, 137, 145-6, 151, 172-4, 177, 180-5, 194, 195, 206, 208, 279-80, 300
*Anthology of American Folk Music*, 31-2
Anubis, 45
'Anyway You Want Me' (Presley), 73
Apollo, 44, 47
Aquarius, 190
Armstrong, Louis, 91, 348
AS I WENT OUT ONE MORNING, 261, 265, 277
Astor, Peter, 296
*At Budokan*, 297
'Autumn Serenade' (DeRose), 110

**B**a-lue Bolivar Ba-lues-are' (Monk), 88
*Baal* (Brecht), 142
'Back Water Blues' (Smith), 112
Baez, Joan, 123, 124, 133, 163, 186, 260
Baker, Josephine, 110
BALLAD IN PLAIN D, 127-8, 180
BALLAD OF A THIN MAN, 226
BALLAD OF FRANKIE LEE AND JUDAS PRIEST, THE, 209, 262-4, 265, 272-3
BALLAD OF HOLLIS BROWN, 125, 143-4, 150, 154, 167, 181, 312
Band, 256, 273, 294, 299, 301
Bangs, Lester, 317
'Bard, The' (Gray), 9, 10
Barnett, Ross, 157
*Bartholomew Fair* (Jonson), 24

*Basement Tapes, The*, 194, 196, 198, 253, 254-6, 257, 264, 299, 360
Baudelaire, Charles, 293
Beatles 3, 34, 50, 57, 69, 74, 80, 118, 120-1, 122, 134, 147, 203-4, 307, 352
Bechet, Sydney, 91
'Before the Deluge' (Browne), 305
*Before the Flood*, 294, 299, 301-2
*Beggars Banquet* (Rolling Stones), 285
'Belle Dame Sans Merci, La' (Keats), 10
Bennett, Tony, 187
Berlin, Irving, 109, 110, 111
Berry, Chuck, 69, 72
'Big Hunk o' Love' (Presley), 74
'Biggest Thing That Man Has Ever Done, The' *see* 'Great Historical Bum, The'
*Biograph*, 52, 94, 125, 131, 187
BLACK CROW BLUES, 125, 180
BLACK DIAMOND BAY, 105, 310, 328-36
'Black Diamond Express to Hell' (Gates), 331
'Black Star Liner' (Culture), 164
Black, Bill, 76
Blake, William, 38, 41, 102, 121, (& Catherine) 190, 250, 264, 280, 311, 350
Blakely, Ronee, 306
BLIND WILLIE MCTELL, 345, 354
*Blonde on Blonde*, 10, 117, 145, 181, 182, 183, 185-8, 194, 197, 203, 235, 239, 240-2, 244-52, 255, 256, 271, 277, 278, 281, 306, 337
'Blood and the Moon' (Yeats), 228
*Blood on the Tracks*, 194, 196, 198, 203, 239, 291, 299, 303-4, 307, 324, 337, 353, 354, 360
Bloomfield, Mike, 78
BLOWIN' IN THE WIND, 19-20, 55, 104, 148, 149, 203, 205, 302, 353
*Blue* (Mitchell), 293, 304
'Blue' (Mitchell), 304
'Blue Bonnet – You Make Me Blue', 110
'Blue Moon of Kentucky' (Presley), 71
'Blue Suede Shoes' (Presley), 288
'[The] Blues Had a Baby (And They Called It Rock'n'Roll)' (Dixon), 33
Bo Diddley, 240
*Bob Dylan*, 3, 41, 100, 137, 146, 148, 149, 185, 187-8, 194, 353
BOB DYLAN'S 115TH DREAM, 43
BOB DYLAN'S BLUES, 148, 149
BOB DYLAN'S DREAM, 148, 149
'Boogie Chillen' (Hooker), 88
Booker T and the MGs, 284
*Bootleg Series, The, Vols 1-3*, 131, 135, 297
BOOTS OF SPANISH LEATHER, 127, 144, 150
*Born Again* (Newman), 345
BORN IN TIME, 11
*Born to Run* (Springsteen), 61-2, 63
'Born to Run' (Springsteen), 61-2
*Bound for Glory* (Guthrie), 16-20, 38-9, 42, 51-5, 106, 210, 254-5
Bowie, David, 301

Brecht, Bertolt, 142-3, 163, 351-2
Brer Rabbit, 45
***Bringing It All Back Home***, 51, 57-8, 117,
    128-9, 135, 186, 194, 196-7, 208, 238,
    255
Brockman, Polk, 30
Broonzy, Big Bill, 13, 82, 86
Brown, James, 90, 123
Brown, Willie, 83, 86
Browne, Jackson, 59-60, 293, 304-5
BROWNSVILLE GIRL, 11, 61, 202, 346, 354
Buddha, 310-1, 313
Burke, Solomon, 122, 123
[Paul] Butterfield Blues Band, 34
Buttrey, Kenny, 248
Byrds, 80, 286, 307

Cain, 167
Campbell, Joseph, 43
CAN YOU PLEASE CRAWL OUT YOUR
    WINDOW?, 235-6, 237-9
Canned Heat, 286
*Cannery Row* (Steinbeck), 209-10, 226
[Gus] Cannon's Jug Stompers, 79
*Careless Love* (Guralnick), 75
CARIBBEAN WIND, 45, 343
Carr, Leroy, 85
'Carrie Brown' (Earle), 30
Carroll, Hattie, 181
Carson, Fiddlin' John, 30
Carter Family, 30, 31, 37, 38, 175, 176-7
Carter, Rubin 'Hurricane', 312, 313, 330
*Casablanca*, 329
Cassady, Neal, 120
Cash, Johnny, 77, 281, 284
CAT'S IN THE WELL, 204
'Cautious Man' (Springsteen), 64
Cézanne, Paul, (& Hortense) 190, 356
Chagall, Marc, 248
'Change Is Gonna Come, A' (Cooke), 122
CHANGING OF THE GUARD, 46-7
Chaplin, Charlie, 42, 43, 45, 48
Chapman, Mark, 285
Charters, Sam, 90
Chatterton, Thomas, 9
CHIMES OF FREEDOM, 124, 127, 130, 172,
    174-80, 181
*Chocolate Kiddies*, 110
'Christian Automobile, The', 164
Church of God in Christ, 81
CLEAN CUT KID, 171, 346
*Close Encounters of the Third Kind* (Spielberg),
    165
CLOTHES LINE SAGA, 253-5
'Coal-Owner and the Pitman's Wife, The', 26
Cochran, Eddie, 72
Coleman, Ornette, 91, 114
Coleman Smith, Pamela 46
Coleridge, S.T., 8
Collins, William, 7-8
Coltrane, John, 91, 114
Columbia Records, 118
*Come Fly With Me* (Sinatra & Riddle), 147
*Common Muse, The* (de Sola Pinto &
    Rodway), 24, 26
*Confidence-Man, The* (Melville), 49-50, 264
Conrad, Joseph, 310, 330
Cooke, Sam, 122
Coppola, Francis Ford, 321

CORRINA, CORRINA, 148, 149
*Country Blues Bottleneck Guitar* (Ferguson &
    Gellis), 84
COUNTRY PIE, 354
Covay, Don, 123
Cowper, William, 7
Coyote, 44, 45
Crabbe, George, 7
'Crazy Blues' (Smith), 29-30, 109, 114
Cream, 286
Crosby, Bing, 139
Crowe, Cameron, 52, 187
'Cry' (Ray), 139
Culture, 164

Dali, Salvador, 248
'Dancing in the Street' (Martha & the
    Vandellas), 122
Daniel, 209, 273
'Daniel and the Sacred Harp' (Band), 273-5
Dante, 232, 308
DARK EYES, 11, 102, 345, 354
*Darkness on the Edge of Town* (Springsteen),
    62, 63
Dave Clark Five, 34
David, 96, 267
Davis, Bette, 218, 240
Davis, Miles, 147
de la Beckwith, Byron, 156-7
De Rose, Peter 109, 110
DEAR LANDLORD, 258, 265
'Deep Purple', 110
DELIA, 11
'Demoiselles d'Avignon, Les' (Picasso) 18
'Deserted Village, The' (Goldsmith), 7
***Desire***, 33, 46, 105, 194, 197, 198, 239, 299,
    305, 306-41, 343, 353
*Desolation Angels* (Kerouac), 209
DESOLATION ROW, 104, 201, 203, 206,
    208-34, 235, 237, 242, 244, 245, 247, 248
Deuteronomy, 272
DIGNITY, 354
Dirty Dozens Brass Band, 92
DISEASE OF CONCEIT, 171, 204
Dixie Hummingbirds, 81
Dixon, Willie, 33, 82
Dodds, Johnny, 91
Domino, Fats, 92
Don Voorhees & His Earl Carroll's 'Vanities'
    Orchestra with Harold Yates, 110-1
Donne, John, 65, 183, 202
Donnegan, Lonnie, 68-9
DON'T FALL APART ON ME TONIGHT, 102
*Dont Look Back*, 186, 220-1, 223
DON'T THINK TWICE, IT'S ALL RIGHT,
    142-3, 144, 148, 149, 201, 203, 205,
*Doors of Perception, The* (Huxley), 279
DOWN ALONG THE COVE, 259, 265, 277-8
***Down in the Groove***, 11, 194, 198, 300, 346
DOWN THE HIGHWAY, 148, 149
DRIFTER'S ESCAPE, 264, 265
*Dust Bowl Ballads* (Guthrie), 147
***Dylan and the Dead***, 296
Dylan, Sara, 184, 309-10, 340

Eagles, 286
Eaglin, Snooks, 90
Earle, Steve, 30
*Earthquake*, 329

Eastwood, Clint, 4
*Eat the Document*, 252, 268
Ecclesiastes, 100
*Ed Sullivan Show, The*, 120
Einstein, Albert, 215, 219, 221, 225, 240
Eisenhower, Dwight D., 293
Eli, 266-7, 270
Eliot, T.S., 69, 71, 185, 187, 208-9, 228, 229-31, 232-3
Ellington, Duke, 110, 114, 348, 356
*Elvis Is Back!*, 75
*Elvis: The '56 Sessions*, 73-4
*Empire Burlesque*, 11, 102, 194, 198, 300, 344, 345-6
*Enemy Within, The* (Kennedy), 322
Estes, Sleepy John, 123
ETERNAL CIRCLE, 131
Evans, Gil, 147
Everest Records, 15-6
Evers, Medgar, 155, 157, 181
Evers, Myrlie, 156
EVERY GRAIN OF SAND, 45, 105, 203, 352, 354
Ezekiel, 102, 164

FATHER OF NIGHT, 289-90
*Feel Like Going Home* (Guralnick), 77
'Fern Hill' (Thomas), 165
Fishbone, 36
*Fistful of Dollars, A* (Leone), 4
Fitzgerald, F. Scott, 240
Flatt & Scruggs, 16
Folkways Records, 31, 36
'Fool Such As I, A' (Presley), 74
FOOT OF PRIDE, 345, 354
*For a Few Dollars More* (Leone), 4
Foster, Stephen, 109
'Fountain of Sorrow' (Browne), 305
*Four Quartets* (Eliot), 230
Four Tops, 121
Franklin, Aretha, 348
Free, 286
Free Speech Movement, 119
*Freewheelin' Bob Dylan, The*, 41, 100, 118, 126, 140-1, 142, 145, 148-9, 157, 194, 196, 304
Freud, Sigmund, 13, 221-3, 225, 234
*From Elvis in Memphis*, 78

*G.I. Blues* (Presley), 75
Gallo, Joey, 317-25, 327, 328
Ganesh, 219
*Gang That Couldn't Shoot Straight, The*, 321
Garvey, Marcus, 164
GATES OF EDEN, 216
Gates, Rev., 331
Gemini, 44, 189, 190
Genesis, 289, 330, 332
Gentry, Bobbie, 253
*Ghost of Tom Joad, The* (Springsteen), 65
'Ghost of Tom Joad, The' (Springsteen), 65
*Ghosts of Mississippi* (Reiner), 156
Gifford, William, 24
Ginsberg, Allen, 120, 121, 174
*Girl Can't Help It, The*, 92
GIRL OF THE NORTH COUNTRY, 10, 140, 148, 149, 181, 281, 296
'Go Slow' (London), 72, 138

God, 5, 48, 102, 103-4, 111, 157, 160-2, 164-5, 184, 262, 266-7, 269-70, 273, 289-90, 325-7, 329-30, 335, 344
GOD KNOWS, 204
Goddard, Donald, 319-22, 324
*Godfather, The* (Coppola), 312, 321
GOING, GOING, GONE, 293-4
Goldberg, Whoopi, 156
Goldsmith, Oliver, 7
*Good As I Been to You*, 11, 194, 197, 198, 300, 347, 354
'Good Morning School Girl' (Williams & Williamson), 86
*Good Old Boys* (Newman), 345
'Good Rockin' Tonight' (Presley), 288
*Good Rockin' Tonight: Sun Records & the Birth of Rock'n'Roll* (Escott & Hawkins), 77
*Good, the Bad and the Ugly, The* (Leone), 4
'Goodnight Irene' (Leadbelly), 36
Gordy, Berry, 121, 122
'Grand Coulee Dam' (Guthrie), 54, 103, 175, 177
Grant, Bobby, 84
*Grapes of Wrath, The* (Steinbeck), 141-2, 210
Gray, Thomas, 7-8, 9, 10
'Great Historical Bum, The' (Guthrie), 159-60
*Greatest Hits*, 299
Grimm, Brothers, 23
GROOM STILL WAITING AT THE ALTAR, 45, 343
Grossman, Albert, 104, 128, 220, 221
Grossman, Sally, 186
*Gunsmoke*, 94
Guralnick, Peter, 75, 76, 77
Guthrie, Charlie, 211
Guthrie, Woody 5, 14, 16-20, 26, 27, 36-7, 38-9, 42, 51-5, 56-7, 68, 103, 106, 140, 142, 143, 145, 147, 159-60, 174-5, 177-8, 210, 211-2, 254-5, 261, 348, 360
Guy, Buddy, 90

Haggard, Merle, 284
Hall, Adelaide, 110
HANDY DANDY, 204
Handy, W.C., 78-9
Hannah, 266, 267
*Hard Rain*, 297
HARD RAIN'S A-GONNA FALL, A, 51, 98-104, 141, 142, 148, 149, 201, 205, 227, 229, 247, 268, 311
*Hard to Handle*, 297
*Harpers & Queen* magazine, 319
Harris, Emmylou, 286, 306, 307, 326
Harvard University, 40, 119
Hawkins, Coleman, 114
HEART OF MINE, 354
'Heartbreak Hotel' (Presley), 74, 288
'Heavenly Aeroplane' (Watersons), 164
'Hellhound On My Trail' (Johnson), 83, 86
'Hello Lola!', 114
Hemingway, Ernest, 69
Henderson, Fletcher, 109, 113-4
Hendrix, Jimi, 119, 307, 348, 354
Herman's Hermits, 34
Hermes, 44, 49
Heylin, Clinton, 168
*Hiawatha* (Longfellow), 68
*High Plains Drifter* (Eastwood), 4
'Highway 29', (Springsteen), 65

HIGHWAY 51, 89
'Highway 61' (McDowell), 66
*Highway 61 Revisited*, 51, 57-8, 66, 68, 69, 78, 92, 186, 194, 196-7, 210, 215, 226, 235, 238, 239, 240, 242, 251, 255, 356, 359-60
HIGHWAY 61 REVISITED, 353
*His Hand in Mine* (Presley), 75
Hitchcock, Alfred, 329
Hitler, Adolf, 175, 225
'Hold What You've Got' (Tex), 122
Holliday, Billie, 348
Holly, Buddy, 211
Holmes, Sherlock, 5, 120
Holocaust, 222-4, 225, 227
HONEY JUST ALLOW ME ONE MORE CHANCE, 148, 149
Hooker, John Lee, 35, 82, 87
Horus, 309
HOUSE OF THE RISING SUN, 263
House, Son, 35, 82, 83, 84, 85, 86, 88, 123, 360
Houston, Cisco, 16, 56
'How's the World Treating You?' (Presley), 73
*Howl* (Ginsberg), 174
Howlin' Wolf, 34, 35, 77, 82, 88, 122, 348, 360
Huck Finn *see Adventures of Huckleberry Finn*
HURRICANE, 306, 311-4, 315, 317, 321, 336, 340
Hurt, Mississippi John, 35, 82, 123
Huxley, Aldous, 279

I AM A LONESOME HOBO, 258, 265
*I Am the Blues* (Dixon), 33
I AND I, 135, 202, 354
'I Believe I'll Dust My Broom' (Johnson), 84
'I Can't Be Satisfied' (Waters), 88
*I Ching*, 132
I DON'T BELIEVE YOU, 127, 129, 180
'I Don't Care If the Sun Don't Shine' (Presley), 288
I DREAMED I SAW ST AUGUSTINE, 261-2, 265
'I Got Stung' (Presley), 74
'I Need Your Love Tonight' (Presley), 74
I PITY THE POOR IMMIGRANT, 258, 265
I SHALL BE FREE, 126, 148, 150, 151
I SHALL BE FREE No. 10, 126-7, 180
I SHALL BE RELEASED, 201, 351
I THREW IT ALL AWAY, 282
'I Want to Hold Your Hand' (Beatles), 120, 121
I'LL BE YOUR BABY TONIGHT, 277, 278-9, 282, 283
I'LL REMEMBER YOU, 11, 345
'I'll Twine 'Mid The Ringlets' (Irving & Webster), 176-7
'I'm a Loser' (Beatles), 50
I'M NOT THERE, 253, 256
IDIOT WIND, 201
IF DOGS RUN FREE, 286, 353
IF NOT FOR YOU, 287
*Iliad*, 4
Impressions, 122, 129
IN MY TIME OF DYIN', 100
IN THE SUMMERTIME, 11
*In the Wee Small Hours* (Sinatra & Riddle), 147

*Infidels*, 48, 100, 101-2, 191, 194, 300, 344-5, 353, 359
International Folk Music Council, 21, 22
Isaiah, 258
Ishmael, 42-3
ISIS, 308-9, 314, 315, 334
IT AIN'T ME, BABE, 130, 146, 180, 182, 183, 296
IT'S ALL OVER NOW, BABY BLUE, 58, 201, 203
IT'S ALRIGHT, MA (I'M ONLY BLEEDING), 141-2, 205, 216, 247
*It's Too Late to Stop Now* (Morrison), 307

Jackson, Chuck, 122
Jacob, 103
James, Elmore, 82
James, Jesse, 318
James, Skip, 35, 82, 123
Jefferson, Blind Lemon, 35
Jennings, Waylon, 96
Jesse, 96
Jesus Christ, 5, 99, 100, 141, 160-1, 178-9, 202, 209, 224-5, 266, 267, 270, 273, 290, 301-2, 308-9, 324-5
'Jim Crow', 109
*John Wesley Harding*, 50, 117, 181, 184, 194, 196, 209, 248, 255, 256-73, 277-80, 283, 339, 360
JOHN WESLEY HARDING, 259-61, 265, 318
'Johnny B. Goode' (Berry), 69
Johnson, James P., 112
Johnson, Lonnie, 77
Johnson, Robert, 20, 35, 83-7, 88, 113, 129, 360
Johnson, Tommy, 84-6, 89
Johnson, Willie, 77
Johnston, Bob, 281
JOKERMAN, 45-6, 47-9, 100, 101, 354
Jones, George, 96
Jonson, Ben, 24
Joplin, Janis, 300, 354
Jordan, Louis, 72
Joyce, James, 176, 335, 349
Judas Iscariot, 27, 160-2, 264, 270
Jung, Carl, 43, 97, 189
Jupiter, 47, 123, 189
JUST LIKE TOM THUMB'S BLUES, 210

'Kansas City Blues', 59
Karpeles, Maud, 14, 21, 22, 23
Keats, John, 10, 349
Keisker, Marion, 76
Kennedy, John F., 118, 155, 157, 322
Kennedy, Robert, 155, 157, 322
Kerouac, Jack, 61, 98, 209
Kesey, Ken, 119
*Key to the Tarot, The* (Waite), 48, 310
'Kind Hearted Woman Blues' (Johnson), 85
King, Albert, 82
King, B.B., 78, 82, 88
King, Dr Martin Luther, 81, 155, 157
*King Lear*, 253
*King of the Delta Blues Singers* (Johnson), 20, 82, 85
Kingman, Daniel 25-6
Klein, Joe, 211
*Knocked Out Loaded*, 194, 300, 346, 354

KNOCKIN' ON HEAVEN'S DOOR, 201
Kokomo, 307

Laine, Frankie, 187
*Last Train to Memphis* (Guralnick) 75
*Last Waltz, The*, 301
*Late for the Sky* (Browne), 305
Law, Don, 85
LAY DOWN YOUR WEARY TUNE, 131, 132, 133, 134, 168-9, 179, 201
LAY LADY LAY, 283
Leadbelly, 36, 56, 68
Leary, Timothy, 119
*Leaves of Grass* (Whitman), 42, 67, 70
Led Zeppelin, 286
Lennon, John 50-1, 344
Leone, Sergio, 4
Levy, Jacques, 306, 308, 312, 320, 321, 332
Lewis, C.S., 352
Lewis, Furry, 35, 78, 82
Lewis, Jerry Lee, 72, 77, 90
Library of Congress, 83
LICENCE TO KILL, 171, 359
LIKE A ROLLING STONE, 58, 226, 236, 302, 353, 354
'Lilacs in the Rain' (DeRose),110
LILY, ROSEMARY AND THE JACK OF HEARTS, 239
'Little Boy Lost' (Blake), 250, 264
Little Milton, 82
Little Richard, 36, 72, 92
*Live 1961–2000*, 296, 298
*Live 1966*, 297, 298
Live Aid, 154
Logan, Horace, 71
Lomax, Alan, 31, 83
Lomax, John, 31
London, Julie, 72, 138
*London Labour and the London Poor* (Mayhew), 25
LONE PILGRIM, 12, 58
Lone Ranger, 4
LONESOME DEATH OF HATTIE CARROLL, THE, 103, 145, 150, 166-8, 181, 207, 311
Longfellow, Henry Wadsworth, 68
'Looking Into You' (Browne), 60
'Lord Franklin', 149
'Lord Randal', 102
Lot, 330, 331, 332, 333, 335
*Louisiana Hayride*, 71
*Love and Theft*, 194, 198, 356-361
'Love in Vain' (Johnson) 85
LOVE IS JUST A FOUR-LETTER WORD, 186-7
'Love Me' (Presley), 73
*Love Me Tender*, 73
'Love Me Tender' (Presley), 74
LOVE SICK, 353
'Love Song of J. Alfred Prufrock, The' (Eliot), 69, 208, 231, 232
*Lucky Town*, 64-5
'Lucky Town' (Springsteen), 64
Lynn, Loretta, 284
*Lyrical Ballads*, 8

MTV, 297
*Mabinogion*, 97
McClennan, Tommy, 86, 89
McCoy, Charlie, 248
MacDonald, Ian, 34, 271

McDowell, Mississippi Fred, 66, 84, 123
McKenzie, Red, 114
Macpherson, William, 7
McTell, Blind Willie, 35, 85
Magic Sam, 82
Malachi, 290
MAN IN ME, THE, 287
MAN OF PEACE, 101, 171, 359
MAN IN THE STREET, 145
Manson, Charles, 119
Marcus, Greil, 32, 77, 86
*Marriage of Heaven and Hell, The* (Blake), 311
'Marshmallow World, A' (DeRose), 110
Martha and the Vandellas, 122
Martin, Fiddlin' Joe, 83
Marvelettes, 122
Marvell, Andrew, 302
Mary Magdalen, 330
Mason, Rev. C.H., 81
MASTERS OF WAR, 88, 141, 148, 149, 312
(John) Mayall's Bluesbreakers, 34
'Me and the Devil Blues' (Johnson), 83
Melville, Herman, 42, 49
'Memphis Blues' (Handy), 79
'Memphis Blues, The' (DeRose), 110
Memphis Jug Band, 79
Mencken, H.L., 69
Mercury, 44, 190
Merry Pranksters, 119
Michelangelo, 10, 356
'Milkcow Blues Boogie' (Presley), 288
Miller, Henry, 245-7 256, 271
Miller, Mitch, 187
Milton, John, 350
Mingus, Charles, 147
Miracles, 122
Miró, Joan, 248
Mississippi, University of, 157
'Mr Pitiful' (Redding), 122
MR TAMBOURINE MAN, 105, 124, 133-5, 137, 179, 181, 204, 206, 216, 217, 236, 238
Mitchell, Joni, 293, 304
*Moby Dick* (Melville), 42-3
Mona Lisa, 240, 248
Monk, Thelonious, 88
MOONSHINER, 135
Moore, Scotty, 76
*More Bob Dylan Greatest Hits*, 297
Morrison, Van, 307
Morton, Jelly Roll, 91
MOST OF THE TIME, 11, 204, 354
MOTORPSYCHO NITEMARE, 126, 180
Motown, 121
Mound City Blue Blowers, 114
*Mountain, The* (Earle), 30
MOZAMBIQUE, 314-5, 326
'Muddy Water (A Mississippi Moan)', 109-14
Muddy Waters, 34, 35, 82, 85, 88, 89, 113, 122, 360
Mugabe, Robert, 314
Murray, Charles Shaar, 112
MY BACK PAGES, 127, 172-4, 179, 180, 201
'My Black Mama' (House), 81, 84
*Mystery Train* (Marcus), 77

*NME*, 113, 352
*Nashville Skyline*, 194, 203, 281-6, 306, 353

National Association for the Advancement of Colored People, 155, 157
Nationalist Movement, 156
Nelson, Lawrence, 211
Neptune, 227
Never-Ending Tour, 299, 353
'New Highway 51' (McClennan), 89
New Jerusalem, 164, 178
*New Morning*, 194, 195, 196, 198, 203, 285, 286-90
Newman, Randy, 345
Newport Folk Festival, 34, 66, 123-4, 128, 184, 221
Newport Jazz Festival, 34
'Night, The' (Springsteen), 61
'Night Train' (Brown), 90
NINETY MILES AN HOUR (DOWN A DEAD END STREET), 11
'No Food Is Blue' (Astor), 296
NO TIME TO THINK, 47
Noah, 98, 103-4, 179, 219, 227
NOBODY 'CEPT YOU, 94
NORTH COUNTRY BLUES, 150, 154, 181
NOT DARK YET, 303
NOTHING WAS DELIVERED, 253
*Notorious* (Hitchcock), 329

'**O**de to Billy Joe' (Gentry), 253
Odysseus, 5
*Oh Mercy*, 92, 194, 196, 203, 204, 300, 346, 354
OH SISTER, 315, 316, 326, 334
'Old Ship of Zion, The', 164
Oliver, King, 91
*On the Road* (Kerouac), 61, 98, 120
ONE MORE CUP OF COFFEE, 315, 316, 333, 334
ONE MORE WEEKEND, 287, 289
ONE OF US MUST KNOW (SOONER OR LATER), 187
'One Step Up' (Springsteen), 64
ONE TOO MANY MORNINGS, 144-5, 150, 169
ONLY A PAWN IN THEIR GAME, 150, 154-7, 163, 181, 312
Orbison, Roy, 77, 121
Orioles, 81
Osiris, 309, 334
'Out of Sight' (Brown), 123
*Oxford Book of Ballads*, 14
OXFORD TOWN, 148, 149, 157

**P**age, 'Gatemouth', 33
Page, Patti, 187
Paine, Tom, 258
Paramount Records, 83, 84
Parker, 'Colonel' Tom, 76
Parker, Charlie, 114, 348
Parsons, Gram, 286
*Pat Garrett and Billy the Kid*, 195
Patton, Charley, 35, 83, 86, 87, 88, 360
*Pearl* (Joplin), 300
Peer, Ralph, 29-30, 31
PEGGY DAY, 282
Pennebaker, D.A., 220, 221
'People Get Ready' (Impressions),122
Percy's *Reliques*, 7, 9, 14
Perkins, Carl, 77
Phillips, Sam, 76, 77, 78

'Phonograph Blues' (Johnson), 113
Picasso, Pablo, 18, 248, 349, 356, 361
Pickett, Wilson, 122, 123
'Pirate Jenny's Song' (Brecht/Weill), 163
'Pitre Châtié, Le' (Mallarmé), 106
*Planet Waves*, 194, 196, 198, 203, 287, 291-4, 299
'Please Don't Go' (Williams & Williamson), 86
'Please Please Me' (Beatles), 203
POLITICAL WORLD, 204
'Poor Boy' (Presley), 73
*Portrait of the Artist as a Young Man, A* (Joyce), 335
*Poseidon Adventure, The*, 329
POSITIVELY 4TH STREET, 235, 236-7, 239
Pound, Ezra, 12, 228, 229
Presley, Elvis, 3, 18, 38, 71-7, 78, 80, 97, 120, 139, 263, 282, 287-9, 348, 352, 354
Presley family, 96
'Pretty Boy Floyd' (Guthrie), 36, 261
'Pretty Woman' (Orbison), 121
Pride, Charley, 284
Profaci, Joseph, 320-1
'Promised Land, The' (Springsteen), 62, 63
Proust, Marcel, 332
Psalms, 237, 266, 267, 289-90

*Q* magazine, 34
Quiller Couch, Sir Arthur, 14

'**R**acing in the Streets' (Springsteen), 62
RAINY DAY WOMEN #12 & 35, 271-2, 360
RANK STRANGERS TO ME, 11
Raphael, 10
Ray, Johnny, 139
*Real Live*, 296
Redding, Otis, 122, 123, 354
Reed, Jimmy, 82
Reiner, Rob, 156
*Remembrance of Things Past* (Proust), 332
*Renaldo & Clara*, 46, 297, 338-9
RESTLESS FAREWELL, 146, 150-2, 156, 168, 169, 261
Revelation of St John, 97, 99, 164, 178, 268-9, 273
Rich, Charlie, 77
Richman, Harry, 109, 110
Riddle, Nelson, 147
Righteous Brothers, 121
Rimbaud, Arthur, 186
RING THEM BELLS, 204, 346
*River, The* (Springsteen), 60, 62
Rivera, Scarlet, 307, 330
Robertson, Robbie, 273
Robin Hood, 215, 219, 318
'Rock Island Line' (Leadbelly, Donnegan), 36, 68-9
'Rock Me on the Water' (Browne), 59
Rodgers, Jimmie, 30, 31, 37-8, 90, 96, 360
'Rollin' Stone' (Waters), 88
*Rolling Stone* magazine, 318
Rolling Stones, 3, 34, 69, 122, 285, 307, 352
Rolling Thunder Revue, 293
ROMANCE IN DURANGO, 326-7, 328
Rotolo, Suze, 142

**S**AD-EYED LADY OF THE LOWLANDS, 181, 184, 188, 244, 251, 337, 339

*Sail Away* (Newman), 345
St Augustine (of Hippo, of Canterbury), 261, 262, 266, 268
St David 96
St Elvis 95, 96
St John, Gospel of, 5, 160, 161
St John the Baptist, 240
'St Louis Blues' (Handy), 58, 79
St Luke, Gospel of, 161, 270
St Mark, Gospel of, 273
St Paul, 224, 240, 262
St Peter, 99
St Stephen, 272
St Teilaw, 95, 96
Saintsbury, George, 7, 8
Samuel, 266-8, 269-70
SARA, 105, 316, 337-41, 343
Sarah, 332
Satan, 101, 161, 308
Saul, 267
*Saved*, 45, 194, 197, 300, 326, 343, 344
Savio, Mario, 119
Scaduto, Antony, 209
*Seasons, The* (Thomson), 7
SEE THAT MY GRAVE IS KEPT CLEAN, 146
SEEING THE REAL YOU AT LAST, 345
*Self Portrait*, 194, 283, 286, 354
SEÑOR, 47
*Sergeant Pepper's Lonely Hearts Club Band* (Beatles), 147
SERIES OF DREAMS, 354
Shade, Will, 79
Shakespeare, William 9, 18, 23, 240, 245, 253, 349
Sharp, Cecil, 14, 21, 23, 29
'She Loves You' (Beatles), 203
*Sheet Music* magazine, 110
SHENANDOAH, 11
Sherrill, Billy, 285
'Shetland Pony Blues' (House), 83
Shirelles, 122
SHOOTING STAR, 11, 201-2, 203, 204
*Shot of Love*, 45, 105, 194, 196, 198, 300, 344, 346
SHOT OF LOVE, 344, 354
SIGN ON THE WINDOW, 286
Silber, Irwin, 124
Simon, Paul, 314
SIMPLE TWIST OF FATE, 239
Sinatra, Frank, 139, 147, 187
*Sing Out!* magazine, 124
*Sketches Of Spain* (Davis & Evans), 147
*Slow Train Coming*, 45, 194, 197, 299, 343, 344, 353
SLOW TRAIN COMING, 164
Smith, Bessie, 87, 90, 109-14, 117
Smith, Harry, 31, 32
Smith, Mamie, 29, 109, 114
'Some Other Kinds of Songs', 279-80
*Song Talk* magazine, 216
SONG TO WOODY, 56, 137, 140, 148
*Songs of Experience* (Blake), 250
Sony Music, 298
'Souls of the Departed' (Springsteen), 64-5
*Sound of the City, The* (Gillett), 122
*Sound, Sound Your Instruments Of Joy* (Watersons), 164
Sounes, Howard, 339

SPANISH HARLEM INCIDENT, 125, 127, 129, 130, 180
Spann, Otis, 82
Spector, Phil, 121
Spielberg, Steven, 164
Springsteen, Bruce, 60-5
Spurgeon, Charles, 172
*Stage Fright* (Band), 273
Staple Singers, 88
Staples, Pops, 82, 88
Stax Studio, Memphis, 78
Steinbeck, John, 141-2, 209-10
Stoner, Rob, 307
*Street-Legal*, 46-7, 48, 117, 194, 197, 239, 322, 324, 335, 343, 353
Strong, Barrett, 122
STUCK INSIDE OF MOBILE WITH THE MEMPHIS BLUES AGAIN, 244-7, 251
Student Non-violent Coordinating Committee, 119
Students for a Democratic Society, 119
SUBTERRANEAN HOMESICK BLUES, 69
Sun Records, 76-8, 289
Supremes, 121
Swallows, 81
Swan Silvertones, 81
SWEETHEART LIKE YOU, 354

**T**aj Mahal, 84
TALKIN' NEW YORK, 40, 137, 148
TALKIN' WORLD WAR III BLUES, 121, 126, 148, 149
TALKING TV, 171
Tampa Red, 84
TANGLED UP IN BLUE, 60, 63, 203, 296, 354
*Tarantula*, 252
Tarot, 46-9, 184, 310-1
TEARS OF RAGE, 253
Temptations, 121
Ten Years After, 286
Terry, Sonny, 16, 56
Tex, Joe, 122, 123
'That Revolutionary Rag' (Berlin), 111
'That's Alright, Mama' (Presley), 71, 288, 289
'That's How Strong My Love Is' (Redding), 122
*Theatre Owners' Booking Association, 79-80
*There Goes Rhymin' Simon*, 314
'There'll Be a Hot Time in the Old Town Tonight', 109
'There'll Be No Teardrops Tonight' (Williams), 140
*This Is Spinal Tap* (Reiner), 156
'This Train Is Bound for Glory', 164
THIS WHEEL'S ON FIRE, 253
Thomas, Dylan, 94, 95, 165
Thomson, James, 7
THREE ANGELS, 286, 290
*Threepenny Opera, The* (Brecht & Weill), 163
'Throw a Boogie Woogie' (Williams & Williamson), 86
'Thunder Road' (Springsteen), 61
'Ties That Bind, The', (Springsteen), 62
TIGHT CONNECTION TO MY HEART, 345, 354
*Tijuana Moods* (Mingus), 147
*Time* magazine, 220
*Time Out of Mind*, 11, 92, 186, 188, 194, 198, 300, 303, 347, 352, 353, 356, 359

*Times They Are A-Changin', The*, 104, 118, 124, 125, 126, 127, 129, 131, 132, 135, 143-5, 146, 149-70, 172, 181, 194, 197, 207, 280, 281, 306, 311
TIMES THEY ARE A-CHANGIN', THE, 104, 125, 150, 151, 152, 154, 167, 169, 181, 311, 351, 358
*Titanic*, 215, 227-9
TO BE ALONE WITH YOU, 281-2
*To Have and Have Not*, 329
'To His Coy Mistress' (Marvell), 302
TO RAMONA, 124, 129, 130, 146, 180, 182-3
Tom Petty and the Heartbreakers, 297
TOMBSTONE BLUES, 58-9
TONIGHT I'LL BE STAYING HERE WITH YOU, 283
'Too Much Monkey Business' (Berry), 69
TOO MUCH OF NOTHING, 253
*Topographical Dictionary of Wales, A*, 95
TOUGH MAMA, 287
'Tougher Than the Rest', (Springsteen), 64
*Towering Inferno, The*, 329
Townshend, Pete, 300
'Travelling Riverside Blues' (Johnson), 87
Travelling Wilburys, 77
Trent, Jo, 109, 110
Trickster, 5, 43-5, 50
TROUBLE, 346
*Trouble in Paradise* (Newman), 345
*Tunnel of Love* (Springsteen), 64
Twain, Mark, 42, 69
*Two Sevens Clash* (Culture), 164

UGLIEST GIRL IN THE WORLD, 354
UNBELIEVABLE, 204
*Uncut* magazine, 271
**Under the Red Sky**, 194, 204, 300, 346, 353, 354
Unofficial Free Bob Dylan Tape Library, 298
**Unplugged**, 58, 194, 195, 197, 198, 297, 298, 360
UP TO ME, 63
Uranus, 189-90

Van Gogh, Vincent & Theo, 190
Vasari, Giorgio, 10
*Veedon Fleece* (Morrison), 307
*Victory* (Conrad), 310, 330
Villa, Pancho, 328
Vincent, Gene, 72
VISIONS OF JOHANNA, 11, 145, 201, 244, 247-50, 251, 263
von Schmidt, Ric, 39

'Wabash Cannonball' (Carter Family), 175, 177
Waite, A.E. 46, 48, 184, 310
'Walk Like a Man' (Springsteen), 64
Walker, T-Bone, 77, 90
'Walking Blues' (Johnson), 84
Wallace, George, 157
'Was a Sunny Day' (Simon), 314
*Waste Land, The* (Eliot), 69, 206, 208, 230, 231, 232
Watersons, 164
'We're Gonna Move' (Presley), 73
Weathermen, 284
Weberman, A.J., 281-2, 284-5
WEDDING SONG, 292

Weill, Kurt, 163
Wenner, Jann, 318
WENT TO SEE THE GYPSY, 286, 287-9
Wexler, Jerry, 344
WHAT CAN I DO FOR YOU?, 354
WHAT GOOD AM I?, 204
WHAT WAS IT YOU WANTED, 204, 354
'When It's Night Time Down in Dixieland' (Berlin), 111
'When That Midnight Choo-Choo Leaves for Alabam'' (Berlin), 111
'When the Saints Go Marching In', 81
WHEN THE SHIP COMES IN, 104, 150, 157, 163-5, 166, 167
WHERE ARE YOU TONIGHT?, 47, 322
'Where Did Our Love Go?' (Supremes), 121
WHERE TEARDROPS FALL, 346
'Which Side Are You On?', 228, 242
'White Cockade, The', 137
White, Bukka, 82, 84
Whitman, Thomas Jefferson, 70, 71
Whitman, Walt, 42, 61, 67, 70-1, 74, 350
*Who's Next* (Who), 300
WICKED MESSENGER, THE, 259, 264, 265, 266-70
WIGGLE WIGGLE, 204
'Wildwood Flower' (Carter Family), 176-7
Wilkins, Robert, 82, 123
Williams, Big Joe, 35, 86
Williams, Hank, 13, 18, 30, 33, 72, 96, 139-40, 203, 316
Williams, Leroy, 83
Williams, Paul, 294, 297, 344
Williams, Ralph Vaughan, 14
Williams, Robert Pete, 123
Williamson, Sonny Boy, 86
Williamson, Sonny Boy, II, 35, 82
Wilson, Brian, 36
Wilson, Tom, 126
WINTERLUDE, 287
WITH GOD ON OUR SIDE, 124, 125, 150, 157-63, 181, 311
Woods, James 156
'Woodstock' (Mitchell), 304
Wordsworth, William, 8, 9, 14, 25
**World Gone Wrong**, 11-2, 58, 194, 197, 198, 299, 300, 347
Wyeth, Howie, 307

Yeats, W.B., 154, 228, 356
'Yiddle, On Your Fiddle, Play Some Ragtime' (Berlin), 111
YOU AIN'T GOIN' NOWHERE, 253
YOU ANGEL YOU, 287
YOU'RE NO GOOD, 137, 146, 188
'You've Lost That Lovin' Feeling' (Righteous Brothers), 121
Young, Lester, 114

Zantzinger, William, 166, 207
Zappa, Frank, 282
Zechariah, 270
Zeus, 44
'Zip Coon', 109
Zollo, Paul, 216

**Erratum, p.331:** 'The Black Diamond Express to Hell' (in three instalments, 1927-30) was recorded by Rev. A.W. Nix, not Rev. J.M. Gates.

At 5 Cwmdonkin Drive, Swansea                    *Bernard Mitchell*

**John Gibbens** was born in Cheshire, grew up in West Germany and West Cumbria and lives in London, where he has been a copy typist, secretary, typesetter, receptionist, playwright, actor, jazz doorman, printmaker, dog-walker and journalist. *Play*, the first album of his music with the Children, was released in 1999. His *Collected Poems* were published by Touched in 2000. More of his work can be found at www.touched.co.uk

Photographer and painter **Keith Baugh** lives and works in Gloucestershire with his wife and two sons. He exhibits regularly and has work in numerous private collections. He has been a member of the Chelsea Arts Club since 1982 and a selection of his paintings can be seen at www.chelseaartsclub.com